PRAISE FOR THE CALL OF DUTY SERIES

"Featuring a well-paced plot and an engaging protagonist, Mills's new series launch is a solid . . . suspense title."
Library Journal on *Breach of Trust*

"[*Breach of Trust* is] jam-packed with twists that will leave readers breathless. Intriguing characters, a crisis of faith, and the element of surprise make this novel a must-read for any avid suspense reader."
Romantic Times, 4½-star review

"Once again, Mills has crafted an engaging page-turner with intriguing characters facing difficult choices."
CBA Retailers + Resources on *Breach of Trust*

"A fast-paced, character-driven thriller. . . . Readers who enjoy the works of Dee Henderson, especially her O'Malley series, will love *Breach of Trust*."
Midwest Book Review

"Mills has spun an action-packed tale of romance, deception, redemption, and trials. Recommended to anyone who enjoys a little romance and a lot of adventure."
Church Libraries

"If you have been waiting for a story to match Dee Henderson's O'Malley series or Susan May Warren's Team Hope, look no further than *Breach of Trust*, the first in the Call of Duty series."
TitleTrakk.com

PURSUIT of JUSTICE

DiAnn Mills

Tyndale House Publishers, Inc.
Carol Stream, Illinois

Visit Tyndale's exciting Web site at www.tyndale.com.

Visit DiAnn Mills at www.diannmills.com.

TYNDALE and Tyndale's quill logo are registered trademarks of Tyndale House Publishers, Inc.

Pursuit of Justice

Designed by Jessie McGrath

Edited by Kathryn S. Olson

Published in association with the literary agency of Janet Kobobel Grant, Books & Such, Inc., 5926 Sunhawk Drive, Santa Rosa, CA 95409.

Scripture taken from the Holy Bible, New International Version,® NIV.® Copyright © 1973, 1978, 1984 by Biblica, Inc.™ Used by permission of Zondervan. All rights reserved worldwide. www.zondervan.com.

Library of Congress Cataloging-in-Publication Data

Mills, DiAnn.
 Pursuit of justice / DiAnn Mills.
  p. cm. — (Call of duty; 3)
 ISBN 978-1-4143-2052-6 (pbk.)
  1. United States. Federal Bureau of Investigation—Employees—Fiction. 2. Murder—Investigation—Fiction. 3. Revenge—Fiction. I. Title.
 PS3613.I567P87 2010
 813'.6—dc22   2010014466

Printed in the United States of America

16 15 14 13 12 11 10
 7   6   5   4   3   2   1

To the dedicated men and women of the FBI

Little Miss Muffet
Sat on a tuffet,
Eating her curds and whey.
Along came a spider,
Who sat down beside her
And frightened Miss Muffet away!

★

"For where your treasure is, there your heart will be also."

MATTHEW 6:21, NIV

★

Many thanks to all who made this book possible:
Special Agent Shauna Dunlap of the FBI field office in Houston,
Texas; Steve Ener; Debbie Fowler; Veronica Heley; Richard Mabry;
Dee McMahan; Mark Mynheir; Barbara Oden; Naomi Taplin;
James Wigington; and Linda Windsor.

★

CHAPTER 1

THE MOMENT BELLA accepted the reassignment to the FBI's field office in Houston, she realized the past had stalked her to the present. And she was ready, or at least she told herself so. Her training and experience had sharpened her skills and provided tools to solve crimes the average American deemed unspeakable.

Fear and memories had climbed into her luggage for the relocation to Houston, but she resisted their hold. Bella had made the decision to work hard to build her credentials and help curtail the endless barrage of crime, especially in the country's fourth-largest city.

Her BlackBerry interrupted her thoughts and her drive to work with its rendition of "That'll Be the Day." A quick glance showed the caller was Frank.

No way, superagent. I don't have a thing to tell you. She answered on the third ring. "Morning, Frank. What can I do for you?"

"Lunch?"

She laughed. "You heard I have an appointment with Swartzer, and curiosity is killing you."

"Me? I wanted to talk about spending the weekend in Galveston."

"Right. Frank, we broke up nine months ago."

"Nine months, huh? As in giving birth to a new relationship?"

She envisioned a slight smile spreading over his face—a good-looking one, but not for her. "No thanks. Remember, we tried and it didn't work. I don't want to put my heart in that place again. See you later."

"But—"

"Bye, Frank."

Bella tossed the phone into her purse. Regret over the failed relationship with Frank settled like a day harboring poor air quality. She'd known from the start a relationship with him wouldn't work. He wanted a wife who'd stay home and raise kids. She refused to give up the bureau, no matter how much she cared for him. The only thing she'd ever formed a lasting attachment to was the FBI, and mistakes in the name of love were not in her playbook.

A promotion had been in her path for the past few months, and she desperately wanted it. Ambition always ruled over her logic, but she didn't view her objectives as selfish. The meeting this morning with her supervisor might be a jump in her career. A coveted opportunity to prove her mettle sounded almost too good to be true, and like a kid at Christmas on this early June morning, she drove toward the field office to see if she had a gift marked *promotion*.

Bella moved into the right lane of 290 to take the feeder road off the highway. For certain, battling traffic at 7 a.m. had hardened her for criminal activity—or destroyed any trace of patience. Her mind raced with anticipation over her meeting with Swartzer. This meeting could be about a number of ongoing investigations or possibly a new one. No matter; she'd take the assignment and keep climbing the ladder.

She swung into the parking lot of the eight-story, glass and steel building and stopped in front of the guard shack. After displaying her creds, she eased into the covered parking area and hurried inside. Her heart pounded against her chest, and she sensed the familiar excitement of something new to challenge her. She scanned her badge and keyed in her security code at every door and made her way to the second floor, housing the violent crimes task force team and the office of Larry Swartzer, her supervisor. While his secretary informed him of her arrival, Bella took several deep breaths in an effort to settle her nerves and will away the anxiousness making her feel like a kid sent to the principal's office.

Swartzer opened the door. "Mornin', Bella. Come on in."

Her heavy shoulder bag shifted and slipped from her arm to the floor. Thank goodness it was zipped. She cringed at the idea of her Glock, handcuffs, and all of her other equipment—not to mention her makeup bag and wallet—dropping at her feet.

"Little nervous, are we?" He chuckled, and her confidence fell to somewhere between diffused and lack-of.

She laughed and hoisted her bag. "Add curiosity to the mix."

He ushered her into his office, and she took a seat across from his desk. The wall behind him intimidated her with its framed certificates and honors earned over his twenty-year career. Most likely his wife refused to have them all displayed at home. Bella attempted to read his face, but Swartzer prided himself in being unreadable, and this morning was no exception. Although short and stocky, her supervisor had the neck and shoulders of a man who must bench nearly 275 pounds. He removed his signature black-framed glasses and turned to retrieve a couple of files from atop his credenza. She hadn't seen him without his glasses. Swartzer's military haircut and polyester pants still made him look nerdish, but then superintelligent people usually were.

Where did that leave her? Shoving aside the bazillion thoughts darting in and out of her mind like mosquitoes over a stagnant pond, she realigned her focus and gave the impression of professional calmness.

"I have an assignment for you." He tapped the file and eased back in the chair that was made for a much taller man, at least physically.

"What kind?"

"Murder. Three bodies were found Monday afternoon on a ranch in West Texas." His calculated gaze met hers. "Sixty miles south of Abilene."

He had her attention, and he knew it. "Runnels County?"

"Ballinger area."

She nodded and forced aside the implications of what the location meant to her. "Why the FBI?"

"It's linked to a man on our fugitive list."

Suspicion flared, and she opened the file, complete with photos of the victims. She pressed her fingertips into her palms. "Who?" But she already knew the answer.

"Brandt Richardson."

"Murder for hire." She stated the fact while memories in apoc-alyptic proportions slammed against her mind. "Also obsessed with finding the so-called Spider Rock treasure."

"The victims were hunting for this treasure and believed their clues led them to the High Butte Ranch, owned by Carr Sullivan. They sought permission to dig, and he refused. Ran them off. One of the victims wrote *Spider Rock* in the dirt before he died."

"Runnels County doesn't fall within the triangle of where the gold was supposedly hidden."

"You know more about it than I do."

"What were the victims' names?"

"Forrest Miller, a history professor at the University of Texas; Daniel Kegley, a geologist from Austin; and Walt Higgins, a retired oilman from Waco."

She didn't recognize any of them. "Family?"

"Miller has a wife and three teenage girls, Kegley was engaged, and Higgins has been divorced for over thirty years—no ties there. The families have all been interviewed. Professor Miller's wife said a fourth man was in the mix, but that's all she knew.

Nothing else at this point." Swartzer slipped on his glasses and steepled his fingers. "You know why I want you on the assignment. Or would you rather I brief Frank Nielson?"

Not on her life. Both of them were up for the same promotion. "I'll take it."

"I thought you'd accept. The updated report has been sent to your e-mail. I've also arranged for you to have access to classified files this morning and anything else you need. Here's the bite: The ranch owner and a man who works for him found the victims. Sullivan phoned the local deputy sheriff and reported the bodies. When Sullivan learned their names, he told the sheriff about his conversation with one of the men. Said the three wanted to dig for treasure and he refused. When the Spider Rock legend came into the discussion, the FBI became involved. Richardson is out there somewhere with his own treasure-hunting expedition, and murder is one of his specialties."

"Any idea who's working with him?" Bella turned the pages in the file, ignored Brandt's latest photo, and read his vital information. "He's been quite successful at staying undercover."

"The classified information will help you there. Twelve years ago he left the area for Peru with a woman. She's never resurfaced. He probably got tired of her." Swartzer leaned over his desk. "You know how these people in West Texas think, and I imagine you know the superstitions surrounding the legend."

"Richardson won't stop searching and killing for the treasure until someone clamps handcuffs on him." Dread filled her while memories from the past threatened to paralyze her, but she refused to show it. She took a deep breath, one meant to clear her thoughts and help her think like a special agent, not a woman who swore she'd never set foot in Runnels County again.

"I have a difficult time believing anyone would spend their lives looking for lost treasure."

"If the three victims believed the gold was on Sullivan's ranch, his refusal wouldn't have stopped them," she said. "By him denying the men access, they'd believe he was searching for the treasure too. And it would have spurred on their efforts. Even caused them to dig at night."

"And your knowledge of the area makes you the best agent for the investigation."

"I appreciate your giving me this opportunity, sir."

"Since this is in Dallas's territory, they will furnish you with what you need. There's also a satellite office in Abilene. But keep me informed."

"I'd rather use one of our analysts, since I have a rapport with them."

"No problem."

Finding the killer would end the nightmares for those families whose loved ones he'd killed and terrorized. If the killer happened to be Brandt Richardson, then that was an added bonus for all concerned.

"Sullivan is also under suspicion for the murders. Richardson may not even be involved with these killings in light of Sullivan's ordering the three to stay off his property. Additional investigation shows the bullets found in the bodies came from a Ruger Mini-14 rifle. One is registered to Sullivan, and it's missing. He claims it was stolen, but he hadn't reported it. And he has an alibi for the estimated time of death."

She turned to another section in the file. *Carr Sullivan, former real estate developer, Dallas, Texas.* He had blond hair and deep blue eyes. A pleasant-looking man, but not a lady-killer. "Tell me more about the rancher."

"The man has a history of violent behavior. Used to be a high roller in Dallas. Made his money in commercial real estate. Drugs, alcohol, and being known for his wild parties along with a propensity to fight. Quite a colorful reputation. He spent a fortune in rehabs, but it never lasted. Then when his girlfriend

OD'd about five years ago, he sold his business and bought a ranch in West Texas. Since then he's settled down."

"So the girlfriend's death scared him into going straight?"

"The word is he got religion."

"Which one?"

"Found Jesus. Claims he's born again."

She stashed that info away for later reflection. "How does he spend his time?"

"He's turned himself into a rancher and a respected member of the community—done all the right things to alter his former reputation. His latest project is turning his ranch into a home for at-risk teen boys. He's already applied for the licenses."

"A real Boy Scout, huh?" She peered into Swartzer's face. Couldn't tell if he thought the change in Sullivan was legit or not.

"Sullivan's past wheeling and dealing in Dallas fits the MO of a man obsessed with finding a lost treasure and potentially hooking up with Richardson."

"I see." She closed the file. "Sullivan could be working with Richardson." *Manipulated* sounded more like Richardson's method.

"You're a good agent, Bella. You've demonstrated your commitment to the bureau with an impeccable record. All of your investigations have been conducted professionally and with excellent results. You lived there for fifteen years. Need I say more?"

"I appreciate your confidence in my skills and experience."

"Then I'm assigning you as lead agent in this investigation to help solve these murders and possibly the opportunity to arrest Brandt Richardson."

Her pulse raced. At last an opportunity to prove her training and determination. "I don't know what to say, except thank you. I'll not disappoint you." Bella couldn't stop the smile. "When do I leave?"

"I'd like to see you on the road by lunchtime. Reservations have been made at the Courtesy Inn in Abilene near Highway 83—the same hotel where the victims stayed. Special Agent Vic Anderson from Dallas will meet you at your hotel at nine in the morning."

"Thank you again." Bella couldn't get to her computer fast enough to review all the reports on the murders and Brandt Richardson.

"If you find yourself in over your head, don't hesitate to contact me." He gave her a tight-lipped smile. "Go for it."

CHAPTER 2

CARR TOSSED HIS PILLOW across the room. He gave up on sleeping. He'd tried everything but counting sheep, and nothing had slowed down his mind—not even prayer. Anger, the old demon that too often wrapped its chains around him, threatened to seize control of him. Over five years had come and gone since he'd imprisoned the dragon, and he refused to release the animal again.

Throwing back the sweat-drenched sheet, he made his way across the wooden floor, down the hall, and into the kitchen for a bottle of cold water. Green numbers flashed 2:47 on the microwave above the oven. Hours before daylight. Hours before the county sheriff's department planted themselves at his front door again. Hours before anyone might possibly have answers about the three murdered men found on his property and shot with his rifle. The past two days and the investigation had added years to his life and wrinkles to his face. A little sleep would have been nice.

He'd never seen dead men before, except at funerals, and Carr didn't dwell on a body in a casket. The horror of finding those three victims continued to replay in his mind. He recalled the soaring vultures, the awkward positions of the bodies, the dried blood, the vacant eyes, and the realization that the act was deliberate. He'd have preferred a nightmare that could have been shaken off with a dose of reality.

Stupid. Stupid. Stupid. Only an idiot failed to report a missing rifle. If he hadn't been negligent, all of this could have been avoided, and maybe those three men would be walking around and enjoying life now instead of waiting for a proper burial.

Carr could have been arrested for those murders. Still might be. Evidence stacked against him to the point he wondered why he hadn't been charged. He thanked God he hadn't been. As he reached into the refrigerator for the water, the pungent scent of jalapeños and cilantro met his nostrils. Normally Lydia's cooking left his mouth watering long after the food disappeared, but tonight had been merely an extension of the miserable day. And just like the sleep that escaped him, so did his appetite. He uncapped the bottle and drank deeply, the cold rush springing life into his weary body.

Sweat beaded on his brow and dripped into his eyes. If he didn't know better, he'd swear high blood pressure and a fever had invaded him. A drug would solve a medical problem, certainly not the kind he used to ingest to eliminate stress and help him appear charming. Thank goodness the past and all of its imprints didn't contain murder. But he'd come close, as the police records about his fiery temper indicated.

With his new life, one dedicated to Christ, he'd hoped he would be immune to tragedy. Shouldn't following God provide some kind of special protection? Why would God do this to him?

Whoa. Carr reined in his thoughts. God had not stolen his rifle. Neither had He pulled the trigger, killing those men. Someone made a conscious choice to steal and murder. None of those choices were a part of God's plan.

Yet nothing looked likely to clear him of this atrocity. He clenched his fist and forced down the gut-punching fury, the unfairness of the whole mess. The authorities probably had their hands on his background and were searching for ways to nail him. If he were investigating the murders, he'd be doing the same thing. He looked guilty to anyone who viewed the colorful habits he had supposedly left behind.

The timing of all this. *Rotten, lousy timing.* But did a man schedule three murders on his land like a businessman recorded dates and appointments on his BlackBerry? What season of the year best fit that kind of disaster? Carr moaned in the darkness, once more feeling the impact of what had happened on his ranch, his haven from the cruelty of the world. Acid burned in his stomach.

Where was his compassion for others? What about those men's families? Did they have anyone to comfort them? Should he step forward to offer sympathy, or would that make him look guilty?

Recapping his bottle of water, he dragged his hand over his damp face. *Focus, Carr.* God had gotten him through bad times before, and He would again. All he had to do was crawl into the little red wagon labeled *Radio Flyer* and let God pull him along.

"Carr, you don't have to face this alone," a sweet, older voice said with a slight Hispanic accent.

He nodded in the dark, more an acknowledgment of Lydia's presence than an agreement with her words. "You and Jasper had my back."

"But we weren't the ones falsely accused."

"Tell that to the county sheriff's department, since they need someone to arrest. The media has me judged and convicted. My own fault, Lydia. I discovered my rifle was missing about a week ago, but I didn't take the time to report it." He blew out his frustration in a sigh that sounded more like a hiss. "Darren and I have been friends since I moved here, and there's no excuse. He's the sheriff and deserved to know about the theft. Actually I thought maybe Jasper had borrowed it, but he'd never open my gun case without asking."

"Obviously you're innocent, and Sheriff Adams thinks so too."

"I keep telling myself if they had found credible evidence, I'd be sitting in jail. Then again, it doesn't matter, since they're coming back this morning."

"To search for more evidence?"

"Yes, and to question all of us again, as if we're involved in some conspiracy to cover up the killings. I'd never heard of the Spider Rock treasure—a stupid legend that seemed important enough for one of the men to write it in the dirt before he died. I shouldn't have . . ."

"What?" Lydia's soft voice had a calming effect on him, even when the woman raised it a notch with an air of wisdom and superiority.

"I threatened one of them—the geologist," Carr said. "He called me from a bar or a restaurant in Abilene. I could hear the music and people in the background. When he asked again for permission to dig, I told him if I found any of them on my land, they'd be run off with buckshot in their rears."

Lydia snapped on a light over the sink. Like him, she still wore the clothes from the night before. The dim fluorescent bulb made him blink. "Did you tell Sheriff Adams about the second call?"

"No. And Sunday night, Miller made a third one. Now I'm wondering if my withholding information is grounds to arrest me. I'm an idiot, so wrapped up in my own little world that I failed to take responsible action. I never met any of those poor men, and they turn up dead on my ranch."

"Men have died since the 1700s in search of the Spider Rock gold."

"And I can't believe these murders are about a treasure hunt."

"It's buried out here in this part of the country—somewhere. But no one has ever been able to find anything but more clues and Spanish artifacts." She smiled, and he saw the beauty of lost youth still in her eyes. Dark hair and dark eyes with smooth, latte-colored skin. But it was her faith that endeared her to him the most. As the light above the sink slowly grew brighter, it intensified the gold cross around her neck. "It's real, Carr. That's why those men were murdered."

"I have no reason to think otherwise." Carr bit back his opinion of how ludicrous it sounded for a cache of lost Spanish gold to be buried in this part of the country, like someone believing Nicolas Cage's claims in *National Treasure*.

"I understand." Her motherly instincts reached out to him, and for those qualities, he couldn't fault her for believing in a legend.

Once more he uncapped the bottle and took another long swallow of the water. "If the victims had been illegals, maybe I could make some sense of all this. Blame gang warfare or a drug cartel. Doesn't matter that I don't believe in the treasure theory; they did. The only thing I can figure out is greed led them here, and greed killed them." He stared into Lydia's tanned face. "And whoever wanted them dead used my weapon."

"I don't understand who could have broken in and taken your rifle. Someone is here most of the time. The doors are kept locked. And—" she took in a deep breath—"I refuse to think the thief, the killer, is someone we know."

"Me either, unless the rifle was stolen while we were at church. In the meantime, I'm trying to figure out if I need a lawyer or a shrink because this is driving me nuts. We were all ready to turn the High Butte into a home for at-risk teen boys. Wish I could calm down, relax. But I'm angry. My future is in the gutter, which means the home for at-risk boys is at best on hold."

"We must trust God. You were sure He wanted this to be a haven for them just as it was for you. You have all the credentials and licenses and everything."

Guilt pelted him for not being able to stop the anger eating at his soul. "I'm feeling sorry for myself. Actually, I'm worried. Not only did someone want those three guys killed, they wanted me blamed. Smart person. Too smart for my liking." He leaned on the kitchen counter. "I made enemies in my day, men and women who despised me. But I don't recall anyone who'd frame me for murder."

"Are you praying?"

"Like breathing. God's probably tired of me pounding on His door."

"I don't think so. I'll brew a pot of decaf, and we'll pray together."

Since he was fresh out of options, he reached for his worn Bible on the counter. "I heard Darren say the FBI has been called in on the investigation."

She pulled the coffee beans from the cupboard and dumped a generous amount into the grinder. "I don't know what justifies an FBI investigation. What did Sheriff Adams say?"

"There's a man on their fugitive list who's wanted for murder-for-hire and has been searching for the Spider Rock treasure." Darren had told him more, even given Carr the fugitive's name, but Carr had been too overwhelmed with what was happening to ask questions. First he had to get past the repulsion of what he and Jasper had discovered. At least his temper was beginning to subside.

"When will the FBI be here?" Lydia poured water into the coffeemaker.

"Tomorrow." He glanced down at his Bible and then into her sweet face. "I'm scared. Real scared."

While driving to Abilene, Bella considered the investigative reports about the murders. Most of the information concerning Brandt Richardson's involvement with the Spider Rock treasure, subsequent murders, and embezzled money had been declassified, and the names of potential suspects were now stored on her laptop and BlackBerry. One of the men was listed in *Forbes*.

Another man held the office of U.S. senator, and another was a professor at the University of Texas, a friend of the professor who had lost his life. Two others were prominent businessmen affiliated with both government and private-sector enterprises. All of the men must have been convinced of the authenticity of the Spider Rock treasure, which wasn't illegal. Murder, on the other hand, had all of them on the FBI's radar.

Since her briefing this morning, she'd attempted to put together the pieces about Brandt's possible involvement. She'd seen him in action, and he was more than capable. His Apollo-looking features had thrilled her until she saw the evil lurking below the surface. His weaknesses were money and women, with an unyielding desire to find the Spider Rock treasure. His strengths were his charisma and the mind that never shut down. It simply spun new webs.

Carr Sullivan's background fit easily into the treasure hunter's picture. The rancher had all the characteristics of someone in cahoots with Brandt Richardson, someone who'd do whatever it took to find the hidden cache of gold. But she also understood Brandt's tactics. Although the rancher had a history with Dallas police due to his partying days and temper problems, and his rifle had fired the bullets that killed the three men, she couldn't discount Brandt's ability to orchestrate the shootings and place the blame on an innocent man. Bella had learned a long time ago that murder brought in an interesting cast of players, and not all were guilty.

Pulling her BlackBerry from her shoulder bag, she phoned FIG—the Field Intelligence Group—at the Houston field office to request complete reports on the high-profile businessmen. Sullivan's former days in Dallas could have put him in contact with any of them, even Brandt Richardson.

She fixed her attention on the trail of lawlessness Brandt had left behind him. Her conscience niggled at her. Protocol required she state her past association with Brandt, even if she was only fifteen years old at the time. But she hadn't because she couldn't.

Yesteryear floated like a vapory figure too real to be cast aside. Fourteen years later and the mention of the man's name still sent a coil of fear up her spine. Too many times today, she'd second-guessed the wisdom in taking on this assignment. She could have recommended Frank and eliminated the heartburn and queasiness this investigation would generate. For that matter, she and Frank could have worked this together with Special Agent Vic Anderson from the Dallas field office. Except Frank would want to reignite their love affair, and she had no intentions of putting herself under that pressure. Not that he wasn't a capable agent. He had the qualifications and intellect to figure out how a twisted man's mind worked. The two worked well together. His confidence would have compensated for her personal fears of Brandt. But she'd chosen a different path, and she would plod ahead to find a way to deal with years that were best forgotten.

The thrill of arresting an FBI fugitive was worth keeping her eyes glued to her back. She'd work with the Violent Crime Task Force to complete this investigation and learn who murdered those men. Arresting Brandt came as an added bonus.

As Bella drove to her hotel at twilight, she glanced around Abilene. She'd dreaded seeing the city again, but it had changed so much. For a moment she wondered if she'd driven to the wrong place. The colors of sunset in vibrant yellows and oranges looked inviting, masking the violence that had summoned her to the isolated ranch miles from the outskirts of the growing city.

Pulling into a Chili's restaurant near her hotel, she ordered takeout. A good meal and hours poring over the information stored on her BlackBerry and laptop awaited her. What she needed was an open mind to the truth and the ability to sort out facts from presumption. And a handle on how she'd manage an interview with Brandt.

CHAPTER 3

THE FOLLOWING MORNING, Bella woke refreshed, and she needed every second of rest until this assignment was completed. At 5:45 a.m., she slipped a baby Glock into an ankle holster and pulled on a pair of sweats and a T-shirt. Once her tennis shoes were tightly laced, she stretched out, anticipating a good run.

After copying the case's file onto a memory stick and tucking it into her pocket, she secured her computer with a cable lock and grabbed her room key and BlackBerry. Anyone attempting to see what her computer contained would be hit with more than one security blockade.

She made her way from the hotel room and down the stairway to the lobby. The property had a fitness center, but this morning she needed to clear her head outside. This part of her life, the relished run, might take a vacation while she carried out her assignment. But at least for today, she'd start the day with her normal routine.

She positioned her earbuds as though she were listening to music on her BlackBerry instead of observing the people and vehicles around her and proceeded onto the street that swung right toward Abilene's mall. All the while, she focused her mental acuity toward anything out of the ordinary. A Hispanic man and woman sat in a late-model car in the hotel parking lot arguing. A landscaping truck slowed, then turned in to the hotel, its bed filled with shovels and a mound of mulch. As she ran past a Popeyes and the Sherwood Hills apartments adjacent to the fast-food restaurant, she spotted a dark green SUV parked along the curb with no visible driver.

After an hour of running around the outskirts of the mall, she retraced her steps to the hotel. A few vehicles lingered, and she took note of colors, makes, and license plates. But nothing had impressed her as out of the ordinary.

Back in her room, she showered and readied herself for the day in jeans and tennis shoes. Already at eight o'clock the sun beat down hard and ensured a scorcher. As soon as breakfast and her token two cups of coffee had powered her up, she grabbed her tools for the investigation and piled them into her car, often referred to as the office on the go. Vic Anderson would meet her at nine, but she didn't know if he'd ride with her or drive his own vehicle.

She'd grown fond of her midsize Ford and how it weaved easily in and out of traffic, as well as its performance on the road. In the past, company-issued vehicles with their mile-high antennae stuck out like lighthouses on a foggy night, but with new technology, the issued vehicles now slipped by the public—and most criminals—undetected.

Promptly at nine, a prematurely gray-haired man dressed in jeans and a light blue button-down shirt walked into the hotel lobby and caught her attention. *Vic Anderson.* He looked just like his photo.

"Special Agent Jordan?"

"Yes, sir."

"Mornin'. Agent Anderson." He stuck out his hand, and she grasped it. "I understand the High Butte Ranch is calling our names."

"So I hear. My car's outside if you don't mind me driving."

He nodded. "I'll get my equipment."

In the parking lot, Anderson transferred his raid jacket, Kevlar vest, and tactical belt to her trunk. He pointed to her vest folded in the corner.

"That looks like it would fit a kid."

"It's all I could get."

He eyed her with a grin. "You look about the size of my daughter—five-two?"

"Right."

He picked up her vest. "What do you use for pockets?"

"My creds, handcuffs, and gun slip nicely in the back waist-band of my pants. I also use an ankle holster."

He shook his head. "Size has its advantages."

"So does being a woman."

He shut the trunk. "I've worked with women agents, and they were able to get into places and secure information where a man didn't have a chance."

"And I've been in a few places where I wished I were a man."

He laughed. "Okay, we're even. Let's get this investigation on the road. We've got three murders too many. Did you happen to talk to the manager of the hotel again?"

"He's off today, so I'll catch him tonight."

"Just wondered. His report seemed vague to me."

Bella liked Vic's Southern gentleman drawl. His success rate of running down criminals was impressive, and she could learn much from him.

First thing on this morning's agenda was a sixty-five-mile drive to the southern part of Runnels County and an interview with Carr Sullivan and his workers. Tomorrow morning, she'd talk to the manager of the Courtesy Inn and his staff about the murder victims who'd stayed on the property prior to their demise.

As soon as they left the city limits, Bella punched in the number for the Runnels County Sheriff's Department. A woman with the voice of one who'd smoked for thirty years answered the phone.

"Sheriff Darren Adams, please."

"Who's calling?"

"Special Agent Bella Jordan from the FBI."

"Yes, ma'am. I'll put you through."

While she waited for Sheriff Adams to answer, she pressed in the address for Carr Sullivan's ranch on her BlackBerry's GPS and proceeded south on Highway 83. Finally the sheriff answered the phone.

"Special Agent Jordan, this is Sheriff Adams. I've been expecting your call."

"I'm driving to the High Butte Ranch with Special Agent Vic Anderson. What time will you be there?"

"I'm here now with some of my deputies."

"Good. I have your findings with me, and I'm looking forward to working with you on this task force. From what I've seen, you've done a top-notch job with the investigation. You've already seen to dusting Professor Miller's SUV and requesting phone records. The field offices in Houston and Dallas speak highly of you."

"Thanks. We believe in our job. I haven't contacted the Texas Rangers since I knew you were on board. We haven't found a single thing to link a shooter to the crime scene, but we're scouring the area."

"Did you place a rush on the car sweep?"

He chuckled. "Nothing out here is done fast, but I'm doing my best."

With the limited resources available to them, the sheriff's department had done quite well. Perhaps she could speed along the car sweep.

"Sounds like Sullivan is our prime suspect since it was his rifle that turned up missing." She waited for the sheriff to fill in more of his thoughts.

He cleared his throat. "I . . . I don't think he's our man. Carr Sullivan is a fine man. In church every Sunday. Volunteers there and in the community. Likable. I read his past record, and this is not the same man. He has too many good things on his side to pin three murders on him. I'd say there was more to these killings than a rancher gunning down three men for trespassing."

Bella inwardly moaned. With the sheriff on the side of one of the suspects, the FBI's job would be harder. "I understand he has an alibi."

"His employees vouched for him."

That's worthless. "What can you tell me about them?" Bella had read the background checks on the two people, but the findings hadn't come from someone who knew them.

"Jasper and Lydia Flores are over sixty years old and devout Christians. Jasper knows more about ranching than anyone I know, and Lydia is the best cook in the county. Both of them have been with Carr since he bought the High Butte."

"Let me guess. They've lived in this community all of their lives."

"Yes, ma'am."

Oh, how she remembered the loyalty of these people. "How did they come to work for him?"

"Carr indicated to the pastor of our church that he needed help, and our pastor knew Jasper and Lydia were in a bit of a bind financially. It worked out well for the three of them. They're like family."

So Adams and Carr attended the same church. She filed that away for future reference. "Can you assist Special Agent Anderson and me with this case objectively, knowing your friends may be involved with three murders?" Bella wished she could see his face and better read how her question affected him.

"Special Agent Jordan, those people may be my friends, but that doesn't mean one of them isn't capable of concealing a crime. On the other hand, I trust my instincts." Irritation ripped through his voice.

She needed to make friends with Sheriff Darren Adams,

not alienate him. "I apologize if I sounded like you were not a professional."

"Yes, ma'am."

"Were you briefed as to why the FBI has been called into this investigation?"

"Brandt Richardson's involvement in the Spider Rock treasure. He's on your wanted list for murder and may be involved." He recited the explanation as though she were testing him. Not good. She needed to befriend him.

"Do you believe in the treasure?"

"Lots of folks around here swear by the old stories."

Those old stories had nearly been her demise.

"The clues are everywhere, strung out in several counties, but the likelihood of the treasure being buried in Runnels County is slim. In response to your question, I've more important things to do than waste my time and money on searching for a supposed treasure."

"Thanks, Sheriff. I'm hopeful this assignment will be completed in days and not weeks or months. I'll be at the High Butte within the hour." Bella disconnected the call and turned to Vic. "Do you know much about the sheriff? I heard a wild tale about him, but I don't know if it's true."

Vic ran his hand through his hair. "Probably is. We call him Daredevil Adams. He's been known to climb out of the passenger side of a moving patrol car and jump onto the bed of a pickup loaded with bundles of marijuana." He laughed. "I've been known to pull a stunt or two, but I'm not sure I'd risk my neck for a little grass."

"The story I heard had him standing up to half a dozen gang members who attempted to crash a high school dance. Adams and his wife were chaperoning in plain clothes. When one of the knife-wielding boys threatened a teacher, Adams used martial arts to settle all of them down."

"That's Daredevil Adams."

"I look forward to meeting this West Texas hero." And she hoped he had the integrity her report claimed.

Bella set her BlackBerry on record and fed it the information she'd gathered from her conversation with Sheriff Adams. This also gave Vic the opportunity to hear the other side of the conversation.

The farther she drove south on Highway 83, the more remote the area and the drier the air. An eerie feeling swept through her, as if she were driving from one world into another. In essence, she was. In some of the outlying areas, the nearest large town could be an hour's drive or more. There the folks lived by their own rules and ethics. She should know; she'd witnessed the evil that could dwell in a man's heart in this part of Texas.

"Sheriff Adams's friendship with Sullivan bothers me," she said. "I've read the sheriff's career stats, and they're admirable. Yet the church loyalties could mean a cover-up, a way for those involved to look like good Christian citizens while breaking the law."

"I agree. The sheriff could be purposely ignoring clues. I'll take a look at his reports and see if anything's missing. When it comes to a violent crime, I don't care whose toes get stepped on."

"Good. While you're at it, could you check on the vehicle belonging to Professor Miller? It was at the crime scene and hauled in for a complete sweep. The sooner we have the results, the better."

Vic drummed his fingers on the dashboard. "I have a few questions about why you're the lead agent."

Here it comes. Vic's talk about respecting women agents was about to get flushed down the toilet. "I'm surprised you weren't informed. I spent the first fifteen years of my life in Runnels County. I know the locale."

"I see. Is your family still here?"

"My aunt raised me, and she lives in Pennsylvania."

"You're a long way from home. Or close to it."

"Depends on what a person calls home."

Vic didn't seem pleased with her response, and she couldn't blame him. With his tenure at the bureau, he expected to be the lead. She considered explaining a little more, but why be defensive? She took a deep breath to rid herself of the animosity inching across the car seat. Nothing in her life had ever been easy, and nothing had led her to expect the road would be smooth now.

The countryside sprawled out on both sides of them: rolling land with little vegetation, harsh and unforgiving. Like most of her memories. Mesquite trees with their featherlike leaves and live oaks dotted the land. Cacti bloomed in yellow, adding color to the bland countryside. Everything here was a postcard of a place she vowed never to revisit.

She entered Runnels County on the north side, a little more rolling and flat. To the right of 83, fields had been plowed and irrigated. Memories, like haunting nightmares, swept over her. She needed this assignment for more reasons than she cared to list.

Once through the small town of Ballinger, the county seat, she took 67 toward Coleman and Valera, according to the GPS recommendations on her phone. These were towns she remembered from school days. She had about another six miles to the High Butte Ranch, passing over Long Branch Creek, then Bearfoot, Butternut, Mustang, and Middle Mustang creeks. More time to think and plan, and Vic wasn't a big talker. She couldn't tell if he was sulking about not having the lead or simply quiet.

Bella drove past a Dodge pickup caked with red dirt. The driver lifted a finger from the steering wheel. It reminded her of old neighbors—neighbors who smiled and went on with their lives, neighbors who thought Christianity meant minding their own business. Neighbors who thought they knew each other.

As much as she didn't want to relive her younger days, if something embedded in her mind led to finding Richardson or solving the case, she'd bring it to the surface.

Opposite a cemetery, she turned right onto a narrow dirt road that was supposed to lead to the High Butte. She moaned. Railroad tracks, then a locked gate strung across the narrow road—not an unusual sight for this area, but she'd hoped for clear passage to the ranch. A sign read, *6187 Acres. No Hunting, No Fishing, No Firearms.* Someone should have told the shooter. A solar panel to operate the gate was mounted high on a pole, and a call box was affixed about five feet from the ground.

"I've got the number for the ranch and the sheriff," Vic said, opening the car door. "I'll get one of them to open the gate."

A few moments later, he shook his head and walked back to the car. "The call box doesn't work. Imagine that."

Bella pulled her phone from her purse to call Sheriff Adams. Rats. No connectivity. She turned to Vic. "Can you call out?"

He glanced at his BlackBerry. "Nope."

"We could walk, but I don't want my rear filled with buckshot." What a way to begin the investigation.

"Neither do I want to carry our equipment or leave it behind."

Groaning, she backed onto the paved road and headed back the six miles to Ballinger. Once inside the city limits, she parked at a feed store and saw she had the ability to call out. Again she pressed in the sheriff's number.

"The gate's locked on the 67 entrance," she said after he answered.

"I entered on the west side, where there isn't a gate. Same entrance where the victims entered. I'll get Carr to open the gate on 67."

"Thanks. We're on our way." Bella exchanged an exasperated look with Vic and drove back toward the High Butte's gate. She drove slower this time, taking in what she could see of the ranch to the right of her. In the distance a butte rose up to meet a cloudless sky. Many of the ranches had wind power farms to generate electricity, and Sullivan's property had them too. Frankly, she thought they were ugly.

A sharp bang startled her. *A blowout.* Bella lifted her foot from the gas pedal and gripped the steering wheel while maneuvering the car to the right side of the road. The left rear wheel bumped metal to the pavement as the car slowed to a stop, and she turned off the engine.

"Someone just shot out your tire." Vic pulled his weapon from his pocket.

Another bang leveled the front left tire. "A rifle." She leaned toward the right side of the car and retrieved the Glock 26 from her ankle holster. She lowered the windows and strained her ears, listening for more rifle fire. Only the quiet sounds of birds and insects met her.

Vic slowly lifted the handle on the passenger side, then kicked it open. He peered in all directions. All seemed quiet. "I don't see a thing," he whispered.

Seconds passed with her pounding heart keeping her company. So they'd been followed. A crow soared above them and called out to another. Cat and mouse was not her favorite game.

She gathered up her phone in her palm and hoped for a signal this close to town. Redialing Sheriff Adams, she realized a little good luck would fit the bill. He answered on the second ring.

"Special Agent Jordan here. We've got a little problem." Bella peered up slightly through the driver's side window. A faint dry breeze met her. "Someone's shot out my tires."

"Are you two okay?"

Until I run into Brandt Richardson. "Yeah. Fine. Wondering where the shooter is hiding. The shots came from the property to the north of the road."

"Any more shots?"

"No. He's had time, unless he only meant to scare us." Which did scare her a little. No way would she confess that to a twenty-year seasoned agent.

"Where are you?"

She slid her finger across the GPS portion of her phone. "About three miles out of Ballinger."

"Sit tight. We'll be right there."

The longer Bella waited for Sheriff Adams, the more restless she became. *This is ridiculous.* "Know what, Vic? I'm not sitting here waiting for the county sheriff's department to save my hide."

"And I don't plan to read in the local newspaper about how the sheriff's department saved two FBI agents."

She caught his attention. "Our egos are bad."

"But we're honest. Are you calling your supervisor about the shooting?"

Bella didn't want to inform Swartzer about the shots, but she was supposed to report the damage done to a government vehicle.

"I will later. I want to check out the tires first."

Vic eased out the passenger side, using the door and the car as a shield. Bella crawled over the console and followed suit. A few head of Black Angus cattle grazed on the High Butte, unaffected by the rifle fire. Across the road, a clump of trees stood about six hundred feet from the car. Thick enough to hide the shooter, especially if he had a high-powered rifle. If he'd wanted to pick them off, he'd have done so before now.

"I sure would like to know if those bullets are still in my tires," she said. "The rear is metal to the road, but the front tire should have the bullet."

"I can take a look."

"No thanks. I'll do it." She pulled a pocketknife from her purse and proceeded to the front driver's side of her car with the knife in one hand and her Glock in the other. Vic covered her. Kneeling, she studied the terrain again to the left. Nothing, not even a breeze. She saw where the bullet had lodged in the tire, but it was too deep for her pocketknife.

Hearing a siren, she and Vic stood to view the approaching flashing lights of the county sheriff's car. The vehicle kicked up dirt and dust behind it like a posse on the move. Behind that one was another county sheriff's car and then a red Ford F-250 King Ranch Crew Cab. One of the other agents had just purchased one, and he'd given every agent in the field office a tour.

The deputies emerged from their cars with their guns drawn. For Bella, a heavy dose of frustration and embarrassment lingered in the dry air. What a way to begin an assignment.

Bella and Vic stepped out from behind the open door and walked toward the sheriff. The man who emerged from the driver's side was anything but the stereotypical country law enforcer. Sheriff Darren Adams stood nearly six feet three, was tanned, and was definitely in shape. No spare tire there. Definitely the daredevil type.

She stuck out her hand. "Sheriff Adams, good to meet you. Special Agent Bella Jordan. This is Special Agent Vic Anderson."

She reached for her creds from the back of her waist, and Vic pulled his from his jeans pocket.

The sheriff gripped her hand lightly and made good eye contact. He gave a cursory glance at their creds. "Looks like the FBI needs to do a little field training in West Texas."

Ouch. That hurt. "You're probably right. Thanks for coming when you did."

The sheriff scanned the area around them. "Any more activity?"

"No."

"And you *are* okay?" He peered at one, then the other.

"Oh yes." Bella turned to view her FBI-issued car. It looked sad, reminding her of one of the vehicles in the animated *Cars* movie. "I could have flipped it."

"Could be the shooter wanted you to lose control."

"Then he lost round one." But she figured the shooter wanted them to understand they were being watched, and he probably got a good chuckle out of the episode.

The sheriff motioned to two officers beside him and pointed in the direction where the shots had been fired. "Take a look behind those trees in the pasture." He shook his head at the crippled condition of her car. *Deflated* had taken on a whole new meaning. The driver from the pickup strode toward them.

"The bullet should be embedded in the front tire," she said. "I'm anxious to trace the rifle to see if it's the same as the murder weapon."

"Let's hope not," the jean-clad man said. He held out his hand, and she got a glimpse of his face under a cowboy hat: clear blue eyes, lashes too long for a man, thick blond hair. Shock rode on the wind as recognition swept over her.

"You're Carr Sullivan."

"That's right." He smiled and shook her hand. He wore a pale yellow shirt with silver snaps, faded jeans, and dusty boots. A portable radio and a cell phone were clipped on his belt. In the five years he'd lived here, he'd definitely learned to fit in. He stuck out his hand to Vic and introduced himself. "In better circumstances, I'd have welcomed you to Runnels County with a barbecue."

Some things never changed. He still liked to party. "In better circumstances, I'd not be here."

He nodded at Bella. "That's a good one."

She didn't particularly care for his confidence, more akin to cockiness. "You have a pretty good attitude for a man suspected of murder."

"I'm innocent, and I'm out to prove it."

She caught Sheriff Adams's attention. "I assume Mr. Sullivan has been with you the whole time?"

"Yes, ma'am." The sheriff turned to Sullivan. "Special Agent Jordan is the lead on this investigation."

Sullivan looked none too happy. So he had a problem with women too. They were going to get along just fine.

"What can you tell us about what happened?" Sheriff Adams stuck his thumbs inside his belt. Now he looked like a cowboy law enforcer.

"Nothing to tell. We left Ballinger and drove back toward the gate. Didn't see a single vehicle."

"But someone saw you."

"Someone had to have an idea about what we were doing." Could the sheriff be behind this? After all, he was the only one who knew when she and Vic would be on the road toward the High Butte.

"Possibly having someone watch your hotel and phone ahead when you left," the sheriff said.

She and Vic were supposed to conduct surveillance work, not the shooter. "I hadn't noted anyone following us, so your explanation is probably right. What do you suggest about my car?"

"I can tow it to the county sheriff's department in Ballinger. We need that bullet."

"Sounds like a plan."

The lack of wheels and being at the mercy of a county sheriff plummeted her spirits. *Nothing like being humbled, and I deserve it.* Too many times she took on a brisk attitude simply because of her gender and her stature. "Should have brought my bicycle."

Sheriff Adams chuckled. "I'll get your car back as quickly as I can."

"Are you returning to Sullivan's ranch?" Bella said.

"I am."

"Good. We can spend some time going over the investigation." She turned to Carr. "Mr. Sullivan, I have a lot of questions to ask you." She wasn't about to ask him if he had an attorney.

"Call me Carr. In fact, why don't you ride back to the ranch with me? We can start the questioning en route."

Did he think she'd lost her mind along with her ride? "No thank you. I really need some one-on-one time with Sheriff Adams."

"And the idea of riding with a suspect doesn't appeal to you?" Carr's words twisted toward sarcasm. "Would you prefer that Agent Anderson ride with us?"

"Easy, Carr." Sheriff Adams's voice rumbled low. "Special Agent Jordan has a job to do. We all want this over with and the real killer found."

Bella's opinion of the sheriff raised a notch. No, two notches. The caverns beneath Carr's eyes indicated he hadn't slept for a few nights. She wouldn't want a friend of hers suspected of murder. *Friends on the edge.* A twinge of compassion swept through her for these two men. How far would the sheriff go to protect Carr? A good question, and she didn't have an answer.

"Mr. Sullivan—I mean, Carr—I understand the past few days have been a nightmare for you. Three murder victims killed with a rifle belonging to you—"

"Stolen."

"Yes, sir. No doubt if the bullet in the tire of my car is from your rifle, then the suspicions about you are greatly diminished."

"Will I be exonerated?"

"That will happen when substantial evidence points elsewhere."

Carr rubbed his forehead. "I understand. Never thought I'd be involved in a murder case. Neither did I ever think I'd find dead bodies on my ranch."

Was his regret staging? "We've got to talk about all of it." Bella looked at Sheriff Adams. "I changed my mind; I'll ride with him. Do you have reports for me to see?"

"In my car."

She could examine them later, and Vic had already indicated a need to follow up on the work done the previous day. Right now her prime suspect was tired and upset. And under those physical and mental stresses, he might let something slip.

"I need to get my equipment first."

"Would you like some help?" Carr said.

She was definitely in West Texas.

CHAPTER 4

Carr slowly drove Highway 67 toward the High Butte, sparse trees and grazing livestock dotting the landscape on either side of the road. He hadn't expected a woman, especially a petite one, but her feisty attitude made up for her tiny frame. If he chose to cast an admiring glance, he did like auburn hair and deep, sea green eyes.

What am I doing admiring a woman who's investigating me for murder?

The last two nights without sleep had affected him worse than he thought. Carr's temples began to throb at the thought of the evidence stacked against him. With Agent Jordan sitting in his truck, she could watch his every move and analyze him. He imagined she was weighing his body language, every word he said, and mulling over his past record as a high roller who had a nasty temper. If he were in her shoes, he'd clamp on the handcuffs.

He swallowed what seemed like a boulder and forged ahead. "Look, I think we got off on the wrong foot. I'm sorry." He gripped the steering wheel. "I know this situation looks bleak. But I didn't kill those men. I want you to know I'll do whatever it takes to prove my innocence."

He assumed she'd heard a lot of innocent pleas from criminals who were guilty as sin—and murder was a sin. And here he was trying to persuade her that the evidence against him was a setup. What could he say or do to convince her that the authorities suspected the wrong man?

"Did the men come to see you prior to the shootings?" Her voice rang soft, sweet, as if she cared about his stress. Obviously she'd learned how to use compassion to wile a suspect's confession.

"No. One of them called me, Daniel Kegley. That was a shocker, since only a handful of people have my cell phone number. Don't know how he got the number, but if someone wants something bad enough, I know the information can be found." Carr moistened his lips. "Kegley said he represented a team of three men who had proof the Spider Rock treasure was buried on my ranch. They wanted to dig for it and would give me 15 percent of the findings." He reached for his can of Mountain Dew, not knowing what he needed more—the caffeine rush or the sugar to fill the empty pit in the bottom of his stomach. "I turned them down. Told them to stay away from my ranch, or I'd report them to the sheriff."

"How did Kegley respond?"

"Told me I was throwing away the opportunity of a lifetime. I could be rich beyond my wildest imagination. Buy anything I wanted. He went on and on, so I hung up."

"When did Kegley make the call?"

Carr mentally calculated the days. Today was Wednesday, and the call came last week. "Last Thursday."

"Did you hear from them again?"

Carr had kept the other calls to himself, most assuredly a mistake. His head pounded harder. The idea of being arrested for withholding information stomped across his mind. But he had to be transparent and tell her the truth. "Yes. Two more times after the first one." He shot her a quick look. "And I didn't tell Sheriff Adams about the other two calls. I don't have an excuse except that I was trying to make the whole thing disappear."

"Understandable, Carr. This is a tragic occurrence. So what happened?"

"Friday night, Kegley phoned me with the same request. He

claimed to be with his two partners in Abilene. I heard music and talking in the background, which led me to believe they were in a bar or restaurant. I told him to stay off my land, or I'd run them off with buckshot in their rears."

"So Kegley made contact twice."

"Right." Carr paused, thinking through the last call to see if he'd missed something. "The professor phoned me on Sunday night. He had a different tack. I termed it a threat. Said my past would catch up with me if I didn't cooperate. He had the means to destroy me financially. I figured they were all nuts, and I'd report them to Sheriff Adams after Jasper and I rode fence on Monday." He shrugged. "You know the rest."

He could feel her gaze branding him. "I don't understand why you didn't reveal this earlier."

"I told you. I wanted it all to go away. Stupid, but true."

"That doesn't make sense for a man who was a prominent business professional."

His blood pressure zipped from borderline high to nearly uncontrollable. "Managing a business and making an error that costs money is not the same as finding three bodies on your property that costs someone their life."

"Same man. Same mental faculties."

"Believe what you want. I told you the truth to assist in the investigation."

"Are you hiding anything else?"

"No, ma'am." Anger rippled across his chest. Oh, great. A heart attack would solve the FBI's dilemma. His coffin would seal his guilt.

"If you do remember something, please call me." She reached inside her purse and pulled out a business card. From the corner of his eye, he saw her write something on the back of it before placing it on the console. "I wrote my cell number on the back. I don't make a habit of handing mine out either."

"I'll keep it to myself." He took a deep breath to steady his nerves.

"Thanks. And you're not to take any trips from the immediate area until the investigation is over."

"I understand what *prime suspect* means." Which also meant his dream of establishing a home for at-risk teen boys would remain a dream, at least for the present. "I also understand from Sheriff Adams that I'm not the only suspect. I believe there's a man on your wanted list who could be behind this."

"Right. Tell me about your missing rifle."

Why did she have to be so abrupt? "As I told the sheriff, I have no idea how long it's been missing."

"And why didn't you report it?"

Hadn't she already read his report? "My mind was on other things."

They rode in silence with only the rumbling of the truck engine keeping them company. Ten years ago, he would have been contriving ways to seduce her, complimenting her, asking her to dinner, looking for an angle to impress her. How pathetically selfish he'd been then by not valuing women as human beings with sharp minds and tender feelings. He'd never been afraid of a woman until today. Special Agent Bella Jordan had the power to charge him with three counts of murder.

Carr considered flipping on the radio or playing a CD, but the music might offend her. *Who cares?* He punched the Play button for a CD. Ah, Michael W. Smith. Carr needed some reassurance that he wasn't alone in this nightmare.

Bella stared at the road while the male singer eased the silence between her and Carr. She'd been right; he was hiding something. But he'd spilled his guts without coercion from her. In fact, he offered the information. In one breath she saw and heard sincerity, and in the next she viewed a polished businessman disguised as a good old boy from West Texas. And she didn't care for the man's confidence masked as "poor me who's been set up for murder" syndrome.

Murderers were desperate people who thought through their actions in hopes of stopping the authorities who sought to bring them to justice. Three men were dead on his ranch, shot with his missing rifle. How much more evidence did she need?

She noted the mobile radio that acted as a repeater for his portable radio and probably for others who worked for him. Mr. Sullivan had all of the toys. Was he accustomed to always getting what he wanted?

A heavy dose of reality halted her accusations. A man was innocent until proven guilty, not the other way around. Carr Sullivan deserved respect until evidence proved otherwise. She knew better. Bella glanced his way. He was visibly upset. Aunt Debbie used to say Bella had a mental block when it came to males, and she needed to forgive those men who had disappointed her instead of blaming every male on the planet. Aunt Debbie was usually right.

"Good song," she finally said, though she hadn't been paying much attention.

"Do you listen to his music?"

"No. A little classical now and then. By the time I'm alone in my car or at home, I want quiet."

"Michael W. Smith is an icon in the Christian music arena. Performed for a lot of audiences, even Billy Graham Crusades."

"That's impressive." Billy Graham she knew. Aunt Debbie believed he was as good a preacher as the apostle Paul, only better, because Billy Graham had that singer with a deep voice and a three-part name—George . . . George . . . She couldn't remember. Oh, it didn't matter. A three-part name who sang with a deep voice. Bella had more questions for Carr before they reached his ranch. "Tell me what happened in Dallas."

He stiffened. "What are you referring to?"

"Let's start with the last arrest." She forced herself to sound more like a counselor than an agent seeking to pull out a confession.

"I imagine you have it all in your records. Wouldn't surprise me if you had the information downloaded to your BlackBerry."

Smart man. "I prefer to hear it from you."

"All right. I partied a lot in those days. One night at a club, after having too much to drink, I slugged a guy who made a pass at my girlfriend. When he got up, I hit him again. Didn't know he was a popular country-western singer. Went to jail for a few hours. Paid a fine. That's it."

"Do you still have problems with your temper?"

He tried to cover his obvious annoyance, but she saw it—his brows arched and his jaw set. "God has shown me how to rely on Him instead of using my fists. Do I still struggle with my temper? Sure. But it's a whole lot easier to control when He's walking beside me." He turned down the dirt road where the locked gate had previously kept her from entering the High Butte. She couldn't even see a house or a barn.

Carr put the truck in park and stepped out to unlock the gate. He swung it wide, then climbed back inside, drove through, and locked the gate again.

"What do you know about the Spider Rock treasure?" Bella said.

"Never heard of it until those men wanted to dig for it on my land. If you're asking if I believe it exists, the answer is no. Treasure hunters are those who want to get rich without working."

Exactly. "Some folks spend a lifetime looking for . . . let's say the Spider Rock treasure. They look for clues and follow them. When those are exhausted, they look for more and justify spending money and deserting their families for the sake of the find. The addiction is as strong as cocaine."

"Not me," Carr said. "I don't have the time or the inclination."

"You run cattle and a few horses?"

"That's right."

She allowed a comfortable silence to settle between them. "This is definitely peaceful with all the sights and sounds of nature. Do you enjoy living out here instead of the city?"

He splayed his fingers over the steering wheel. "I do. It's quiet. Cows don't talk back. I choose my own company."

"But it's so desolate."

"This is true beauty to me—a wild, untamed freshness that brings me closer to God. No sounds of traffic or smells of polluted air. No taste of disgruntled people or the stress of business to tend to. Just me and God in the nature He created for the world to enjoy. This is where I belong."

Did Sullivan truly believe this or had he carefully rehearsed his words? "It doesn't look like you get many people selling magazines." She purposely turned to stare out the passenger side window at cattle-filled pastures. Typical ranch. Neatly kept. The barns and a house came into view.

"I've never had a problem with anyone bothering me until Monday."

Not exactly what Carr Sullivan should have said to prove his innocence. "Don't forget: no trips or vacations until this is settled."

His face pinched. "How long do you think it will take?"

"Depends on how quickly we can work through the investigation and make an arrest."

"What can I say or do to show my desire to help find the killer?"

She took in a breath. They were nearing a picturesque farmhouse with a huge wraparound porch. Two Australian cow dogs ran to greet them. "That's a 'should' question."

He stopped the truck and focused on her. "I don't understand."

"You *shouldn't* have threatened those dead men, and you *should* have reported the missing rifle, and you *should* have told Sheriff Adams the whole truth."

CHAPTER 5

C<small>ARR HAD WALKED</small> into business meetings where every person there opposed what he was presenting. He'd gambled and lost, gambled and won. Critics had labeled him ruthless when it came to cutting a deal, and those within his conglomeration praised his ability to shuffle priorities and continue making money under his corporate umbrella. The *Dallas Morning News* repeatedly called him snarky, and Carr guessed it was because they couldn't print profanity. Six years ago, his life existed under those circumstances. Now he never spoke the vocab that partnered with wheeling and dealing. None of his cutthroat tactics staged in an Italian suit prepared him for false murder charges. Now, as he glanced around *his* kitchen and viewed Special Agent Bella Jordan enjoying the air-conditioning in *his* home, he realized she was ready to bring out the handcuffs.

Whose house is this?

Carr sucked in a breath. *Your house.* He kept telling himself God walked beside him, but it sure would be nice if he could feel a hand grip his shoulder or a whisper in his ear. Lydia once told him the Bible said, "This too shall pass," but he hadn't been able to find it. All he did have was a thin thread of hope woven with trust. He smiled at Darren and the two agents in dark blue FBI jackets while telling himself when this was over, he'd have a good life lesson to teach at-risk boys.

Standing in the kitchen of the home that once symbolized new beginnings, Carr caught Lydia's smile and the compassion in her eyes. He saw what he needed to keep going. The woman had more wisdom in each strand of her gray hair than he ever hoped to have in a lifetime. If Lydia ever chose to take on the big city, look out organized crime, drug cartels, and pedophiles. Her no-nonsense approach to right and wrong would have them behind bars in a day.

Carr wrapped his arm around Lydia's waist. "I'd like you to meet the FBI agents sent to investigate the problem here. This is Special Agent Bella Jordan—she's the lead on the investigation. And this is Special Agent Vic Anderson."

Lydia's wide smile coaxed one from Vic, then Bella. "Welcome to the High Butte. We wish you were here under better circumstances."

That's my girl.

"Thank you. Call me Bella."

"Call me Vic. I apologize for the inconvenience to your home. Hopefully we'll get this wrapped up today."

Lydia glanced at Darren. "I have fresh coffee and warm cinnamon coffee cake, plenty for all of you and your men outside."

Darren leaned on the kitchen counter. "I'll take a refill on the coffee, but we have lots of work to do. This isn't a social event, Lydia. I'm sorry."

Lydia pressed her lips together, and her eyes pooled. Carr walked her to the coffee bar and squeezed her side. "This will be over soon," he whispered. "Then we'll go on with our lives."

"I know. It's the waiting that's so hard on all of us. I can't stop thinking about those poor men. What about their families?"

"It is tragic for them, and they've all been notified." Bella's voice rang with kindness and sympathy. "A cup of coffee would be nice, but I can help myself." She glanced around the tiled kitchen. "I like the Southwest flair—more like New Mexico or Arizona. This is beautiful, Carr."

"I can't take the credit. When I moved here, I hired a decorator from Abilene. She has great taste."

Lydia turned to the coffee bar, and Carr pointed to everything the group would need. The leaders of the task force wanted privacy to discuss the case, and as much as he wanted to hear every word, he didn't make the cut.

"No one brews better Starbucks than Lydia," Darren said.

Carr forced a smile for Lydia's sake. "Help yourself. I'll be upstairs in my library. Lydia will be in her room on the first floor behind the kitchen. Jasper is taking care of things outside."

"Once we're finished here, I want to take a ride to the crime scene." Bella poured a tall cup of coffee. She picked up the bear-shaped container of honey and read the label. "Good. Local honey. I'll need this to fight allergies." She measured a dripping spoonful and stirred it into the coffee. "Thank you both for your hospitality. I appreciate it."

Carr caught her eyes, green edged in gold. They were bright but not with sparkles like his Lydia. Odd, how he used to look at a woman for other characteristics, and now his interest focused on a woman's eyes and hair. Must be God. Bella's auburn hair, pulled back into a no-nonsense ponytail, had lighter shades of red. It shone in the morning sunlight streaming through the window. Strange how he admired her physical attractiveness while she looked for ways to pin him with murder charges.

With a nod, he excused himself and disappeared upstairs carrying a huge cup of black coffee. He'd already started the day with prayer and Scripture, and now he needed to call his pastor. He stepped into his library, which was also his study, a cozy room with floor-to-ceiling bookcases in light oak and a heavy desk in the middle made from distressed oak. His favorite room—other than the barn. With that he chuckled. His sense of humor was still intact despite his world crumbling around him.

He remembered a time in his life when he nearly succumbed

to madness and suicide, the night Michelle overdosed. And with what was discovered on his ranch and what was being discussed downstairs, it still did not compare to those days when he didn't have God to keep him strong and show him the way to peace.

He stared at his desktop, an array of books with his Bible spread out where he'd been studying Paul's missionary adventures. He'd planned to continue the study on Tuesday evening, which never happened. As he eased down into his massive brown leather chair, his attention swept to the right-hand corner of his desk, where he'd piled files and licensing information regarding the potential home for at-risk teen boys. He refused to remove it from his desk or give up hope. He focused on a Spanish cross sitting on the center of his desk and pulled his cell phone from his shirt pocket.

Seconds later he had Pastor Kent on the line.

"I heard what happened," Kent said. "Tried to call you a few times yesterday."

"I know and I apologize. Didn't want to talk to anyone. *Humiliated* and *angry* best described my attitude. Not sure I feel much better today."

"I understand. How are you doing—honestly?"

"Like a seasoned broker on Wall Street when the stock market hit bottom in 2008." Carr leaned into the back of his chair. "Kent, I can't figure out why God would allow this to happen right before we were ready to launch our plan for a boys' ranch. Why would He do that? It's an incredible need, especially with the state of our nation and world. I mean, we've read the stats with all of the fatherless boys and the climb in drug and alcohol abuse."

"I wish I had an answer for you, but my comments would all be speculative."

"Lydia thinks Satan doesn't want us to continue our plans. Or I'm like Job and need to be stronger. But the truth is, I don't need to know why as much as I want it all to end. Find the murderer and get the sheriff's department and the FBI out of my house and off my land."

"You have all of us praying. How're Lydia and Jasper?"

"Supportive. Jasper's not saying much. I think he's as angry as I am. The news reporters swarmed here yesterday. Like vultures." Carr stood and walked to his window. "Oh, they've returned in full force."

"I'm really sorry. What has your lawyer suggested?"

"You mean the lawyer who's been handling the paperwork for turning the ranch into a home for at-risk boys? I don't want to talk to him about this, especially since his specialty is contracts. Besides, I'm innocent, and that's what's going to vindicate me."

"Are you sure you want to eliminate good representation?"

Did Kent think he was guilty? Carr stiffened. They'd been friends since the beginning. A shiver rose on his arms. "If I'm charged, then I'll consider an appropriate lawyer. In the old days, I had lawyers on retainer to take care of every rough spot in my life. But those days are gone. I don't want to go back there. To me, calling in an attorney for this says I have something to hide."

"I hear the conviction in your voice, and only you know what God is telling you. But remember there are Christian lawyers who could defend you with God and the law on your side. We have a church member who's—"

"I know, Aros Kemptor."

"He's a good man. You know how he drives all the way from Abilene to attend New Hope. And he volunteers to help with projects and folks in need."

"So you're thinking I'm being bullheaded about this?"

"No. Well . . . maybe I am. You're my friend and my hunting and fishing buddy. I want you open to whatever options are tossed in your path."

Carr had been called stubborn a few times with an assortment of vivid adjectives thrown in. "All right. I'll give him a call. Guess I'd rather talk to a fellow Christian about this than the attorney who specializes in contracts."

"Would you like for me to come over?"

Carr considered Kent's request. Did he really want to drag his friend and pastor through the fresh manure? "No thanks. And I appreciate the offer. If you'll keep remembering me in your prayers, that would be great. The FBI has sent two agents to work on a task force investigation. Looks like a fugitive may be involved with the murders."

"I saw that in the Abilene newspaper. Brandt Richardson is wanted for several murders. He used to live in these parts, but as far as I know, he and his wife haven't been seen in about twelve years."

"I'm going to ask some questions of my own once the meeting is over downstairs."

"Okay, bud. From where I'm at, looks like you could use peace, guidance, strength, wisdom—for both you and the investigators—and an end to this tragic set of circumstances."

"Add comfort for Lydia and Jasper. And don't forget the families of the victims. In fact, would you send out a prayer request for those families?" Carr thought about what he'd just said. "God has to be working hard in my life for me to be thinking about someone other than myself."

"He's in that business. I'd like to pray with you, but first I'd like to recommend a few passages of Scripture."

"Sure. I need all the help I can get. Early this morning I thought of Valium and a bottle of Cutty Sark." Carr reached for a small pad of paper inside his desk drawer. "I'm ready."

"Start with 1 Peter 5, verses 6 through 10. When I'm down, these always help me put life into perspective. Then Psalm 23 and Psalm 139 are a good dose of reality. I also like Hebrews 11 to help me understand I'm not the only man in history who has been through hell."

Carr finished jotting those down. Familiar passages, but powerful. "In the early hours of this morning, Lydia suggested I start a list of things I'm thankful for. Sounded like a childish assignment at first, but it's starting to make sense. I'm ready for that prayer."

★ ★ ★

Bella sat at the kitchen table in Carr Sullivan's house, drinking his coffee and discussing a murder he'd probably committed. She doubted she'd be a model of congeniality if in the same situation. Sheriff Adams had a file in his hand, but she guessed she'd already seen most of the findings.

Back at the field office in Houston, the task force would be working shoulder to shoulder to solve the crime. The FBI, Houston police department, Field Intelligence Group, and in some instances the Secret Service would be in a conference room exchanging information. Here she met with Sheriff Adams and Vic.

"The ballistic report states the victims were shot from about five hundred feet, about the same distance as the stand of trees the shooter could have used to blow out my tires," she said. "Looks like we have a marksman here. Anyone know Carr's skill?" She directed her question at Sheriff Adams.

"He's a fair shot. Nothing to brag about." He jotted down something on a notepad. "He does some hunting with our pastor. I'll find out and get back to you."

Bella thanked him, appreciative of the extra step, considering his friendship with the suspect. "I'm wondering about vehicles at the scene. The shooter had to get there by some mode of transportation."

"We found one set of tracks belonging to Professor Forrest Miller. The SUV is parked at the sheriff's department and is in the middle of a complete sweep. So far, the only fingerprints were the ones left by the murder victims." Adams lifted the coffee to his lips. "And we found horse prints about seven hundred feet from there. However, no boot prints were found. Looks like the shooter used a leafed branch to cover his tracks."

"What entrances could he have used to gain access to the ranch?" she said.

"West side," Adams said. "And my thoughts are he must be a professional."

Brandt Richardson spun into Bella's mind. In the past, he did his own dirty work with perfection and precision. She studied Adams's body language while she drank her coffee. "Our killer is a man who goes to all the trouble of stealing a rifle and planning his moves. I don't think we can rule out Brandt Richardson as the shooter or working with the real killer."

Vic picked up the file folder on the kitchen table. "I disagree. Carr Sullivan is our man. He has motive, the weapon, and a past record that slides him into the murder corner."

"Or the two could be partners," she said. "Have you had any other shootings of late?"

"No," Adams said. "What is the last known whereabouts for Richardson?"

Bella recalled Richardson's latest report. "A year ago he was seen in Abilene at a bar. He'd changed his hair color to black and added a mustache and beard. A woman was with him, but she didn't fit the description of his wife. When he started asking the bartender, who was a college student working on a criminal law degree, about the Spider Rock legend, she got suspicious. After Richardson left, she took his glass to the police department. A quirk of circumstances that aided the authorities in trying to apprehend him." She scribbled a note to have Vic contact the girl again.

Bella saw a deputy's car drive up. The two deputies who emerged were the men who'd remained at the shooting site to wait for a tow truck. She really needed her car. More importantly, she wanted the bullet dug out of her tire. Vic saw the deputies and rose from the table to meet them outside.

Sheriff Adams took a deep breath. A spark of determination flared in his eyes. "Sure would like to catch the man who brought murder to our community."

"We all would," she said. "Any idea what happened out there?"

"Speculation, Agent Jordan. I hesitate to say because I haven't found a single lead."

"That's why we're working together. What have you done to this point?"

"Interviewed Carr, Lydia, and Jasper. Another man helps part-time, but he's been in Mexico."

Probably undocumented. But his citizenship status doesn't make him guilty of murder. "I'll want to talk to them too." She wrote down more memos.

Adams lifted a couple of sheets of paper from his file and pushed them her way. "Here is the transcription of our findings. Oh, I've ordered the phone records on the three victims and Carr."

"Thanks. That will help so I don't duplicate things. Anything else I need to be aware of?"

"We've searched through the house and brushed for fingerprints. We're working on the barn, horse stalls, and tool shed. I've gathered up every bit of trash and assigned a couple of men to that detail. I believe they have some obscure items you might want to examine, but nothing substantial." Adams sat calm and relaxed. His gestures were not demonstrative, neither did he sit rigid, and he hadn't touched his face. Eye contact was good but not forced. Unless Sheriff Darren Adams had acting experience, he was not deceiving her.

"You're thorough." She met his gaze and hoped he saw the respect. "I'd like to talk to the men who've gone through the house and whoever is working trash."

"Sure. You planning to give trash detail a little help?"

"Actually, I am."

"Gotta hand it to you," he said. "You don't mind getting dirty."

"Oh, I brought gloves."

He chuckled and she joined him. She desperately needed to trust Adams, and although all the signs were there to believe him, the truth could bite her in the backside if she wasn't careful. "I'd also like the cell phone records for Lydia and Jasper—if they have cell phones."

"I'm sure they do."

Bella picked up the file, anxious to get started on her part of the investigation. "How soon can we visit the crime scene? I'd like to look around before diving into other areas."

"Sure. I need to check on a couple of my men first. And I have a call to return."

"Guess I'll check with your men about the trash, see what they've put aside for me."

Vic cleared his throat from the doorway. "Uh, Bella, I've got a message from the field office in Dallas. Then I want to talk to Jasper and Lydia."

"I'll be outside." Adams rose from the table. "It'll most likely be tomorrow before I have the results of the bullet dug out of your tire."

Bella remembered country time versus city time and the resulting frustration. She'd have to put a little rocket fuel into the investigative engine.

CHAPTER 6

BELLA STRODE DOWN the back porch steps toward Sheriff Adams, who still had his phone to his ear. While he handled his call, she made small talk with the deputies who were going through trash. The temperature was rising, so she wrapped her jacket around her waist. One of the men handed her a pair of rubber gloves, no doubt thinking she wouldn't assist. But she pulled them on and laughed about the large size. Her own were in her bag, but this appeased the deputies, and she needed to demonstrate she was a team player. She'd dive into it until the sheriff completed his call.

All of the trash from Carr's house and barns had been gathered the day of the murders and, according to Sheriff Adams, the men found nothing. Since then, they'd added more green bags with the nifty yellow ties to the growing pile from the house and barn. One of the bags had shredded papers from Carr's library. She tagged that one to send to the FBI lab in Quantico, Virginia. A special department there would piece it together.

In the heat, the stench from the food waste wafted through the morning air and gagged her. She'd seen a compost heap on one side of the barn and was thankful she didn't have to go through that. But the findings might add critical evidence to the case, so she continued to work alongside the deputies and echo their displeasure with the task. As she completed each bag and grimaced with the maggots pilfering through them, she wished for once that Frank had been assigned to this case too. Not because this part of the investigation was unpleasant, but because she felt unsure about her assignment. However, she'd not ask for any partner other than Vic, even if it meant working 24-7 to solve the murders in a reasonable amount of time.

She stretched her back and glanced at Sheriff Adams, still involved with his call. One of Carr's dogs nuzzled at her leg. She pulled off her stinky glove and let the animal sniff the back of her hand before patting his head. Snatching up another bag, she noted this one had come from the barn. What luck.

"Do you think this is going to take all day?" Sheriff Adams said, startling her. She hadn't seen him approach. From the look on his face, he'd taken her handling of the trash as a personal affront rather than a willingness to help, and she could feel the iciness.

"It could, but it won't."

"Glad to hear you've decided the Runnels County Sheriff's Department does know how to handle routine procedures."

She didn't need an enemy here. Time to rein in her controlling personality with a generous pinch of Southern charm. "Sheriff, I have no doubt you and your people have followed this investigation to the letter. I'm not second-guessing you or doubting your ability. I'm simply the type who has to see things for herself." She gestured to the two deputies, who were listening to every word. "And I wanted to help."

"I understand, ma'am." He relaxed slightly. "This investigation has all of us edgy. Anything I can do here?"

"Nothing, really." She pointed to the tagged bags. "Those are finished. I need to know where to place for disposal." She didn't envy the deputies assigned to this mess. "Can you take me to the crime scene?"

"I'm sorry, but there's been an accident on 277. That and two other emergencies need my attention. Unfortunately, I need a couple of my deputies. One of the perils of the county sheriff's department. Never enough personnel."

She masked her irritation with a smile. "That's a problem everywhere."

He shifted and glanced toward the house. "What about Carr? Two of my deputies are at the scene if you feel uncomfortable about being alone with him."

The sooner she got her car back the better. But as much as she detested riding in a truck with a suspected murderer, this would give her time to befriend Carr and see if he spilled any more of his guts. "That'll be fine, Sheriff."

"How about first names? We're going to be spending some time together with this investigation."

"You're right, Darren. I'm Bella."

Once in Carr's truck, she allowed the air-conditioning to chase away the perspiration trickling down the sides of her face. The leather seats were cool too.

"Brought you a cold water." He set the bottle in the cup holder between them.

"Thanks. Just what I need." She wrapped her fingers around the icy wetness, then twisted off the cap, listening for the familiar snap to release the seal. *Drop the paranoia. Carr Sullivan, even if he had shot the three men, wouldn't poison me at a ranch swarming with deputies and another FBI agent.*

"How's the trash detail?"

The sarcasm in his voice annoyed her, but she'd keep her feelings shelved. "Smelly and filled with maggots."

"You're not going to find anything, unless the person who stole my rifle planted incriminating evidence."

"This is part of my job." She took a long drink. The water, mixed with the air-conditioning, gave her a new spurt of energy.

"Must be why I didn't choose law enforcement."

"Real estate, right?"

"Oh, I'm sure you know everything about me, including my

blood type and whether I prefer my Mountain Dew in a bottle or can."

"Bottle." She laughed. "AB positive."

"Good job. Where are you from?"

"Houston." At least right now.

"This dry heat must be a shock to your body."

More shock than he could imagine. "I think I might get real seasoned out here."

He pressed his lips into a lopsided grin. "Oh, the relentless sun has softened me up."

"Wasn't it hard? I mean leaving Dallas and the good life to go cold turkey in total isolation?"

"I welcomed it, like a deer pants for water."

Carr Sullivan wasn't the first murder suspect to quote Scripture—or kill, as if God had sent him as an avenging angel.

"But," he continued, "there were a few adjustments. I traded using my head for dirtying my hands. Tossed the gym for break-ing my back. Swapped my three-figure cologne for sunscreen."

Witty. She liked that. Kept life interesting. "Any regrets?"

"Only the events over the past few days."

"You mentioned that before. Have you remembered any-thing else?"

"Not a thing. I've turned my mind inside out, even rethought the phone conversations to see if I missed a clue or detected an attitude. Nothing."

"If something comes to mind, no matter how insignificant, I want to know right then."

Carr pulled his pickup alongside a deputy's car and disengaged the engine. "Here we are."

Bella peered up at the magnificent stone butte. Amazing. Even when she lived in this area, the structures had captured her atten-tion, as if a giant had taken a sword across the top of a mountain, then used it as a table.

"Gorgeous, aren't they?" Carr said.

"I wonder what secrets lie there."

"Centuries of stories, I'm sure. What can I do to help?"

Bella drew herself back to the present. "All I need is for you to wait until I'm finished. I want to check out the crime scene and walk the area."

"I haven't done any searching myself. Darren spent most of the day combing the area yesterday, and I steered clear of their investigation."

She raised a brow, ready to recite the law regarding entering a crime scene, but he raised his palm. "I'm not talking about the taped section but the outlying area. So can I join you once you're finished there?"

"I think you already know the answer. Darren couldn't risk your jeopardizing the investigation and neither can I." When Carr frowned, the banner of whether or not he was guilty marched across her mind.

"The protocol here stinks."

"I don't make the rules, Carr. I simply do my job."

He gave her an obligatory nod and stepped out of the truck. She opened her door and slid out of the seat into a boiling temperature that felt about as welcome as the rattlesnakes and scorpions lurking under the rocks. Carr waited for her near the hood; then the two walked together toward the deputies.

Carr shook each one's hand. "Mornin', Sam, Wesley. I'd like for you to meet Special Agent Bella Jordan from Houston."

She chose to keep her creds tucked in her purse and flashed a smile instead.

The older deputy shook her hand. The younger man greeted her. "I'm Wesley Adams. Welcome to West Texas."

Bella made the same small talk with them, just as she had at the ranch house.

"Her car met with a little accident this morning," Carr said. "And I'm being her chauffeur."

"A good one, too," she said, adding as much friendliness as possible. "I'm going to look around. Don't mind me." She hoisted her heavy bag onto her shoulder, remembering she'd added a camera and handheld voice recorder. While the men talked, she made her way to the yellow-taped area. Kneeling to the side of where each body had lain, she checked to see if anything caught her eye. Nothing. If there had been anything, it was gone now. She snapped a few pictures to go over later, even if they were over two days old.

The report stated each man had been shot in the head execution-style. That seemed more like Richardson's mode or that of someone he would hire. Whoever had done this had to be a crack shot. Just like the one who had destroyed her tires.

"Ma'am," Deputy Myers said. "I'll show you where we found the horse tracks."

She followed him west of the crime scene.

"The footprints you see here are the deputies'. Out there is where I think the killer dismounted." He pointed, and she followed.

The fading horse prints were a disappointment, but he informed her that the area had been swept for any traces of hair follicles. She snapped a few more pictures and wrote a quick note to see if horseshoes could be traced. As Darren stated earlier, the shooter had brushed away any traces of where he'd walked across the dry earth. A mesquite branch lay near the horse's tracks, probably the one used to conceal the evidence. But the shooter had to have slipped up somewhere. She stood. Wide-open spaces in every direction, except for the butte. According to Deputy Myers, the horse's tracks led beyond the High Butte to a county road where tire treads indicated the killer had parked a truck and trailer. That was the sheriff's department's theory.

All before six in the morning. *Why didn't the killer walk from the road?* She spoke into her handheld recorder and wrote the question on her notepad.

Bella turned to take in a 180-degree view. The killer had to know the layout of the land and exactly where the victims were digging. But there were no signs of a dig. For that matter, did the three find what they were looking for? If Carr didn't kill them for trespassing, then they must have uncovered something of value—valuable enough to pay for in blood. As much as she wanted to believe the business executive–turned–rancher hadn't killed them, the suspicions continued to mount.

Off to her right, several feet away, a figure moved, and she swung her attention in that direction. Carr walked slowly northwest from where she'd planted her feet.

"What are you doing?" Annoyance sent a memo to her logic. Was he looking to cover up his own tracks? "Are you destroying evidence before anyone finds it?"

Carr stopped and motioned for her. "If I wanted to look innocent, I certainly wouldn't be out here. I'd be home talking to a fancy attorney about my rights. Anyway, I've found something."

She hurried toward him while biting back a caustic remark. "What is it?"

"A candy bar wrapper." He pointed to the ground. "I'm not picking it up and putting my fingerprints all over it."

She stood beside him. Her mind spun, and she reached inside her shoulder bag for her gloves and a plastic bag. "Thanks. It'll be interesting to see the prints on this one." She picked up the wrapper and sealed it in the bag.

"Hope so." He studied her every move, making her uncomfortable. "You see, Jasper is diabetic, and even if it came from Ciro, his favorite is Snickers, not Godiva, like this one. This brand costs a few more pesos."

They were at least eight hundred feet from where the authorities believed the shooter had killed the men. With the wrapper secure in her bag, her gaze followed a straight path to the road. Could it be the sheriff's department had not looked this far?

Carr joined her, which set in the uneasiness again. Just because he'd found a shred of evidence didn't mean he'd been cleared.

"Not a law written says I can't walk across my own land."

"True, but if you try to obstruct my investigation, you're out of here."

He chuckled. "Yes, ma'am. And for the record, I'm not a candy connoisseur."

She'd like to cram his humor back down his throat. Her gaze swept around them. Trodden underbrush indicated someone had passed through en route to the road.

"The likelihood of one of my men or even me using that road is slim." Twice he bent to examine the brush but then moved on without a remark.

They continued to make their way along the edge of his property where the deputies had scoured yesterday.

"Let's walk north and see what we find," Carr said. "Darren told me this morning they didn't search much farther from here."

"As if the killer looked for his best advantage." She questioned why the deputies had been satisfied with what they'd found and not extended their search.

Bella was the first to see a heel print dug into dry earth. She reached into her shoulder bag and pulled out her camera. Several more prints took form until tire treads revealed the man had driven away. She snapped a few more photos.

Carr measured the boot print with his own foot. "This is about a size twelve. I'm an eleven."

Bella sensed a catch in her chest. *Control.* She peered around him. Jasper and Ciro most likely had small feet with their Hispanic ethnicity. "Could be one of the deputies."

"Possibly. But it's the best we have so far."

We? And she didn't need a reminder of her lack of evidence. "Mr. Sullivan, you are not a consultant on this case."

"You're right. I'm a suspect determined to prove my innocence."

Bella snapped a picture of the boot print. Recognition software would provide some answers. She climbed over the fence and walked a few feet down the dirt road away from where it looked like the killer had parked. Her father wore a size twelve. So did Brandt. Two details she remembered about these men.

Her father. She hadn't wanted to consider him involved in this, but he very well could be. Fourteen years ago, he'd been obsessed with finding the Spider Rock treasure. The entire family had suffered when he either spent household money to purchase treasure-digging tools or gambled it away. He and Brandt were partners back then, both men determined to get rich by finding the buried cache of sixty-four million dollars in gold on their dirt-poor ranch. But as much as she detested her father and what he'd done, would he resort to murder? She took in the surroundings, keeping her emotions deep inside. Of course he would.

If she had cell phone access, she'd have called Pete at Houston FIG to request a full report on Stanton Warick. Bella rubbed her finger across her forehead. She'd see if a text to Pete would go through and at least get him started on the process. Three men dead, all looking for the Spider Rock treasure. Brandt Richardson was wanted for murder-for-hire. Carr Sullivan had a record of violence and evidence against him, and her own father could be knee-deep in the whole mess.

CHAPTER 7

CARR SENSED HIS anger festering like a boil. Special Agent Bella Jordan believed he'd killed those men, and no matter what he did or said, she continued on the same dead-end road. Bad pun. His stomach churned with what the future might hold. The charges. A trial. The weeks and months of waiting. He eased the truck into reverse, turned around, and drove through the pasture back toward the house. Three hours in the blazing sun while she talked to deputies and snapped pictures. When she wasn't speaking into her little handheld recorder, she made notes.

Bella looked at him with a half smile, as if he were nothing more than a cockroach. What happened to a man being innocent until proven guilty?

"I want to know why you think I'm guilty." He stopped the truck and hung his left arm over the steering wheel. Angus grazed peacefully on both sides. Two mares and their foals added to a picturesque memento of how he'd viewed his life until Monday.

She tossed him a curious look. "Who said I did?"

"You. Every word spoken or unspoken. I read people well enough to tell when hostility rules the moment. Is this another rung in your ladder toward a fat FBI promotion?"

She winced for a fraction of a second, and he caught it.

"Be careful, lady; your fangs are showing."

Anger peaked in her green eyes. "I resent your unfounded accusations."

"And I resent your assumption that I murdered those men."

His voice had risen with each word. "Seems to me you're looking for ways to pin this on me instead of looking for evidence leading to the real murderer."

"I really don't care what you think. I have a job to do."

"I bet the sooner you get back to your air-conditioned office in Houston, the sooner you'll be sitting in a new office." He looked away. Losing his temper didn't prove a thing but his lack of control—and lack of control was what killed three men. His outburst would do nothing but move him higher on her list of suspects. He took a deep breath and then another. Putting his truck into drive, he drove on.

Once at the house, he saw Darren had not returned. Two deputies lingered with Vic on *his* back porch drinking *his* bottled water. Carr exited his truck and made deliberate steps to the back door, forcing himself to greet the three men. Anger jutted from the pores of his skin like barbed wire. He paid taxes and obeyed the law. He followed Christ and studied His Word. What more could he do?

Swinging open the door, he ushered Bella inside like a proper gentleman. But his thoughts were not conducive to attributes of a godly man.

Lydia met them in the kitchen. She blinked but said nothing about his apparent dissatisfaction with what had transpired. "Sheriff Adams said he'd be back around four."

Not soon enough, in his opinion. "I'll be upstairs."

"I have more questions for you," Bella said.

"I'll be upstairs."

Silence drummed on between them.

"I'm being a jerk," he said. "Sorry."

"I've been known to have better people skills." She blew out a sigh. "I'm sure there are more bags of trash for me to sort through. There's an outhouse behind the barn that better fits my attitude."

He lifted a brow. Comic relief he could use. "And what would you find?"

"More of the same. I'm sure."

"Excuse me?" Lydia's voice seldom took a high note, but it rang with a tone of authority. "Are you two squabbling or trying to get along?"

"We're attempting civility." Bella took the bottle of water that Lydia offered. "Neither of us has any answers. If we did, the killer would be in custody."

"I'm innocent. How do I prove that to you?" The bickering had to stop. Hurling words at Bella made him look immature . . . and guilty. Again he took another deep breath and asked God—no, begged Him—to muzzle his mouth. This time he began with control. "I apologize for my lack of manners. This whole thing has me upset, out of focus."

"Perhaps if I'd ever been in your situation, I'd understand." She crossed her arms over her chest, then unfolded them.

Carr desperately wanted to show her he wasn't a killer-psycho, but how? "I want to cooperate, not alienate the investigators. Seems like I left my faith and my ethics in the barn." What was she thinking? Had he dug himself in so deep that she could arrest him?

"You know, the Spider Rock treasure is cursed." Lydia's voice broke the awkwardness while he waited for Bella to comment. She stood between them, first eyeing Carr, then Bella. "Those men may have been murdered, but the curse of the treasure makes this tragedy no surprise."

Bella slowly nodded. "Knowing more about the treasure— the legends, the history, and those involved—might provide the motivation for the murderer."

"You're a smart lady, Agent Jordan." Lydia turned toward the hall leading to her and Jasper's room. "Now, if you two could discuss your differences instead of fussing like two children, this investigation might go a lot smoother."

Carr felt like he'd been disciplined by one of the sisters in parochial school, who had tried unsuccessfully to make him take his life and God seriously.

Lydia started down the hall, then whirled around. "And Carr did not shoot those men. The sooner you accept that fact, the better we'll all get along."

He hoped the stoic look on Bella's face wasn't the makings of an arrest. She could claim he interfered with the investigation or was hostile or who knew what else.

Finally she met his gaze. "Lydia makes sense."

"About my innocence?"

"About researching the Spider Rock treasure."

"The kind that leads to men getting killed?" Carr studied her—poised, a trained professional, type A personality. He didn't like her, but he didn't dislike her either. "I don't know a thing about the Spider Rock legend."

Bella uncapped her bottle of water. "I have a little knowledge. Looks like I need to acquire a lot more. Right now, I'm checking with the deputies who sorted through the trash."

Silence weighed in heavily, and she wore the boxing gloves.

He took in a gulp of air. "Can I help?"

Bella walked outside into the heat, which reminded her of what she'd left inside Carr's house. So many questions and so few answers. Aunt Debbie had told her that God had led her to this assignment, and the dear woman's voice echoed around her.

Learn more about the Spider Rock treasure? Memories slowly crept to the surface, despite the fact that she'd shoved them to the empty corner of her heart, then locked the door and hidden the key.

She took a breath to calm herself and studied the ranch house.

The two-story beauty rose up and sprawled out to well over six thousand square feet. If the circumstances were better, she'd have asked for a tour. Exquisite, but inviting. What she'd seen in the stone kitchen and the outdoor patio and summer kitchen said much for a man who liked to entertain, but Carr had chosen the life of a hermit. Well, until recently, when he decided to venture into the business of offering a home to at-risk boys.

The beauty of the perfectly landscaped surroundings, including the flowers and shrubbery on a timed sprinkler system, reminded her of one of her aunt's *Southern Living* magazines—even though she lived in Pennsylvania. Everything at the High Butte had been planned, right down to the Mexican heather with its tiny purple flowers, the rosebushes kissing the sun, and the bunches of pink and white impatiens within the shade of centuries-old oaks. In the rear, she'd noted a pool butted up against a rock waterfall. The rushing water pouring into deep blue depths gave the feeling of peacefulness—even if peace had exploded into turmoil two days earlier.

Oh, to have grown up in an architectural masterpiece such as this. Her thoughts turned to where she'd been reared amid the dirt and weeds. At least that had been home until she was fifteen. Her father had been in her thoughts since she'd flown into Abilene. And finding the size-twelve footprints had added layers of regret. When she was much younger, he'd slapped a huge photo of the Spider Rock map on his bedroom wall. Blown up in huge proportions like a shrine—the altar that ruled his every decision, even his heart.

A different shift of deputies arrived at three, and around four, Sheriff Adams returned and continued to work. Shortly after seven, she and Vic decided to call it a day. Bella wiped the perspiration trickling down her face and tossed her gloves in the trash. There were plenty more where those came from.

After informing Darren that she and Vic were ready to head

to Ballinger for her car, he introduced them to Deputy Roano, who'd be their transportation to town. Bella made a point of telling Lydia, Jasper, and Carr good night, if for no other reason than to have closure for the unpleasantness of the day. Sliding into the air-conditioned comfort of the deputy's car, Bella allowed her mind to dwell on what had happened during the last nine hours. The various pieces of paper found in the trash appeared meaningless, but she and Vic would follow up on those tomorrow. The thought of asking for assistance from the field office either in Houston or Dallas crossed her mind, but she refused to call for additional resources on the first day.

Perhaps tomorrow she'd have a report on the bullets lodged in her tire. The candy wrapper had led to the boot prints, which seemed to be the only substantial find. The print size affected her more than she cared to admit. Brandt Richardson and Stanton Warick were the two men who had caused her to run from this area in the first place.

Brandt Richardson. Her nemesis had frightened her long enough, and she would not stop until he was behind bars.

"Are you planning to return to the ranch tomorrow?" Deputy Roano said. The young man looked like he'd just graduated from the police academy.

"Yes." She smiled. "I hope a shooter doesn't decide to use me for target practice again."

"Ma'am, I know you're FBI and all that, but you and Special Agent Anderson need to be careful. The long stretches of road out here can be dangerous, especially if someone's after you."

Conscientious man to offer them a warning. "We'll be careful. Right, Vic?"

"After twenty-two years, I've learned a thing or two. But thanks for the warning. You have the advantage of knowing the area."

Roano nodded and they passed pleasantries between them. He didn't ask about the case, which she found odd. Neither did he inquire about the FBI—refreshing, because she didn't have enough words floating around in her mind to respond intelligently. Neither did she want to burden Vic by having him answer all of the questions. Food and crawling into bed zoomed to the top of her priority list.

After picking up her car, her confidence resumed, mostly because she had her own wheels again and didn't have to depend on a deputy or Carr Sullivan.

"What do you think?" she said to Vic once they were on the road.

"Something's not right about Sullivan. I think he killed those men."

"What about his plans to open a home for at-risk boys?"

"Ever been around an abortion clinic after a bombing? Those nutcases believe God wanted the clinic destroyed."

Bella understood Vic's reasoning, but she didn't quite agree. Of course, she hadn't revealed that Brandt wore a size-twelve shoe, and she had no idea if he had a favorite candy bar. "Well, we don't have enough evidence to arrest Sullivan yet."

"Maybe tomorrow." He lowered the temp on the air-conditioning. "Hope you don't mind. I can't seem to get cooled off."

"No problem. What do you think of Sheriff Adams?"

"Despite his friendship with Sullivan, he's followed the law. After all, he ran fingerprints and contacted us with the possibility of Richardson's involvement."

Bella agreed, but she couldn't help but believe something was missing, something they'd overlooked. "He had his deputies hard at work in the hot sun."

"Want to have dinner together?"

Vic was a nice guy, and she'd like to hear about his years in violent crime, but she wanted to be alone. "No thanks. I'm bushed and still have work to do."

"Sure. What time do you want to get started in the morning?"

"Early. I'd like to leave Abilene around seven."

"I have an audio conference at eight, so I'll drive myself when it's over."

"Okay. I know you said the interviews with Lydia and Jasper cleared them, but did you pick up on anything else?"

"Not a thing. We'll both stay on it."

Bella dropped him off at the hotel parking lot, then swung back into the street toward a chain restaurant and ordered carry-out grilled salmon. The tempting smell in the car drove her to distraction. Then her stomach growled to make matters worse.

At the hotel, she greeted the front desk on the way to her room. She slid the magnetic card into the door and eased inside. The soft hum of the air conditioner greeted her, and if not for the need to check e-mail and think through the day, she'd take her dinner to bed. Snapping on the lamp light, she relaxed in a soft chair and propped her feet on a matching ottoman.

After taking a couple of bites of the tender salmon and buttering a warm roll, she plugged in her computer, quickly got online, and responded to her work e-mail. After a few more bites, she checked her personal e-mail. A message from Aunt Debbie grabbed her attention.

Hi, Bella,

By now you've been on the job for a day, so I'm wondering how you're holding up. Oh, I know you're a top-notch special agent and all that, but my concern is the scene of the crime. West Texas, for heaven's sake. I'd rather you were in the Middle East. Keep your eyes open, one eye over your shoulder, and your weapon close by.

How very strange that we carefully hid our addresses so they couldn't find you, and now you've returned to another crime scene.

Now for the mundane things here in Pennsylvania. The

church plans two sessions of vacation Bible school. They asked me to be a teacher or an aide, but I had to refuse. I'd lose my mind with all of those little kids. About the first time a hyper little boy got the best of me, I'd be asking him if he was ready to meet Jesus. I'll bake cookies and deliver them at night.

Let's see . . . Got my hair done yesterday morning. Instead of the color corn silk, I went wild with strawberry blonde and requested a few maroon highlights. My aerobics class loved it.

I'm praying for you.

Love,
Aunt Debbie

Bella laughed until tears rolled down her cheeks. She needed to save all the crazy and witty quotes from her precious aunt and read them on bad days.

She whisked off a lengthy e-mail to the field office and finished her dinner. She'd refused to look at the bed for fear she'd toss back the quilt and sheets and not open her eyes until morning. Actually, not a bad idea.

With her teeth brushed and her face squeaky clean, weariness tugged at her eyelids while her shoulders ached. Her gaze swept over the flowered quilt, and she realized she'd better set her BlackBerry for five o'clock in the morning or she'd sleep till noon. In the shadows, she saw a long, narrow, hoselike shape in the bed. *What in the world?*

Bella touched the shape and jerked back her hand. *Surely not.* Her heart thudded against her chest. She moved around to the opposite side of the bed, grabbed the bedclothes, and flung them back.

A rattlesnake clicked its warning.

CHAPTER 8

CARR PRESSED IN the phone number for Aros Kemptor, the attorney Kent Matthews had recommended. He didn't know Aros's experience with criminal law, but he had witnessed the attorney's faith more than once in the last year since Aros joined New Hope Church. Volunteering time and money went a long way in showing a man's character.

About six months ago, a church member lost his house in a fire, and Aros stepped in by finding temporary housing for the family of seven—and paying for it. Another time, a young woman diagnosed with cancer no longer had medical insurance. Aros arranged for a county-wide benefit dinner and concert and then brought in a popular Christian singer from Dallas. Carr used to wonder why the man drove all the way from Abilene to attend church in Ballinger, but he said Kent's sermons and the community of believers were worth a little inconvenience.

Carr checked his watch and saw it was 6:30 a.m., mentally confirming what Kent had said about the attorney beginning work by six. With all of the problems connected with his involvement in the murders, he needed legal advice about his assets. Mainly his ranch. Aros answered on the third ring.

"This is Carr Sullivan."

"Mornin', Carr. Pastor Kent said you might be calling me. Sorry to hear about the unfortunate circumstances on your ranch. Anything I can do?" Aros's voice held a mixture of sympathy and friendliness, but the sound reminded Carr too much of the high-dollar attorneys who had been on his payroll in Dallas. He envisioned the dark-haired man leaning back in a plush leather chair in a tastefully decorated office in Abilene. Perhaps this wasn't such a good idea. He shrugged off his misgivings and focused on the reason for his call.

"Thanks. I'll feel better when the murderer is arrested and my name is cleared."

"How can I help you?"

Taking in a breath meant to erase the memories of some of the overpaid and obnoxious attorneys from his past, Carr plunged ahead. "I'm concerned about my assets in light of the murder victims found on my ranch. I wanted to verify that Texas property rights are supreme."

"Yes, sir. If you'd purchased the property with money obtained by illegal means—let's say drugs—then you could lose your ranch. The good news is, if you were charged with a felony, your property would still be intact."

Relieved, Carr tossed that worry aside. "Thanks. I needed confirmation."

"Do you need representation?"

"Not at this time. If I'm charged for those killings, then I'll be camping on your back doorstep."

"I understand how you feel. Regarding your concern about property rights, are you facing a lawsuit?"

"I don't think so. There was nothing dangerous about where the victims were digging. Except how they met their demise."

"A very sad and tragic situation. Would you like to get together and discuss this matter? I understand the sheriff's department and the FBI have taken up residence at your ranch. Are you sure they aren't in violation of your rights in your willingness to help with the investigation?"

The thought had crossed Carr's mind, and he wondered if his overexuberance in helping could be used against him. But he had to follow what he felt was the right thing to do. "I appreciate your help. But I'm fine with how the authorities are conducting their work."

"I hope you haven't made a foolish decision. Being a suspect in a murder case can damage your reputation for a lifetime. Legal representation is not an option; it's a necessity."

Aros had clearly demonstrated his faith, and he was a wise man with legal expertise, which Carr lacked. And yet the dilemma of whether or not to engage the attorney's services . . . "Let's see how the investigation progresses."

"I'm only giving you legal advice, Carr, nothing else. And I certainly don't want to undermine your convictions. Are the authorities still linking the deaths to the Spider Rock treasure?"

"The last I heard. It's a hoax, if you ask me."

"Call it what you want, but if people are dying for it, then it's a problem." Aros cleared his throat. "Carr, do you know anything about the Spider Rock legend?"

Great, here it comes again. "Not a thing."

"I suggest you ignore the tall tales. It'll only waste your time. Can't imagine three men giving their lives for such foolishness. Now look at what it's done to them and their families—and you."

"I thought I'd look into what's available online and read a book or two about it. I'm not in the treasure-hunting business, but I'd like to know what those men died for."

"I'm merely suggesting not getting involved. If you're arrested, your interest could be used against you."

Aros made good sense about an angle Carr had not considered. "All right. The sheriff and one of his deputies suggested the same thing. However, sitting around while the FBI and the sheriff's department continue their investigative work is driving me crazy."

"I'm a phone call away if you need representation or simply need to talk. Day or night, feel free to call. As you already know, I'm a single man. A call won't disturb me."

"Thanks. I'll give this a few more days."

"Be careful."

Carr ended the call and contemplated Aros's advice to ignore the talk about Spider Rock. The attorney made sense, but knowledge was power. At least he'd always believed so.

As Bella drove toward the crime scene, she hoped her second day at the High Butte Ranch would prove more productive than the previous one. Yet as the sun began its slow rise in the sky, she already had misgivings.

Last night, after she found the rattler in her bed, a young female manager with purple highlighted hair assisted her in changing rooms. Odd, since the report stated a man was the manager. Another matter she'd need to check into. The woman trembled so much that Bella ended up comforting her. Once in a new room, the manager sent a male worker to assist in searching for any signs of other unwanted reptiles. He tripped over his words and offered one apology after another about his uneasiness. More than once Bella considered sending him back to the lobby.

The snake had all the characteristics of a Brandt Richardson tactic. If he'd meant to kill her, then two bullets wouldn't have been aimed at her car tires or a snake planted in her bed. She knew changing hotels wouldn't matter. If someone had gotten into this hotel, he'd find access into another. What would the killer try next?

Although Bella had grandiose ideas of solving this case in a matter of days, she'd been fooling herself. Reports, interviews, motives, and follow-ups were in line for the entire task force. Another suspect floated to the top of the brine. *My father could be involved.* She shuddered. Although she detested him, the little girl in her didn't want to think of him as a murder suspect, and she couldn't bring herself to call FIG for a report. He wouldn't come after his own daughter. Or would he? When she examined the past, the probability reared its head like the rattler in her bed last night.

Returning to this part of the country could very well have been a mistake. The dry and barren land filled her with an intense fear, while an ache deep inside matched the wasteland surrounding the High Butte. She wanted to run from all it represented. But not this time, not with the prospect of ending what should have been finished years ago.

Bella considered herself a woman of logic and rationale, and still she had a feeling deep in the pit of her stomach that Brandt had orchestrated the three deaths and the threats on her life. Even worse, she knew he wasn't finished. Although she sensed she might not be strong or clever enough to outthink his next move, she'd chosen to face him and bring the past to the present before one more person died.

For a few moments she let her mind wander back to her three younger half brothers and a half sister and calculated their current ages. The oldest brother would be eighteen, then seventeen, sixteen, and her sister would be fourteen. They'd been sweet babies, often turning to her instead of their mother. She couldn't fault Mair too much because the woman had a tremendous burden in being married to Bella's father. All of them had gone hungry. Given the same situation, she might have reacted with some of the same apathy. Had those kids escaped the craziness of their parents, or were they walking the same road? Aunt Debbie said the time would come when she'd need to find her siblings and make peace with them. Even with her father.

The gate to the High Butte was open, a good omen as far as Bella was concerned. As she pulled the car to a halt beside Sheriff Adams's vehicle, gravel crunched beneath her tires. No one was in sight. She grabbed her shoulder bag and strode to the back door, where she figured Carr and Darren would be having coffee.

She took one quick, longing gaze at the pool, the early morning sun sparkling off its blue waters like a million twinkling diamonds. The door opened, and the sound of conversation reminded her of the murders and why she'd driven to the High Butte.

"Good morning, Agent Jordan." Lydia's wide smile could charm the moon. "Come on in and join us for breakfast."

"Call me Bella. Remember?" The scent of bacon and eggs and a waft of maple syrup tempted her. She hadn't run this morning. Been in too much of a hurry to get there. "When this is over, I'm making reservations here." What was she thinking? These people weren't friends. They were murder suspects. Then again, she needed to secure their trust.

"You'd be welcome." Lydia's silver and black hair was tied back in an elegant bun at the base of her neck. Long red and silver earrings and a turquoise blouse trimmed in red over dark blue jeans did make her look like she was welcoming guests at a resort.

Bella greeted Carr and Darren while pouring herself coffee. She *really* wanted some scrambled eggs and one, only one, piece of bacon. What was it about bacon and chocolate when it came to women? She gave in when Lydia handed her a plate. Once she lowered herself into one of the wooden chairs, she refocused on her job. "Vic will be here later on this morning. How long have you been here?" She aimed her question at the sheriff.

"About twenty minutes. Wanted an early start. How was your evening?"

Bella lifted a brow and poked a mouthful of eggs into her mouth. The sheriff might already know.

"Hope you got a good night's rest." With the dark circles beneath his eyes, Carr looked like he should go back to bed.

"Not exactly." Bella stirred honey into her coffee mug and

lifted it to her lips. "Someone put a rattler in my bed." Before either of the men could respond, she continued with her story. "However, I did get a free night at the hotel, which will help the looks of my expense report at the FBI."

"How ever did you crawl into bed after that?" Lydia's face had grown ashen.

Bella laughed. The woman's question reminded her of how she'd felt. "I changed rooms, and the manager sent a worker to help me tear everything apart—twice."

Carr leaned on one elbow. "Do you have any idea who did it?"

Bella bit into the bacon. With questions and details about the case swirling in her mind, her food no longer had appeal. "Obviously I'm being warned to leave this case alone."

"And?" Carr said.

"No way." Bella gave Sheriff Adams a curious look. He hadn't said a word, and his face appeared intent on her account of the previous night. His pale face was a sharp contrast to the man she met yesterday. "Is there something I should know?"

"I want to think about a few of the things we uncovered yesterday. In short, this investigation concerns me as to where it leads."

"We're all concerned." Carr scooted out from behind the table and helped himself to another cup of coffee. "What's going on, Darren?"

"In my opinion, more than one man is involved. I think it's a team of players, and last night at Bella's hotel proved it."

That's when she noted Darren hadn't touched his food. Sweat dripped down his temples, and his pale face indicated something was going on. "Are you sick, sir?"

Darren offered a tight-lipped smile. "I'm trying to talk myself out of it." He shook his head as though mentally chasing away whatever had attacked his system. "There's more to this than treasure hunters who are out to find the cache of gold. These are murderers who are well organized and out to derail our investigation."

"I agree we're not looking for just one man," Bella said. "But what brought you to the same conclusion?"

"Strange occurrences. Give me some time to mull it over." He pointed at Bella. "Be careful. Third time's a charm, and I don't want to be informing the FBI that one of their agents is out of the game permanently."

Bella appreciated his concern, but—"I'm a trained professional. I can take care of myself."

"Figured you'd respond like this was nothing." Darren moistened his lips. "I have the report on the bullet dug out of your car's tire: .223 Remington ammunition. The same make of bullets pumped into our victims."

"Like the ones from my stolen rifle," Carr added.

"You're right. It may be your gun, but you didn't fire it yesterday morning." Darren hesitated and drew in a deep breath. Sweat continued to bead his face.

Carr's brows narrowed. "You look horrible."

"Thanks. You don't look like fashion runway material yourself. Truth is, I have a nasty stomachache, and it's gotten steadily worse. Think I have a fever too."

Lydia walked across the kitchen and touched his forehead. "You're on fire, Sheriff. You need to be in bed."

He attempted to stiffen but failed miserably. "There's too much work to be done here for me to take off."

"Delegate it. And what your deputies can't do will have to wait." Lydia picked up the phone. "Do I call your wife, or are you going home?"

Darren slowly rose from the table and made his way to the back door and outside.

"Men." Lydia crossed her arms over her chest. "Stubborn as mules. He'll be out there for a while."

"I'll take him home when he's ready." Carr carried his plate to the sink. "He doesn't look like he's in any shape to drive." He glanced at Lydia and Bella. "Either of you feel sick?"

"Not me," Bella said.

"Or me," Lydia said. "He needs to be in bed."

Carr turned on the water. "I'll take him a washcloth and a glass of water."

Bella let his words sink in. Carr pulled a cloth from a kitchen drawer, held it beneath the faucet, and wrung it out. He filled a glass with water and walked outside. Carr Sullivan was either a clever liar, pretending to care about Darren Adams, or he was genuine. She'd like to think the latter. "I'd better get to work."

Bella kept checking on Darren. But he repeatedly vomited until Carr finally convinced him he should be at home.

"I can take him," Bella said. "The deputies are busy, and I need to stop at the sheriff's department afterward."

"No way," Darren managed. "Carr, you take me. I don't need a woman to nurse me. One of the other deputies can drive my car back to the station later."

Bella asked Lydia a few questions and then found Jasper in the stables. Their stories matched what Darren and Vic had reported. In the beginning she wanted to believe the two were covering for Carr, but her instincts, including all of her training, sensed they were innocent. Yet she'd proceed with caution. Trust had to be earned, not handed out like candy. *Candy* . . . Bella made a mental note to check into Jasper's alleged diabetic status. While sitting on the front porch swing, her new office, she wrestled with what she knew about the crime and the possibilities.

The victims' wives and Kegley's fiancée termed the men's interest in the Spider Rock treasure as a hobby, an obsession, and a diversion from the mundane—in that order. The women knew of no danger and were equally shocked and upset, including Walt Higgins's ex-wife. Bella needed to talk to them one-on-one and question them further. Once the funerals were over, they might remember important information. Bella wanted to ask them about Brandt Richardson. He changed his identities like women changed lipstick, but the man had a raspy voice that could not be masked.

Midmorning, Vic arrived and found her on the front porch. She relayed her evening and the newest findings.

"Who do you think is after you?" Vic leaned against the porch railing.

"You mean your bed didn't have a guest?"

"I'm not as lucky. My theory is still that Sullivan and someone else are working together. Possibly Richardson." He shrugged. "Whoever our killer is doesn't care for women. Or maybe he doesn't like women FBI agents."

Or maybe an old vendetta is still alive. "How do you feel about a day trip to Waco and Austin to interview the families again? I have a few more questions."

"Sure. Right now, I want to inspect the crime scene. I want to find out who did the fingerprint sweep." He glanced around. "Where's the sheriff?"

"He got sick shortly after I arrived. Carr took him home."

Vic frowned. "You let our suspect drive a sick sheriff home? Smart move for the lead agent. Did you hand him a few thousand for expenses?"

His sarcasm miffed her, but maybe she did need her brains jarred loose. "If Carr doesn't return, then we have our answer."

"You think he's innocent."

"The jury's still out." She tilted her head. "But it's leaning farther away from him."

"Don't let his charm fool you." He started to say something else, but he must have changed his mind.

Bella studied the man before her. Granted his over twenty years of experience meant she should listen to him, but what she should have done and what she sensed was the truth didn't match.

"When you're ready, let's take a drive to Ballinger and see if some of our reports are in," Vic said.

"I want to talk to the county coroner."

He nodded and left. Special Agent Vic Anderson didn't care for her, but it wasn't the first time a male agent disrespected a female agent. Maybe he was right. The investigation was going nowhere. She'd had more productive cases in Houston, where the criminal made stupid mistakes or a witness came forth with the truth.

The sound of robins and a lark piqued her attention. A mourning dove moaned its lonesome song, and she thought how very much it mimicked her life. The lark crooned again. Before her mother died, she used to tell Bella the lark sang "pretty, pretty." Warm remembrances swept over her of sea green eyes peering into a little girl's face while gentle hands stroked her hair. A lump formed in Bella's throat, and she thought she'd gone far beyond a child's grief. The lark sang out its tune again. It had to be the birds . . . and this part of Texas . . . and thoughts of her family.

The screen door opened, but not with the creak she remembered from the rickety farmhouse of her youth. Lydia stepped out with a cell phone in her hand. Her lips quivered, and tears pooled in her eyes.

"What's wrong?" Bella said as a hundred sketches of more tragedies beset her.

"It's Carr. He wants to talk to you." With a trembling hand, Lydia held out the phone.

Bella held it to her ear, her attention focused on the woman. "This is Bella."

"I'm at Ballinger Memorial Hospital."

"With Sheriff Adams?"

"I'm afraid so. He's dead."

CHAPTER 9

BRANDT RICHARDSON TOYED with a pen on his desk, the anticipation of treasure swelling his mind while frustration with the lack of progress filled his belly, like chasing a shot with a beer. He'd make the call in a few minutes. Some things were worth the sweat, especially those things that propelled his search. Another glance at the clock on his computer showed 2:56.

Good things come to those who wait.

He had the satellite imagery and topography of the area memorized. At three o'clock he walked outside and drove six blocks to a convenience store. After purchasing a Dr Pepper and getting change for the pay phone, he ambled outside and flipped the top on the can. *No police cars. Good.* Neither did any people loiter around the phone.

A pickup slid in front of the store. He glanced away and took a long drink of the Dr Pepper while the woman and child exited the truck and made their way inside.

"Handsome boy you have there," Brandt said.

"Thank you," the woman said.

He turned and slipped coins into the phone.

"I'm here," the man answered.

"Good. Did you take care of the little matter we discussed?"

"It's handled."

Ah, good news. "We're going to be very rich men, but it has to happen according to the plan," Brandt said. "Any screwups, and we've lost it all."

"I understand. The plan's working. Our man's about to be charged with four counts of murder."

"Maybe more." Brandt took another long drink. "Where's the map?"

"In a safe-deposit box at First National Bank of Ballinger."

"Did you make a copy for me?"

"It's there too."

"What about getting access to his land?"

"I'm working on it. Sullivan won't have much of a choice with this one." He laughed.

"I'll be at our normal meeting place at six thirty. Bring the map, and I want to hear more about how we're going to dig. I'm not against getting rid of him, Lydia, and Jasper. But we have to wait until the sheriff's department and the FBI clear out."

"Can't make the meeting. I have a six o'clock appointment."

Stupid fool. "This is more important than your golf game. You can buy your own course when we're finished." He disconnected the phone and crumpled the empty can in his hand. Tossing it into the trash, where flies buzzed around the garbage, he nodded at a tattooed kid who walked his way.

"Finished with the phone?" the kid said, his eyes glazed over like doughnuts.

"All yours." With that, Brandt walked back to the temporary junk heap he used for errands. The next item on his agenda had him driving south of town to another convenience store.

He would not lose this time. Six men knew the plan; four of them were dead.

CHAPTER 10

BELLA HANDED the phone back to Lydia. News of Darren's death had jolted her and left her numb. Judging by the pale look on Lydia's face, the woman felt the same shock.

Bella glanced down at her notes. "I had a list of questions for Darren." Was it only yesterday he'd asked her to call him by his first name? She whipped her attention back to Lydia standing before her. "That's not what I mean."

"How . . . how does a man die from flu that quickly?" Lydia slumped into the swing next to Bella.

Unless it wasn't flu. "I'm sure there's a good medical reason."

"He and Carr have been good friends for five years, and I've never known him to be sick." Lydia's words sounded flat. "Tiffany must be paralyzed with grief. They have three boys—the oldest will be a senior in high school."

"Are you going to her?"

"I can do no less. She has a large family, and the church will rally to her and the children's side. But I can't stay here when I can be doing something. But first I must tell Jasper."

"I'm so sorry." Bella stood and reached for her shoulder bag stuffed between her and Lydia. The bag slipped between her fingers, its contents spilling out like a sacrifice to a man who had given his all to the community. *Daredevil Adams. What a legacy.* She stuffed her keys, phone, recorder, and makeup bag back inside along with her standard gear. However, the gathering helped her gain control from the devastating news. She offered a slight smile. "I'll tell the deputies before I leave."

"Thank you. Make sure Wesley at the crime scene is told. He's Sheriff Adams's nephew. They're close."

"I will. Do you need some help?" Bella started to reach out for her, but they weren't friends. Not when Bella looked to charge Carr with murder. Lydia grieved for a real friend, and with her sorrow came the turmoil of the past few days.

Lydia shook her head. "I need to be busy with my hands."

After Lydia disappeared into the house, Bella hoisted her shoulder bag and approached the two deputies in the barn. They'd soon be finished going through all the contents of the outbuildings and stables.

"Hey, fellas. Got a minute?"

"Sure," said Deputy Roano, the man who had driven her and Vic to retrieve her car.

She glanced at the two men, regretting what she had to say. "I have some bad news. Carr just called and said Sheriff Adams died."

Deputy Roano took a step back. "Died? What happened? He was vomiting before Carr helped him into the truck, like he'd gotten food poisoning—"

"All I know is Carr took him to the hospital in Ballinger, where he died."

The other deputy stared at the dirt. "I don't remember Sheriff Adams ever taking a day off from work."

"Yeah. He was on duty before anyone else and there long after the others on his shift went home." Deputy Roano's face looked more like granite. "Something about this isn't right."

"I'm sure we'll have the doctor's report soon. I'm on my way there once I inform a few more people. I'm sorry for your loss."

Roano cursed. "He has a family. We were all family."

Bella didn't respond. Like Lydia, the deputy grieved for a highly respected man. She left the two men and walked to her car.

Deputy Roano made his way to her side. "Death number four and again Sullivan looks guilty."

Bella still didn't believe Carr was guilty—not really. "It's too coincidental."

"Go figure. Darren's wife and family need support more than I need this job." He cursed again, relaying how he felt about Carr.

She left Roano and drove to the crime scene to tell Deputy Wesley Adams.

"He's dead?" The young man's eyes pooled, and he blinked. "I talked to him this morning. We arrived here at the same time."

"He became suddenly ill. I'm driving to the hospital now."

"Wish I could go." Grief etched his face. "Sure seems strange my uncle dies while investigating a triple homicide." He glanced away, then back to her. "I'm going to find out what happened to Uncle Darren, and I won't stop until I find out the truth."

Bella had the same sentiments, and the scenarios mounted. *Darren said he wanted to think about a few of the things he uncovered. Did he discover vital information?* "I'm sorry. Lydia said you two were close."

"Darren recruited me, then mentored me through my training and then on the job. His three words of advice for all of us were to be conscientious, diligent, and caring. He said a good deputy settled for getting the job done. An excellent deputy went over and beyond what was necessary. Everyone looked up to him."

Bella's insides churned. Yesterday she'd silently made fun of his daredevil feats, downplaying the man because he worked a rural area. "When is your shift over?"

"Three o'clock."

"Can you call anyone to relieve you?"

"I'll see what I can do. Today is the last day we were scheduled to stay at the crime scene."

"Again, I'm sorry; and I hope you're able to leave your shift early."

Bella got back into her car and drove to Ballinger Memorial Hospital. She pulled into the small, orange brick facility with its grand total of twenty parking spaces. As soon as she had a signal, she called Vic's cell phone. No answer, so she left him a message. Time to call Swartzer in Houston. Hitting speed dial, she learned he was not in the office.

"This is Bella Jordan," she said. "We have another problem. Sheriff Darren Adams of the Runnels County Sheriff's Department is dead." She went into what happened a few hours before. "I'm on my way inside the hospital to find out more about how Adams died. You can call me there."

Carr was with him before I arrived, supposedly drove him home, and then he died. That was too obvious. A setup. If Adams's death was not a natural cause, then suspicion exponentially mounted toward Carr, and attention shifted from the real killer. How long had the killer, whoever he was, planned his every move and made provision for any alternative? Maybe she could grapple with that until one of the members of the task force uncovered concrete evidence.

The motivation for these murders needled her, and she didn't want to discount the Spider Rock treasure playing a role. What she knew about the hunters came from eavesdropping on her father and Brandt. The random clues whispered in obscure places and the over sixty million dollars' worth of gold lured far too many people.

Her cell phone jangled its familiar tune. A quick glance showed it was Swartzer.

"How are you doing?" he said.

"My mind's racing." He didn't need to know about the rattler.

"Two days and you've got yourself another body."

"That's right. I'm looking into the cause of death. Sullivan's involved."

"What's your take?"

"Setup. Too obvious, unless Sullivan believes his money can buy him innocence."

"Does he seem like a man obsessed with money—possibly gold, as in the Spider Rock treasure?"

Bella formed her thoughts before speaking. "He's either up for an Oscar or he's genuine."

"Trust your instincts and keep probing. In the meantime, I'll send additional people to assist the task force."

"I think I'm okay without more help. The sheriff's department is doing a good job." She didn't have substantial leads, but no point in admitting her assignment was not proceeding as fast as she would like.

"I believe in your skills as an agent. Keep me posted, and be safe."

"Thanks. I will." Encouragement always helped. She should have told him about the rattler, but for sure he would have sent more agents to help. In her opinion, it discounted her ability to lead out the investigation, and she desperately wanted to prove Swartzer had not made a mistake.

Shaking off the rule book, she focused on the questions to be directed at Carr Sullivan. So where did the former party animal, now Christian advocate for at-risk teen boys, fit into the case? Did she dare trust her instincts that he was being used as a scapegoat, or had he become so fanatical about the Spider Rock treasure that he resorted to murder? Her hunch led her to Brandt, but had Carr thrown in with him too? Now she needed to find where either of them might have slipped up. But the first thing she needed to do was find out how Sheriff Darren Adams had lost his life.

She exited her car and entered the hospital. Unfortunately, due to the nature of the deceased's unusual death and connection to Carr, she needed to order an autopsy, including toxicology tests.

Carr watched Tiffany from across the waiting room at the hospital, where she hadn't moved since the doctor pronounced Darren dead. They'd spoken briefly when she first arrived at the hospital with her three sons. The four were in shock, in disbelief that a beloved husband and father was gone from their midst. Carr remembered what Darren had said when the two drove away from the High Butte.

"I'm not supposed to be sick. I'm the sheriff who's investigating three murders. I have more important things to do than throw up."

"You can resume the investigation later," Carr had told him.

Darren had moistened his lips. "This is bad. Worse than what you could imagine."

Carr knew Darren was not referring to the flu. When his friend felt better, he'd planned to ask what he meant. Too late now.

A voice over the intercom requested a doctor and pulled Carr back to the present. He glanced at Tiffany surrounded by family and friends who had arrived initially to pray for a man to be healed; now they offered sympathy and comfort. Soon they'd be arranging a funeral. Too many well-meaning people shoved their way through the crowd and intruded on those offering condolences. Carr would rather sit back and pray, then make his way to her when the others parted.

Tiffany took Pastor Kent's hand and bowed her head. Her graciousness to those around her seemed to exceed the sorrow of losing her husband. She was a role model for all men and women who walked through similar losses.

Darren's oldest son stood and walked into the hallway. Carr caught the boy's eye. Too young to be fatherless. Too young to have the responsibility now resting on his shoulders. The boy nodded and stepped into the restroom. No doubt to cry where no one could see him.

The cause of death ate at him like acid. Darren had the same symptoms as flu or food poisoning—severe vomiting, fever. But as Carr drove him through Ballinger and north of town toward his home, the man had begun to convulse.

"I'm taking you to the hospital." Carr had whipped the car around and stepped on the gas.

Darren didn't respond, and shortly thereafter, Carr realized he was unconscious.

He never understood why so many prayers went unanswered. He hadn't known God when Michelle lay dying, but he'd prayed for *something, someone,* to save her. When he and Jasper discovered the bodies of those men, Carr prayed for them to have a spark of life. But it had been too late. A few hours ago, he prayed for Darren to fight whatever had attacked his body. He died too. Perhaps the words spoken to the great Healer weren't the right ones.

Carr walked down the hall to the drinking fountain. His thinking bordered on ludicrous. A man's prayers were heard because of the condition of his heart and his relationship to God, not his choice of words. Yet the grieving for Darren brought back Michelle's overdose and the raw ache of finding the murdered victims on his land earlier in the week.

God, when will this end?

Deputy Roano followed Carr into the hallway. "What happened once you left the ranch with Sheriff Adams?" He leaned on one leg and crossed his arms. Hostility oozed from the pores of his skin.

The hospital was not the place to argue. "He continued to vomit and then began to convulse. When that happened, I rushed him to the hospital."

Roano's fiery gaze raked him. "Don't you think it's odd Sheriff Adams has been working the murder case and now he's dead?"

Carr understood how the deputy felt. "Darren Adams was my friend too. And yes, I've thought about the implications. I'm sure an autopsy will be ordered to satisfy all of us."

"You'd better hope there's a good explanation for his death, and it had better come fast."

CHAPTER 11

EXHAUSTED, MENTALLY and physically, Bella drove back to Abilene from Ballinger Memorial Hospital in what she termed "autopilot." Hunger gnawed at her stomach, and she had a ton of online work to do. Those things could wait until later. She wanted to talk to Vic, but he had yet to respond to her phone messages. Strange work ethics for a veteran agent.

The scene at the hospital had deepened her resolve to restore peace to the community. Not that she hadn't witnessed tragedy in past investigations. But in this case, maybe she could have done something fourteen years ago to put a stop to Brandt Richardson's rapacity. She shrugged. Who would have believed a fifteen-year-old runaway?

Friends and family reminisced about Sheriff Darren Adams's daredevil escapades and how much he was loved and respected. She'd watched Carr, too. He shed a few tears of his own—not the behavior of a man who plotted murder on his own property.

Shock and grief among the deputies turned to animosity when Deputies Roano and Adams turned on Carr, pelting him with questions about how Darren had died. Carr handled it well and held his own while displaying compassion for Tiffany. Bella admired his composure when the scene could have erupted into a fistfight.

Putting aside her ruminations, Bella swung her car into the parking lot of the Wings and Beer Bar, where, she'd learned from phone records, Daniel Kegley had phoned Carr last Friday night.

She exited her car and stepped into the noisy bar, where the sound of country-western music blared from all four corners. This was where she should have had Vic beside her. This was where she needed another agent as witness to an interview.

The smell of barbecue sauce and chicken again reminded her she hadn't eaten since breakfast. Ignoring her protesting stomach, she focused on the information she needed to acquire. After studying the layout, she eased onto a stool at the bar and studied the patrons and waitstaff. Tonight was a mix of young twenties and good old boys. What a combination, and none of them looked like company for three men determined to find the Spider Rock treasure.

Bella glanced up when the laughter of a ponytailed woman, who tended bar, caught her attention. A couple of guys on the opposite side of the bar were making fools of themselves by trying to balance shot glasses on their chins. When one of the young men mentioned classes in the fall, Bella assumed they were college kids.

The woman made her way to Bella's corner of the bar. "What can I get you?"

"A Coke."

"Sure you don't want something else?"

Bella flashed her creds. "Special Agent Bella Jordan. I'm investigating three murders, and I understand the men were here last Friday night."

Even in the dim lighting above the bar, Bella saw the color drain from the young woman's face.

What do you know? "Did you work that night?" When she nodded, Bella pulled photos of the three men from her shoulder bag. "Do you remember these men?"

She nodded and swallowed. "Did you say they were murdered?"

"Yes. And what's your name?" The woman must not pay attention to media news.

"Lexie Bronson. I remember them. They sat over there." She pointed to a nearby table.

"What else do you remember about that night?"

She paused and took in a deep breath. "They were celebrating something. At least for most of the evening."

"Hey, I need another beer," a middle-aged man said.

She held up her hand. It trembled. "Just a minute."

"Go ahead. I'll wait." Bella smiled.

As soon as the man received his beer and the college guys ordered another round of tequila shots, Lexie returned to Bella.

"I don't want to keep you," Bella said. "But is there something about the men or the evening that could help with the investigation? Whoever murdered them is free to kill again."

She appeared to contemplate what to say. "One of them—the younger man . . ." She looked at the photos again. "That one." She pointed to Daniel Kegley's image. "He made a phone call and was really angry. Strange, because up until then they were laughing and having a good time."

"Did you hear any of the conversation?"

She nodded slowly. "Couldn't help but hear him. I thought I might need to ask him to leave, but he hung up. Too much noise that night to make out anything he might have said."

"Were any names mentioned? anything you recall?"

"Actually, there were three calls. His ringtone was a trumpet call—like a cavalry charge. The first one was probably a woman from the way he was acting. You know, all smiles and sweet, and he walked outside for a while. The second one seemed short. And the third was the angry one."

Carr said Kegley had placed a call to him. "This is important. Think hard. Did anything else happen?"

Lexie took a breath. "During the last call, he stood and slammed the chair into the table. The other two guys tried to calm him down."

"Were those the only times he used the phone?"

She hesitated. "I think so. We were really busy, Friday night and all. Like I said, his ringtone was obvious."

"I understand. Thanks. You've been very helpful." Bella jotted down the girl's name and handed her a business card. "If you remember anything else, would you give me a call?"

"Sure. Hope you catch the killer real soon."

Bella nodded. "As long as people like you are willing to help us, we should be able to make an arrest soon."

"Do I need to be afraid?"

Odd question. "Why would you need to be afraid?"

Lexie glanced away, then back to Bella. She drummed her green fingernails on the counter. "Daniel Kegley went home with me that night."

That's why you were paying attention to the calls he made. "What did he tell you?"

"We . . . we didn't talk much, and he left before I woke up the next morning."

Bella studied her face. From her darting eyes, she was clearly terrified. "If anyone else contacts you about the murdered victims, please let me know."

"I will. Believe me I will."

★ ★ ★

Holding a to-go bag of food for dinner, Bella opened the door leading into her hotel room. A healthy grilled chicken salad with lots of veggies awaited her. But first she intended to search every inch of the room for unwanted varmints—including the kind who packed a gun.

In the open doorway, she considered leaving another message for Vic before eating. He'd phoned while she was at the bar to tell her that an emergency had taken up his day. Bella wanted to discuss Darren's death, but Vic said he'd talk to her tomorrow morning at the High Butte. Said he'd found evidence and wanted to discuss it with her. Why at the ranch when the crime scene investigation had disbanded? But he didn't have time to talk.

"Miss Jordan, I saw you come into the hotel," a male voice said behind her.

She dropped the bag of food while reaching for her firearm. With her fingers wrapped around her gun, she read his name badge: *Charles Habid, Manager.* Who was the woman from the preceding night who had claimed to be the manager?

He immediately raised his hands. Fear etched the features of the good-looking man of Eastern ethnicity.

"Does this property have more than one manager?" Bella said, suspicion mounting.

"Uh, just me, except for an assistant who works evenings."

"FBI, sir. I'm an agent. You can lower your hands." She set her shoulder bag on the desk and pulled out her identification. "Can you describe your assistant?"

"She's about five feet four. Dark hair except for a few purple streaks—"

"Is her name Sissy?"

"That's her. Earlier this week I gave the FBI what little information I had about the three men staying here who were found murdered on a ranch south of town. But Sissy didn't say a word this morning about an FBI agent staying here as a guest. Is this connected?"

"Yes, it is. I'm conducting an investigation about the deaths of those three men."

He frowned. "I need to discuss communication with her. Now I understand last night's disturbance."

Bella laughed, but she was not amused. "*Disturbance* is a good description. She told you about the snake in my bed?"

The manager peered up and down the hallway. "That's why I'm here. I'd appreciate it if you'd keep your voice down."

"The young woman whom I spoke to last night said she was the manager."

"I assure you, ma'am, that I've been the manager here for the past four years."

Sissy has an ego problem. "I could use a little help in conducting a search. It may not be as exciting as last night."

He gulped. "That's my job."

"It's *my* job, but you can assist."

"My pleasure." He retrieved her upside-down salad from the floor—an authentic tossed salad. The Coke had not spilled.

With the door flung open—she snapped on all the lights. The manager followed her inside. "Let's do this thing so you can enjoy your dinner and have a good night's sleep," he said.

Fat chance of either of those happening. "Honestly, I can take care of the search." Bella grinned at him. "Don't let anyone take my food."

"They'd have to rip it from my hands." The manager watched her strip the bed, and then he set her dinner on the desk to help her check every inch of the room.

"Do you need to do a dusting for fingerprints?"

Amusement sprang to her thoughts, but he was serious. "Not at this point. However, I do need a list of your guests since the victims stayed here. I requested it last evening."

"My assistant should have had that for you last night. As soon as we're finished, I'll get on it." He picked up the phone and ordered the list. "I want fresh linens sent up immediately and new pillows. Thank you." He glanced at Bella and nodded. "Make that a change-out of everything—the ice bucket, glasses, bathroom accessories, etc." He ended the call and turned back to her. "I assume you'd like all of the items in this room tagged like you requested last night?"

"I would." She observed his detailed mannerisms, and respect crept to the forefront of her mind. "If you're ever looking for another career, I think the FBI would be a consideration."

He chuckled, the first she'd heard from him. "I've been to the Web site. And I speak four languages."

"Which ones?"

"Arabic, Korean, Russian, and English."

"Whoa. How did you manage that?"

"My parents were in the military. My father . . . Well, he never told us what his exact job is, but I'm sure it has something to do with U.S. security."

She took one last look under the bed, then straightened. "How did you end up in Abilene?"

"I chose hotel management. Seemed a little tamer than my dad's profession. Nothing personal, but I sorta enjoyed tonight."

She'd laugh about that later. Bella filed everything from this conversation into her mental database. Later this evening, she'd do a search on him and the sweet gal who wanted the title of manager without the responsibility. "Do you remember anything unusual about the three victims? any visitors? conversations?"

"Not a thing. They were guests. That's all." He studied her for a moment. "I find it odd that you are the third FBI agent to question me about the crime."

Three? "Who else has been here?"

"Two men from the FBI. And you."

Her nerves flew into overdrive. "Who were the agents?"

"Steward Nostrom and William Bonney. They came two separate times."

William Bonney, as in Billy the Kid? Had to be Brandt Richardson. "Did they leave cards? show you their credentials?"

"Mr. Nostrom did, but not Mr. Bonney."

Figures. "What did Mr. Bonney look like?"

"Dark hair, mustache. Late forties. Limped when he came in."

Limp? Last she knew, Richardson didn't limp. But it could easily be part of his latest disguise. As could the rest of the appearance Mr. Habid had described.

Her gut feeling told her it must be him. *Brandt Richardson.*

CHAPTER 12

DAY THREE of the investigation and Bella had a fourth body. Not good stats for a lead agent. But she'd made progress, something solid. Clearly she wanted to give Houston a stellar performance. Clearly she trembled at the thought of squaring off with Brandt. Clearly she feared she would shatter before the assignment was completed.

Last night she e-mailed Swartzer about the new link to Brandt Richardson. This wasn't the first time Brandt had posed as a law enforcer in an attempt to hinder an investigation. After evaluating Lexie's story at the Wings and Beer Bar, Bella understood Brandt could have been one of the three phone calls to Kegley.

Brandt may be a master of disguise, but he couldn't change the sound of his voice. She'd learned from the victims' families' interviews that one man outside of the three initiated the treasure hunt and offered partial financial support. But none of the family members mentioned the man had a raspy voice, which indicated at least one more person was involved.

During the wee hours of the morning, while the thumping sounds of the air conditioner kept jarring her awake, Bella reached another conclusion—the need to find her father and question his involvement with Brandt. At 3 a.m., Bella whisked off an e-mail to Pete at the FIG and requested a full report on Stanton Warick. She chastised herself for not following up sooner. Depending on what she learned about him, she would inform Swartzer about her past. No point diving into that nest of scorpions until after she saw her father's report.

After a 4 a.m. workout in the hotel's fitness room, Bella downed a cup of coffee and headed to the High Butte Ranch. Vic would arrive later, so while she waited for him, she wanted a complete tour of the property. Other items fighting for priority on her list were the fingerprints on the candy wrapper, any updates on the cause of death for Sheriff Adams, and getting closer to Carr.

The more time she spent with Carr, the more she'd be able to confirm his guilt or innocence and piece together the clues about the four deaths. The question persisted as to whether Carr and Brandt had worked together. Or could Carr have been implicated in the murders as part of a master plan? He didn't seem motivated by money, especially when he'd walked away from a lucrative income in Dallas to change his destructive lifestyle.

By six o'clock, she was well on her way to the ranch. She grabbed her phone from the car seat and hit the speed dial she'd assigned for Carr's number. He answered on the first ring.

"Good morning. This is Bella." It occurred to her that she'd made a friend. Strange, and yet she needed to make sure she didn't allow friendship to influence her assignment. "I'll be there in about thirty minutes."

He yawned. "Early bird, huh?"

"Did I wake you?"

"No. I didn't go to bed last night."

That could be for a number of reasons—the unsolved murder case, the disgruntled and grieving deputies, possible guilt. "Anything I should know?"

"How about a black eye for starters?"

"I could list about a dozen who might want to accommodate you. Who did it?"

"No clue. It happened when I drove back home last night. I spent some time with my pastor until around midnight. When I reached here, I got out of my truck and someone grabbed me from behind."

"What was said?"

"A muffled voice told me to mind my own business."

"As if being a murder suspect was not your business?"

"Whatever. Since the county sheriff is dead, and the power behind the fist could have been one of the deputies, I kept my sentiments to myself."

Possibilities rolled across her mind like roll call on the first day of school.

"Are you up to giving me a tour of your ranch this morning?"

"Sure. Have you learned anything new?"

"Possibly," Bella said. "I'm beginning to think you might have been set up." That information should cause him to lower his defenses. If he'd lied, then maybe he'd make a mistake or two thinking he was in the clear.

"That's worth a black eye, but not the loss of a good friend. Still can't believe Darren's gone."

Silence settled between them. She remembered the devastation of losing a fellow friend and agent who took a bullet in the line of duty. "I'm sorry. Losing a friend is never easy." She waited a moment longer. "Before I get there, have you remembered anything else to aid us in this investigation?"

"As a matter of fact, I did. About six months ago, a woman called and asked if I was interested in selling the ranch. I told her no. She persisted and offered a generous amount."

Brandt had a history of using women for small things and eliminating those who served as barriers in his thirst for more lucrative ventures. "Did she give you her name or a real-estate company?"

"I didn't ask because I had no plans to sell the place. Remember, I've been working to open a home for at-risk teen boys."

"What about a reason for wanting to make the purchase?"

"She mentioned an investor from LA who wanted a retreat."

"I have your phone records. We can begin there."

"Is Vic with you?"

Was Carr uncomfortable with him? "No. You're stuck with me, but he may join us later."

"I'm surprised you don't mind being alone with me."

She should have waited for Vic or one of the deputies, but impatience overruled her better judgment. "I can handle myself, Mr. Sullivan. But if you're worried about yourself, call the sheriff's department for an escort."

"I'm fine. I'll have coffee ready. Black with a spoonful of local honey, right?"

"Thanks." Next time she'd follow protocol and have someone with her.

★ ★ ★

Carr swallowed three extra-strength Tylenol with half a can of Mountain Dew. Now on to his coffee. Between the three, the pain in his head and the throbbing in his swollen eye should diminish. Lack of sleep, however, could not be pacified or squelched. Rest would be postponed until time permitted a payment toward the three nights' debt of sleep.

Rubbing his temples, Carr walked onto the front porch and stared at the driveway and the road beyond the gates welcoming visitors to the High Butte. *Special Agent Bella Jordan.* He rather liked the FBI agent sent to lead the task force and solve the murders. Even though he shared the title of likely suspect with Brandt Richardson, he admired her professionalism. He chuckled at her earlier comment—as if *he* were afraid of *her*.

Yesterday at the hospital, many of the people stayed with Tiffany and the boys long after Darren was pronounced dead. No one wanted to believe he was gone, and all wanted to do something to help. When the majority of people had left, Bella took the Adams boys to supper and brought Tiffany a sandwich and coffee. Bella even held her hand. Strange combination for what he termed a type A personality, a woman who asserted control and power with a twist of quirkiness. The combination earned her respect in his book.

His book. What a joke. The book was God's book, and Carr had wondered on more than one occasion if she followed it too. Maybe he'd ask. His devotion time for the past few days had left him weak and leaning on Truth. His pastor called it faith.

How were Tiffany and the kids faring this morning? The shock of Darren's death certainly became reality as funeral preparations took over what should have been the beginnings of a summer weekend. Darren loved spending time with his family. Although the boys were older and had friends and part-time jobs, Darren did his best to plan at least one family activity each weekend.

I'll miss him. Darren attended his boys' ball games and swim meets, and he worked in the church and the community. Sure made Carr want to throw down the why-do-bad-things-happen-to-good-people card. He, Lydia, and Jasper planned to take food to the Adams household later.

Carr believed the deaths this week were linked, but how? He wished he had the answers to so many things, but one thing stayed fixed in his mind: whoever had brought tragedy to Runnels County had done so with planning and precision. No sloppy evidence. Darren's autopsy would take until the middle of next week, but the funeral was scheduled for Monday. He hoped Tiffany was prepared for a memorial service and possibly a later burial. He'd have to ask Bella about how fast the cause of death would surface.

Bella's white car slowly rolled up the drive toward the house. He sighed, not certain if he welcomed another day of interrogation or looked forward to ending the nightmare for all of them. Questions pelted him like rock-size hail.

When sleep escaped him last night, he'd pulled up various

Web sites and ordered a book about the Spider Rock legend. Aros would frown on his probing, but Carr had not abandoned his interest in what had driven the three victims to their deaths. The FBI agents might be the investigators, but Carr had much to lose. And for that reason, he intended to keep probing the treasure's legend in hopes of discovering who and why. A quote he'd heard somewhere continued to ripple through his mind: "What man deems as gold and priceless, God deems as naught."

Bella's car door shut, breaking nature's morning songs. He waved and offered a prayer that the barrage of deaths would end and the killer be exposed today. With an inward groan, Carr understood the futility of his prayer. But he could hope for evidence freeing him from the suspect list.

After Lydia insisted Bella and Carr eat breakfast, despite the memories from the previous morning, the two climbed into his truck and began the tour of the High Butte. They crossed bumpy pasture and drove around rocks and ruts he called his ranch. Carr noted their talk was shallow. If her mind was a mass of intricate gears, he could hear them grind and squeak.

"When are you planning to tell me the rest of the story about your shiner?"

"How was your evening?" he finally said. "Any surprises in your hotel room?"

"So the deputies ganged up on you?"

"You first." He tossed her a grin, hoping to melt her demeanor. But he was so tired mentally and physically that any thoughts of congeniality seemed disrespectful to Darren.

"Busy, and the hotel room lived up to its expectations. Got maybe three hours' sleep."

"What else have you learned?"

"It's your turn to answer questions." Her voice lifted. "So how's the black eye working for you?"

"Very funny. It's my red badge of courage."

"To do what?"

"Find out who's behind this."

"Noble. How many jumped you?"

"Have no idea who or why."

"What else did he say?"

"I'd fallen under the curse."

"Interesting. What have you learned about the Spider Rock treasure?"

"Makes me wonder if you're researching it too." Trying to get information out of her was like lassoing a mosquito. "It might not be a hoax."

"At least in some people's eyes." Bella lifted a bottle of water to her lips. "Have you changed your mind about becoming a treasure hunter?"

"I prefer living a little longer."

"So you believe all of the reports?"

"No. I spent about three hours doing online searches." He swallowed hard. "Darren was onto something."

Her attention riveted on him. "He told you that?"

"Yes. He called me from home yesterday morning. Said he was on his way and to tell Lydia that he was hungry. He sounded fine. No hint of feeling bad. He said this could be the day we find evidence leading to the killer. Then he said something was bothering him, and he hoped he was wrong. He wanted to pray about it when he got there. But it didn't happen."

"Wish we had the autopsy report, but that may take days. No doubt in my mind Darren was murdered." She pulled out a notebook and wrote for the next few minutes. "Have you received any calls from a man who had a raspy voice?"

So early in the morning for a Q and A. "No. So you think Brandt Richardson called here?" When she lifted her brow, he continued. "I've been doing a little research on my own. Plus

Darren told me a few things. One of the reports about Richardson stated he had a raspy voice."

"I see."

"Did Richardson have contact with the victims?"

She shrugged. "Maybe."

Carr had no intentions of stating another thing until she revealed some of what she'd discovered. The FBI probably had special procedures in matters of investigation. But Richardson's notoriety was what brought her to Runnels County. If she had any idea where he was hiding, she didn't let on. "I understand divulging certain information might be against the bureau's guidelines. But their lives aren't on the line, simply their reputations."

"And integrity and the need to capture those who fall under our jurisdiction."

He'd press her later. "Where's Vic been keeping himself? Haven't seen him since yesterday morning." Was the other agent onto something?

She glanced at her watch. "I imagine he'll show up before noon."

The three-hour drive around his ranch, which consisted of more stops and starts than he cared to mention, turned up nothing. Back at the ranch, Bella wanted to see the stables again. With a firm resolve never to enter law enforcement or investigative work, Carr led the way to the stables. He had a small office there, and he invited her inside. She'd seen it before, and at this point, all he wanted to do was show his sincerity in finding the killers.

Jasper worked at the other end of the stables, readying a stall for a mare about to foal. Carr should be helping him. A man Jasper's age needed to take it easy. As he grabbed the office door to close it behind him, Jasper's voice clamored for attention.

"Well, I'll be."

Curiosity snatched hold of Carr. "What is it? Has she foaled?"

Jasper didn't answer, as though he'd been struck speechless.

"Jasper?"

"I'm in the stall. Not sure what to do with this. Looks like we might have a problem."

Carr trod down the concrete walkway with Bella beside him to where Jasper leaned against the open stall. The man pointed to a corner. "Found this under a fresh pile of hay—hay I didn't put there."

Carr's stolen rifle lay in the corner of the stall.

CHAPTER 13

Bella instructed Carr and Jasper not to touch the rifle. She tugged on her gloves, then carried the weapon to her car to transport later for prints. She'd been in this same stall yesterday, and nothing had been there but a pile of loose hay and the lingering odor of horse. The rifle had been planted as if the FBI were a group of children playing a game of hide-and-seek. She blew out an exasperated sigh. The likelihood of anyone's fingerprints but Carr's being on the rifle was slim. So why would the killer go to this length to frustrate all concerned, except to prove he could?

Today's incident sounded like Brandt was up to his old tricks of control and maneuver, as though the investigators were marionettes. She sure would like to be the one to handcuff him. Had he arranged Sheriff Adams's untimely death? Most likely so. Daredevil Adams must have stumbled onto something that pointed to the killer, but what?

Piece it all together. The answers are there. She had to keep looking at it from different perspectives. *Think like a criminal. Where does his motivation lead him?* She had to wear his head. Feel with his cold heart. Walk where he stalked.

"I've read and reread online what I could find about the Spider Rock treasure," Carr said, without an attempt to hide the aggravation in his voice. "So the killer is after the treasure, which means the three victims knew or found something that resulted in their deaths." He stared out the window of his library and continued to voice his thoughts to Bella and Vic, who had arrived around noon. "But none of the past searches or findings indicate the gold could be on the High Butte. Nothing in the rock etchings lead here. Period."

Bella crossed her arms over her chest. "Let's compare notes, because we're missing something. I'm familiar with the indecipherable maps, and like you, I agree the idea of the gold on your ranch is against anything the legend claims."

Carr turned to face the two agents. Since he and Bella had returned from riding across his acreage, they'd discussed and explored possibilities with nothing making sense. Vic had joined them in the library but had merely listened.

"One story is that the gold originated with Francisco Pizarro, a Spanish soldier-explorer who landed in the New World in search of wealth for Spain," Carr said. "He had this insatiable thirst for gold, which led him to barbaric treatment of the Incas to attain their wealth. One of his captains became greedy for the treasure and convinced some of his soldiers to steal a portion of it. They hightailed it north from Peru, up through Mexico to the current Texas panhandle in search of safety. Who knows why they hid the treasure? Could be the Indians stalked them. The captain is the one who supposedly made the original spiderweb map and then burned it onto parchment with charcoal."

"That's a whole lot more than what I know." Vic lifted a glass of iced tea to his lips. "You know, Bella. It would have been *nice* if you'd waited for me before you took the ranch tour. Not really smart to examine a crime scene with a suspect."

Bella raised her glass as if to toast him. "I believe you did the same yesterday with one of the deputies. But point well taken."

Vic offered a faint smile. More like a smirk. "Touché."

These two did not mix. Carr had questioned their compatibility the previous day: young female lead agent working with a seasoned veteran.

"What did you observe yesterday?" she said.

"I've searched the perimeter of the butte three times, and I have yet to see any indication of digging or carved rock. My theory is Professor Miller signed *Spider Rock* in the dirt because he knew he no longer would have an opportunity to search for it."

Carr didn't share the same mind-set, but he needed to hear their viewpoints.

"Carr and I must have read the same information," Bella said. "The soldiers loaded forty mules or llamas, depending on the source of history, of gold and silver for the trek north. A priest, who carried his Bible, also accompanied them. Maybe so God would bless their endeavor. The men disappeared along with any traces of how to read the map. I don't think contemporary experts ever learned which came first—the parchment map or the rock etchings."

Carr picked up several printed pages about the Spider Rock legend and handed them to Vic. "The three Spider Rock locations formed a triangle of sorts, stretching from Aspermont near the Brazos River to Clyde and Rotan."

"Our killer may have deciphered how to read the signs and lines that supposedly lead to the treasure," Vic said. "It's amazing how all of modern technology hasn't been able to figure it out. The soldier who drew the map had to be a genius." Sarcasm ignited his last phrase.

Bella paced the library. "Oh, I think the treasure was dug up long ago, and the one who found it kept it to himself. He'd probably seen enough men killed."

"Possibly. But the three victims on my ranch obviously believed in the legend." Carr wished one of them could tie the treasure and his ranch into one package. He peered first into Vic's face and then into Bella's, capturing her gaze. For a fleeting moment, a peculiar twinge settled in his stomach. He assumed it was the talk of treasure.

"Definitely they met with the curse," she added.

The three had worked together too many hours and needed rest. Carr cleared his throat. "I'm not superstitious, but this almost makes a believer out of me. Look at how history depicts the lives of those who tried to find it. In the twentieth century alone, men were murdered, lost their families, died penniless, and some even went crazy looking for it. Sounds like a curse to me."

Vic paused from taking notes. "You two sure have spent a lot of time working on this aspect of the case. However, I've been doing a little researching on my own." He eyed Bella curiously. "Did your family search for the gold?"

"Doesn't everyone out here?"

"I don't know, which is why I asked you." Vic's tone sharpened.

Carr sensed the conversation was again propelling in an antagonistic direction. Darren would have nipped this unprofessionalism at the root.

Bella smiled, and Carr silently cheered her on. "I believe I told you I was selected for this assignment because I'm from the area."

Vic nodded with a slight sneer. "Indeed you did."

Not a muscle moved on Bella's face. "Are you looking to take over the lead in this investigation?"

"If I wanted it, I could have it."

"Okay now." Carr interrupted the silence thick enough to cut with a machete. "This treasure talk makes me want to find out what Lydia knows. Recorded legends and locals' opinions sometimes conflict."

"Sounds good," Bella said. "What do you think, Vic?"

"I have things to do. I'll call you later. Want to drive home to see the wife and grandkids for the weekend."

"Be safe and enjoy. See you Monday morning."

"Right. I'll check in on Sunday night."

Carr couldn't ignore what he'd witnessed between Vic and Bella, even if none of it was his call. Vic said his good-byes and left them alone in the library.

Bella pressed her lips together in a thin smile. "Maybe he needs a good dose of family to sweeten his disposition."

Or a five-pound bag of sugar. "Let's go find Lydia."

Lydia sat in the shaded courtyard reading, seemingly engrossed. Carr wished she'd give up the suspense novels until this was over. Whatever happened to women reading romance?

Bella and Carr seated themselves on the comfortable patio furniture in vivid Southwest colors of red and gold, much like the area sunsets. He did love his home. Had he really appreciated the beauty before the tragedies?

"What can you tell us about the Spider Rock treasure?" Carr said. "We've read online information, and I've ordered a book about the history of the legend."

Lydia lifted a finger to silence them and finished reading a page. She inserted a bookmark and closed the book. "I thought you two were researching that information."

"We are," Carr continued. "But we'd like to hear your take. I'm sure you've heard a lot of stories through the years."

Lydia's eyes widened, but he saw the smile. "I'm sixty-seven, not a hundred and seven. But I've heard rumors and the like."

"Like what?"

"Since I haven't seen proof, all I can do is repeat the stories."

"I want to hear it all," Bella said.

Lydia took a deep breath and tilted her head. "This may sound bizarre to you, but you asked. Ancient Indian ghosts who haunt the seekers. Men and women who disappear. Dreams that become obsessions and drive men to murder—even their own families."

Carr could easily believe the latter. He glanced at Bella, who seemed to agree.

"Many times in an investigation, friends and neighbors know more than we do," Bella said. "I ignored much of what I heard when I lived here, so I'm no help."

"Let's see." Lydia hesitated. "I've been told some of the families who've found Spanish relics hoard them, passing them from generation to generation and not revealing their finds to anyone. A lot of superstition layers these tales too. I imagine if all of the finds were laid out, the treasure could be found." Carr thought she'd finished; then she focused on him. "I've heard rumors the treasure is buried here on the High Butte. But you already figured that out."

"Do you know the source?"

"This could be a key to what's happening in your community," Bella said.

"Hmm. I'd have to ask around. There's supposed to be an old man in Junction—older than dirt—who believes the clues point to the gold buried in Runnels County. He's done quite a bit of research."

Carr chuckled at Lydia's description of the old man.

"I imagine you've heard of Brandt Richardson," Bella said.

Lydia's eyes snapped up to meet first Carr's, then Bella's. "Yes. He's one of those who's obsessed with finding the treasure. No one has seen him for a long time since authorities are after him for murder."

"Do you know who was the last to see him?" Bella said.

"Not really. About twelve years ago, he broke up a marriage west of here. The woman left her husband and kids for him. At the time, the husband swore to kill him and didn't mind letting folks know about it. Then about eight years ago, Richardson surfaced again and supposedly hired a killer to get rid of a couple of treasure hunters. But most of us believed he'd done his own dirty work."

Richardson had his fingers in several pots—from stealing

wives from their families to murder. Darren must have uncovered evidence to end up dead. "Nothing since?"

"No." Lydia's long silver earrings bounced against her cheeks.

Carr stood from his chair. "Don't discuss another interesting fact. I want a bottle of water. Oh, I'll get three."

★ ★ ★

Bella watched Carr disappear inside the house. A sweet breeze cooled her face, temporarily alleviating the gravity of the circumstances before her. How pleasant to sit and enjoy the beautiful home with the sounds of nature to pacify the chaos surrounding the community. She turned and smiled at Lydia. What a dear lady.

"About fourteen years ago," Lydia said, "I remember a young girl from this area disappeared. *Ballinger News* and other local papers covered the story and printed her picture. Her parents feared something horrible had happened to her. The girl was on every prayer list in the state. Then the story faded into oblivion for the next local excitement."

Bella kept her composure, but inside, where the demons of yesterday clawed at the mask of today, the gnawing fear of being recognized surfaced. "Interesting. Anyone ever find her?"

Lydia's dark eyes bored into Bella's soul. "Not back then."

All the training and self-control, all the martial arts and target practice, and her desire to forget the past and leave it behind didn't stop the fragmenting of emotions. "What would you have me say?"

"Say? I don't know. Why did you take this assignment?"

"It's my job."

"Or your destiny. God has brought you home for a reason, but I don't think you realize it."

"God and I aren't on good terms. Never have been."

"Doesn't stop Him from pursuing you."

Lydia sounded like Aunt Debbie. "Not interested. If He remotely resembles my own father, then I'll pass."

"Anyone ever talk to you about God?"

"My aunt took me with her to church and made sure I learned all about Christianity. But I'd already formed my own opinion."

"I see. Are you happy?"

No. Not really.

"No need to answer, Bella. I see the misery in your eyes."

The door from the kitchen opened, and Carr returned with the bottles of water and a pitcher of lemonade.

"Thanks." She turned to Carr. "I'll take the water and a rain check on the lemonade. I need to run a few errands before I set off for Abilene."

Carr set the pitcher on a small table. "I'll walk you to your car."

His gesture warmed her despite the uneasiness with what Lydia knew about her. Carr would find out soon enough, but not right now. "That's all right. You're ready to relax."

"But I'm a gentleman."

Yes, he was. Once they were outside and walking toward her car in the intense heat, reality snagged her again. "Do you understand why I keep returning to your ranch?"

"Sure do. Three men were murdered here, and your job is to find the killer."

Does he really understand? "You are a suspect along with Brandt Richardson." She said the words slowly, deliberately. "And you might hit the charts again once the autopsy report is in for Darren."

"Don't think my status with the FBI is anything I've forgotten." Carr snapped the words like a crack of thunder. "The sooner you realize I'm on the side of the law, the sooner you'll be able to find the real killer."

Bella allowed his anger to settle before she responded. Given the same situation, she'd be worried about the future and testy too. She considered telling him the truth about herself, even more than what Lydia knew. *Wait. Vic thinks Carr is involved, and he has twenty years of experience.* But her gut feeling was that he was innocent. If she learned later he'd murdered those men, then she'd need to resign.

"I've never been suspected of murder, but I have lost a close friend to a fugitive. I remember being furious and grief-stricken at the same time." She stopped at her car and turned to face him. "I'd wanted it all to end and justice to be served. Just like you."

"I'd like to believe you have compassion and sympathy for all that's happened." The lines on his face deepened. "And I hope you aren't befriending me because you think I've had a part in all of this." He opened her car door. "No need to answer that. You have an investigation to conduct."

She wanted to assure him of her belief in his innocence, but she could be wrong. An urgency to turn tail and run back to Houston pierced her heart. Vic could finish the investigation; he'd said so. Houston could send Frank to assist him. The two men would work well together.

Last Monday, a new assignment and bringing in Brandt challenged her skills. The idea of a promotion was an added plus. Now she felt inept, and fear threatened to confiscate her ability to peel off layers of lies to find the truth. Fear was not a bad thing unless it overruled sound judgment and made the truth harder to face. And that was what bothered her. She could be wrong about Carr. Very wrong.

CHAPTER 14

"MY WIFE NEEDS emergency surgery," Vic said to Bella on Saturday night. He'd phoned while she was en route to Abilene from Ballinger. "She's being admitted to the hospital on Monday morning. I had a feeling this would happen." Angst threaded his words. "Been on my mind all week. And I apologize for my lousy attitude."

"What's wrong with your wife?"

"Cancer. Stage four."

How horrible. "I'm so sorry." Bella regretted her resentment of Vic. If she'd only known how worry had eaten at him. "Is there anything I can do for you?"

"Do me a favor and don't contact the Dallas field office. I have my reasons, and I'll explain after her surgery is over. I have a responsibility regarding this assignment, and I will do my best to follow through."

Strange. The Houston office always rallied behind their agents. "Sure." Bella didn't look forward to working by herself this week, but she could.

"My question is this: Can you continue working the investigation with the county sheriff's department until I get back to you? Looks like the county commissioners appointed a good man in Deputy Roano to take Adams's place."

"I can. Roano has been helpful, and he can call in the Texas Rangers if necessary."

"Stall Roano on that aspect. I'll not be gone too long. A week at the most."

The Texas Rangers often assisted the county sheriff's departments. Odd that Vic was against it. "Are you onto something about this case?"

"Hmm. Hard to concentrate on the investigation."

In his position, she'd be useless. "Okay. Take care. And I hope the doctors are able to put your wife's cancer in remission."

"Thanks. But that's doubtful. Right now I want her pain free. Just keep the information to yourself. Don't trust Sullivan. I feel in my bones that he's mixed up in the murders."

After the call, Bella replayed the conversation. She'd honor Vic's requests unless his absence was prolonged or she saw the need for more help. What did he see in Carr that she'd missed? To date, Bella had never been wrong in judging a person's character. And she'd seen nothing in Carr that resembled deceit.

On Monday, Bella learned the fingerprints on the candy wrapper belonged to Sheriff Darren Adams. She hadn't yet received the complete workup on Stanton and Mair Warick. But she did learn the boot print found on the High Butte was a size thirteen, and the brand was sold in Walmart. In the afternoon, she attended Adams's memorial service and sat as far away from Carr as possible. His presence in the church bothered her. The *why* nestled deep inside, but she refused to even consider what the uneasiness meant.

Late afternoon, she received a call stating the fingerprints on Carr's rifle were his and Jasper's. Vic's warning from Saturday evening swept over her like a hot, dry south wind.

Tuesday morning, she received an e-mail with the autopsy results, which revealed Adams had been killed by a recently developed poison called thanatoxin. Her mind spun with what these new findings meant. Darren had been murdered. He'd been onto something the morning of his death. Had he shared any of it with Carr or his deputies?

She immediately phoned Sheriff Roano, who was reading the autopsy report while she spoke with him. His offensive language charged Carr with a fourth murder.

"I suggest sending a team of deputies to sweep his house for traces of the poison," she said.

"I'm on it. Are you heading there too?"

"You bet. I have a few e-mails and calls to make here at the hotel, and then I'm on my way."

"Good. I'm not going to allow Sullivan to walk away from these murders."

Bella drove to the High Butte to question Carr. On the way, she phoned Swartzer with the latest development and asked for information about thanatoxin. Once the call ended, her mind wandered.

Carr had a rugged gentleness about him, certainly something he had acquired since moving from Dallas to his ranch. Her mind lifted and bent, twisted and turned, like a poem that had no ending. A truth about herself and how she felt about Carr took form, and the realization hammered at her heart, as though she'd been tricked into taking the wrong fork in a road. How had he begun to stir her heart? The part of her she kept hidden, protected. Even from herself.

She took a deep breath and remembered the sage advice of the only person she trusted. "Emotions are like scorpions," Aunt Debbie always said. "If you ignore them, they will sting you when you least expect it. They won't kill you, but there are times you wish they would."

Insight surfaced like acid churning in Bella's stomach. She had broken one of the first rules of good investigative work. A prime suspect had gotten under her skin—and in the worst of ways. She actually liked him, respected him, valued his input, not to mention his incredible eyes. But Carr Sullivan kept sticking his nose into her assignment. Wanted to be a partner of sorts. Always had an opinion.

Great. The very things she liked about him, she also detested.

Perhaps she should resign from the case because her objectivity had evaporated. In Bella's opinion, she jeopardized the assignment by having feelings for Carr. She'd never allowed a man to affect her this way, not even Frank. Her heart had betrayed her when she least expected it, just like Aunt Debbie had warned.

Her thoughts moved on to her father and stepmother. For a lot of years, Bella had blamed her father for what happened, and rightfully so. Yet Mair could have stopped the whole thing with one word. Instead, the woman silently condoned the fate of a fifteen-year-old girl. How could Bella consider herself any better than Mair when she had ignored the welfare of her brothers and sister? She'd tossed them aside like a woman who stuffs out-of-date clothing into a donation bag. Why hadn't she searched deeper for their whereabouts? She owed her siblings an opportunity to better themselves. More importantly, she owed them love.

The report about her father hadn't arrived, and she needed it—desperately.

At the High Butte, Sheriff Roano and his deputies swarmed the house. Bella found Carr in the privacy of his library, reading his Bible and drinking coffee from a mug with the word *Faith* printed on it. She watched him from the doorway, his face intent on whatever Scripture had captured his attention. Aunt Debbie used to have the same look on her face when she read her Bible.

"Good morning," she finally said.

He lifted his gaze. New lines had been added to his face. "I figured you'd be here sometime this morning."

"I should have called." She pointed to his Bible. "I can wait till you're finished. But we need to talk about what's going on downstairs."

"That's why I'm here looking for strength and wisdom." He studied her face. "Darren was poisoned."

She nodded. "The substance is called thanatoxin—only recently discovered by the CIA—and has its origin in the mountains of Peru. The poison kills its victims within a few hours. No known antidote."

He gestured for her to sit down. "Roano claims he'll have the evidence to charge me by midafternoon."

Will he? Roano had an issue with stubbornness, but his tenacity might reveal incriminating information. "He questioned you?"

"In a manner of speaking. I'm sure he wanted to use waterboarding. I've been reading from Proverbs 6 about what God detests in a man. One of them is pride, and I know I have a tendency to be prideful. So if you have more news, I'll do my best to handle it with my faith intact."

"Like the words on your cup?"

His shoulders lifted and fell. "Yeah. Guess God directed my hand when I reached into the cabinet this morning."

"The fingerprints on the candy wrapper were Darren's. He must have walked out farther than the other deputies."

"I don't recall ever seeing him eat a candy bar. I sure had hoped the prints would lead to the killer."

"We all did." She took a deep breath. Talking to Carr was awkward after her own revelation of friendship—not that it went beyond that. She had no business acknowledging feelings for him of any sort. Her dealings were to be professional only. Devastating emotions had slipped in on the sly, and she dared not reveal any of them.

Carr rose from his desk and walked to the window, where gray clouds hinted of rain. He jammed his hands into his jeans pockets. "Tell me more about the poison."

"It's a powder—colorless, odorless, and tasteless."

He turned, and his eyes emitted sadness with the weight of

the news. "You know I was on a mission trip a year ago in Brazil. Does that make me more of a suspect?"

"I don't think so."

"Praise God," he whispered.

Bella took a deep breath. "Brandt spent time there. What if you were set up . . . and Lydia too, since she cooked for Darren that morning?"

Carr covered his face. "There's not a sweeter, more godly woman on the planet. Can this get worse?"

"Sure it can." For a moment, she thought he might break down. Odd, for she'd never seen a man grieve openly.

"Darren didn't deserve to die like a tormented animal. And I don't think it was an accident. What's your professional take on this?"

She studied him, looking for telltale signs of guilt. "I haven't seen enough to make a qualified decision."

"Do you think he was poisoned because he got too close to the killer?"

She moistened her lips. "Absolutely." She stretched her neck muscles, longing for a few hours' sleep to get her mind and body in gear. "Someone who had the ability to obtain the poison and then administer it unbeknownst to him."

"As in a friend?"

Bella shrugged. She allowed the silence between them to settle. Both needed time to ponder the implication of someone close to Darren ending his life. "How well did you know him? I saw the crowd of people at the hospital and at the memorial service. The newspaper bannered him a model citizen, a hero in the community who died in the line of duty. I heard the nickname 'Daredevil Adams' and the stories. His pastor read line after line of the people he'd affected with his countless good deeds."

"You're wondering if he lived a double life."

"Did he?" *Tell me more, Carr.*

"He was not the kind of man to be involved with murder or any kind of a ridiculous treasure hunt."

"Did he say anything to you the morning of his death?"

"In fact, he did, except I wondered at the time if his comment was about his sickness or the case. He said, 'This is bad. Worse than what you could imagine.'"

"What was said prior to that?"

"Oh, he was complaining about not being able to work on the investigation, and I responded it would still be there or something like that."

Darren was onto the truth. He must have discovered who was behind the killings, and he'd died for it. She stood and walked to the window beside Carr, taking careful measure of the steadily graying sky and the distance between them. "Did he say anything else?"

"Nothing. But whatever he learned upset him. I could tell by the look on his face." He shrugged. "But he was dying in front of me too."

"Did he get along with all of his deputies?"

"As far as I know."

"Were he and his wife getting along okay?"

"Yeah. They always held hands, kissing. Loved each other and in love. Once a week they had a date night or breakfast, whatever they could fit in."

Later on she'd talk to Tiffany Adams to see if she could find a chink in their marriage or if Adams might have discussed information about the murder case with his wife. Could be another link . . . or a wild card.

"I've holed up here long enough. Lydia was devastated with the news, and I need to be with her. Really selfish of me when she's downstairs."

"I like her." *And she knows the truth about me.*

An hour later, Bella drove to the Adams home. From Tiffany's reddened eyes, it was obvious she was not doing well. The news about the poisoning deepened her private abyss.

"Poisoned? It doesn't make sense." A tear slipped from her eye. "I'm afraid the coroner won't release his body for burial."

"I have no idea, but I'm sure it won't be too much longer."

"Who despised him enough to kill him?" Tiffany said.

"A good question. We're working on it, and that's another reason why I'm here. Just like you, I want to find out where he was poisoned. Did he mention having problems with someone recently released from jail or another deputy?"

"Not at all. Everyone respected Darren."

Someone didn't. "Did he have breakfast that morning?"

Tiffany dabbed her eyes and blew her nose. "No. Lydia had invited him to eat with her and Carr." She gasped. "Do you think Carr or Lydia is responsible for this?"

Bella smiled and took her hand. "I don't think so. The sheriff's department was at the High Butte when I left, and they hadn't found a thing to connect Carr or Lydia. What time did he leave for their house?"

"Six o'clock. I remember because I'd glanced at the kitchen clock and realized I needed to get the boys up for their summer jobs."

"And it takes about thirty minutes?"

"Twenty-three minutes. I know for sure because Darren had clocked it. He and Carr often did things together."

"Did he have any stops to make along the way?"

"Oh no. He wanted to be there before you that morning and talk to Carr about the murders." The moment Tiffany spoke her last word, tears trickled over her cheeks. Bella squeezed the woman's hand while her own thoughts raced.

"Are you sure? Because Lydia said he didn't arrive until 6:35. She remembered distinctly because the timer for her biscuits rang the moment he knocked on the back door."

Tiffany's eyes widened. "Where did he go during the extra minutes?"

"The sheriff's office maybe?"

"I don't think so."

"Tiffany, I'm headed there now, and I'll check to see if he made any calls."

"Would you call me when you're finished?"

"Sure."

Tiffany stood with Bella. Hope leaped across her face. "Someone could have poisoned him during those extra minutes. I hope you're able to find out who did this to my Darren. I'm going to be praying for that very thing."

"I'm doing my best, and so are all the others working on this investigation."

Tiffany glanced toward the kitchen, where one of the boys was opening the refrigerator. No doubt listening to every word. "You think the men found dead on Carr's ranch are linked to Darren's death too."

"Possibly."

"I'll talk to my boys, see if they have any idea where their dad could have gone. This may have a simple explanation. Plus, it will give me something to do—to stop my mind from thinking about it."

Bella remembered a murder case in which a woman recorded her thoughts about a deceased parent. When she shared the contents with Bella, the murderer was found. "Do you journal?"

"Why, yes. I do. It's a part of my quiet time with God."

"Are you writing down your thoughts and memories about Darren?"

"Of course."

"I'd like to see it if you don't mind."

"Of course, especially if it helps find who did this to him." Tiffany stumbled over her words, then committed to help in any way she could. "I'll go get my journal now."

Bella drove into Ballinger and snatched up her phone as soon as she had coverage. She called the FIG in Houston. "Hey, Pete. I'd like a complete workup on Sheriff Darren Adams."

"I'll get on it. Anything else?"

"Yes. Transfer me to Swartzer's office." She waited until he answered.

"Any closer to a solution?" Swartzer said.

"Maybe. There's a few minutes' time lapse from when Sheriff Adams left home to when he arrived at the High Butte. His wife has no idea where he might have stopped, but his kids may know."

"What about his habits?"

"He looks squeaky-clean, but a few things raise a flare."

"Like what?"

"Very nice house and his wife doesn't work. She drives a new Toyota hybrid SUV, and they have three teenage boys, stair steps in age; one's going off to college in another year. I'd like to see Adams's bank records and a list of cases he's worked on. His wife told me they've been married twenty-two years. She used to teach school until the kids came along. There could very well be a legitimate reason for how they live, but the doubts are still there. I've asked Pete for a complete workup."

"Keep me informed. I have a meeting in ten minutes."

Bella had wanted to toss around a few other thoughts, but she could talk to him later. "One quick question. Who interviewed the families of the murder victims?"

"An agent out of Dallas. In fact, your partner, Vic Anderson."

Why hadn't Vic told her about the interviews? "I'm going to talk to them again. Something is missing, and I think it's there." She changed lanes, leaving a late-model truck far behind in her rearview mirror. "Another thing: I learned that Richardson caused a divorce about twelve years ago, and the husband threatened to kill him. Hadn't seen that in our report before. It's worth a follow-up. Richardson's appearance on the fugitive list happened about ten years ago. I'm wondering if the husband is dead or if he's available for me to talk to."

"I'll get back to you once you receive your reports. I think the candy wrapper prints are insignificant unless something comes up in Adams's background. It will take a while to trace the boots from Walmart."

Bella started to protest, but she'd wait. "I have a few loose ends here; then I'll drive to Waco and Austin to talk to those families. Probably Friday."

"Bella, slow down. Your mind is moving faster than I can keep track of. Is Agent Anderson going with you?"

She wanted to mention Vic's absence, but she'd let this week coast by first. "I doubt it."

"Why?"

"He's involved in other things."

"Don't go alone. Not safe and you know it. One more thing," Swartzer said. "Richardson could have easily obtained the thanatoxin. I have my doubts Sullivan killed the sheriff."

"Me too." Relief flooded her that she'd not allowed her feelings for Carr to override her investigation. "The evidence tells me he's being used as a scapegoat."

"Looks that way. But it could be part of his tactic, especially if he's working with Richardson."

Bella remembered the conversation this morning with Carr. The conversation had been laced with sincerity, and she doubted he was lying. She had puzzle pieces, and she knew Brandt was part of it, but none of them fit together—yet.

When the afternoon sun slipped behind storm clouds and the sheriff's department and county poison control had finally left the High Butte, Carr stepped outside in hopes that physical work would help relieve the stress of the day. Lydia had opted for a nap, but he was too restless.

The whys and whos of the week stalked him day and night. He had no answers and the web—yes, the Spider Rock web—continued to entangle him. Brandt Richardson, the fugitive who had drawn the FBI into this case, had to be in the center of it all. *Darren.* Had his friend and accountability partner stumbled onto clues that convinced the killer to poison him? Or was his death something isolated from the case? The memory of how the fast-acting properties of the poison caused Darren to suffer made Carr physically sick. How was he poisoned? Carr blew out a sigh and a prayer at the same time.

Poor Lydia had faced the shame and mortification of having her kitchen turned upside down by the county officials and deputies looking for the poison or the ingredients to it. He'd stayed right there with her until they finished tearing through all the cabinets, refrigerator, freezer, pantry, and yes, the trash again. They found nothing but took a number of pantry items and unmarked containers from the barn and stable.

Carr recognized his fury—the senseless killings, the grieving families, the loss of a dear friend, his name along with Lydia's and Jasper's splattered with blood, and the female FBI agent who acted like he was innocent one minute and guilty the next. However, Vic Anderson was convinced of his involvement, so maybe having Bella partially on his side had kept him from being formally charged.

He pounded his fist into his hand. *Why, God? What have I done to deserve this after I turned my life over to You?*

CHAPTER 15

"Good things come to those who wait."

How many times must Brandt remind himself of this adage? In truth, it was a campaign slogan for ketchup from the eighties. However—and he chuckled each time he thought about it—the slogan fit his plan. And he'd followed it ever since.

How long had he been seeking the gold? Some days it seemed like forever, especially when it was the first thought of the morning and the last delicious morsel at night—that and Rachel. Ever since he read about the lost gold in college history, ever since he'd first seen Rachel, both had become an obsession. One entwined with the other. Pure treasure.

"Good things come to those who wait."

The maps with their clues kept him focused on the prize. He'd chased down the meanings of the so-called indecipherable carvings—the tunnel inscription, the Roman numerals, the turtle, the arrows—and talked to experts and dirt farmers. The years he'd spent in Peru studying the Incas and their culture had given him an appreciation for their religion. His travels, his work had paid off. Some parts of the journey had been disheartening, especially when he couldn't locate the Spider Rocks that had disappeared from Aspermont and Clyde. The sketches helped, but he'd wanted to touch the real thing. When he was able to place his hands, his fingertips, on the artifacts, life flowed through him. He heard the cries of those who had lost and gone on before him, but their obsession urged him on. At one time, he talked to those near Aspermont who were convinced the Spaniards had mined copper in the area and buried their vast storehouse of gold nearby.

He'd been up and down Salt Fork and to Kiowa Peak. He'd searched Knox, Jones, and Haskell counties and walked the same trail as those who had gone before him. He'd memorized the web, studied the copper relics with their carved symbols, and drank in every clue.

Many people had spent their entire lives and everything they had in vast diggings that turned up nothing. The longing, the yearning for the treasure kept Brandt alive. No one dared to get in his way. The gold belonged to him, and in Peru he'd found the answer.

The treasure had been traced to the High Butte Ranch, Carr Sullivan's land, far away from where others had searched, and Brandt couldn't touch it. Not until arrangements were made to eliminate those standing in his way. But no one would hurt Rachel. Those who worked for him understood that from the beginning. He'd purchased an estate in Brazil where the two of them could live forever. How very hard to see her every day and not reach out and pull her into his arms. As a girl, she'd refused his advances, but as a woman, she'd welcome him and all he offered. Perhaps his voice had repulsed her, but that would no longer hold her back.

He glanced at his watch. Once again Aros was late. He'd have an excuse; he always did. The habit irritated Brandt.

A charcoal gray sedan pulled onto the dirt road and eased to a stop at the foot of the bridge. Attorney Aros Kemptor climbed out and met him halfway. Dressed in a suit, he looked like a member of organized crime. In essence, he was. Brandt's organization.

"Sorry about being late. Accident coming out of Abilene."

Brandt skimmed a stone across the creek. His knee hurt to stand. Hurt to walk. "Do you have everything in place?"

"I do."

"The media are our friends, and I'd better not have any surprises."

Aros studied him, then loosened his tie. "Who is the real you?"

"Why?"

"Every appointment you're in a different disguise."

Brandt might have laughed if he hadn't been so disgusted with the jerk's disregard for scheduled appointments. "It means you haven't earned my trust."

"But we're partners."

Aros's whining grated at Brandt's nerves. He had more likelihood of winning the lottery than ever collecting a dime from the Spider Rock cache.

"Of course. But you don't have the FBI on your tail," Brandt said.

"From the looks of Bella Jordan, it might not hurt getting caught."

Brandt tossed him a halfhearted grin. Rachel belonged to Brandt long before she formed an alliance with the FBI. Time had taken her girlhood charm to classic beauty. Longing tugged at his body. Soon all he'd waited for would be his.

Staring at Aros, Brandt reached into his khaki pants pocket with a glove-clad hand and handed the man a typed piece of paper. "Here's the contact. I want it done now."

"Why me?"

"Why not you? You're paid to take orders, not question them."

CHAPTER 16

BELLA CHECKED her e-mail. As the flood of messages filled up her in-box, she looked for one from Aunt Debbie. How she'd like to hear her aunt's voice and soak up her wit and wisdom. A smile turned at the corner of Bella's mouth as she clicked on Aunt Debbie's name.

> Hi, Bella!
> Expect your birthday present when you arrive home in Houston. Hope it's okay. I went to the leather handbag Web site you recommended and picked out a good one. You certainly go through the purses. Must be all the heavy gun stuff. Gives me the creeps.
> I miss you, sweet girl. The house is lonely without your every-other-weekend visits, and my animals don't respond to my conversation. Rockefeller, and you know how much I love my dear sweet terrier, has taken to having accidents in the house. I guess it's because he misses you too.
> We've talked.
> He has issues.
> Yesterday was my volunteer day at the nursing home. Didn't help that one of the staff members thought I was a resident. When I told her of my elevated status as a volunteer who fixes hair and paints tips and toes, she thought I was a bit . . . Well, *eccentric* would have been a compliment.
> On the serious side, I've been wishing you hadn't burned

those letters from your father years ago until you'd read them. Of course, hindsight is better than foresight, and his letters were sent before we moved to Pennsylvania. I was determined not to leave a forwarding address so he and that Richardson jerk would not try to come after you. And now you're back there in the thick of evil.

And I mean evil.

Anyway, those letters might have helped your investigation.

I'm praying for you.

Love you bunches,
Aunt Debbie

Once Bella finished laughing about Rockefeller and his issues, she read and then reread the section about her father's letters. The frightened fifteen-year-old had cut the unread letters into tiny pieces and tossed in a match. But Aunt Debbie was right. They would have given her more insight into the case today. The years had come and gone, but rarely did men change their personality, and Bella hadn't forgotten.

Her cell phone rang while she was midway through responding to her aunt's e-mail. A quick glance didn't reveal the caller.

"This is Bella."

"You're in too deep," a muted male voice said. "Sullivan is hiding a secret that needs to be exploited."

"What kind of a secret?"

"His cover-up to four murdered men. That makes him a serial killer."

"Possibly."

"He's about to spring. Last I heard, he's escaping to Mexico. Check it out. His pastor knows all about it."

"I will."

"Once he's gone, all you can do is recommend he be placed on Texas's ten-most-wanted fugitive list. Of course your career would be finished."

If only she had a way to trace the call. "Guess you need to explain all of this to me."

"He's clever, and he's playing stupid. Watch him. Whatever evidence surfaces exonerating him, he's behind it."

"Really? Can we meet and talk?"

The man chuckled. "Now, why would I want to be the next victim? I have no desire to find myself at the receiving end of Sullivan's rifle. Have you seen the paper today?"

"Not yet. Listened to the local news about two hours ago how the evidence is stacked up against Carr for all four murders."

"Smart girl. This is a warning. You might be on the killer's list."

Who is this guy? "I've heard that before. What's your name?"

"Doesn't matter. My point is, Sullivan is a murderer, and he'll have no problem eliminating you. For your own protection, you should arrest him and file charges. And don't believe a word from Lydia and Jasper. They've always covered up for him."

"What if he's innocent?"

"He's not."

"What's it to you?"

"I'm a man of justice." The man ended the call, leaving Bella wondering who led the brigade against Carr. Couldn't be a law-abiding citizen when he refused to give his name. A couple of deputies had given Carr a rough time, and someone had given him a black eye. The caller wasn't Brandt, but who was it?

Bella studied the notes she'd taken during the conversation. The man was stringing her along, but first she'd call Pastor Kent Matthews, then check out the latest news. The pastor answered on the third ring.

"Pastor Matthews, this is Special Agent Bella Jordan. A few

minutes ago I received an anonymous phone call from a man who claimed Carr planned to leave the country and you had knowledge about it. The caller suggested I talk to you."

"Carr did plan to go to Mexico, but he canceled his part in the mission trip after those men were killed."

The caller knows Carr's every move. "I see. Is the trip still on?" As Bella suspected, she'd been strung along with just enough truth to cause her to follow up.

"Postponed. Darren Adams and Carr were on the planning committee to build a church for a pastor we support there. The mission team decided to wait six months."

"Sounds like a good idea." Bella toyed with the pen in her hand. "Can I have a list of the others on that committee?"

"Why?"

"Curious. I'm following up on anything in which Carr and Darren were involved. Whoever poisoned Darren may have other motives—or victims."

"Okay. It was a small team: Carr, Darren, Tiffany Adams, Jasper, my wife, and myself."

"Thanks. I appreciate your help." Bella disconnected the call. Nothing there either.

Carr closed the book about the Spider Rock treasure. He'd read a section that fascinated him; then the information would drift into detail, and he grew bored. His interest peaked and lagged about Dave Arnold, the heavyset man who at the turn of the twentieth century entered the area carrying a parchment map of the treasure. Claimed to have gotten the map from an old Mexican sheepherder. As the years rolled by, rumors claimed he'd murdered for the map.

Arnold had a knack for conning others into helping him dig

for the Spanish gold. He located one of the three Spider Rocks and claimed to be able to read the hieroglyphics. Maybe he could, since he found a number of artifacts. Others came after him searching for the treasure, and all were obsessed in finding the hidden cache. The biggest mystery to Carr came in the presumed location of the gold, which wasn't anywhere close to the High Butte. So Carr continued to read, some reports and accounts conflicting with others. Many opinions. Many missing clues. Was it worth all this effort, and did it have anything to do with the murders on his ranch?

He'd never been superstitious, but the trail of misfortune from those who sought the treasure was beginning to make sense. The book he was reading recorded the exploits of treasure hunters on into the sixties and seventies who had tried and failed to find the meaning of the web of intrigue.

His phone rang, and he saw Bella's name on the caller ID.

"Have you seen the five o'clock news?" The slight rise in her voice clued him that trouble had knocked on his door again.

"No. Sounds like I should."

"Are you near your computer?"

Carr stood from his favorite chair in his library and walked behind his desk. "I can be. Give me a moment."

"Have you talked to any reporters?"

"What do you think? I'd run them off—"

"Like you did those three men?"

Heat rose from his neck to his face.

"I'm sorry. Out of line," she said. "No reason to hit you with my lousy mood."

He mentally flipped off the switch on his fuse box of anger. "All right. But before this conversation is over, I want to know whether you believe I'm innocent or guilty."

"Are you online?"

"Dial-up, remember?" What a time for slow Internet.

"Right."

"I'll take your answer now." Exoneration for the three men's murders would give him a good night's sleep and make a nice deposit on his self-respect.

Silence met him.

"Bella, do you think I'm responsible for the deaths of those men or for Darren Adams?"

"It's not a simple yes or no."

Carr practiced his breathing techniques. In the five years he'd lived on the High Butte, he'd never fought to control his temper so many times. "It's either you do or you don't."

"Are you online yet?"

He was, but she could wait. "My answer."

"We've been through this before. The evidence pointing to you is too obvious, sloppy."

"Then you believe in my innocence."

"Maybe."

He couldn't win with this woman. "I'm connected." As he browsed, the latest news updates filled the monitor, and Carr's spirits plummeted as he read an inflammatory editorial aloud.

"'New information has cast a suspicious eye on Carr Sullivan, the owner of the Runnels County ranch where three bodies were found. Not only were the men shot execution-style by his rifle, but he was heard threatening the three men to stay off his land. The county mourns the death of Sheriff Darren Adams, who was poisoned on Thursday while investigating the murders. Adams arrived at Ballinger Memorial Hospital in Sullivan's truck after Adams allegedly complained of flu-like symptoms. The county sheriff's department refuses to comment, stating the FBI is involved in investigating the murders, which brings us to another interesting addition to the case. The three victims found on Sullivan's ranch were looking for the Spider Rock treasure. The question tonight is why Carr Sullivan hasn't been arrested.

The answer may be in an anonymous tip received earlier this afternoon. Sullivan and the FBI agent assigned to the case have been romantically linked. Is this your definition of justice? Leave a comment and tell us what you think.'"

"That's . . ." The words describing his reaction weren't the kind honoring God. "*Inaccurate* sounds good." "*The devil prowls around like a roaring lion looking for someone to devour.*"

"My adjectives are a little more colorful," Bella said.

Truthfully, so were his. "What does your supervisor have to say about it?"

"Ignore the media. Do my job. If the slander gets worse, they'll address it. But I wanted you to know the media is out to crucify you with this."

Carr cringed at the word *crucify*. Not a pretty picture. "I figure if enough evidence had been found to arrest me, then I'd be sitting in jail."

"True."

"So even if you refuse to admit it, you're convinced of my innocence." When she didn't respond, he chuckled.

"Glad you have a sense of humor in this mess."

"That and a strong belief in God." Again she didn't respond. "Is there anything I can do about the report?"

"I've been thinking if there is anything in it we can use to our advantage. Possibly contacting the editor and asking for a chance to air the other side of the story. But taking the offense might backfire and make you look guilty."

"Or contacting a TV station for an interview?"

"Hmm, let me think. Doing nothing may be the best move." She sighed. "Guess we'll have to stop the late dinners in Abilene and the bar hopping afterward. You're a wild dancer, Carr Sullivan."

Surprised at her candidness, he complimented her wit. "We could play into the report."

"What?"

"Consider this: if we were seen openly together, acting as though the report was correct, wouldn't we throw the killer off guard?"

"Possibly. I'd need to let that suggestion rattle around in my brain for a while. Run it by my supervisor. So you're suggesting we play into their hands in hopes the killer exposes himself?"

"Just a thought. What if you charged me with the crime?"

"Without evidence, it's not wise."

"Can't you talk to your supervisor to see if I could sign something that allowed you to pin the charges on me?"

"You are innocent, aren't you?"

He heard the conviction in her voice. "Yes, Bella. I did *not* kill those three men, and I did *not* poison Darren. I'm ready to do anything to prove that to you."

CHAPTER 17

WEDNESDAY MORNING, Bella played catch-up with the various reports that needed her attention. Under no circumstances was she going to tango with the media, which meant no social scenes with Carr or false arrests. To Bella, courting reporters for favorable ratings ranked below her professionalism. She'd leave that dance for those who had nothing better to do.

First on her list were the telephone records from Carr's landline and cell phone. Although the Houston field office had gone through them, she wanted to make sure the calls had occurred when Carr claimed. Kegley phoned him twice, and Miller phoned the night before the murders. The calls were short. All of the numbers traced to legitimate numbers. The day of Darren Adams's death, the deceased phoned Carr at 6:00. Jasper's and Lydia's cell phone records were absent of any of the numbers of those involved. It all matched Carr's testimony.

"Help me here," she said to her laptop. "This is killing me." *Poor choice of words.*

The cell phone records of Forrest Miller, Daniel Kegley, and Walt Higgins showed that the three men had been in contact with each other for about six months. Various numbers repeated on all three phone records, and those numbers led to public phones, most of which were in Abilene, but a few were in Ballinger.

Bella picked up her cell phone and speed-dialed Pete in Houston. "Hi, Pete. I've got a few calls made from public phones in Ballinger. Can you run down the addresses and e-mail them back to me?"

"Sure. Anything else?" Pete's skills were better than a wife's. She chuckled.

"What's so funny?"

"You wouldn't understand."

"Try me."

"I'd embarrass myself. Get back with me, okay?" She ended the call, glad for the temporary humor break. Her neck and shoulders ached, and she had nothing, absolutely nothing, to show for it.

Her e-mail alerted her to a new message with an attachment. She opened it, silently praising all those in the field office who helped agents.

Professor Miller's records displayed nothing out of the ordinary. Neither did Walt Higgins's. Kegley appeared to be the spokesman for the group, and he originated the calls to the others. His fiancée's number appeared frequently—Yvonne Taylor. Bella thought about the bartender who stated she'd taken Kegley home. Clearly he had commitment issues.

Later on in the afternoon, Bella phoned Professor Miller's wife in Austin and set up a time for another interview in the morning. Yvonne didn't respond, and she was the one Bella wanted to question. She wanted to explore Kegley's unfaithfulness and their relationship. Vic's interviews appeared devoid of specific information that Bella wanted. Perhaps his wife's health had affected his work.

Vic still hadn't contacted her. She felt bad about his wife's medical condition, but he'd been a part of the FBI long enough to understand responsibility. And why didn't he want the bureau notified about his absence? If Vic didn't call her by Sunday night, she'd alert Swartzer to the problem on Monday morning.

Bella focused on her online reading, continually weighing information in her mind in case she'd missed something. Her phone rang.

"Special Agent Jordan?" Bella recognized the voice of Pastor Kent Matthews.

"Yes, sir. What can I do for you?"

"May I have a moment of your time?"

Anticipation charged through her. Could he have remembered valuable information about the murders? "Go ahead."

"I've known Carr Sullivan for five years. I'd known Darren and Tiffany Adams for nearly twenty, since they were newlyweds. Carr and Darren were friends. Solid friends. It's ludicrous to think Carr poisoned Darren."

"I see. What about the three men found on the High Butte Ranch?"

"No matter what the media says, Carr's a good man. Why, he's been taking biblical studies distance-learning classes for the past three years in an effort to gain more knowledge of Christ and Christianity."

As much as she believed in Carr's innocence, she refused to allow anyone to deceive her. Ulterior motives, cover-ups, and lies were the makeup of criminals—no matter what their interests. "He wouldn't be the first delusional psychotic to murder in the name of God."

"That is *not* Carr Sullivan."

Immediately she regretted her impudence. "I'm sorry. I realize Carr is your friend, and I made an insensitive remark. What can you tell me about his temper?"

"Around five years ago, Carr asked for counseling to help curb his temper problem. I met with him weekly for over four months. I've never seen his temper in action."

"But you heard about it."

"Agent Jordan, don't put words in my mouth. I've never seen or heard anyone speak of Carr having anger issues. The purpose of my call is to let you know the media have accused the wrong man."

"I appreciate your concern and your loyalty to Carr. I really do. These murders have everyone in the community upset and pointing fingers, but my job is to help put an end to the nightmare. If I insult or upset anyone, it's simply part of the process. Do you have any idea who could be behind the tragedies? anyone who might have pertinent information?"

"Uh . . . no. Not at all."

So what was Pastor Kent Matthews hiding? "Is there something you'd like to tell me?"

He sighed while heavy seconds passed. "I can't accuse someone simply because I have problems with his personality."

"I assure you any name given to me will be kept strictly confidential."

"Let me have a little time."

Urgency raced through her. "Pastor Kent, don't approach the man yourself. We have enough victims without adding one more."

"This may mean nothing."

"The FBI needs to be the judge of your information." When Pastor Kent didn't respond, she continued. "I could drive to your office right now. We could talk through this, explore your reservations."

"Not yet. I'll let you know. I have a feeling, that's all. That isn't enough to subpoena me."

Curious and frustrated, Bella thought through the reports and names on all of the interviews. Without the name of the person Pastor Kent suspected, she had nothing.

Carr drove to see Kent in Ballinger. Long overdue. He should have gone to see his pastor when he first discovered the dead men. Phone calls helped, but not like a face-to-face meeting. And Carr needed prayer. At the hospital, Kent offered to meet regularly until the chaos ended, but again Carr felt like he was an imposition. The media last evening had shaken him, even if Bella admitted her belief in his innocence. Then the onslaught of calls started—noisy reporters wanting interviews; anonymous calls, which he assumed were from the sheriff's department. One call from a well-meaning man said God would judge Carr for his murdering ways. *Whoopee.*

The truck hummed over the highway while Carr played a Spanish guitar CD. A month ago, he and Darren had discussed the upcoming mission trip to Mexico. They were excited about the building project and being a part of what God planned. *What God planned* . . . The calamity besetting them all hadn't been listed on Darren's and Carr's to-do lists. Granted, God allowed the murders to happen for a greater purpose. But that kind of reasoning was easier to accept when catastrophes weren't happening to him or his friends.

Lately Carr had read so many viewpoints and opinions about why bad things happened to good people that he didn't want to see another piece of Scripture or hear another prophetic voice. All he could deduce was that God was still in control. And Carr had problems accepting it. Period.

When would this be over? His cell phone rang, interrupting his thoughts—mostly feel-sorry thoughts. He should be praying for wisdom and guidance and strength and all of those other pious things. But he was fresh out of spirituality.

"Carr, this is Aros. How are you doing?"

Maybe he did need an attorney. "All right. What can I do for you?"

"It's what I can provide in the way of legal assistance. Caught the latest news from Abilene. Thought you might be ready for representation."

Many fine Christians were attorneys, and he'd spent much of the night contemplating Aros and his expertise. He'd seen the man in action more than once. And he claimed to pray for his clients. "I'm considering your services, but I haven't decided yet."

"I hate to bring bad news, but don't be surprised if you're arrested."

A twinge of apprehension attached itself to his heart. "I have an alibi for when those men were murdered. And Darren and I were accountability partners."

"I understand. If money—"

"Money is not the issue. Faith and trust in God will see me through this."

"God can use other people to fulfill His purpose. Our small group just talked about those whom God uses. We're all praying for you, but I'd like to do more—to help."

Which was exactly what Carr had been thinking. "I need time to make sure I'm doing what I'm supposed to."

"I understand. This whole mess makes me angry. Anyway, I'm here, and I'm glad you're considering legal representation."

"Certainly. I'll get back to you. Thanks for hanging in there with me."

"One more thing. As a deacon, I want you to know I've volunteered in an advisory role to help the church in the upcoming building campaign."

Carr had placed the new education addition to the church on hold. "Are you calling a meeting?"

"Not yet. I suggested Pastor Kent acquire a few more estimates first. Then we can look at those and make recommendations before submitting it to the church body."

"Good. I can't take on anything until the murders are solved."

"Understandable. My thoughts are to have the project paid for before we hammer one nail. One of my ideas to raise money is for ranch owners to assign their mineral rights to the church."

Talking about church business relieved Carr's load, something else for him to think about beside his problems. "I have mine. But other ranchers may not."

"It's a way for the church body to help finance the new building project."

"I agree, and it's an excellent idea. In fact, I'll take a little time today and pull out the paperwork on my mineral rights. I don't have any plans to ever do anything with it anyway."

"Are you sure, with all of the other pressures?"

"Absolutely. I welcome the diversion."

"Take care, and I hope the FBI solves the case today."

Today would be nice. More than nice. Having the murderer arrested meant he would have his life back, his integrity restored, and the plans for at-risk teen boys put back into action.

Some of the folks in the area had never accepted him as a part of the community. He understood the skepticism of small-town people toward outsiders, but with the media dragging him through the manure, he'd never be trusted. He ached all over for things he could not prove. All the adverse publicity probably ended any hope for the High Butte Ranch showing teens how to become Christian men. At least his mineral rights could go to a godly cause.

CHAPTER 18

LATER THAT MORNING, Bella met with Professor Miller's widow in Austin and picked up a journal belonging to her deceased husband. Mrs. Miller had not detected anything that could help in the investigation, but details about the responsibilities of each of the four-member team were documented. Mrs. Miller pointed out that a man referred to as simply "Morton" had provided a map and funding. However, the professor indicated Morton had a bad knee, which limited his walking. This could have been another of Brandt's disguises.

Shortly after one in the afternoon, Bella knocked on the door of Yvonne Taylor's luxury condo. She'd seen the woman enter about twenty minutes before, but Bella had waited for her to get settled. Yvonne worked as a Realtor for an upscale firm, which caused Bella to wonder if the woman could have been the one to phone Carr about selling his ranch.

The door slowly opened. The tall, attractive brunette in an ivory silk pantsuit sipped a glass of wine.

"Hi, Miss Taylor. I'm Special Agent Bella Jordan from the FBI." She pulled her creds from her purse and gave the woman time to read the information. "I'd like to talk to you about the death of Daniel Kegley."

"I've already talked to another agent, Vic Anderson." She cast a skeptical glance. "Told him all I knew."

"I know, and we appreciate your cooperation. I have a few questions that the other agent didn't have in his report, crucial questions in solving not only Daniel's case but the murder of the other two men as well."

Yvonne hesitated. Her shoulders slumped, and her eyes reddened, revealing her grief—or at least giving that impression. Bella had her own hunch about that one. Knowing Kegley had been unfaithful to her once indicated he could have done so on numerous occasions. Yvonne might have been aware of his indiscretions and reciprocated.

Bella smiled. "I'll make it as brief as possible."

"All right. Come in. I do want to help." She gestured to a sofa.

"Thank you." Bella took a quick glance around the living room—sleek, contemporary lines in stark black and white with splashes of vivid red and yellow. Bella pulled her pad and pencil from her shoulder bag and sat on the edge of a white sofa.

Yvonne eased onto a matching chair, clutching her wineglass as though it held her life together. "I was supposed to have my first wedding shower on Saturday."

"I'm so sorry for your loss. When were you to be married?"

"In September. Daniel frequently traveled, so we set a date nearly a year ago."

"I'm sure you had many wonderful conversations when he was on the road."

"Not really. Daniel was very caught up in his work and focused on his dreams and goals." Her eyes pooled. "We were very much in love."

Really? "I can tell you miss him. We are doing everything we can to find his killer. When you say Daniel's work, do you mean as a geologist or the team's search for the Spider Rock treasure?"

"Both. One complemented the other. He was very close to finding the treasure. Said we'd never have any financial worries."

"Did you ever accompany him on the searches?"

"I wasn't interested in rocks or digging for lost treasure. All I did was arrange for hotel accommodations and make phone calls."

New information. "The other agent failed to mention that in his report."

Yvonne stiffened. "I didn't tell him. Saw no need for it."

"I see. Did you ever phone Carr Sullivan about the purchase of the High Butte Ranch for the team?"

Yvonne crossed her legs. "I may have. I don't remember all the calls. My work for them and as a Realtor could have crossed."

"Sounds like you are extremely busy. This morning I met with Professor Miller's wife, and she gave me her husband's journal. I briefly examined the contents, but it will definitely assist the task force team."

Yvonne lifted a brow. "I'm glad she could be of help. I met her briefly at the funeral."

"So did you act as a secretary for the four men?"

"Uh, yes, I did. Once they formed a team, someone needed to keep records."

"How did the men team up?"

Yvonne pointed to Bella's notebook. "Did Professor Miller's wife give you a similar report?"

"She said the men met online during an open forum about the Spider Rock treasure."

"Correct. They met that way for about three months before a face-to-face."

"Is that when plans took form to search out the treasure for themselves?"

"More or less."

Bella took her time in recording Yvonne's statements. She wanted the woman to think through every word. "I understand there was a fourth man who organized the search. Did you meet him?"

Yvonne slowly brought the glass of wine to her lips. "Many times. He and Daniel were the most involved."

"What was his name?"

"Morton Thomas."

"Did he accompany the other three on their treasure hunts?"

"No. He has terrible allergies."

Bella pulled out a picture of her dad. She didn't know if she wanted Yvonne to recognize him or not. "Have you ever seen this man?"

"No."

On the glass table in front of them, Bella laid out six eight-by-ten photos of Brandt Richardson. In each one he wore a different disguise. "Is this him?"

She picked through each one and then smiled. "No. None of those men are Morton."

"He must be quite the lady's man," Bella said.

"Morton? What do you mean?"

"Oh, other women I've interviewed have dated him. He does get around."

"Really? He seemed like the studious type."

Bella caught Yvonne's intense gaze. "I've been disappointed in men enough times to know none of them can be trusted."

Yvonne took another sip of wine. "How many women claimed to have known Morton?"

Bella shrugged. "I didn't count. Some of the reports came from Peru and Mexico. Another agent relayed the information. I do know the man's real name is Brandt Richardson, and he's on the FBI's fugitive list. He's also been implicated in a fourth murder—a sheriff in Runnels County." She leaned in closer to Yvonne. "Are you sure there isn't anything else you can tell me?"

She moistened her lips. "Nothing. I'm sorry."

"I'd like to see the records you kept for the team."

"Sure." Yvonne rose from the sofa. "The file's on my laptop. But nothing's really there except where they'd looked and what they found—if anything."

"I really need to take it with me as evidence."

"Do I have a choice? My work contacts are stored there, but I could put my info on a memory stick."

"I'll get your laptop back to you as soon as possible."

Yvonne's lower lip protruded slightly. "I guess it's okay. If the information helps solve Daniel's murder, then you can keep it for as long as you need." She disappeared and returned quickly with the laptop, bringing a memory stick with her. Good. She didn't give herself enough time to delete any files or make any calls.

"Thanks, Miss Taylor. By the way, has Morton contacted you since the deaths?"

She handed Bella the laptop and sat down. "No need to."

"Wouldn't he be interested in the files about the treasure or how you're doing?"

"Oh, he wasn't the social type, and he has a copy of everything."

Bella didn't believe her for a minute. "Do you have a way of contacting him?"

Yvonne's foot wiggled. "He initiated the phone calls, and he didn't use e-mail."

"That's a shame. We really need to ask him a few questions about his dealings with the deceased and some of the allegations from women he's known."

"Sounds like he's a jerk."

"Then I can count on you to let me know immediately if he contacts you?"

"Certainly."

Bella thanked her again and handed her a business card. Yvonne took the card and clenched her fists.

Once outside, Bella left the parking area of the condos and drove until she found a side street close by where she could leave her car. She had FBI surveillance waiting on standby. Walking behind the condos and a three-story apartment house, she made her way back to where she could keep an eye on Yvonne.

Within fifteen minutes, a taxi pulled up, and Yvonne exited

her condo. Now why didn't she drive her own car, unless she'd been given directions not to? Once the taxi pulled away from the curb, Bella phoned the surveillance team to keep an eye on Yvonne, the taxi, and her little silver BMW.

CHAPTER 19

CARR TIGHTENED THE CINCH and led his gelding from the stable. Normally while saddling up, he took a few minutes to appreciate the squeak of leather and the fresh scent of hay. Until five years ago, he'd never been on a horse or appreciated them. When Jasper came along, he made sure Carr was put on "the fast track to ranching" and learned as much about horseflesh and ranching as Jasper could squeeze into one man's brain.

But this morning things were different. Jasper awaited him, and the two were on a mission. Early this morning both of them had heard rifle fire—six shots, to be exact—and Carr wanted to make sure another dead body hadn't dropped on his land.

Calling Bella crossed his mind more than once, which was why he'd asked Jasper to join him. In light of the media reports, it made more sense for the two men to search the ranch than for Bella and him to find another body. Carr regretted her name had been splattered across the TV and newspaper headlines with his when he knew she was a conscientious professional.

He swung up into the saddle. "I sure hope we don't find another problem out there."

The leathery old man mounted his saddle like a twenty-year-old. "But we both are thinking otherwise, or we wouldn't be doing this."

Apprehension ground in Carr's gut, but he couldn't sit back and do nothing. "We were caught off guard when we found those three men, but since Darren's death, I'm more angry and determined to get to the bottom of this than afraid."

"A healthy dose of fear is better than stupidity."

"You're thinking I should have called Bella?"

"She carries a weapon."

"We have our rifles."

"But we're not trained FBI agents assigned to solve murders."

Jasper made sense, but not enough for Carr to change his mind about going. However, he could appease his friend. He pulled his cell phone clipped to his belt and punched in Bella's number. Staring at the butte in the distance, he waited for her to answer. Her soft voice rattled him, not about the investigation but what he realized were his steadily growing feelings for her.

"Bella, this is Carr. Jasper and I heard rifle fire shortly after midnight, so we're taking a look on horseback. Thought you might want to know."

"Did you call Roano?"

Carr had a hard time being civil to the newly appointed sheriff. "He's busy."

"That happens to be part of his job. Wait and I'll go with you this afternoon."

"Too late. We're saddled and riding."

"What if you find a situation out of your control?"

"Won't be the first time."

"This isn't a game, Carr. Wait until I get there."

"Not this time. It's my ranch, and I'm making sure there aren't any bodies. I'm not leaning on a . . ."

"Woman?"

"Bella."

"Don't say another word. Do you have mush for brains? Think about it. You're a major suspect in four murders, not the Lone Ranger on a crusade with your sidekick Tonto."

"I'll talk to you later." He ended the call and clipped the phone back onto his belt. "Satisfied?"

"I suppose." Jasper's voice sounded tired, old. And who could blame him?

"If you're afraid, stay here. Doesn't bother me at all."

"Nope. You're stuck with me. My reservations are about where this is all headed. You look guilty to most folks."

Carr had assumed Jasper believed in his innocence. "What about you?"

Jasper tossed him an exasperated frown. "I think I know you better than anyone else, except for Lydia. Being a woman, she has insight I wasn't born with. You don't have a streak of meanness to deliberately hurt someone."

"Thanks. I'm praying for God to vindicate me, but the problem is growing worse right before my eyes. Can't sleep for worrying about it."

"Maybe you need a lawyer."

Carr studied his friend. "I've been thinking about Aros Kemptor."

"Me too. He does a lot of good in the community, but I've never heard of him representing anyone in serious trouble."

"He's called me a few times. A little pushy but sincere."

"It's your decision, Carr. My thoughts are like yours. The situation is going to get worse before it gets better." Jasper shrugged. "Could be I'm an old man who doesn't like what he's seeing."

"You're a good friend, and I need all the friends I can get. Over the past five years, your advice has kept me on track in my spiritual and personal life. My dad tried to teach me what life was all about, but I didn't listen. He loved God and wanted me to follow in the faith. Now he's gone. You've given me a chance to honor and respect you the way I should have done for him."

"We've talked a lot about your past and what brought you out of Dallas. But what brought you to this part of Texas?" Jasper studied him with a narrowing of his left eye, which meant his questioning was steered in a particular direction.

Carr sensed irritation rising in him. Jasper knew all about him. Why did he ask again? "I'm sure you remember how I needed a fresh start."

"Didn't Jesus give you that in Dallas?"

"He did." Confusion crawled across Carr's emotions. "I told you what I did there." Did Jasper have doubts about his integrity?

"You did. I have a point to make."

"Figured."

"You believed by living out here, the temptation to party in ways that don't please God, use folks for your own means, and socialize with women would be easier to avoid." Jasper's voice had a spiritual tone to it, lower and more reverent.

"And I was right."

"I agree, and I think for your circumstances you made the right move. You aren't the same man who hired me to help run this ranch."

"But what, Jasper? Where's this leading?"

Jasper grinned. "You know me pretty well. I have a question for you. Did you think that by avoiding those sins, you could avoid sin entirely?"

"Of course not." Carr stopped himself. Had he thought he was immune to sin simply by leaving Dallas and avoiding those triggers? Had he set himself up as a pious, monkish man a level above other men, as though he had an immunity to sin? *Have I done exactly that?*

"I made you think. Good. And I don't believe what you're wondering about yourself will be figured out today. Sometimes realization is the first step to lettin' Jesus in to do His work. At least it is with me."

Carr rode a few more feet. Thinking. Praying. Questioning. "Sin's going to find me wherever I go."

"My point. Since you've lived here, it's been easy to love God and be obedient. And when you felt Him guiding you to start a home for those boys, you accepted the challenge."

"Right. Here in the silence, I seem to hear God better." He shrugged. "But I get your point. I still sin."

"God knows your heart, and Satan is after you big-time. He's not happy about your change of life and commitment. So all he can do is hammer you with situations causing you to doubt your faith."

Like how he felt about Roano. Carr had turned the other cheek when the man blacked his eye, and he felt real smug about it. Big old Christian from West Texas out to show the world what being like Jesus was all about. But inside, Carr despised Roano. The newly appointed sheriff was disagreeable, and he'd taken Darren's place.

Now Carr understood. "The four murders and my suspected involvement have weakened my faith instead of making me stronger." He took a deep breath. "Trials are to strengthen our faith."

"You're not going to let Satan win." Jasper's words were a statement, a declaration.

"Absolutely not. I'm riding this bull until it's over."

Jasper laughed. "That's why you have me."

"Guess so. The worst pain I ever had was when Michelle died, and with it came an invitation to follow Christ. But I suppose I'm not the only man who heeded the Holy Spirit at a funeral. I've hurt plenty lately, which says to me if I stay strong, I'm about to take a spiritual leap."

"I agree. Don't give up on the Lord. There's a reason for all of the tragedy."

Carr hoped so. Too many times of late, he wanted to quit life. "Any other sage advice?"

"Just know that Lydia and I are praying for you." Jasper rubbed his whiskered jaw. "God sure didn't intend for His creation to act like this."

"I know He can handle it, but man's behavior must grieve Him."

"I'm sure it does. He has emotions that are deeper than ours." Jasper hesitated. "One other thing: there's more to Miss Bella than meets the eye."

Strange remark. "Such as?"

"She's been through a lot of pain. Has she told you about her life when she lived here?"

Carr shook his head. "I know she doesn't have much use for God."

"Understandable. Considering."

"You're not planning to tell me a single thing, are you?" How could one man make him so frustrated?

"Nope. Not my job."

An hour later, the two men rode along the northwest corner of the ranch. The need to know more about Bella would not let Carr go. He couldn't ignore his growing feelings for her, and he hoped she might have the same for him.

Carr drank in the beauty of the land—God's ranch. Nothing looked out of the ordinary as they rounded small hills strewn with rock. A rare summer rain drenched them both, but neither man wanted to ride back until they checked every section of the ranch.

Jasper was the first to see the fallen livestock. Carr audibly moaned with the realization of what the rifle fire indicated. The rain grew heavier, sure to wash away the tracks, as though the shooter had ordered up the gully washer. The two men dismounted. Four heifers and two horses were shot.

Bella's progress in solving the case looked like a sixth grader's work. Actually it was dismal. If she took the time to dwell on what Brandt might have in store for her in his bag of tricks, she'd run back to Houston. But she wasn't a fifteen-year-old kid any longer, and this time she intended to stand her ground.

To make matters worse, Carr and Jasper were on some crazy escapade to find out why they'd heard shots fired on the ranch.

While in her hotel room, Bella phoned Pete in Houston and asked him to dig deeper for any rumors about Brandt, no matter how remote. She'd fly with whatever they could find. Somewhere in all of this was the key to unlock the investigation.

Roano had been helpful, but hostile toward Carr. His words nailing Carr for the murder of the three men and Adams weren't conducive to a pleasant working environment.

And she hadn't heard a word from Vic. Why hadn't she asked for his wife's name so she could check the hospitals in Dallas? Another stupid move. She shouldn't think disparaging thoughts about a fellow agent, but she did.

Gathering up her shoulder bag and laptop, Bella took the stairs to the lobby and parking lot. Earlier rain had fallen like sheets, but now the sun peeked through the clouds and dried the pavement. Definitely a good omen, except for Carr's fool trick to look for the source of the rifle fire. She made her way into the parking lot and noted muddy footprints leading to her car. The footprints stopped by the driver's side, and a white, business-size envelope had been tucked under the windshield wipers. She noted it was dry—a recent addition. Closer inspection revealed her first name printed with a black marker: *Rachel.* Bella took a cautious glance around and saw no one. Bending to the ground, she measured the muddy footprints with her own sandal.

Paranoia must have set in because the print looked like a size twelve. She reached into her shoulder bag and pulled out a tape measure: 11¼ inches. Before she touched the vehicle, she wanted to make sure there were no surprises. Taking a few steps back, she disarmed the car's alarm and waited. For the next ten minutes, Bella watched various vehicles pass, studied the parked ones, and paid attention to any walkers. Nothing about her car looked unusual or suspicious.

A Hispanic man walked by dressed in jeans and a long-sleeved shirt. He had a slight limp. "Have you seen anyone by my car?"

He cupped his ear.

She repeated her question, this time in Spanish.

Again he cupped his ear and pointed to it.

Great. The man was deaf. She smiled and directed her attention to a couple leaving the hotel, their fingers entwined and her head nestled into his shoulder. They'd be oblivious to a tornado.

Bella lifted the envelope from the windshield and slipped her index finger beneath the flap to the folded piece of typed paper inside.

Rachel, be careful. You're safer in Houston. Brandt plays for keeps.

CHAPTER 20

WHEN BELLA DROVE to the High Butte Ranch on Friday afternoon, she repeatedly checked the mirrors of her car for a trailing vehicle. What a life. Actually, driving defensively through Houston rush-hour traffic seemed safer. In the big city, she expected motorcycles to weave in and out of three lanes and good old boys in pickups to attempt to outrun police cars. *But in West Texas, anything goes.*

She passed two trucks while the dazzling sun blinded her. The temps were over a hundred, making the paved road hot enough to fry burgers. Perhaps whoever had shot out her tires nine days ago would be inside in air-conditioning and not waiting for her to drive by.

She knew Brandt was behind all of the deaths. She understood his motivation, his lust for the Spider Rock gold. But how could she prove it? Where had he slipped up? Those three men had found something on Carr's ranch connected to the treasure, but what? Lydia claimed an old man in Junction said the maps were wrong, that the treasure was in Runnels County. Bella needed his name for an interview.

As Bella allowed her mind to wander, she discarded the idea of Darren Adams playing a role in the scheme of things. Tiffany Adams had inherited a sizable sum in the early nineties when her parents were killed in a car crash. The person who poisoned Daredevil Adams had to have caught him unawares—probably a friend. If she could discover that person, the case would take a huge step forward.

Over and over she toyed with scenarios looking for the weakest link. So one more time, she wanted to see the murder site and search for evidence that might have been overlooked. She hoped Carr and Jasper hadn't found anyone hurt or dead this morning. Perhaps it was kids on the butte messing around. But rifle shots in the middle of the night didn't sound good.

At the ranch, the surroundings looked peaceful. She enjoyed coming here, but she'd prefer more pleasant circumstances. She paused to watch a frisky colt race across the pasture and listened to the peaceful sounds of cicadas and songbirds. If her life had been like this fourteen years ago, she might still be here.

At the back door, Lydia invited her inside. "Carr's upstairs in the library," she said. "Have a seat and I'll get him."

Bella slid into a chair, realizing how her body ached from lack of sleep. No matter how tired she was at night, visions of the rattler's form in her bed kept her awake.

Lydia reappeared. "He said for you to come on up. Would you like a cool drink? Just made a fresh pitcher of iced tea." She sighed. "He had a rough morning. Has a decision to make."

Bella's internal alarm poured adrenaline into her veins. If Carr and Jasper had found a body, the place would be swarming with deputies. Considering how the caffeine would give her a jolt, Bella accepted the tea. She climbed the staircase that wound to the loftlike upstairs. The walls held framed art of Texas's history beginning with the Alamo and continuing on with oil wells and ending with space travel. Someday she'd take the time to study each picture. She turned left and made her way to the library that doubled as Carr's office.

She paused in the doorway. "Good morning."

Carr lifted his head from a book about the Spider Rock treasure, one she'd seen him reading in the past. He offered a grim smile. The deepened lines around his face and eyes probably matched hers. "Sit down." He gestured toward the leather chair across from his desk. His gaze failed to meet hers, not a common occurrence. As much as she didn't want to admit her attraction to him, it fueled her wandering thoughts. The last time they spoke, she told him she believed in his innocence.

"What did you find this morning?" she said. "I expected a call."

"Four dead cattle and two horses. All shot with the same type of bullet." He opened his desk drawer and pulled out the bullets. "All of this is a warning to scare me off my land. And these are the same shells used in my rifle, the type used to kill those three men and blow out your tires. And I'm fed up with it. These guys are not giving up, and neither am I."

"Did you call the county sheriff's office?"

"Sure. Roano said he'd check in later. Other things had more importance."

She'd seen law enforcement officials give up on investigations when days passed without solid answers. But that didn't sound like Roano. "Why do I think he said more?"

Carr lifted his chin. "For whatever it's worth, he said, 'Too bad the shooter missed the real target. I feel bad for the animals.'"

She winced. "Nice guy. Is he a suspect in shooting your animals, or is he the one who blacked your eye? or both?"

"Neither one is important. Roano lost a good friend, and he's retaliating the only way he knows how. But I doubt he shot my livestock."

"Right. Rather immature. I saw real tears at the memorial service."

Bella listened to Carr voice his thoughts, always analyzing his statements, always reading his body language. She believed in his innocence, but she had to be looking for an error. Allowing her feelings for him to blind her meant someone else could be killed. Yet she sensed something else bothered him. "What else is on your mind?"

His gaze bored into hers, cold and calculating. "When were you planning to tell me?"

"Tell you what?"

Carr's eyebrows narrowed. She hadn't seen him angry before, only heard about his temper. "When I talked to Roano today, he had a few questions about Darren and me having a disagreement regarding our church's building project." He folded his hands on his desk, and she didn't understand what had gotten him so hot. "For the record, I thought the project should be debt-free. Darren wanted to secure a loan for half of it. Once Roano was finished, he told me something interesting. Said you and he had gone to school together. Why didn't you tell me you grew up in Runnels County? that your father was a Spider Rock enthusiast?"

Uneasiness chased a chill up her spine. Why hadn't the deputy questioned her about her life there? She didn't remember him from school, but much of those days were a blur. "The information hadn't come up in the investigation."

"But you pretended ignorance about the Spider Rock."

He had no idea what nightmares the legend procured. "I said I didn't believe in it, and I knew very little about the legend. And for the record, my father was the treasure hunter, not I. What I know is minuscule compared to what we've researched online or what you've relayed to me from your book."

He leaned back in his chair. Still no sign of his infamous temper, unless his rage lay dormant until it exploded in a burst of fury.

She silently dared him to challenge her. "I've seen how the Spider Rock treasure affects those who forsake everything to find it. I don't have specific clues. Sure I've heard the stories and seen the map. But as far as I know, the gold could be anywhere."

"I've done all I could think of to help you, and you played me for some kind of a fool. I understand I was a suspect in the murders. Probably still am. I also understand you're an FBI agent sent to find out who committed those murders and under no obligation to tell me anything. But I thought we were friends, on the same side."

In his shoes, she'd be upset and feel betrayed too. Perhaps a little information for friendship's sake was in order. "I lived in this county until I was fifteen years old. My father was obsessed with finding the treasure, which is why I left the area."

"You left the area? But not your parents?"

"Right. I went to live with an aunt."

"Seems strange. Do they still live here?"

"I have no idea."

"Are you going to tell me any more? Because I have a hard time believing you don't know where your parents are."

"Believe what you want. Doesn't matter. Because of those early years, the FBI assigned me lead agent in the investigation."

He studied her as though weighing what she'd said—or perhaps what she hadn't said. "What prompted you to join the FBI?"

She smiled and his animosity appeared to diffuse, if there had been much at all. She'd been asked this question before, and the answer had motivated every step of her career. "Concern for violent crime. I believe good and decent people deserve to walk the streets and country roads of the U.S. without fear."

"I see. But there's more, isn't there?" Intensity crept across his face. "We all have our secrets, Bella."

No point in getting in his face. He saw straight through her avoidance. "I haven't been back here since." Bella wrestled with how much more to tell Carr. She'd allowed her feelings for him to affect her logical, matter-of-fact method of processing information in the investigation. Yet deep in the pit of her stomach, where reason collided with intuition, she knew Carr was one of the finest men she'd ever met. Her original impression of him being arrogant and guilty of violent crime changed when she watched how he led his life. His role in the crimes lay in circumstantial evidence, and at this point, she'd learned nothing to convince her otherwise.

"I'm sorry for not telling you the truth." She hoped he believed her.

Silence wafted about the room. Uneasiness warred against her normal mode of wanting to be in control. But beyond her domineering personality traits was how she felt about truth and justice.

"Earlier today, I found footprints leading to my car. A note had been placed under the wiper blades." She pulled it from her shoulder bag and read the typed note, omitting her first name. "'Be careful. You're safer in Houston. Brandt plays for keeps.'"

"Someone wants to make sure you're safe."

"Maybe. Would have been nice if the person had signed it."

He paused. "Footprints, huh? It must have rained in Abilene too. What size shoes?"

"What do you think?"

"But the note says to stay away from Richardson."

"He's not the only one involved who wears a size-twelve shoe."

Carr's openness urged her to take another step forward. But was this the right thing to do? Vulnerability had never been a part of her adult life, and she wasn't so sure she wanted to start now. Bella stood and walked to the window—the light streaming in had come to represent clarity of thought. From the view there, the butte appeared to hold up the sky. Wasn't she the special agent who supposedly had her act together, sent to locate a murderer and make an arrest?

"Who is the other ghost?" His words were spoken barely above a whisper, coaxing her. She feared making a mistake, and yet she detested looking over her shoulder like a coward afraid of her own shadow.

"My father."

Carr scooted back his chair, and in an instant, he was beside her. "The FBI assigned you to a case in which your own father may be involved?"

"I don't think they're aware of his possible role in what is happening here."

"I haven't heard of a man named Jordan in this case."

"His name is Stanton Warick."

Carr's eyes softened.

Her pulse raced. "Do you know him?"

"I know the name. While getting my feet wet about ministering to troubled teen boys, I visited a couple of churches in the county—sort of to see if I could relate to teens. I spoke to them about my life before becoming a Christian." He hesitated, his eyes capturing hers. "I remember a couple of boys with the last name of Warick."

Must be a mistake. "They were in church? I find that hard to believe."

"Yep. These boys came from youth groups."

Did she really want to venture into this? But how could she not explore the possibility? "First names?"

"I don't remember."

Bella doubted the boys were a part of her family. She couldn't remember any other Waricks from her childhood. However, she'd look into it. The Stanton Warick she remembered had no use for church or anything that didn't profit him. This evening when she was able to get online, she'd have Warick's info, which would give his address and how he spent his time. She'd have the information now if her BlackBerry had a signal. Still, she'd made a commitment to Aunt Debbie to find her siblings, and she intended to keep her word. They might need her.

"Was Pastor Kent with you during those visits?"

Carr nodded. He stepped to his desk and pulled out a pad of paper and a pen. "I'm assuming those boys could be related to you. Why don't you give me their names?"

Why not? What did she have to lose? "Ty, Alex, Zack, and a girl—Anne."

"All right. I'll see what I can find out. Are they cousins?"

"Something like that. I'd hate to involve kids in all of this. But it may be necessary."

"Wish I could figure out how your mind works."

"With this investigation?" She knew exactly what he meant.

"For starters."

"It's always a puzzle, but unlike a jigsaw where you start with the corners and sides, the pieces are all random."

Carr stuffed his hands into his jeans pocket. "In the middle are three dead men, and Darren's body may or may not fit."

"I'm inclined to believe it does," Bella said.

"What else goes into the puzzle?"

"The Spider Rock treasure, Brandt Richardson, Stanton Warick . . ."

"I can almost hear the gears grinding in your head. What else are you thinking?"

Bella reached for the pad of paper on his desk, tore off the names of her brothers and sister, and drew a square on a clean piece. "What if the treasure is in the middle of the puzzle with the High Butte in the background? And in one corner are the three victims. In another corner is Brandt Richardson, and in the other two corners are other players?"

"Like Warick?"

"Yeah." She doodled on the bottom of the paper while mentally processing what she remembered about her father and Brandt's relationship.

"So who else could be in those two corners?"

Bella allowed her mind to clear. "Maybe Darren. We both know he heard or saw something that bothered him. Maybe someone who was close to the victims—or someone close to Richardson."

"What are Richardson's habits?"

She started to tell him he didn't qualify for the information.

But then again, he might have answers for her. "He's manipulative, charming. Uses disguises like a chameleon. The one characteristic he cannot alter is the raspy sound of his voice."

Carr moistened his lips. "No one with that kind of voice has contacted me. Let me be a part of this investigation. I can help. The killer won't suspect me."

"You aren't trained, and it's too dangerous. Out of the question, and I don't want to bury a friend."

He chuckled, the deep resonating sound that she'd grown to welcome. "Glad to hear you'd miss me."

"This isn't a child's game, Carr."

"I figured that out when Jasper and I found those bodies. The more I think about it, the more complicated it gets. You came here looking to arrest me or Brandt Richardson for the murders. Possibly both of us. So in addition to four dead men, who shot out your tires, planted a rattler in your bed, returned my rifle, left a note on your windshield, and whatever else he's done?"

"If I had answers to those questions, I wouldn't be here."

"What else has happened?"

"Small change."

"Aye, a stubborn woman you are," he said with a thick Irish brogue. "You must possess a handful of four-leaf clovers, or the bad guys wouldn't be wasting their time."

"Nice to think I can scare them."

"I don't want you as a statistic on the FBI's hero list. I did my own research on Brandt Richardson, and I'm perturbed only two agents were sent to conduct the investigation, and one of them isn't even around. Is this a part of economic cutbacks?"

She crossed her arms over her chest. "You and my aunt Debbie would get along just fine."

"If she's concerned about your ornery hide, I imagine so."

"Now you sound like a local."

"Good. Nothing worse than being shunned in the community

because of your city-slicker ways." His features softened. "I have another motive. When this is over, I'd like the opportunity to get to know you better."

A strange sensation snaked up from her stomach to her throat, rendering her speechless, and it had nothing to do with the case. She hadn't seen his interest coming, and thus she refused to respond.

"Your face is red," he said.

"It's a first."

"To blush or for a suspect to want to court you?"

She laughed. "Court? As in the nineteenth century?"

"Whatever it takes." He nodded as though accenting his words. "I'm serious."

"Interest in me isn't a good idea." What if Carr had read her emotions?

"Let me be the judge of what's a good idea or not."

The importance of maneuvering Carr from this topic crept to the forefront of her mind. "I need to talk to Lydia. She recognized me, and I haven't addressed it properly."

"Sure. But I'm not apologizing for making you feel uncomfortable."

"I didn't think you would." Maybe things would change when this was over. But until then, Carr was off-limits in the romance department.

CHAPTER 21

WHEN BRANDT WAS fourteen years old and read the side of a cigarette pack, he saw those expensive nuggets that made him look cool could kill him, so he threw the cigarettes away. Hadn't touched one since.

When he read his body might last longer if he jogged, he bought a pair of running shoes, and he still had the body of a twenty-year-old. Except for his left knee.

When he realized his four-point average could land him a free ride in college, he dug into the books and now held a degree in business and a minor in history.

When he learned about a lost Spanish treasure buried somewhere in the triangle of Aspermont, Rotan, and Clyde, Texas, he decided the cache of $64 million in gold belonged to him.

And fourteen years ago, when he first saw Rachel Bella Warick, he knew she had to be his. He craved—no, needed—the green-eyed beauty.

He intended to have the gold and Rachel. Yet neither was in his awaiting hands. But he was growing closer, and he could taste and smell the sweetness of pure bliss.

CHAPTER 22

HALFWAY BACK to the hotel on Friday evening, Bella considered pulling over and reading the information on her BlackBerry about Stanton and Mair Warick, but she wanted to give the report her full attention. With the highway winding ahead of her, Bella's mind drifted back to when her father married Mair. He'd promised Bella their new life would be like a storybook. What a joke. She wanted to believe there'd been good times during her childhood, but she couldn't remember them.

Bella's siblings had been on her mind since she first took on the assignment in Houston. But how did she right all of those years when she'd deserted them? She'd been selfish in not making contact. Ty, Alex, Zack, and Anne. Beautiful children. She'd missed them terribly in the beginning. Would she recognize any of those angelic faces from the past? If their lives had been anything like her first fifteen, they needed encouragement and support—and counseling. She was in a position to take care of them, and it was time she began.

She pulled her car into the hotel parking lot, weary and needing a break from the stress of an unsolved murder case. Tomorrow, she and Carr planned an early morning horseback ride to take the edge off the stress of the case and begin the weekend.

Bella had no intentions of burning daylight on the FBI's dollar, and she had plenty of work to do once they finished. She'd take clothes to shower and change before enjoying one of Lydia's mouthwatering breakfasts. Lots of leads were on tomorrow's lists, including an afternoon drive to Austin to see Yvonne Taylor again.

Carr promised to show her a sunrise unsurpassed by any she'd ever seen. He must have forgotten she'd spent the first fifteen years of her life under those sunrises. Memories of nature's beauty had slipped from her thoughts along with any semblance of pleasantness.

Tonight, she'd load up on caffeine and work late on those puzzle pieces that she and Carr had attempted to fit together. But first she wanted to read e-mails and study the report on Stanton and Mair Warick.

At the hotel, she hoisted her bag onto her shoulder, grabbed her laptop, and hurried inside. She greeted the female attendant behind the desk, the one who had claimed to be the manager, and made her way to the elevator and second floor. As the elevator closed, a man dressed in a gray silk suit stepped in behind her, with silver-rimmed glasses and eyebrows that were joined in the middle. He smiled and she returned the gesture, noting she could have seen her reflection in his glasses.

"Have a good evening." She exited the elevator on her floor.

When he didn't respond, she jerked back to see why. In the crack of the closing door, the man offered a slight nod. Instantly, Bella realized the man was Brandt Richardson.

She pressed the elevator button up, but her reflexes weren't fast enough and the door closed. Racing down the hall, she flung open the door to the stairs and took two steps at a time up. By the time she stood in front of the next floor's elevator, Brandt had disappeared. She shifted the laptop and shoulder bag and rushed down the steps to the lobby, but no one had seen a man in a gray business suit.

He could be a guest.

How many other times had she encountered Brandt and not realized he was following her? Surprise did not assault her, only the frustration that Brandt had continued to outsmart her. The dreadful cat-and-mouse game.

The implication seized her, and fear dug its claws into her heart. Brandt had planned the encounter on the elevator. He could have killed her, and no one ever would have known. In the past when she worked at outthinking a criminal, she took all the findings about him and slipped into his shoes. In this case, size twelve. The same size as her father's. They were working together. She was positive.

Carr looked forward to tomorrow's ride with Bella like a kid who anticipated a birthday surprise. She'd be at the ranch by 5:45, and they'd grab a cup of coffee before saddling up to leave by daybreak. They'd ride east into the sunrise—Bella and the sunrise, two beauties who were equally breathtaking. One he could only admire from a distance, and the other would ride beside him, off-limits until her investigation cleared both of their lives.

Not since before finding the three victims had he looked forward to anything with enthusiasm. The deaths he regretted, and he mourned losing Darren. Soon this would be over. All of the families involved needed closure, and the murderer needed to be in custody.

Carr leafed through the stack of mail on his desk. Most of it could be tossed into the trash unopened. An envelope bearing his church denomination's return address captured his attention. Rather than ponder its contents with the understanding he'd not contacted them since the ordeal started, he lifted the flap of the envelope and listened to it crack and complain.

Dear Mr. Sullivan,

It has been brought to our attention that you are being investigated for three homicides found on your property. I'm sure you will understand the necessity of our stance in this grave matter.

Carr shook his head at the bad pun before he continued reading.

Until the situation is resolved, we cannot endorse your application for the facility housing and rehabilitating at-risk teen boys. In addition we cannot offer financial assistance. We wish you success with your endeavor.

"Cowards." He resisted the urge to crumple the letter in his fists. They couldn't pick up the phone and talk about the crimes that had taken place on his property.

He inwardly groaned, feeling like he'd been kicked in the teeth. What good did it do him to have these thousands of acres if he couldn't use them for the glory of God? The bunkhouse had already been renovated with a full, new kitchen to accommodate twenty boys. He'd received estimates to construct a building that would house an auditorium and game area. He'd walked an area beside the proposed auditorium for an Olympic-size swimming pool and basketball court. Now it all was put on hold.

The whole ugly mess regarding the murders made him want to sink his fist into the wall. He wouldn't, but the temptation made his fingers tingle.

Lydia appeared in the doorway. "I heard you pound your desk, so I thought I'd check on you."

"Did I?" He lifted a brow. "Must have affected me worse than I thought."

"What?"

"Oh, the endorsement and funding from my denomination has been withdrawn. I'll need to contact the psychologist we hired, the physical activities director, and the teacher."

She frowned. "I'm sorry. So they canceled everything?"

"No, they need the situation resolved, which isn't that bad.

Can't blame them in the least. Who wants a killer attempting to rehabilitate the hope of the future?"

"I'm sure it will get back on track once the investigation reveals who is responsible." Lydia slipped into a chair across from him. "Aren't Bella or Vic any closer to solving the crimes?"

"Haven't seen Vic, and if Bella has made progress, she hasn't let on."

"What did you and I talk about before all of this began?"

"Pleasant things. And we debated our political differences."

"And quite adamantly, as I remember." Lydia smiled, and it coaxed one from him. "Our discussions made Jasper nervous."

"I believe, given the choice, he'd rather have our politics on the forefront than what's there now." He stuffed the rejection letter into the envelope and dropped it into a desk drawer. "Bella and I are going riding early in the morning."

"I think that's a wonderful idea. She looks pale and tired, and the ride should relax her."

"I'm taking her to the butte and back. Won't be long." He studied Lydia's face. "Do you think that's a mistake?"

"The butte provides the best view of a beautiful sunrise. It was breathtaking before the killings and will continue to bless us."

Good. "My thoughts too."

"She's a good match for you—sweet when she needs to be sweet and firm when the occasion arises."

"Hadn't thought about it that much."

Lydia laid her hand on the desktop. "The first step is admitting there's a crisis of the heart."

He laughed. "Her confession about living here must have gotten to you. You're a bit dramatic, don't you think?"

"I'm a woman, remember?" She rose from the chair. "Seriously, I'm sorry about the letter. I'm praying for all of this to end and bring our lives back to normal. God wants you to learn from the tragedies, but I have no idea what or why."

"Jasper and I discussed the same. The only path forward is to trust God and realize He wants the best for me."

Lydia left him alone, but restlessness filled him. The silence that usually blessed him with peace now thundered in his ears. He had plenty to do outside. Anything beat trying to outguess God.

He rubbed his fist in his hand. He wanted to help those boys, show at-risk teens how to follow Jesus and be real men. Disappointment cut through him like a bolt of lightning. If God had something better in store, then he sure wished He would give him a preview.

CHAPTER 23

AFTER SEARCHING her hotel room like someone with obsessive-compulsive disorder for anything Brandt might have done or left behind, Bella washed her face and resolved to shake off the reality of the stalking demon. Trained professionals used their training, not their scarred pasts. This wasn't the time to allow emotions of any kind to take precedence over her assignment.

She scrolled through her e-mails, looking for the report about Stanton and Mair Warick. And there it was. She clicked on the message and fixed her eyes on every word. Once she finished the report, she stood from the chair and walked to the window. Rubbing the chill bumps from her arms, she mentally fit a corner piece into the crime picture.

Mair left the country with Brandt twelve years ago. She'd been seen last in Rio de Janeiro as well as Peru. Recent findings revealed the woman now went under the name of Lynne Michaels and had successfully dodged the FBI's radar.

Peru . . . as in the source of the poison that killed Darren Adams.

When Bella had read the report in Houston, she'd skimmed over the information about Brandt's leaving the U.S. twelve years ago with a woman. She hadn't probed to find out the woman's name, and neither did she have the foresight to deepen the research. After all, the woman had disappeared. According to the original report, Brandt and the woman had parted company a few years ago. Bella had allowed her personal feelings to get in the way of the investigation.

Vic had been right. So right. Shame filled her for what she'd failed to do or accomplish with this assignment. No wonder Brandt had successfully implemented his plan.

Stupid. Stupid. Stupid.

As of right now, Bella's method of investigation was changing.

Bella's siblings were being raised by a selfish animal—their father. Stanton Warick could have killed all of those victims on Carr's ranch, including Darren. He currently worked as a foreman on a cattle ranch, where he lived with his children. His record was clean of arrests or suspicions, except for a DUI after Mair left him.

She picked up her cell phone and pressed in Tiffany Adams's number. The woman answered on the first ring.

"Hi, Tiffany, this is Bella Jordan. I'm sorry to bother you, but a recent development has come to my attention."

"What . . . what is it?" The woman's voice shattered. "Have you found out who poisoned Darren?"

"I'm getting closer. Are you okay?"

"Some days are better than others. It's all part of the process. We're all grieving, and each of us has our own way of showing it. I want to help you, so please ask what you need."

"Did Darren ever mention Stanton Warick?"

"Darren didn't talk work with me. He was afraid it would upset me, a habit he started years ago. But the name sounds familiar. Hold on a minute."

Bella waited while Tiffany asked whoever was nearby if the name Stanton Warick was familiar.

"Agent Jordan? I just asked my sons about the name. They said two boys with the name of Warick are basketball rivals from a neighboring high school."

Bella scolded herself for trembling. "Ty and Alex?"

Tiffany repeated the names, and Bella heard a young man respond affirmatively.

"Do they know if the boys are often in trouble with the law?" Tiffany posed the question, and Bella waited again.

"Neither of them thinks so. In fact, Ty was a junior high counselor at church camp last summer."

Bella's stomach did a flip. Maybe one of the kids had come through this okay. "Thanks so much. If anything comes to mind about the Waricks, would you call me?"

Bella disconnected the call and laid the phone beside her laptop. She reread her father's background check. Brandt had broken up her father's marriage. Mair had deserted her four children and left them with Stanton. As though her father knew anything about rearing kids. Could he and Brandt possibly have mended their differences with Mair absent from the picture? What if the two of them were leading her brothers and sister down the same greedy path? Maybe not Ty.

The longer she peered at the screen, the more she faced the ugly truth about herself. As soon as she finished her ride with Carr in the morning, she planned to take a drive to see her brothers and sister. Destiny had arrived. Why had she waited? Fear? Selfishness? Did she think by ignoring them, her family would disappear? Regret rippled through her for ignoring those who needed her. What Aunt Debbie had done for her, she could do for them. It would be hard, but investing in the future of her siblings was the least she could do. If she faced the truth head-on, she realized she needed them as much as they needed her.

Stanton Warick. His parting words had been a threat, and she hadn't forgotten a single word. But hadn't she claimed courage a long time ago? The analyst's report had an address and a phone number for her father. She wrapped her fingers around her cell phone and took another thirty seconds to gather strength. Her heart sped up to match her thoughts. Finally she pressed in the numbers. A young man answered on the second ring.

"Ty?"

"No. This is Alex."

She swallowed her nervousness. "This is Rachel. Your sister."

"Hey. Dad said you went by Bella now."

"I do. Are y'all going to be around tomorrow late morning? I'd like to stop by and see you."

"Awesome. What time's good? We'll be here."

"Great. Ten thirty sounds good." Bella moistened her dry lips. She'd been less shaken when criminals were shooting at her.

"Can't wait. We've been following the investigation. You rock, Sister."

Bella forced a chuckle while too many thoughts chased through her mind about how and why her siblings were following the case. She ended the call and drank in several deep breaths.

After working through the rest of her e-mails, Bella opened a message from Aunt Debbie. Oh, how she needed to hear the voice of her dear aunt, even if it was in an e-mail. She didn't dare call, or she'd cry, and then Aunt Debbie would find her way to Abilene. That would never do. Bella could only imagine the life her brothers and sister had spent with their father, knowing their mother had left them for a fugitive.

The subject of the message read, *A long dog's night.*

Hi, Bella!

The longer you are on this case, the longer I spend time on my knees. I find myself remembering the years when you first came to me, the frightened and determined fifteen-year-old, and the fine woman you've become.

Everything here is okay, but I had a bad night. The cat somehow got into the house, and you know how I despise cats in the house. Can't sleep right knowing those sneaky little varmints are prowling about. Anyway, the cat must have decided to get even with my banishing her to the out-side. She did her business in the bathroom—at least she had the right room. I woke up to a frightful smell and had to chase her around the house three times before I could catch her. Then I had to clean up the mess before I could go back to sleep.

Shortly after midnight, Rockefeller decided if the cat could enlist her free spirit, it was okay for him too.

It wasn't.

I sent him to his kennel. About four o'clock, Rockefeller's crying got the best of me, so I got up and let him out. We talked. Everybody is happy again.

I know you can't tell me everything about the case, but can you fudge a little and fill in some of the details for this middle-aged lady who's glued to the news? I'm ready to set the media straight about their bizarre accusations.

Have you seen your dad, Mair, or your brothers and sister?

Love,
Your zany aunt Debbie

"Tomorrow, I will have much to report," Bella whispered.

CHAPTER 24

"So how soon after the papers are filed can we get in and dig?" Brandt fired one question after another at Aros on the other end of the phone. This needed to be wrapped up soon and completed according to every letter of the law.

Brandt had the map, and three members of the team had located the entrance when Brandt had eliminated them from the equation. If the three hadn't wasted so much time, he would have the gold by now.

"Told you, I have a plan," Aros said.

"I'm paying you, not the other way around. What is this foolproof plan? Because I haven't seen anything that's helping the cause."

The man blew an exasperated sigh into the phone. Brandt let him huff and puff all he wanted. He had a special reward for him.

"The plan, Aros. Now."

"Okay, but I deserve a bigger cut after you find out about this one. Sullivan learned about his church's denomination stopping the funding and support for his project to help teen boys. I'm going to call him about the progress with the investigation and lead into church business. When he gives me his sad story, I'm going to suggest he might be the next target. With a little persuasion, I think he'll will his land to the church. We'll then have the land and the mineral rights. With my current responsibilities at the church, I'll make sure we get our hands on what we need."

"You'd better make sure it's done right."

"Don't worry, Brandt. The—"

"Do not use my name." Hatred for the weasel who thought he was indispensable nearly cost Brandt his composure.

"Sure. I forgot. Let me remind you how often you use mine. Like I started to say, the locals who attend this church have put their trust in God first and me second."

"I'm not so believing."

"You will be. The gold is almost in our hands."

My hands.

CHAPTER 25

"I REALIZED THIS MORNING that you've seen more sunrises in West Texas than I have." Carr handed Bella a steaming mug of freshly brewed coffee. He'd slept little last night in anticipation of sharing his favorite time of the day with her. In truth, he was concerned about her welfare and the lack of help from Vic.

"But I haven't seen them on horseback." She lifted the mug to her lips. "This coffee is fabulous."

"Thanks. In my old days, I was known as a coffee snob." He shrugged. "Guess I still am."

"I'm glad it carried over from city to country."

He stole a glance at the jean-clad woman, the freshness of morning still on her face, beauty as perfect as God created in Eve.

"Mr. Sullivan." Bella laughed.

He raised a brow.

"Thank you."

"Oops. I need to watch my transparency. Let's take our coffee to the stable and get saddled up. Any longer in the house, and I'll be in trouble."

"Trouble?"

"Yeah. I can't be trusted with a pretty woman."

"Is this the man who was furious with me yesterday?"

"The same."

"Have you forgotten who I am?"

"Not at all. It's Saturday. Time to take a break."

She didn't reply, and he realized she intended to work as hard today as any other.

Within a short while, the horses were saddled and ready. When Carr reached for a rifle, she asked him to leave it.

"I have my firearm. We'll be okay," she said. "Nothing personal. You know I believe in your innocence."

"How am I supposed to defend the lady from wild animals? You know—lions, tigers, and bears?"

"We women today are independent creatures. I'll take care of you. And you have your portable radio and cell phone."

He tapped them, both clipped to his belt. "Uh, where is your weapon?"

She lifted the left leg of her jeans to reveal an ankle holster.

Carr chuckled. What else could he say? The pair rode out across the field toward the butte and the rising sun.

Bella gasped, and he followed her gaze to the eastern sky. "If I did see a sunrise this beautiful, I don't remember it. It's as if a huge bonfire has ignited the sky."

"No matter how late I'm up the night before, I've got to see the sun bring in the day over the horizon." A couple of the questions about her entered his mind. "This case must be a hard one. I mean personally."

"That's a delicate way to put it." Her voice was devoid of emotion.

"How did you survive without your parents?"

"My mother died when I was three."

"Okay, how did you elevate yourself from a fifteen-year-old runaway to a respected member of the FBI?"

"My mother's sister took me in. She gave me more love and nurturing than I'd received since my mother died. Aunt Debbie legally adopted me, and I took on her name."

"I've heard you mention her. So you're still close?"

"Oh yes. My aunt is quite the character. She loves animals, and she has this rather eccentric and sometimes bizarre outlook on life."

For the next several minutes, Carr listened to Bella expound on one hilarious tale after another about Aunt Debbie. "I'd like to meet her," he finally said.

"You'd be entertained, and you'd love her," Bella said. "She's a humor writer for a Christian women's magazine and on staff for a family-oriented sitcom."

"Are you a Christian?" Surely an aunt who wrote for Christian media had influenced her niece for the same.

"My aunt would like to think so."

"I see." Another topic for them to talk about once this was over.

"I have a question for you."

"Religious or otherwise?"

She laughed. "Both. Your pastor, Kent Matthews—does he do routine counseling?"

"Sure. Young and old. He was a psychologist before becoming a pastor. Why?"

"Oh, nothing. Just wondering."

"*Nothing* with you means you're working. You've got a lead?"

"Possibly. Is his office at the church where the memorial service was held?"

"On the left-hand side. Entrance is off the parking lot in back. Should I call to warn him?"

"Nope. I'm harmless. I have errands to run later on this morning, and I'll add his name to the list."

"Can I ask what else you're doing?"

"Wouldn't do you any good."

"I'm learning." They rode on in silence, and he couldn't quite put his feelings into words. Comfortable . . . more like peace. Strange, but true. The source was God, but the woman beside him had to be a special gift.

"Once I leave here, I'm going to visit them," she said.

"Who?"

"The Warick kids."

"Do you need company?"

She took another swallow of coffee. "No thanks. I have to make this trek alone."

Carr lifted a brow in mock annoyance. "You're a stubborn woman, Special Agent Bella Jordan." He pulled in his reins. "Take a look at that." He pointed to the chalky shades of yellow, orange, and purple slipping over the horizon.

A smile spread over her face. "It's amazing. I regret missing this before."

Rifle fire split the air like a crack of thunder. Bella's horse startled, and Carr grabbed his and her reins. She slumped over the saddle. Blood spurted from her left shoulder and trickled down her back.

Carr jumped from his horse and hurried to pull her from the saddle. Another shot pierced the air. A sharp sting rippled up and down his arm, but he refused to allow the pain to stop him from getting her to safety. His gaze swept to the butte, sensing the shooter had a position where he could see them perfectly.

"I've got you," he whispered.

"It's him." She sucked in a breath. "He promised to get even."

Carr had no idea to whom Bella referred. Later he'd ask— much later. He carried her toward a mesquite tree. A third shot downed the mare Bella had been riding. His gelding galloped toward the ranch.

He was confident the rifle fire had already alerted Jasper, but he yanked his radio from his belt and pressed the Talk button. "Jasper, Bella and I've been shot. We need help and Bella needs an ambulance."

"Got it. I'll call the sheriff's office."

A fourth shot zinged over Carr's head, and he dropped the radio. Hopefully Roano would respond to the call. Carr had more than one enemy wearing a badge there. But if Roano knew Bella was injured, he'd hurry.

Another bullet soared a few inches to the right of him, and he pulled her firearm from her ankle holster, then lowered himself over her body.

"He doesn't give up," she whispered through a ragged breath.

"Who, Bella?"

"Dad."

What tormented her from the past that she'd be convinced her own father would want her dead? He figured their relationship had to be fragile, but not this. Bella needed off this case, and he didn't care how angry it made her. Once she was at the hospital, he'd make a call to the FBI in Houston.

Several seconds passed while he waited for another crack of rifle fire. Nothing. He studied the butte to see if the shooter was closing in. Nothing around them moved. Not a sound but the morning songbirds. Bella moaned, and he took a quick look at her wound, all the while keeping an eye out for the shooter. His attention riveted on the amount of blood she'd lost. The bullet had gone straight through her shoulder, much too close to her heart for Carr's liking. Carr's medical training consisted of a first aid course, but he didn't need a medical degree to see if she didn't receive help soon, she'd bleed out. He pulled his uninjured arm from his shirtsleeve, biting his lip while freeing the other arm. For the first time he caught a glimpse of his wounded arm that felt like a swarm of bees had declared war. Blood trickled to his wrist.

"What are you doing?" she managed. Her eyes had been glued shut since he pulled her off the saddle.

He thought she'd passed out. Strong lady. "Trying to bandage you."

"Hey, cowboy." Her eyelids fluttered open.

He pressed his shirt against her wound. "Hold your praise and rest. I'm sure Jasper will be here any minute."

"Be careful. Four men are already dead."

"The shooter's had plenty of time to finish us off. I think this is a warning, like your tires and the rattler." Carr's thoughts had changed about the situation, but he didn't verbalize them. The shooter needed time to get away, not more time to line up his sights.

She swallowed hard and closed her eyes. "You'd make a good agent."

"I'm in training."

"Can you get out of here, 'cause—?"

"Hush. Jasper will be here in no time, and I'm not leaving you alone."

Her body relaxed, and his mind flew back to the night Michelle overdosed. The memories of watching her die swept through him. She'd slipped into unconsciousness, then quit breathing. Oh, how his life had changed since he'd come to know Jesus. Through the help of understanding Christians, he'd learned to deal with regrets and purposed to live for the future.

Carr drew Bella's body close to him, as though if he held her tight enough, she would hold on to life. Fear for her gripped his heart, squeezing him like a child desperately clings to a favorite toy. *This time I have Jesus.*

"Keep her alive," he whispered. "Lord, I'm trusting You in this. I refuse to react like I did before with Michelle. Help me to rest in the understanding that Bella is in Your hands."

In the distance, Carr heard the sound of a truck bumping over the pasture. His gaze shot out over the rolling field. "Jasper's on his way, and we'll get you taken care of." Panic took over as he realized Jasper could be in the shooter's sights.

His prayer became a repeat of his Savior's name, while his blood-soaked shirt stayed affixed over the gaping hole.

CHAPTER 26

BRANDT FOUGHT THE FURY threatening to spin him out of control as he watched Sullivan's hired hand lift Rachel onto the truck bed. Sullivan climbed in after her. Brandt seldom experienced raw sentiment, but this incident had brought on emotion he normally chose to conceal. Strange how he could love a woman for all this time and despise who she'd become with the same passion. She had guts to come after him, knowing his capabilities. And he admired her strength. It made her all the more mysterious and desirable, and all the more his. Soon she'd understand that he always had her best interests at heart. A woman like Rachel had to be tempered into submission, and Brandt knew how to do it.

He had not authorized this shooting, and the call to be here this morning was supposedly for his benefit.

Bella must have recognized the inevitable, or she wouldn't have taken on the case. That was it. She wanted him to come after her. Brandt felt the certainty rise in him and calm his raging thoughts.

When Rachel was fifteen, when he decided she must be his, the girl had been confused. How ludicrous of Warick to think he could play the role of a father and order her to come home. Brandt should have taken over the communications with Bella's aunt. Warick's stupidity was why Brandt stole Mair away from him. Warick didn't deserve a good woman, and Mair had clever means of keeping a man happy. Brandt cared for her in his own way, but that didn't stop his wandering eyes or his heart for Rachel.

He made his way back to the horse tethered to an oak. His gaze took in the foot of the butte containing his future. *Soon all will be mine.* The gold and the investments would keep him and Rachel forever.

But first he had to make sure Rachel survived the bullet. Then he would make certain Aros understood who gave the orders. And make him pay.

CHAPTER 27

BELLA WOKE to the siren clearing a path of traffic and the wind whistling around the ambulance's doors. She fought to open her eyes, wanting to see Carr beside her but not wanting him to comprehend she craved the sight of him. The fiery pain in her shoulder served as a reminder of the shooter's accuracy. The man behind the trigger had to be her father, who had kept that promise spoken fourteen years ago. This time he'd nearly killed her.

A callused hand wrapped around hers, and she understood from the firm grip that it was Carr's. She forced her eyes to open, only to see his eyes were closed. She didn't need an explanation. The man was praying for her. Neither did she have any desire to stop him. She found comfort in the knowledge of another human sharing a request with a divine being on her behalf, even if her own faith had no substance.

Her attention trailed from the IV attached to the top of her hand up to the pole holding the liquid keeping her alive. A flash of pain seared her body, and she longed for blessed darkness. Closing her eyes, she urged her battered body to give in to a state of no feeling.

"Save her, Lord," Carr whispered.

At the sound of his voice, she opened her eyes. How good of him. Aunt Debbie would approve. His tender gaze met hers, and he squeezed her hand lightly.

"Hold on there, lady. We're on our way to Abilene."

She saw the bandage around his arm and realized he'd been shot too. She wanted to ask if he was okay, but the words refused to form. His smile warmed her, and amid the pain wracking her body, she sensed an unseen hand held her safely.

★ ★ ★

Carr checked his watch and resumed his pacing of the hospital waiting room. Could it be only ten o'clock? Treating his own wound had not taken long, but Bella remained in surgery, and he had no idea of her condition. How long would the doctors take to repair her shoulder? Prayer kept him from falling apart—that and the companionship of Pastor Kent, who had arrived at the hospital a few minutes after the ambulance.

He assumed the hospital, Runnels County Sheriff's Department, or some internal communications department had notified the FBI in Houston about Bella's injury. Abilene had an FBI office, and he expected one of their representatives to be at the hospital—at least to be asking Carr questions. Where was Vic Anderson? Carr hadn't seen him all week. But no one showed up at the hospital but Roano, and the man acted as though Carr had pulled the trigger.

Carr clenched and unclenched his fists. He had no idea how the bureau worked, but he needed to do his part. During this ordeal, Bella needed support from those who had assigned her to the investigation.

With the aid of the hospital receptionist, he located the FBI's number in Houston and made the call. Once he finished, Carr wondered how the bureau viewed the situation. One of the original prime suspects in the murder case waited at Abilene Regional Medical Center while their agent fought for her life in surgery. He hadn't thought to tell them he'd been wounded too, but that was selfish, much like the old Carr who found ways to make himself look good. Bella's aunt deserved to be notified. Perhaps the FBI had a process for notifying family members about wounded agents.

While Kent phoned his wife, Carr took a walk outside. Not until Bella was taken to recovery would he learn anything about her condition.

A familiar dust-covered truck pulled into the hospital parking lot. Jasper and Lydia stepped out. Both waved as though he'd been waiting for them to arrive. Neither of them wasted time in making their way to Carr. He fixed his eyes on Lydia first. The closer she came, the deeper the lines around her dark eyes seemed. When she had heard from Jasper about the shooting, she called for an ambulance in Ballinger and directed them on to Abilene. Lydia had a powerful way of taking control of situations that couldn't be explained in her five feet of spirit and determination. Or her tremendous capacity for love.

"She's in surgery." Carr read her and Jasper's questioning glances, both filled with concern. In a short while, they'd all grown attached to Bella. "That's all I know. Pastor Kent's inside."

Earlier this morning, Bella indicated she wanted to see Kent today. He was on her list. She had something on her mind that had to do with Kent's counseling. She also wanted to see the Warick kids.

"What about Bella's family?" Lydia said.

"I assume the FBI will contact her aunt."

Lydia raised a brow. "What do you know about her family here?"

"Nothing more than what she told you. She planned this morning to see some teens who are related to her. Obviously that isn't happening." Suspicion inched through him. "Let's get some coffee and take it up to the surgical waiting room. I have a few questions for both of you."

"What kind of questions?"

"The kind two locals who have spent all of their lives here could answer."

Lydia frowned at Jasper. "This means you too, old man."

Jasper fell into step with them, taking on his characteristic silent response to Lydia. In the five years Carr had known them, he'd never heard Jasper raise his voice to her.

In the surgical waiting room, they prayed with Kent for Bella's healing and for the doctor's wisdom. Carr watched the doorway for the doctor to emerge while carefully forming his questions for Lydia and Jasper.

"You have that look on your face," Lydia said. "Out with it. If Jasper and I don't have answers, we'll tell you."

"You recognized Bella the day she set foot on the ranch, and you chose to keep the information to yourself. I think her confession about her identity was more for my benefit than yours."

Jasper nodded and Lydia pressed her lips together. "She should be answering your questions."

"But she can't, which is why I need you two. Someone is trying really hard to scare her off this case—or kill her—and I have good reason to believe one of the suspects is her father."

"Maybe." Jasper took a sip of his coffee. "I heard he's kept his nose clean for a long time."

"Stanton Warick?"

"Right. I never had any dealings with him," Jasper said. "But I heard the stories."

"What stories? Bella told me he was obsessed with the Spider Rock treasure, which is why her aunt finished rearing her."

"*Obsessed* is mild." Lydia brushed the leg of her jeans as if it held dirt.

"Why don't you tell me what happened?"

Lydia lifted the lid from her coffee cup, and the steam curled around her fingers. "It's gossip, and I vowed a long time ago not to repeat such nonsense. I suggest you ask Bella when she's able to talk."

"But what if her father is out there trying to find another way to get to her?"

"Why not let the FBI handle this? That's their job." Jasper's words were firm, but the familiar gentleness took the edge off Carr's frustration. These two were aware of Bella's family, and he desperately needed to understand what had happened to her.

"From what you know, is her father capable of murder?"

"Any man can kill if given the right circumstances," Lydia said.

Carr studied his dear friends. Somehow, someway, he was going to find out what happened fourteen years ago. And as soon as Bella was stable, he'd start at Ballinger's library and move on to courthouse records.

The gnawing question persisted: Why had the FBI assigned Bella to a case where she had a conflict of interests?

Unless the FBI didn't know. Could that be it? Had her paternal background been hidden in light of Bella's adoption? Maybe he needed to talk to the infamous Aunt Debbie.

Carr buried his face in his hands. So much blood had been shed, and he still had no idea why.

How many days ago had his thoughts been filled with the anticipation of changing young lives who statistically were headed for criminal records? Now he wanted to strap on a pair of six-shooters and call the killer out into the middle of the street. Only the awareness of who he was in Christ stopped him.

CHAPTER 28

BELLA AWOKE to the sound of voices calling her name. Other attempts of men and women who urged her to waken had been successfully averted. She didn't want to be bothered, only to sleep. Then a streak of white fire sent a gasp of pain to her lips.

"Easy, Bella. Open your eyes."

The voice was familiar. *Frank?* Confusion swept over her. She'd been shot at the High Butte Ranch and then brought here. Carr had been shot too. Had he survived? She forced her eyes to open.

"That's my girl." Frank's soft, mellow voice brought back memories.

"I'm not your girl."

Another laugh sounded behind Frank. "Carr? Are . . . you okay?" He stepped to Frank's right side, wearing a bandage around his left arm. "Good," she managed. "I was remembering."

"Remembering is good," Frank said. "Talking is for later, when you have your strength back."

"Listen to him." Carr pointed to Frank and added a smile. "Seriously. You've come a long way, and you have a long way to go."

Bella moaned, but not from the pain searing her body. "My assignment."

"I've got it handled." Frank's sandy-colored hair and pale blue eyes attracted many a woman. At one time, she'd been one of them. But it was the sun-streaked hair and deep blue eyes of

Carr Sullivan that had captured her heart. "Don't worry about a thing."

Except solving the murders and bringing Brandt and her father to justice. "I'll be back to work tomorrow."

"Don't think so," Frank said. "I've got guards posted outside your door 24-7, and a doctor who says it'll take a few days for you to gain enough strength to return to Houston."

Bella attempted to sit up, but agony made it impossible. She bit her lip to keep from crying out. "I'm not going back to Houston. My work's here. Swartzer gave me the assignment."

"She still has her spunk," Carr said. "Maybe the doctor can take her back into surgery. He must have forgotten to remove something."

The words should have reassured Bella, even amused her, but she hurt too badly. She'd been defeated by Brandt and her father, and her career challenged. If not for the two men before her, she'd have shed a bucket of tears. "How long have I been out?"

Carr leaned over the bed. The thought of touching his face entered her mind. The medication had definitely affected her mind. "This is Sunday," he said.

"I . . . I kept fading in and out."

He smiled, and she caught a light of something she'd suspected before. "You've been real popular. Look at the flowers." He stepped aside.

Pleasure turned the corners of her lips upward. Four vases of fresh flowers and a green plant sat on the windowsill and table. "Just what a girl needs when she's been shot."

"In the future, tell me what flowers you want, and I'll send them without the bullets." Frank chuckled.

"Very funny." She closed her eyes and dug her fingernails into her palms. Should she ask for pain medication in front of them? "Who . . . who are they from?"

"I'll read the cards. Then we're leaving," Carr said. "You need rest."

"Start with the red roses and baby's breath," she whispered, not wanting to admit he was right.

"Oh, that one is from a rancher who thinks you're gorgeous."

"Thank you, Carr. But it wasn't necessary."

"Is it against FBI rules for a former suspect to send the special agent roses?"

She shook her head. "Especially not when he took a bullet too."

Silence hung like the calm before a twister. No doubt Frank didn't appreciate the flirting between her and Carr.

Picking up another card, Carr began to read. "This pink and yellow one is from the FBI."

"Wonderful. Frank . . . please let the office know I appreciate these."

"Of course. Anything you want."

Frank's sweetness would have sugared a lemon tree.

"The plant with fresh flowers is from your aunt Debbie. She called earlier and will call back this evening."

"That'll be nice." If Bella didn't choose her words carefully, Aunt Debbie would be on the next plane to Abilene.

"This arrangement is from . . . Hmm." Carr frowned and turned the card over. "It doesn't have a signature, and it's addressed to Rachel Bella."

Her breath caught in her chest. "I want the florist contacted to see who placed the order."

Frank agreed to the task, and she didn't interrupt.

"The last one is from . . ." Carr glanced away.

"Who?" Her heart still pounded from who had sent her the previous bouquet.

"The card says 'Dad.'"

CHAPTER 29

CONTROL CAME SECOND-NATURE to Brandt. At least he thought so until he began conducting business with a power-hungry man by the name of Aros Kemptor. What began as a recommendation from an unsuspecting Spider Rock enthusiast had grown to parasite proportions. Brandt needed the attorney's expertise, but the man was an employee, not a decision maker. Soon the man's usefulness would expire, like the other men and women who grew beyond their value.

Brandt had the exact location of the treasure. All he needed was a way to get to it, which required time and patience. He swallowed his growing anger and pressed in Aros's phone number.

"You don't call the shots in this operation."

Aros chuckled, a nervous rattle that didn't impress Brandt. "Got to admit, it was a smart move."

"How do you figure?"

"I used the same make of rifle used to kill our friends and shoot out the tires on Bella's car."

"If and when I decide it's necessary to eliminate her, the killing would be blamed on Sullivan."

"Take it easy."

"Who is sending you money?"

"You forget I'm taking a lot of heat here—convincing others of Sullivan's guilt and putting myself on the line to make sure others are warned and eliminated. Any slipups and you don't have the gold."

And neither did Aros. He also didn't have the exact location and the numbers of all the people working for him. "Better men than you have ended up dead because they thought they had all the answers."

"Are you threatening me?"

"Do I need to?"

"You can't get to the gold on Sullivan's ranch until I finish what I started."

And that was where Aros believed he had Brandt cornered. Let him get overconfident. His attitude would play well into Brandt's hands. "When will you have the information I need?"

"Soon. After all, his lady friend—"

"What do you mean, 'lady friend'?"

"Just a phrase. Take it easy. Anyway the agent was nearly killed, and Sullivan was shot. That should convince him to think seriously about his future—or his lack of one. Even if Bella had been killed, he would have been upset enough to possibly leave the area and put his land up for sale."

Brandt had to admit that sometimes Aros's thinking had a few clever storage units. But only if the agent shot hadn't been his Rachel.

"Remember, *Brandt*, without my skills to gain access to the High Butte, you have nothing."

The next time he used Brandt's name, his number would expire. "As long as you remember I have more resources than you could ever imagine. Cross me again like you did with the shooting, and your bones will be bleaching in the sun."

Aros chuckled. "I've protected myself through all of this. Trust me on this one."

CHAPTER 30

C<small>ARR HEARD</small> the lunch carts squeak and groan down the hospital corridor. Kent had left to attend a youth function, and he promised to call later to make sure Bella was continuing to improve. Carr refused to leave her side. While she slept, he watched her, allowing every moment he spent in her company to soothe him. In the ambulance, he'd nearly lost her. *Nearly lost her.* When had his thoughts turned to thinking of Bella as his? His first impression of Special Agent Bella Jordan was less than positive. In fact, her in-control personality had irritated him.

How was he supposed to feel about a woman once determined to pin three murders on him, possibly four? Then Carr realized both of them wanted to be in control, and neither intended to give an inch. She certainly didn't fit the type of woman he once found attractive, but those women were a part of his life before Christ stepped in as CEO.

He resisted the urge to brush her auburn hair from her cheek. Knowing Bella, her green eyes would snap open, and she'd give him a piece of her mind. Probably arrest him. With an inward chuckle, he turned to look at the flowers, and his stomach soured at the sight of the two vases: one from Stanton Warick and another from an unknown sender. Frank had been gone since eleven o'clock to check with the florist about who ordered the anonymous flowers. But finding the flower shop open on a Sunday afternoon was unlikely.

Brandt Richardson and Stanton Warick. A shot of heat burned his face. Bella had indicated that Warick may have shot her. Then the man had the guts to send her flowers. A psycho for sure.

As soon as she wakened, he'd ask her if she'd actually *seen* Warick near the butte.

Bella's eyes fluttered open, and she smiled. Carr took her hand and brushed a kiss across her fingertips.

"Are you taking advantage of me?"

"I am. It's not every day a man gets a chance to kiss an FBI special agent."

"And don't you forget it."

That's my girl. "How are you feeling?"

"Like I've been shot."

"Ever happened before?"

"This is the first. Hope it's my last."

Carr studied her face. He had to ask about Warick. "Do you know who fired at us?"

"I have my suspicions."

"Back at the ranch, before you passed out, you uttered a name." She tilted her head. "Who?"

"Dad."

"Does Frank know?"

"No. I thought you should tell him."

"It's probably time."

Carr took a deep breath. How strange to feel close to a woman he barely knew, to feel the stirrings of love and wonder if she shared the same. A part of him believed he had nothing to offer her but a past filled with imitation life. The part of him who trusted the promises of God said he was a new creation. "Someone is trying to kill you. For heaven's sakes, Bella, tell what you know to those who can stop this madman."

She peered up at him, not at all like the crusty agent who appeared fearless in the face of danger. "I . . . I have no choice but to continue the investigation. This is my job."

The phone rang, and she waited two more rings before asking Carr to hand it to her. "Aunt Debbie, I'm so glad you called."

Admiration for Bella seized him. He believed in her—the things she said and the things she didn't say.

"I'm sorry I upset you, but I'm fine. Just a surface wound." Bella closed her eyes. "Oh, they exaggerated. If they'd told me about the call, I would have contacted you yesterday. As it was, they doped me up, and I slept all afternoon and through the night." She whisked away a tear. "Don't you dare think about coming here. I'm fine, and I'm working. Besides I know how your allergies act up in this climate."

Carr took her hand. He'd read of courage, heard of courage. But he'd never witnessed strength in action like his Bella demonstrated.

"I'm so sorry to have worried you." Her shoulders lifted and fell. "No, I haven't seen any of them, but I'm sure I will."

She must be talking about the Warick cousins. But seeing them made little sense if she suspected Stanton was trying to kill her. What a peculiar family. Maybe the kids' parents were better people. No wonder she ran away.

"Yes, I'll call or e-mail every day. I love you too." Bella disconnected the call, and Carr replaced the phone for her. She blew out a sigh. "That was close. Aunt Debbie had the airline's Web site up to purchase a plane ticket."

"Would that be so bad?"

"If someone wants me dead, she'd be number two."

The hole grew deeper. "Am I right that the murder investigation and the Spider Rock treasure are tied together with a personal vendetta?"

She winced, and he knew it had nothing to do with her wound. "You're close. And I've got to see it to the end."

"Doesn't this convince you to let someone else handle it? After all, there's been a whole task force on this case." He punched his fist into his hand. "Do you think one of them is behind this?"

Bella peered at him. "I did, but he was poisoned. And I do again, but I have no proof."

"Who?"

"The new sheriff."

"Roano? He isn't the one. He's too loyal to Darren."

"Those are the ones to watch. What can you tell me about him?"

"Newly married. Takes his job seriously. Unchurched."

"Does he live within his means?"

Carr thought for a moment. "He's into horses like a lot of folks out here. Everything about his lifestyle seems to be in line with a typical deputy. Or should I say sheriff?"

"A little animosity there? I guessed a long time ago he was the one who blacked your eye."

"Maybe so."

"But you don't suspect him as power- or money-hungry?"

He shook his head. "Have you done your normal cell phone and background check on Roano?"

She laughed. "Yes. He's clean, *Agent Sullivan*. Do you suspect anyone else on the task force?"

Carr shoved his hands into his pockets and walked across the room. He turned, realizing his statement would most likely shake her resolve to not involve him. "I suspect whom you suspect—Brandt Richardson and Stanton Warick. If it wasn't for all the disturbances in your investigation, I'm sure you'd have the information by now. Because of it, I plan to conduct a visit to a certain Warick."

"Don't even consider it." She frowned. "Have you seen Vic?"

"No. Frank asked about him too." Her hair splayed against the pillow like Carr envisioned an angel. Breathtakingly beautiful.

"Would you make a call for me? I need to talk to my supervisor in Houston. I need to find out where Vic is spending his time."

Bella pushed away the liquid-only tray of food. The nurse claimed tomorrow she could enjoy a soft diet. Bella would suck in her growling stomach until then. Bouillon and tea were for tooth-less old ladies, and she had miles to go before she gave in to eating with a straw.

Carr had stepped out to get cleaned up at a hotel. He'd be back within the hour.

"How are you going to get any better if you don't eat?" Frank peered from behind the newspaper in front of his face. His attempt at a scowl gave him a uniquely studious look. "I purposely sat over here and ignored you so you'd follow doctor's orders."

"Bring me a milk shake, and I'll drink my dinner. But first tell me what you learned at the florist."

"I lucked out because the owner was cleaning up after a wedding. He said Stanton Warick phoned in the flower order signed 'Dad.' A woman came into the florist shop of the hospital and paid cash for the one with no signature."

"What did she look like?"

"Tall blonde. Midforties, wearing jeans and red boots. The florist said she was an attractive woman but didn't say much."

"Sounds like Mair, the woman my dad was once married to."

"How was your relationship with her?"

Bella hadn't disliked her stepmother until she learned Mair had teamed up with Brandt. Most likely the hard times had driven her into his arms. But according to the FBI, she was somewhere in South America. "She wasn't the evil stepmother, if that is what you're driving at. She had her hands full taking care of five kids and trying to feed us. I helped her with the younger ones."

He folded the newspaper in his typical everything-has-a-place attitude and stood. "I know you have more to say, so out with it. What about this case aren't you telling me?"

She pointed to her laptop, which Carr had brought in earlier from her car. "It's all right there. I want this killer apprehended. He's killed four people—four people too many. I have a few ideas and leads I want to check into, and it's all documented."

"Good. You told me earlier the clues to this Spider Rock treasure led to a triangle between the towns Rotan, Aspermont, and Clyde. Have you learned anything that points to the High Butte?"

"Only the dead man's words in the dirt."

"I'll get right on it. Swartzer sent me the intel report on the other men associated with Richardson. All of them checked out except the professor at the University of Texas. What's his name?"

"Howard MacGregor. Teaches law. The problem is he took an extended leave of absence before the three victims were found. No one knows where he is. However, we did learn he is an expert rifle shot, which Richardson could use."

"Any family?"

"Not married. No close friends at UT. Neighbors stated he's a loner."

"I'd like to see what he looks like." She shrugged. "Of course, if he's associated with Brandt, then he's learned how to disguise himself."

Frank pulled out his BlackBerry and showed her Professor MacGregor's photo. Something was vaguely familiar about him. "Show his photo to Pastor Kent Matthews and Carr."

"Will do. Why don't you concentrate on getting well and let the task force bring this to an end. Once you're home, you can rest up before going back to work."

She fought the urge to cry—like a girl. Special agents worked together as a team, not hiding their findings so they could secure promotions. "I'm not going back to Houston."

"That's not my call or yours." She saw the old look of caring in his eyes and promised herself not to use it selfishly. As intuitive as Frank had always been, he'd no doubt seen what she and Carr refused to discuss.

"It could be. All you have to do is tell Swartzer you need me on the case."

He twisted his mouth as though she'd asked the impossible. "According to Carr, this isn't the first time an attempt has been made on your life."

"Please, Frank." Desperation crept through her good intentions. "Our job is dangerous. I'm onto something for the shooter to pump lead into me."

"Did you see who shot you and Carr?"

"No. I simply have a strong suspicion."

"Brandt Richardson?"

"He's one."

"Who else are you thinking is involved?"

"My father—Stanton Warick."

Frank's face paled. "I humored you about running down the florist. So this isn't a family squabble? Is Swartzer aware of the possible connection?"

"I told him this afternoon, along with the information about Vic's absence from the task force."

"Maybe you could enlighten me about what's going on." He blew out a huff. "One thing at a time. I did find out about Vic Anderson, what's going on in his life, and why he's absent from the assignment. He took a leave of absence. I understand his wife is in the final stages of cancer. Looks like he'd been missing quite a bit of work for the past several months, and his job was on the line."

"That explains a lot of things. It would have been considerate of him to have notified me about his leave of absence. I couldn't tell if his problem was with me because I'm a woman and younger or something else. Certainly his wife's health weighed on his mind. I'd like to think his personal problems have gotten in the way of his professionalism. I mean, his record is outstanding."

"He's clean—just handling a lot of stress."

That eliminated her suspicions about him being involved with Brandt. "Has anyone taken his place?"

"You're looking at him. Swartzer knew we worked well together."

She read more into his words than a working relationship. Poor Frank. She'd never hurt him intentionally. "We've solved some high-level cases together."

"Your insight and my analytical manner of doing things."

She appreciated him, always had. She simply didn't love him. "When our differences don't have us climbing down each other's throats."

"Now for situation two," he said. "Why are you on this assignment? Because it doesn't make sense to me."

"Remember? I'm familiar with the area. I spent the first fifteen years of my life in Runnels County."

"Must you always be so secretive? Enlighten me as to why you think your father is involved with the shooting and possibly the murders."

She regretted saying a word about her father. Without hard proof, she had nothing to base her suspicions on except his angry threat and greedy craving for the Spider Rock treasure. "He is—or rather, was—a treasure hunter."

"Is he capable of murder?"

"You and I both know the answer to that."

"Have you seen him?"

"Not yet."

"Why?"

She swallowed hard. "No excuse. But here is what I do know. I learned the night before the shooting that my stepmother divorced him for Brandt Richardson. Dear old Dad ended up with their four kids. I can only imagine how they've had to take care of themselves. Anyway, I planned to investigate the whole matter after the morning ride on the butte when someone used Carr and me for target practice."

Frank picked up his notepad. "I want names and addresses."

She would not exploit her siblings. "I can't, Frank. I know you have the means to find names and addresses, but not my brothers and sister. Do what you need with Stanton Warick, but leave the rest of my family to me."

"Honey—"

"I'm not your honey, and don't patronize me. Give me a few days or whatever you can for me to talk to those kids."

"I can't promise you that."

"Yes, you can."

Frank marched to the door. "I need air."

"A few days."

He stopped and swung around. "All right. Then I'm stepping in."

CHAPTER 31

ON MONDAY MORNING, Carr woke with a resolve that no one could squelch. When he lived in Dallas, nothing stopped him from finding answers to questions that ate at him night and day. This was worse, because the problem affected more than him.

"The shooting was not your fault." Lydia carried a basket of dirty clothes to the laundry room. "Any thought otherwise is pure foolishness."

"It is if the shooter meant to get rid of me." Carr paced the tiled floor of the kitchen, stopping briefly to note the setting sun and remembering when it rose Saturday morning.

"From all the unexplainable events over the past two weeks, I think if you were supposed to be the only recipient of some shooter's greed, you'd be at the funeral home."

"Might be a better alternative than Bella in the hospital."

Lydia uncharacteristically dropped the basket with a loud splat. "Feeling sorry for yourself doesn't undo the tragedy that's hit this ranch."

She had a way of scooping him right out of his self-pity. "I'm going to do a little snooping on my own."

Her gaze swung to him. Like fire on kindling. "What are you planning?"

"I'm going to see Kent, then visit a couple of kids in the area."

"You're going to see the Warick kids, aren't you?"

"And any other cousins or uncles."

She shook her finger at him. Her eyes pooled. "Carr, this is not smart. I . . . can't let you put yourself in danger. What about Vic or the new agent or one of the deputies?"

"I'm sure they all have their methods of investigation. I need to do this for myself."

"I forbid it." The three words thundered around him.

If Carr hadn't seen the seriousness in her face, he'd have laughed. "What are you going to do about it?" He understood her fears, but what—? "You're not going to try to stop me by contacting the FBI or the county sheriff's department, are you?"

"Absolutely."

"I don't need a mother, Lydia." He snatched up his keys. "A shooter couldn't do much more damage to me than a few members of the sheriff's department."

"Why didn't you press charges against Roano?"

Carr fumed. "And what makes you think Roano blacked my eye?"

She lifted her chin, hostility in every muscle. "You're asking to be the next warm grave. You can't fight the killers and hotheaded deputies and sheriffs."

"And what would you have me do?"

"Mind your own business and let the law enforcement people take care of solving murders and murder attempts."

"Fat chance. I'm not about to let someone commit murder on my property, poison my friend, and try to kill Bella without a fight."

"Are you going to break the law in the process?"

Carr's thoughts scrambled. Lydia had never reacted with such vehemence. "I'm not that man. Neither do I plan on making an example out of lawbreakers. I'm looking for answers." He took a deep breath. "I don't think the FBI would spend time talking to kids."

"But those kids have a daddy, and you already know what

Stanton Warick is capable of. And those kids have a stepfather who is a serial murderer."

Carr felt as though she'd thrown ice water on him. *How did I not see the connection?* "The Warick kids are Bella's siblings?"

"Half brothers and a sister."

The jigsaw puzzle now took on more meaning. "I thought those kids were cousins or something. That means Brandt Richardson is their stepfather."

Lydia stared at the basket on the floor. "That's it."

"What a mess. Why . . . why did she accept this assignment?"

"A woman like Bella can't leave the past dormant forever."

Carr tried to understand the reason Bella parceled out truth like slices of pizza. "A couple of kids aren't murderers."

"Tell that to the parents who lost kids to the Columbine massacre."

Carr touched her arm. "Please. I'll call Frank as soon as I'm finished. I'll call you too. Besides, I may learn I can't talk to the kids, especially since their dad is Stanton Warick. This is a whim. Kent is going with me. Sort of a summer visit to a few of the kids to see how they're getting along."

"If you leave, I won't be here when you get back."

Carr startled; then his anger mounted. "You do what you have to do. I have to find out who's turned our community into a haven for murderers." He started to add that he wasn't a coward but changed his mind. He left Lydia standing in the kitchen.

Outside in the steadily rising temperatures, he flung open the truck door, flipped on the engine, and headed to the highway while wrestling with his and Lydia's argument. The new revelation about Bella made him crazy with fear for her and furious that she'd kept the information from him.

But this wild, irrational ultimatum wasn't Lydia's normal behavior. They didn't quarrel and threaten like those who didn't care for each other. They were Christians who reacted and responded to each other as they wanted to be treated. He fondly called her Mom. She labeled him her son. Lydia hadn't meant what she'd said. But what did she mean?

Carr stepped on the brakes before he reached the highway and spun the truck around. Cold chills raced up and down his arms and neck. Understanding gripped him, and he hurried back to the house, kicking up dirt in his wake. Lydia hadn't made sense, and in her harsh words, he hadn't heard the truth.

He took long strides onto the front porch and threw open the door. He made his way into the living room and on to where Lydia stood in the same spot in the kitchen, except now she sobbed.

"Lydia, who threatened you?"

CHAPTER 32

BELLA HAD TWO more days in the hospital, and then she was a free woman again. Swartzer urged her to return to Houston to recuperate, but she convinced him to let her stay. Carr offered the hospitality of the High Butte Ranch, and she took it—for professional and personal reasons. The latter she chose to explore after the murderer was arrested. She intended to be in the thick of the investigation and the High Butte looked like headquarters to her. Frank wanted her to stay with him at the Courtesy Inn in Abilene so he could take care of her. Soon they'd have to talk about where their relationship was not going.

She eased out a slow sigh. Neither Carr nor Kent Matthews recognized the picture of Professor Howard MacGregor. Perhaps it was the beard, mustache, and shoulder-length hair. She thought something about him was familiar, but at times her own exuberance in an investigation caused her to leap on details that had nothing to do with the case. This was no exception.

She laughed at an e-mail follow-up regarding Charles Habid, the manager at the Courtesy Inn. He'd cornered Frank with a little of his own investigative work. In his enthusiasm to assist the FBI, he'd gone through various receipts of the hotel's restaurant for the past few months and discovered a couple of matching signatures from different customers. Sure enough, Brandt had stayed at the hotel using different names and disguises. Habid decided to apply to the FBI.

The media had changed its tune about dragging Carr's and her names through the mud. A little plus in the FBI's favor, but she wasn't so sure she liked the cost. The TV news now made her and Carr look like heroes. She preferred to think they were victims. Someone had even run a section on Vic Anderson's wife and her fight with cancer. Reporters sympathized with the veteran agent who made a decision to spend his wife's final days with her rather than continue his stellar career with the FBI. Oh, fickle media. They could turn again tomorrow.

In the meantime, she had much to do. Frank had jumped into the investigation with both feet, just as she expected. He hadn't turned up anything new, but he and Carr had discussed the Spider Rock legend in depth. The two men had established a rapport. Or had they? Frank could have doubts about Carr's innocence. And if Frank's ways of perception were anything like they'd been in the past, then he saw the attraction between her and Carr. What a blow to Frank's heart and an issue she needed to address soon.

I've got to stop worrying about Frank and be a contributing agent in this investigation. Later she'd address personal issues. Now she sounded like Frank.

Bella wanted to see her brothers and sister and begin making arrangements for their future. Her demanding job meant their care would be difficult, but she'd neglected them too long. The boys needed good role models, and Anne . . . Girls had so many needs. Someone must have taken an interest in them, or they wouldn't have attended a church youth event. And the initial contact had to be done before Frank approached them.

Bella blew out an exasperated sigh. Rats. She hated being in the hospital. So much to do, and with the guards posted outside the door, she had to have an escort to walk the halls.

Her relationship with Carr—or rather the beginnings—excited and alarmed her. While lying in the hospital bed counting the holes in the ceiling tiles and then conjuring up the patterns they made, she resorted to logic about the two not having a future together. Once arrests were made for all the crimes, he'd go back to ranching, and she'd go back to her position in the violent crimes department in Houston—and finish raising her siblings. But she did allow herself to dream.

Bella's BlackBerry rang, and she saw the caller was Carr. At the sight of his name, she warmed. "Hey. How are you?"

"Good." But his tone denied it.

Her stomach churned. "What's happened?"

"Is Frank there? He's not answering his phone."

"No. He may be out of range. Had an appointment with Roano. So what's going on that you need to talk to him?"

"I'd rather not burden you with it."

"Carr, you might as well tell me because I won't let up until you do."

Silence swung like a pendulum, and she envisioned his brows narrowing and the tiny lines deepening around his blue eyes. "Lydia received a threatening phone call."

Not that sweet lady. "Oh no. What did she say?"

"A man called yesterday and said she would be next on the hit list if she didn't convince me to stop assisting the FBI."

"What does she know that someone would view her as a threat?"

"I asked her the same thing, and she claims nothing. I also asked her if she and Jasper should visit a relative until this is over."

"And?"

"Told me to forget it. She's planning to see you later on today, and it would take a crowbar to budge Jasper."

"Sure, and I'm not surprised she won't take a vacation until this is over." Bella sensed a mixture of rage and protectiveness rising from her toes. "I'll get someone to keep twenty-four-hour surveillance on both of you."

"The call was made to frighten her, not me."

"I don't read it the same way."

"I have no intentions of hiding out. Lydia is scared and rightfully so. I appreciate what you can do for her, but—"

"Tell me what could be more important than saving your life." Carr could be so infuriatingly stubborn.

"I'm not hiding out like a scared kid. If I was supposed to be dead, it would have already happened."

No point in arguing with him. One thing they had in common was tenacity. "I've been doing some thinking, and I want to talk to you and Lydia."

"We can head over now."

"Do you want to wait until someone is assigned to protect both of you?"

"For Lydia, yes. Not me."

"Okay. I'll make a call and get back with you in a couple of minutes. Then let me know when you're on your way." Carr had taken a bullet for her. He deserved to know the rest of the truth.

★ ★ ★

"Did you drive yourself here?" Fear in mammoth proportions coursed through Bella's body for Carr and Lydia.

"Deputy Wesley Adams was our chauffeur. Roano assigned him to Lydia. He's Darren's nephew."

"Yes, I remember him. Took his uncle's death real hard."

Carr looked exceptionally handsome in jeans and a green striped shirt. She'd always given cowboys a second glance.

She knotted the sheet draped over her waist. If she didn't tell them the truth, the deceit would fester like infection in an open wound. Honesty was supposed to be good for the soul. No. That was confession. Same thing. "I want to tell you what happened fourteen years ago when I left Runnels County." She slid a look first at Lydia and then at Carr. "In a short time, we've become friends, and I think telling you this is fair." When neither of them responded, she took a deep breath.

"My father and Brandt Richardson were partners in searching for the Spider Rock treasure. In my opinion, Brandt supplied the brains, and Dad supplied his back. Brandt claimed the gold was buried on our ranch, but nothing ever came of it. I heard very little about their plans. It was a hush-hush business, like two little boys with a secret. Dad had a big problem—gambling. He couldn't hold on to a paycheck. Mair, my stepmother, did her best to get it from him before he spent it all, but it seldom happened. The two of them had four children together. Those kids . . ." She captured Carr's gaze. "Those kids are the Waricks I wanted to see last Saturday morning. They aren't my cousins, but my half brothers and sister." She waited for him to react.

He frowned. *He already knows.*

"I appreciate your telling me about them. Does your boss in Houston know about your siblings?"

"He does now."

Carr nodded slowly and she continued. "I'm hoping to get them away from Dad. Anyway, his gambling debts exceeded thousands of dollars. Then Brandt offered him a way out of his problem. He'd pay off the creditors if Dad agreed to let him marry me."

"What?" Carr's face reddened. "He wanted to sell you to Richardson?"

Bella nodded. "Mair agreed, and I couldn't change their minds. When I told Brandt I'd never marry him, that I'd run away first, he told me I'd live to regret it. He went to Dad and said the deal was off. Dad was furious. He told me if I ruined his chances to get out of debt and find the gold, he'd dig a grave with my name on it. I ran off and made my way to Abilene."

"You walked?" Lydia reached out for her hand.

"About twenty-five miles of it. A trucker picked me up and drove me into town. I stayed at a women's shelter there for about three weeks. The director took a liking to me, most likely because she realized I was younger than eighteen, and I was so frightened. One day she had me ride along with her to an abandoned women's shelter in Snyder. There, stored away in an old jail built in the early 1900s, were red silhouettes of all the women and children who'd died at the hand of family violence. I cried buckets, the first time I'd allowed myself to grieve for all the troubles in my life. After telling her about what really happened, we talked about my options, and I remembered my mother's sister. Somehow she found Aunt Debbie. When the judge heard my story, Dad denied it, but he did give up custody. Aunt Debbie adopted me. The rest you already know."

Carr stood and paced the floor. He looked drained, and his eyes moistened. "No child, no woman should live with that kind of fear. Why *ever* did you take this assignment, knowing either of those men could kill you?"

"To stop them." She shrugged. "To be honest, I think it was vengeance. And I need to take care of my siblings before it's too late. I've neglected them far too long."

She swallowed the lump in her throat and the tears threatening to make her look like a pathetic woman instead of a lead agent. "Once here, I learned more about my family. Twelve years ago, Mair left my dad for Brandt. They took off to South America, where she changed her name and dropped out of sight. I wouldn't be surprised if he'd killed her, except she may have been the woman who purchased flowers for me. So in the thick of all the mud, my siblings' stepfather is on the FBI's fugitive list."

"Thank you." Carr leaned over the bed. "Earlier today I learned about your brothers and sister. There's so much I now understand. No wonder the flowers upset you."

"I have to get past it and go on with the investigation. I haven't been able to secure enough evidence to put the killings on Brandt or Dad, but I believe both of them are involved."

Lydia patted her cheek. "I'd heard rumors, but I never had any idea your father did all those things."

"Please. I don't want any sympathy." Bella stiffened. "Consider my story an explanation as to why I'm committed to bringing in the killers and taking care of my brothers and sister, and why both men are motivated to kill me. Right now, I think it's a cat-and-mouse game. But the killer could get tired and end it all. Please promise me you two will agree to round-the-clock protection until arrests are made."

Lydia leaned over the bed and planted a kiss on Bella's cheek. "I don't have the spunk I used to have, so I'm going to do exactly what you ask."

Bella peered up into Carr's face, anticipating his reply before he spoke a word. "And you?"

"I'll be more careful."

"You're incorrigible."

He grinned. "I'm in good company."

Bella shook her head. "I refuse to respond to that. Do you mind if I speak with Lydia alone for a few minutes?"

CHAPTER 33

WHEN CARR LEFT the hospital room so Lydia and Bella could talk, Bella formed an apology. "I'm sorry the investigation has come to this. Even more so that you were threatened. The task force is working nonstop to find the killer, and it can come none too soon. In the meantime, I'll find another place to stay."

Lydia scooted a chair beside the bed. "I want you at the High Butte."

"It's too dangerous."

"Nonsense. It's settled. Sounds like I'll have the sheriff's department camped at my door and an FBI agent. The more law enforcement, the happier I am."

"My track record leaves a lot to be desired."

"My mind is made up."

"You're a persistent woman, Lydia."

"The same is said about you. Carr has stated so on numerous occasions."

Bella wagged a finger at her. "Maybe you're right. He probably uses a few other descriptors too."

"Looks like we are a stubborn trio, and don't get me started about Jasper. Sometimes I think that man is part mule. Anyway, we chatted about Darren, shed a few tears, and talked about the community efforts to offer support for Tiffany and the children." Her eyes widened. "See, I told you far more than you wanted to hear."

Bella missed Aunt Debbie. But Lydia made a close second. "Just talk to me. I don't care if it's about brushing your teeth."

Lydia took her hand. "TMI, as the kids say."

Bella couldn't quite shake her concern about someone threatening Lydia. "I'm sorry about the phone call."

She pursed her lips in mock annoyance. "Hush. It's over. If he'd given his name, Jasper would have torn him apart by now. Only a coward threatens a woman."

"Not so when four people are dead."

Lydia immediately sobered. "You're right. I wonder what I thought about before all this happened. For certain, I'll never look at the precious gift of life quite the same again." She patted Bella's hand. "Which brings me to why I'm glad I have you all to myself."

Bella stared into the woman's face. Her eyes held a certain light, the same she'd seen in Aunt Debbie's. "Okay. I hope it's not about my going home."

"It's not." She appeared to consider Bella's comment. "In a way, it is. This is about your spiritual life. But first I want to talk about Carr. I see something special between you two, so don't bother denying it. Love is a gift, and it doesn't come knocking on the doors of our hearts very often. Because of the fondness I have for you, I want to tell you about him and the man he has become." Lydia smiled. "My daughter says I get a bit poetic and dramatic at times, so humor this aging lady."

Bella responded by squeezing her hand.

"Right after Carr purchased the High Butte, he told Pastor Kent he needed a cook and housekeeper. Then he said he needed someone to show him how to ranch. Pastor Kent's secretary is my daughter, and she recommended us. Soon after, Jasper and I came to live and work at the High Butte. We became a threesome, a family of sorts. Jasper worked with Carr around the clock, patiently teaching him about the land, cattle, and horses."

"I can envision him up at the crack of dawn and working alongside Jasper."

"They were and still are inseparable. Jasper also discipled Carr in the process." Lydia hesitated. "Do you know what I mean?"

Bella nodded. "He helped him understand what it means to be a follower of Jesus." *I sure wish this conversation wasn't about religion.*

"Carr was concerned about his temper because of what happened in Dallas. I'm sure you know the story: how he used to drink, do drugs, and get into fights. He also carried a lot of guilt about his girlfriend dying from an overdose. Jasper convinced him to see Pastor Kent for counseling about both problems. Pastor Kent and Jasper and I worked together to help him see how God offers immeasurable forgiveness. His girlfriend had chosen to take the drugs, and any wrongdoing on his part had been forgiven. For five years, the three of us have worked and laughed and played hard."

"I saw right from the start the loyalty and love among you." *And I mistook it for a murder cover-up.*

Lydia beamed. "When Carr decides to take on a project, he jumps in with both feet until he has the knowledge to satisfy him. In fact, he's taking classes about ranching and online classes for biblical studies. The latter wouldn't be necessary if he'd paid attention to the sisters in parochial school—but that's my opinion."

Bella attempted to picture Carr sitting in school and ignoring Bible classes. Oh yes, she imagined he'd been a handful. She'd seen the theology books on the desk in his library and wondered at the time about the depth of his Bible study.

"As you already know, he and Darren were good friends. In fact, Darren encouraged him with the idea of starting a home for at-risk teen boys. That's on hold right now, but I'm sure it will happen once this mess is settled. Carr never mentioned wanting to have a woman in his life. I think he was afraid. Still is. That is, until he met you."

I'm not the only one who's noticed the interest.

"Right from the start he asked us to pray for you."

Acid rose in Bella's throat. She didn't want this conversation. "Pray for me?"

"For wisdom and safety. But Jasper and I could see his feelings deepened every time he saw you. Just like we could see your feelings deepening for him."

Bella wasn't sure what to say. "Why are you telling me this?"

"Go easy on his heart, Bella. He's a good man. But I have a concern about your spiritual life. So I have to ask. Do you have Jesus in your life?"

Bella regretted the whole slant in the conversation. Aunt Debbie used to periodically point out her need for a Savior. "No, ma'am. I mean, my aunt took me to church, and I learned about the Bible. I earned all kinds of awards for memorizing Scripture. My finest was Romans 8. Please don't take this personally, but I'm simply not interested."

"I understand." Lydia's voice was gentle. "Your life has been in danger too many times not to be concerned about what happens to you when you die."

Bella smiled. "You and my aunt Debbie would get along splendidly." She worried her lip. "You know my father. I can't bring myself to devote my life to a divine being when my own father is such a jerk. I mean, let's be real here. The Lord's Prayer begins with 'our Father,' and that is where I end the whole dialogue. Why would I want anything that resembles a father in my life?"

"Which is exactly why you need a Father and Savior."

I don't want to talk about this. "I'll think about it."

"Promise me?"

She couldn't lie to Lydia. "All right."

After Lydia left, Bella sensed depression settling on her. She'd battled with black moods since she was fifteen, and the episodes always occurred after someone talked about her need for Christ. To Bella, severe depression and Christianity were partners—partners she didn't want or need. And when other Christians insisted she pursue God, the whole thought sickened her.

But . . . many times she'd wished all of the things she'd heard about God were true.

CHAPTER 34

CARR SAT OUTSIDE Kent's office while his friend finished a meeting with his secretary, assistant pastor, music minister, and head deacon. Kent wasn't expecting Carr, and he intended to make their meeting brief.

His thoughts waffled between the unsolved murders and his growing feelings for Bella. He refused to mention how he felt until the case was solved. After all, he'd been on the suspect list, and it wasn't fair to her.

Over five years ago, Carr thought he loved Michelle, but actually he was in love with how she looked on his arm. She had people-pleasing skills, and he'd recognized how good they'd look together right from the start. She liked the same things he did, and they were . . . well, friends. They probably would have eventually married if not for her death. The old guilt twisted at his insides, but he shoved the sensation away.

Bella had become his breath of fresh air. He didn't know how it happened. His heart simply let go and let her in. He treasured everything about her—her determination, compassion for others, the way she appreciated a sunrise, the way she always smelled faintly of flowers and herbs, and the softness of her voice. The color of her eyes reminded him of a high mountain lake, deep green and mysterious. Oh yes, he had it bad for the auburn-haired beauty, and he would do all he could to keep her safe.

"Carr?"

He glanced up at Kent and smiled. Caught daydreaming. But

that was okay. Sure beat holding on to the turmoil that kept him awake at night. "Hey. I took a chance at being able to talk to you for a minute."

"No problem. The meeting's over." Kent's freckles had multiplied since he'd spent time with the youth camping. Standing before Carr, he looked very much like one of the kids.

"This won't be long. I don't want to keep you from your family."

Kent leaned against the doorway. "No problem. Lisa planned a late dinner due to the meeting, and I have a counseling appointment with a young man who's thinking about the ministry. He's meeting with the music worship team first and then me. Got plenty of time."

Carr followed Kent into his office and took a seat, the same seat he'd occupied during all those months of his own counseling.

"My appointment is in about twenty minutes. How's Bella?"

"Improving. Anxious to get out of the hospital. Feisty as usual."

"And Lydia?"

"She has a deputy sheriff attached to her side. She doesn't much like it, but the rest of us are relieved. She doesn't want her daughter to know about it."

"Okay," Kent said. "Sure would like to, though. Her daughter deserves to know the truth. What's on your mind?"

"A couple of things about the building project."

Kent startled. "The building project? Why not get out from under the FBI and the sheriff's department sifting through the dirt on your ranch . . . ? That didn't come out right."

"I know what you mean. And I understand what you're saying. The killings and the attempts are why I want to proceed with assigning the mineral rights of the High Butte to the church. I'm also thinking of changing my will to have everything go to the church too."

"Carr, don't you have family?"

"A brother who's a doctor, and he doesn't need money. And our parents are gone."

"Let's wait for all of this to end before you make any rash decisions."

Carr chuckled. "So you think if I will everything over to the church and get 'eliminated' from the killer's list, you might wind up as a suspect?"

"Very funny. At least you can laugh about it."

"Sounds better than having a mental breakdown. Don't think that hasn't crossed my mind."

Kent nodded. "You're one strong man, Carr. Not sure I could walk through this mess as well as you are."

"When I think God knew all about the junk going on before it happened, I add one more item to my 'ask God one day' list."

"Mine has grown to book length. He must have figured you could handle it."

"Wish He'd consulted me first." Both men laughed. Humor did have a way of easing the angst. "I have one more quick question."

"Fire away." Kent groaned. "My word choice tonight is horrible."

"Some subconscious fear of being with me, I'm sure. But I've learned that Bella has three half brothers and a half sister, and Stanton Warick is the father. I thought visiting the kids tomorrow would be good—if you have time to accompany me."

"What about their father?"

"I understand he works as a foreman on a ranch. I'll talk to him later. Most likely with Frank. If Warick's carrying a gun, I want to have an armed agent close by."

"We can do it. I did a little snooping of my own about those kids."

Carr raised a brow. "What did you find out?"

"All in church. Good grades. The boys are in sports, and the girl's class president."

Great news. "How did a lowlife like Stanton Warick manage that?"

"Ask him yourself. He'll be here in a few minutes."

Bella opened the bedside stand and pulled out the Bible. What irony that she knew every book of the Old and New Testaments, memorized Scripture, attended church camp, even worked as a counselor for children, but never gave her life to Christ. That wasn't ironic; it was hypocritical. But here she was scooping up God's Word and looking for meaning in her life after some crazed idiot had tried to kill her and Carr. Why should now make any difference? Except she'd told Lydia and Aunt Debbie that she'd look into the God thing.

Where did she start? Write down all the Scripture she'd previously memorized? She leafed through the thin pages from Genesis to Revelation and back again. Closing her eyes and using the point-and-choose method wasn't recommended by theologians, but neither was her sacrilegious attitude. She did it anyway. *Psalm 139.*

An hour later, exhausted with the wrestling, Bella gave in to the prompting of her spirit. Maybe it was time to open her heart and mind to the tenets of faith she'd learned as a child. She didn't have answers to the tragedies of her life, but maybe she wasn't supposed to. Maybe being closer to God meant she'd have to learn how to trust. For certain, she couldn't unravel the murders and the situation with her family by herself.

CHAPTER 35

BRANDT SAT in a rusty pickup where he could watch New Hope Church. He had an idea. The more he thought about it, the more it grew. The thought began when he followed Vic Anderson to see if the agent was a possible threat. From what Brandt learned, Anderson had over twenty years invested in the FBI. Enough time to pick up a few tricks of his own. Brandt studied his mannerisms, speech patterns, and how he walked. And when Brandt learned the agent had a medical emergency— his wife was diagnosed with stage-four breast cancer—an extra bit of fun settled in his mind. After all, impersonations were his speciality.

Another problem had presented itself. Stanton Warick had decided to pay a personal visit to Kent Matthews, Sullivan's pastor. Yeah, he took his oldest kid with him, but Brandt didn't care for Sullivan and Warick having an opportunity to talk. Unless Sullivan's temper became an ace for the whole situation. Brandt would sit back and watch what happened.

He would have gotten rid of Warick a long time ago if it hadn't been for Mair. Her motherly instincts might have kicked in if no one was left to raise those kids. And then he'd have to get rid of all of them.

What were the three men talking about for so long? Maybe he'd venture inside. Brandt laughed. How ironic if the lovely sound of a police siren made its way to New Hope Church.

CHAPTER 36

CARR HAD NO EXPECTATIONS when it came to Stanton Warick. So when the man walked into Kent's office, sporting auburn hair and green eyes, looking very much like his Bella, Carr wanted to punch him in the nose. Looking into the face of the man who may have murdered four times and tried to kill Bella brought fire into his very soul.

"Carr, this is Stanton Warick." Kent seemed to measure each syllable. Perhaps he remembered the months Carr spent in anger management. Right now, he needed a refresher course. This man had attempted to *sell* his daughter to pay off gambling debts.

Warick reached out his hand. Carr stood and accepted the gesture—reluctantly. If this was going to be confession night for Warick, then he intended to take notes. "I'm not here to interrupt your counseling session."

"It's a meeting," Warick said. "Not sure counseling is part of it."

"I'm a friend of Bella's." Carr knew he should extend Christian love and fellowship and all the other things that he was *supposed* to do. But frankly, his heart denied Warick access to anything remotely resembling friendship or acceptance.

"Rachel needs good friends." Warick's face tightened as though pained. Well, he should be. "I'm trying to get the courage to see her. Did she receive the flowers?"

"Did you shoot her?"

"Easy," Kent said.

Warick stiffened. "No, I did not shoot my own daughter. Does she think that?" He crossed his arms over his chest. "Of course she does, and who could blame her?"

Carr studied him: jeans and a yellow shirt. Leatherlike skin. Worked outside—probably digging for treasure. Strong too. He glanced at Kent, whose face had turned a ghastly shade of white, which looked incredibly odd with his freckles.

"I did *not* arrange for both of you to be here," Kent said. "Carr stopped by about another matter."

"But I would have been here if I knew you were coming." Carr heard the grit of his own animosity.

Warick dropped his arms to his side. "You heard what I did to my daughter."

Carr's fists clenched at his sides. "I did." What was he doing letting his old self take control? He had to get out of Kent's office. His attitude was a disgrace to everything he claimed to believe in. No matter what Stanton Warick had done, God would judge him. *God* would judge him. Not Carr Sullivan. He peered into Kent's face and then Warick's. "Excuse me." He made his way down the hall to the sanctuary and inside, then down to a front pew.

God, I need help here. I can't help Bella or myself by breathing fire. It's as if You never entered my life. He buried his face in his hands. How could he ever help at-risk boys? For that matter, how could he expect to have a relationship with Bella when his life centered on himself—and his temper? The storms that had thrown his world off course had invited the old methods of dealing with problems.

"I thought my temper was gone," he whispered.

Conviction shattered what was left of his pride. He'd denied his anger, shoved it aside, and not comprehended that anger in itself was not wrong. But how he handled it, how he channeled the adrenaline, was the sin. Instead he'd stuck a Band-Aid over the whole ugly situation—said all the right things. Went through all the proper motions.

A cloud of what his life had been like in Dallas streamed across his mind. He'd been forgiven, but in the growing process, he'd allowed himself to believe that living a monastic life meant he was immune from sin. Jasper had said the same thing, as though the older man knew the blackness invading Carr's heart. He thought he understood. How very wrong. He slipped from the pew onto his knees. His temper might always haunt him, but that didn't mean it had to overtake him.

When he finally lifted his head and sensed the burden of trying to fix himself had vanished, he realized unfinished business. He made his way toward the back of the darkened church and saw Warick sitting in the back pew.

"I owe you an apology," Carr said. "It's not my call to judge or condemn you."

Warick slowly stood. "I'd like to tell you my story."

The man deserved a listening ear. "All right."

The two men met midway in the aisle. Carr revisited his commitment and his dedication to placing God first. For the next several minutes, Stanton Warick told about his past greed, his gambling problem, his search for the Spider Rock treasure with Brandt Richardson, and what he'd done to his daughter. Every word matched what Bella had revealed. All the while, Carr prayed for a discerning spirit. Because even though he'd confessed his temper and his judgmental spirit, Carr also had a responsibility to filter the truth.

"Once Brandt confirmed the treasure was not on my land, he grew bored. I continued to dig, but he spent more and more time with Mair. A few months later, she confessed their affair. My ego took a plunge. I loved Mair, and I thought Brandt and I were friends. Soon after, she left me and the kids." Warick shrugged.

"The first few days were a blur. I had no idea what it was like to take care of my own children, so I stayed drunk until the booze ran out. Spending time alone with them showed me what all

Mair had put up with through the years. I couldn't blame her for leaving, any more than I could blame Rachel for running away. The kids were hungry, and their clothes were dirty and ragged. Ty told me I was a lousy dad, and he'd rather go live with Rachel. She loved them—even gave them her portion of food. Anne cried until I took her to a free clinic and learned she had a double ear infection. The doctor didn't spare words about my lack of parenting. In fact, he dialed social services while I was in his office and handed me the phone.

"That woke me up. I got help for them and myself. The only counseling available was through a pastor, and he showed me how to love my children and make changes. More importantly, I gave my life over to a God who was a perfect role model. I sold my small ranch to pay my debts and took on a job as a foreman near here. I've been at the same job, and we've been at that church ever since. I love my kids, and I've repeatedly apologized to them for all the hurt I caused. They're all good kids, know Jesus, and love each other. They say they've forgiven me and their mother. Although she hasn't seen them since the day she left. I doubt if she'd recognize any of them. But it's Rachel who needs to hear my confession." He swiped at a tear.

"At first I thought she'd have a better life with Debbie, and I'm sure she did. But she deserves to hear my apology. Now someone is trying to kill her."

Carr questioned Warick's every word. He glanced toward the back of the church and saw a man standing there. "Are you looking for someone, sir?"

"Is the pastor around?"

"His office is down the hall on the right."

The man, who looked homeless and hungry, appeared confused. "Can you show me? I can wait in one of these pews until you're finished."

Carr nodded while the man limped to a seat behind them.

"Sir, we're having a private conversation. If you'd kindly wait in the back, I'll be right with you."

The man looked none too pleased, but he moved.

"Who do you think is behind the shootings?" Carr whispered.

Warick lifted his chin. "No doubt in my mind it's Brandt. He has a philosophy—what's his is his, and he won't let it go. He claims the treasure and Rachel are his. I . . . I found out what hotel she's staying at and put a note on her windshield to warn her about Brandt."

Question after question burned in Carr's mind. Later he'd ponder the truth, if any, in Warick's words. "Why didn't you go to the police when those men were murdered on my ranch?"

"I feared what Brandt would do to my kids. I never dreamed he'd try to hurt Rachel."

"You don't think your ex-wife would have stopped him?"

"No. She loves Richardson, and she's blind to anything he does. I ought to know." He blew out a sigh. "I haven't seen her in twelve years, and I have no reason to believe they're still together. Brandt was obsessed with Rachel. How Mair dealt with that is beyond me."

Carr chose not to comment. Thoughts poured in and out of his head like running water. The revelations of the late afternoon and evening had left him exhausted and yet at peace. His temper was in God's hands, where it should have been all along. Listening to Stanton Warick with an open mind was another matter. He longed for time to pray about the man, to figure out if his words were true.

The stillness in the sanctuary calmed him even more. "Why are you telling me this?"

Warick gripped the pew in front of him. "I want my daughter safe from Brandt. I also want her off this case. Brandt's clever and manipulative, and he won't give up. Let someone else from the FBI handle the investigation, but send my Rachel home. And lastly, I want reconciliation with my daughter. In that order."

"Why do you think she'd listen to me?"

"I saw the TV report about the two of you."

"Media hype. Not a word of it was true." But Carr wished it were.

"But you spend a lot of time with her. At the very least you're friends."

Carr considered a rebuttal, but perhaps listening to Warick made more sense. "I doubt if she will abandon her assignment. I've tried and gotten nowhere. As far as reconciliation, I can tell her about this conversation. Bella has a mind of her own, and once it's made up, it takes an act of God to change it."

"I couldn't ask for more."

"Why are you here tonight?"

"Ty, my oldest son, is considering the ministry, and I wanted him to talk to several pastors in the community."

He's the young man Kent was talking about? "I'd like to meet him."

"Uh, okay. He had an appointment with the music minister, then Pastor Matthews." Warick glanced at the back of the church and down the hall as though his son waited for him. "Let's find him."

The two men exited the sanctuary together. Oddly enough, the man in the back pew had disappeared.

"I wonder . . ." Warick rubbed his chin. "Oh, never mind. Let's go find Ty."

CHAPTER 37

Tomorrow Bella could escape this prison called a hospital, more like a torture chamber with the daily bloodsuckers in their little white jackets. The doctor had told her she couldn't drive, but Bella had already tuned out such nonsense. All she needed to do was forgo the pain medication and snatch up her keys. Oh, she'd wait maybe two days before a solo flight, but not a day more. Too many things to do.

The recorder inside her purse contained a list of all the follow-ups and questions for Frank, but typing on her laptop with her left arm in a sling was tedious. One item kept pestering her: how had the three victims met and discussed the treasure hunt without mentioning the details to their families? Brandt had surely drawn them into meetings, phoned them, something. But those involved with the victims claimed they were clueless.

Bella's cell phone rang. She answered without looking at the number. The moment she heard the woman's voice, she recognized the caller.

"Mair," Bella said. "It's been a long time. Or are you going by Lynne?" She tucked the phone between her shoulder and her ear, then grabbed the pen and paper on her table.

"I heard you had an accident."

"Clear in Peru? Or are you not there anymore? And you wanted to make sure I was okay?"

"You are my children's half sister."

Bella decided not to ask when the last time was she'd seen them. "But you're no longer my stepmother."

"You've done your homework. The FBI has trained you better than I expected. If you know about my divorce from your father, then you know I'm with Brandt."

Bella forced a laugh. "Better you than me."

"Come now, Rachel. Are you still harboring bad feelings about his little infatuation with you?"

"Not at all. I thought you were a smarter woman than to team up with him. Do you have a fixation for losers?" Bella scribbled their conversation. If only she could get the attention of one of the officers.

"Your father made top billing."

Bella wished there were something close at hand that she could throw at the guard and snag his attention. "So Brandt had you pick out flowers and then call me?"

"He didn't have a thing to do with it. I was concerned."

"About what?" Bella took a purposeful pause.

"You were nearly killed. One of your father's stupid tricks, I'm sure."

"Possibly. What do you want?"

"I don't want a thing. Just a friendly chat."

"Why not a friendly visit? You know my room number."

Mair laughed. "I'm not stupid."

A nurse entered the room, and Bella mouthed, *Police.* An instant later, one of the officers stood at her bedside. She jotted down, *Brandt Richardson's wife. May be in the hospital. Tall blonde in her midforties.* The officer nodded and snatched up his radio. He rushed into the hall.

"Besides, I don't want to be arrested either," Mair continued.

"Brandt's aim might be a little better next time."

"He didn't shoot you."

"I'm sure he knows who did. What about the other four dead men?"

"If they're dead, then it's their own fault."

Mair had hardened. Sad, but true. "Is that the reason you're calling—to warn me?"

"Possibly. I don't really want to see you dead, especially when you helped me with the kids."

Bella needed to keep Mair on the phone. By now the policemen were looking for her. "What do you remember?"

"Oh, the sweet girl who worked hard and never gave us any trouble. Until—"

"You and Dad sold me to Brandt."

Mair laughed. "He wasn't serious."

"Brandt or Dad?"

"Brandt, of course. Hey, gotta run." The phone disconnected.

Mair had been in the hospital, and Brandt could have been with her. Bella leaned back against the pillow. So close. Like in the elevator at the hotel. He might be the master of disguise, but his little game of charades was about over.

CHAPTER 38

THE FOLLOWING MORNING, the doctor released Bella. She had a two-page list to work through and wanted to start today. But she knew her strength would wane before she got to item number three.

From the backseat of Wesley's squad car, Bella turned to Carr, once more thanking him for picking her up from the hospital, helping her gather up her belongings at the hotel, and allowing her to stay at the High Butte until she could again take a hotel room. Hopefully, the murderer would be arrested this week, and all of their lives could go back to normal.

Frank had volunteered to stay at the High Butte until they arrived. He had his own set of questions for Lydia and Jasper about the series of murders. Unfortunately, when Frank learned about Bella's stand as a Christian, he'd be upset. He was agnostic and had no problem defending his views.

"You are amazingly radiant today," Carr said. "Is it my charming personality?"

She laughed, and it felt good. Really good. "I had a date last night."

A pained look spread over his face. "Now I'm crushed."

"Oh, you could never compete."

"Why's that?" All traces of humor vanished from his face, and Bella knew without a doubt his feelings for her were sincere. Yet she refused to confess her feelings until this was over.

"I had a date with God."

He grinned. "You go, girl. Your life will never be the same. Lydia will be ecstatic."

"I want to tell her in person." Bella glanced at her phone and saw she had a message. How had she missed this? Must have been when she was helping Carr pack her suitcase, which had been a little embarrassing. The call was from Frank. A twinge of sympathy for what she felt for Carr swept over her. Her reasons for abandoning a relationship with Frank tugged at her heart. She shared with him that her career came first. After all, part of the reason she wanted this assignment was for a promotion. *Not anymore.*

Shaking away thoughts of romance with Carr and the multitude of problems an affair of the heart could cause, she listened to Frank's message.

"I forgot to tell you I've requested Yvonne Taylor's cell phone records," Frank said. "I think you already did this, but I wanted to see if anything had changed. They'll be sent to your phone, probably today." She texted Frank and thanked him for the information.

"Good news?"

"Just a lead." An idea had struck her while she was in the hospital concerning the technology available for modern medicine. Why not? She pressed in the number for Pete at the FIG in Houston. Glancing at Carr beside her, she realized she didn't need to hide this from him. "Good morning, Pete. I'm looking for information on Brandt Richardson while he was in South America. Is it possible he could have had a medical procedure to repair his vocal cords? If there's a remote possibility this could have happened, do some prying. Thanks. Yes, I'm feeling pretty good." Bella glanced at Carr. "I have a great nurse." She ended the call and dropped her BlackBerry into her shoulder bag.

Carr rolled his eyes. "Nurse? How about a hero or a knight? Better yet, a cowboy, a real John Wayne." He hesitated. "Seriously, if Richardson has shed his hoarse voice, that opens a lot of possibilities. Along with his many disguises."

"Exactly. He could be someone we trust, disguising his looks while we've been looking for a man with a distinct voice pattern."

"So now you wait until they get back to you."

She nodded. "James Bond."

"Instead of John Wayne?"

"It's all in the technology."

Wesley drove on toward Ballinger, making small talk and forcing a laugh from both of them. Bella noted he kept a watchful eye on the rearview mirror. She appreciated what the county sheriff's department was doing for her—and those she cared about. They talked about Carr's childhood: his parents, who'd been professionals; his older brother, who followed in his father's footsteps as a surgeon; and his grandmother, a devout Catholic.

"Tell me about the home for at-risk teen boys."

He nodded. "I simply want it to be an opportunity for a second chance at life, like it was for me. God allowed me to have the High Butte Ranch for a purpose, and I think this is it. Before the investigation, I lined up a reputable fellow who would help with counseling and directing the boys' aggressive behavior toward healthy outlets. Since then, he's withdrawn his acceptance. Can't blame him for not wanting to get involved. I'd also interviewed a couple of teachers to aid the boys in continuing their education or possibly obtaining their GED. Online learning is another option for those who want to advance their education. Lydia would be in charge of food and hiring domestic help, and Jasper would show them about ranching and taking on responsibilities. An activities director would work with Jasper and me for a balance of fun and chores. The one person I hadn't been able to find yet is a youth minister."

"What about yourself?"

"Hmm. Kent suggested I could fill the spot, and I have been taking distance and online classes for a biblical studies degree. Maybe I could."

She so enjoyed talking to him without analyzing his word choice and body language. "You'd be perfect."

"Well, until my name is officially cleared and arrests made, everything is on hold. Used to be, I thought bad luck trailed me wherever I went. But I think God is maturing my faith, taking me through a few challenges so I can better lead those boys."

"I think you're right."

His gaze caught hers. She should look away and break the spell, except she was right where she wanted to be.

"Sure is quiet back there," Wesley said.

Carr cleared his throat. "So now you're a bodyguard turned chaperone?"

"Both. What do you think my uncle would have done?"

"Given us the same hard time as you are," Carr said.

As Bella entered Ballinger, riding in the squad car and enjoying Carr's company, all of her past thoughts about what she wanted for her life faded. How peculiar that here, in a part of the country she detested, she'd found a relationship with God and for the first time discovered honest feelings for a man. The past and the present had collided, and even with the uncertainties of the future, the world felt right.

If she were completely honest with herself, she'd admit that love was an antidote for the ugliness of the world, a euphoria that seemed bathed in tender glances. Without the Divine working in her life, she'd never have accepted what Carr meant to her. How incredibly beautiful.

Wesley drove over the bridge at Elm Creek and past the Ballinger bakery and café that boasted of wireless Internet. Distant and familiar at the same time. They passed the courthouse, a yellow rock building with a statue of Charles H. Noyes on the front lawn—whoever he was. Across the street was a sand-wich shop where, before her trip to the hospital, she and Carr had enjoyed a fabulous lunch—back before she admitted her feelings for him. Deputy Roano, now the acting sheriff, preferred the Tex-Mex food at Alejandras restaurant. He and Carr had fussed about it. Carr won.

Outside the town, a huge cross had been erected on a hill after she'd left the area fourteen years ago. It stood symbolically for who and what she'd become.

Wesley drove past the sheriff's department, a one-story stone building with a metal roof, across the street from the United Methodist Spanish mission. The shopping district was sparse with most of the buildings reminiscent of the turn of the twentieth century downtown. Wesley's phone rang, inter-rupting her reverie.

"Would you believe that was Lydia?" Wesley palmed the steer-ing wheel and laughed. "She needs milk and bananas. So you two get an escort to the Shoppin' Baskit."

The three made a quick stop for the grocery items, and Carr bought a dozen chocolate chip cookies. The locals stared, but Bella didn't care. In fact, she enjoyed every minute of their short excursion. Back in the car, they made their way through the little town en route to the High Butte.

"You're looking at this town as though you'd never seen it before," Carr said.

"Is that why I'm getting a tour? Actually, I don't think I ever paid much attention when I was younger."

"Why do you think that is?"

"New eyes and rose-colored glasses." She meant her faith, but as soon as the words were spoken, she understood both men had assumed something else.

"If I reached over to hold your hand, would I get slapped?" Carr said.

"You have to obtain my permission," Wesley said. "Rose-colored glasses or not. The law is the law."

"Might have to write you up. Damaging government property is a federal offense," Bella said. "I'm sure there's some sort of protocol." She recalled his tenderness when she'd been shot. But until the murderer was arrested, she'd keep her heart intact. "While I was in the hospital, I did a lot of thinking about the case."

"Before or after Mair called you?"

"Both. I've already told Frank this, but now I'm tossing my thoughts your way too." She took a deep breath, pushing aside their lightheartedness. "More players have to be involved in this besides Brandt and my dad. My guess: two others are working with him, doing his dirty work."

"Any idea who?" Carr said.

She smiled. "Not you. But I want to spend the afternoon rereading the books and Web sites about the Spider Rock treasure. I also want to talk to Lydia. She mentioned some things I should have followed up on." She stared out the window as both sides of the road gave way to pasture. "Actually, I was planning to dive deeper into her comments, but someone decided to stop my progress. Or rather, the task force's progress."

"Finally you agree we're a team."

"I'm in on that," Wesley called from the front seat. "Not a day passes that I don't think about Uncle Darren and his dedication to enforcing the law. I want all of those guys found today."

We all do. The day had arrived when she no longer had to face Brandt Richardson or her father alone. Bella thought of her siblings and hoped they hadn't gone too far astray. The boys might very well be candidates for Carr's home for at-risk teens.

"What is Richardson's background?" Wesley said. "What makes a guy do anything for a chance at some lost treasure?"

Bella sorted through all that had been discovered about Brandt.

"He had good parents, the middle child of a suburban couple in Houston. Made good grades until he reached junior high. Then he jumped into puberty, and behavior problems erupted, much of which were attributed to the middle child syndrome of wanting attention. Parents placed him in counseling, and soon after, he was diagnosed as bipolar. Medication and counseling helped, but once he reached his midteens, he refused to take the prescription or have blood work done. However, other areas of his life improved. He gave up smoking, didn't do drugs, and managed a four point in high school. He joined track and earned a scholarship to college. Still he remained a loner but stayed out of trouble. Once he graduated from college, he broke contact with his parents and family. None have heard from him since."

"A decent kid who went bad," Wesley said.

"Oh, I think the psychology was there all along," Bella said. "Just because he didn't act on his tendencies when he was younger doesn't mean he didn't want to."

"I certainly don't understand the workings of the criminal mind like I should," Wesley continued. "But I will. I owe Uncle Darren that much."

"Give yourself some time. However—" she glanced at Carr— "sometimes first impressions are not the most reliable."

CHAPTER 39

CARR WANTED BELLA'S undivided attention before he talked to her about his conversation with Stanton Warick. She needed to get settled in the downstairs guest room and rest. Lydia suggested a nap, and to Carr's amazement, Bella agreed. Although she'd been released from the hospital, she looked too pale to him. No point in upsetting her, and relaying his meeting with Warick would definitely agitate her.

Carr viewed the reformed man with muddled feelings. Warick had convincingly told his story of shame and rehabilitation and how the church and county social services helped him become the father his children needed. But had Carr swallowed a mass of lies? Where would he be if others had not given him an opportunity to prove his convictions?

But what if Carr had been led down a path of deceit? What if Warick's pleas for help to make sure Bella was safe, relieved of her current assignment, and reconciled with her father and siblings were a ploy? Ty seemed like a good kid, but he could have learned the art of deceit from an excellent teacher.

The worst scenario came with Warick and Richardson working together to find the lost treasure and destroying any evidence of their involvement. That also meant eliminating some members of the task force.

Tomorrow he and Kent planned a visit to the Warick family. The boys all worked on the ranch where they lived, and the girl had a babysitting job in Ballinger. The only time to visit was late at night or early morning. Kent and Carr chose morning, and they'd be bringing Lydia's homemade breakfast burritos. He kept the information to himself, which meant he kept his plans from Frank, too. That man had feelings for Bella—something Carr would deal with when the murderer was arrested.

The house had given him claustrophobia, or rather his concerns had caused his mind to reach explosive stage. He needed to get outside and work off his stress.

In the stable, Carr stuck the pitchfork into another pile of wet and matted straw. He emptied it into a wheelbarrow and thrust the pitchfork into the dirty straw again. Cleaning out stalls was a perpetual chore, always out with the filth and in with the clean. Where did Warick fit into the purposefulness of life? Carr sure wished he had the answers.

★ ★ ★

Bella drifted in and out of sleep. The trip from the hospital to the High Butte was harder on her than she'd ever admit. Finally she forced herself to stay awake and check text messages on her phone. At least that part of civilization was available here.

Her cell phone buzzed with a text message. With sleep-laden eyes she read the words: *Call me at this number. Vic.*

She picked up the landline on her nightstand and pressed in the number on the text.

"This is Bella."

"Thanks for getting back to me."

Immediately her senses were sharpened. "How are you doing?"

"Pretty good. Taking each day at a time. I heard you're recovering okay."

"Sure. What can I do for you?"

"Something about the case keeps bothering me."

"I remember when you said you'd found evidence, but I never

heard a thing. I also wondered if you'd followed up on Lexie Bronson—the bartender in Abilene."

"She's clean. Doesn't know a thing. Anyway, my mind's been in a daze worrying about my wife."

"I understand. How is she?"

"Spending more time sleeping. That's what she's doing now, so I thought I'd call. The appointed sheriff, uh—"

"Roano?"

"That's him. I overheard a phone call that led me to believe he might be working with Richardson. Something about 'having more money to spend soon' and 'making sure Sullivan got his due.'"

Bella recalled the many times Roano had sworn to find evidence to convict Carr . . . and the black eye. "I'll get on it. Thanks."

"No problem."

She disconnected the call and phoned Pete at FIG. Vic's observation could mean nothing—or everything.

Carr and Kent drove onto the Circle D Ranch at dawn and followed Carr's directions to the Warick home. The one-story rock and frame home had recently been painted, and the roof looked new. Two dust-covered, older model trucks sat in front of a single garage. All looked quiet, but lights shone through the window of the small home.

"This is it." Carr turned off the engine to his truck. "I hope this convinces me one way or the other about Warick."

"Me too." Kent wiped the perspiration from his forehead, even with the air-conditioning cranked up to full blast. "I've always believed that how a man's children behave is a reflection of their father."

"Good thing you didn't come to my house. I had no respect for discipline, and my dad tried everything he could think of to straighten me out."

"But how did you act when folks came by to visit?"

"Like manners were my middle name."

"Precisely." Kent opened the passenger door of the truck. "I'll grab the doughnuts, and you grab Lydia's burritos. Not sure how much time we'll have since everyone has a job to do."

"I appreciate your helping me arrange this."

"You're welcome. Now let's see what we can find out."

Carr watched Stanton Warick step onto the front porch and wave. Carr and Kent returned the gesture. A young girl joined Warick on the porch. Even in the faint light of dawn, Carr saw the girl's striking resemblance to her father and Bella. His heart sped into fifth gear at the thought of Bella's reaction. He understood her wanting to make a positive impact on these kids, but he hoped their father had taken a step in that direction twelve years ago.

Carr stepped out of his truck and grabbed breakfast. His gaze fixed on a rusted red wagon near the steps. "I don't believe it."

"What?" Kent said.

"It's a Radio Flyer." Carr pointed to the old wagon loaded down with flowering plants. "I had one of those as a kid. That wagon and I were inseparable. We tore up and down the sidewalk like we owned it. Wore many a hole through the right knee of my jeans."

Warick laughed. "My boys did everything but sleep in it when they were little. If they weren't carryin' each other, then they had some project going on. I couldn't part with the wagon once they got older."

Carr peered into Stanton's eyes and saw what he needed to know.

CHAPTER 40

Bella wanted to record every word Carr said about her siblings. At first she was irritated that he went to see them without telling her, but she'd visit them as soon as she could drive.

"Were they receptive to your visit?" She settled back in a kitchen chair.

"Absolutely. They want to see you, and the two older boys remember you. I thought maybe tomorrow night the kids could come for a barbecue. That is, if you're feeling up to it." His shoulders lifted and fell. "Ty said he could drive them here."

Alex had sounded good when she talked to him before her hospital stay. She didn't need to think twice about it. "I'd love a visit."

"Great. I'll arrange it."

"Did they have the look of abuse?"

"Not at all. The Circle D is a good-size ranch, and the foreman's quarters are neat and clean. The boys work there, and Anne babysits during the week for a couple in Ballinger. You should see her. Looks so much like her big sis. In fact, I had to do a double take. They are well-mannered, respectful—prayed before we ate."

How could they not be hardened after a life with their father? "Wish I could see what they look like."

Carr fished his camera from his pocket and laid it on the table. "I took a bunch of pictures. All I need to do is download them. I'll go get my laptop from the library."

"Then I want to talk to you about their father."

"Your father too."

Did she hear an edge in his voice? "I'm hoping he's ready to relinquish custody to me."

"Ty's eighteen and ready for college." He paused, and she recognized his manner of thinking through something before speaking. "I met Stanton a few nights ago at the church."

She frowned. "What was he doing there?"

"Ty is considering the ministry, and his dad had arranged for him to talk to the music minister and Kent before he made a final decision."

"My brother . . . a pastor?" She thought of her siblings as four nearly grown kids who needed guidance. What happened? It was good. God had definitely looked out for them, but this information was not what she expected. Not so sure it was what she wanted to hear either. *She* wanted to take care of her siblings.

"I see the questions on your face, and I'm ready to answer what I can. But first I want you to see their pictures."

Bella took a deep breath, wishing her energy level would return sooner than the doctors anticipated. Confusion about her brothers and sister caused a chill to race up her arms. How was she supposed to feel or act or think? What was she supposed to say when it came to her siblings? Dad and Carr talked—about what? Her dad's ability to fire a rifle from the top of a butte? dig for buried gold by lantern light?

She halted her thoughts. Even if her reflections about Dad were true, she shouldn't dwell on them. The priority was her brothers and sister.

Her fragile faith gave her hope, and the Scripture she'd memorized years ago now had meaning. But the challenges of her family frightened her. She picked up her cell to text Frank about the kids' visit tomorrow night, and she didn't want him there. Knowing Frank, he'd interrogate each one. Another thought took root. Perhaps Carr had found new evidence leading to the killer's arrest. Her dad might want a plea bargain.

★ ★ ★

Carr clicked on the last photo of the Warick teens, fourteen-year-old Anne. He watched Bella's guarded emotions melt like ice.

"She looks so much like me at that age." Bella's soft voice broke with the emotion that he sensed had been building since he showed her the first picture. She reached to the computer screen and almost touched the smiling face. "She looks happy. All of them have beautiful smiles."

He handed her a tissue, and she dabbed her eyes. "Ty looks like Grandfather Warick, and Alex and Zack have Mair's light hair and blue eyes."

Carr peered at the screen. "How can you tell they have blue eyes?"

She laughed and sniffed. "I remember them as babies and toddlers." She took his hand. "Thank you. I will never forget this. Tomorrow . . ." She straightened. "Now I want to see the pictures again."

This time he laughed. "When you're finished, we can have the discussion about your dad."

She nodded, while her attention stayed glued to the computer screen. Once she'd clicked through the photos again, she turned to him. "I'm ready. I've thought about it most of the day, and I'm hoping you've found evidence to solve these murders."

Bella was about to be disappointed—and probably furious at him for what he was going to say. He also understood this might end their relationship before it began.

Carr closed the lid of the laptop. "I met your dad at Kent's office on Monday night. I told you Ty had an appointment with the music minister and Kent, and Stanton came along for moral support. Once I learned who he was, it was all I could do to keep from punching him in the nose." He peered into her eyes and took her hand. "In fact, I had to excuse myself and spend some time in the sanctuary."

"I'm not so sure I'd have had any self-control."

"God used the situation to deal with me about some of my own issues. When I finished my come-to-Jesus meeting, as Jasper calls it, I realized I needed to face Stanton in Kent's office. I saw him at the back of the church and offered my apologies. He asked if he could tell me his story."

"I can only imagine what he conjured up." Her face tightened.

Help me, here. "Your dad relayed the same atrocities about his abuse to you and the rest of his family. He even added a few more events that you omitted. But most of his account happened after you left the area." Carr proceeded to tell Bella about the affair between Brandt Richardson and Mair while he continued to search for the Spider Rock treasure. "When Mair left, Stanton turned to drinking. In short, when he saw Anne was sick, he took her to a clinic. The doctor there gave him a choice of getting help for his drinking and cleaning up his life or losing his kids. Stanton chose fatherhood. He got help, ended up in church, and became a Christian. He's got good kids, which he attributes to God. He also said he'd tried unsuccessfully through the years to contact you and apologize."

Bella nodded through a hardened expression. "I destroyed his letters. Then Aunt Debbie and I moved, and we didn't leave a forwarding address."

Carr saw she was not handling this well, but he had to continue. "His story is much longer, but he wanted to tell you himself."

"Does he think I'm going to forgive him and welcome dear old Dad into my arms?"

He refused to comment because Bella knew the answer to that question. She glanced away, but he saw a single tear drip onto her cheek. He wanted to comfort her, but her hostility was between her and God.

"Tell me what you're thinking," Carr finally said. "I have a good ear."

"For years I had nightmares about him. What he and Brandt did. And that is why I entered the FBI." She rubbed her uninjured hand on her jeans. "If I'm to remain true to my faith, then I have to forgive him." She blinked again. "And Brandt."

"It's tough."

She nodded and swiped at a tear. "Do you know I've shed more tears here than I have since I was a kid?"

"Look where you are. Look at what's happened. Look at the emotional, spiritual, mental, and physical drain on your life."

"But to forgive Dad or even Brandt makes me feel like I'm weak."

"Not at all. It takes more strength to let go of the past and step forward than to darken our hearts with hate."

Several seconds passed, and he waited. How well he understood the turmoil of facing the devil and his wiles head-on.

"I can forgive Dad," she said. "I appreciate the fact he did well for my brothers and sister. But I don't want to ever see him. Never. I can't put myself there."

"It would be hard."

"Brandt will take more time. Maybe never. I feel like he's the devil with skin on."

"Again, I understand."

"Glad you do, because I don't understand myself. One thing I ask."

"What?"

"Dad has to be interviewed for the investigation, but I'll have Roano and Frank handle it. Do not *ever* arrange a face-to-face between us for the purpose of reconciliation. If you find that necessary, my trust in you is gone."

His poor Bella. He could only pray for her heart to heal and for God to give her peace.

CHAPTER 41

BELLA WATCHED a late-model truck pull up to the ranch house. Her pulse quickened. Three teen boys and a girl piled out of the truck. *Where are their seat belts?*

Her babies. She'd rocked them to sleep, fed them, played with them, and then deserted them to a man who apparently had done a U-turn.

A sob caught in her throat, and she covered her mouth.

"Are you okay?" Carr's arm slipped around her waist. "Maybe this is too soon. You're not well by any means."

She forced a smile and blinked back the emotion. "No, I'm fine. Very fine. And I'm excited." She turned to Lydia. "Thank you again for inviting them to dinner. Both of you."

"My pleasure. Can't go wrong with grilled burgers and chicken."

"My job," Carr said. "And I'm on my way to turn on the grill."

Bella's emotions had turned to pure giddiness. "I'm going to meet them on the front porch."

Carr stepped back and gestured toward the door. "Your entourage awaits."

She hurried past him. "I think it's the other way around."

Bella opened the door and gasped. The speech she had planned all day disappeared from her thoughts. Standing before her were four jean-clad teenagers who mirrored the babies and toddlers she'd loved so dearly.

"Rachel?" the tallest boy said.

"Ty?"

He opened his arms, and she fell into them laughing and sobbing. Her other siblings touched her back, uninjured arm, face. Bella embraced an inkling of heaven.

When dinner was ready, they gathered around the table and prayed before digging in. "Alex, tell me about what is going on with you," Bella said midway through the boy's second hamburger. Ty had spoken freely about his call into the ministry.

"I tend to be the black sheep, but Dad and Ty are doing their best to make sure I behave."

"Sure you want to confess crimes to an FBI agent?" However, her laugh didn't match the whirling in her stomach.

"Sounds like a plan to me. After spending a night in jail for drinking, I think I'll be in law enforcement. Sure looks better on the outside than the inside."

They all laughed, but Bella took careful mental notes.

"Going into law enforcement would be something I could do for Sheriff Adams." Alex reached for a chicken leg dripping in barbecue sauce. "Since he's the one who picked me up and gave me the worst lecture of my life."

"Those weren't your exact words, Bro," Zack said. The two boys could have passed for twins with their long legs, straw-colored hair, and large blue-gray eyes. "'In my grill like a redneck on steroids' is what you said."

Alex grabbed the picante sauce. "That's before someone murdered him. And Dad was harder on me than the sheriff. Gave me two hundred hours of community service on the ranch."

Good. Sounds like Dad changed his ways for the sake of the kids.

Alex wiped his fingers on a checkered napkin. "Rachel—or do you want us to call you Bella?"

"It doesn't matter."

"Anyway, I know none of the others will say a word about this. But since I'm the one who has no problem speaking my mind,

I will. We all know what Dad did. It's not a secret. We've all chosen to use how he treated us as a lesson on what not to do." He
tossed a glance at Ty. "See, I do know a few things."

Ty chuckled. "Maybe you should consider the ministry."

Alex pointed a half-eaten drumstick at his older brother.
"Forget it. Zack, your turn."

"Uh . . . I like baseball."

"What position?" Bella said.

"Second base."

"He's good." Anne had spoken little during the meal. "Daddy
says he could get a college scholarship. He makes all of the hits
too. You should see him play."

Anne clearly adored Zack. "Are you playing during the summer?" Bella's shoulder throbbed, but she would *not* break the
spell—this wonderful, magical enchantment.

Zack moistened his lips the way she remembered Mair doing.
"Our church has a team, young guys and old guys."

"Watch it," Carr said. "I play on our church's team, and we
beat you the first game."

"New Hope?" Zack's forehead crinkled.

"Yep."

"We hadn't any time to practice."

Carr laughed. "Neither did we, but I remember you made the
only hits."

Zack nodded. "And don't you forget it when we play you
again. You'll be eatin' dirt. We've got a game tomorrow night.
Wanna come?"

Bella looked at Carr. She wanted to attend Zack's game, but she
didn't want to see her dad. Oh, she was such a brave FBI agent.

"I'll take you," Carr said. "That way I can watch Zack's strategy."

Bella nodded. She could handle it. "We'll be there. So what's
your ultimate goal?"

Zack pressed his lips together and reached for the corn and

jalapeño casserole. "Not sure. Maybe coach high school baseball." He pointed to Anne. "You're next, princess."

"I don't like that name."

"We know," Alex said. "But, princess, it's all you."

Bella studied the face of her little sister, whose resemblance stirred Bella's soul. Was it wrong to welcome her sister's mirrored looks? "I understand you babysit for a couple in Ballinger."

"Yes, ma'am—"

"I'm your sister, sweetie. No need to *ma'am* a sister."

Anne grinned. "Daddy told me to mind my manners."

Another reason to hide her feelings about Saint Dad. *That's wrong. Lord, this is harder than I thought.* "How old is the child you babysit?"

"There are two of them—boys—and they're two and three."

"Sounds like a handful." Bella studied Anne's face. Her green eyes sparkled.

"They are, but I love 'em. We play and do crafts."

"And school? You're going to be a freshman this year?"

"Yes, and I know what else you're going to ask. I want to be a pediatrician."

Beautiful, lofty goals for a sweet girl. For all of them. "Wonderful."

"Rachel," Ty said, "when are you going to eat?"

"Now, little brother. My, how did I get along without you?" She reached for a bun and a burger.

"Tell us about it," Alex said. "Can we ask you questions?"

Oh, great. "I suppose."

"Ever been shot before?" Alex said.

"No. Been shot *at*. Don't care to have it happen again."

"Ever shoot anybody?" Alex continued.

"Alex," Ty and Zack said.

Bella held up her hand to let them know Alex's question was not off-limits. "Yes, but I don't really want to talk about it."

"Fair enough," Alex said.

Ty relaxed a bit, and she was pleased with the way he worked at being a good role model. However, he might take his family position a bit too seriously.

Lydia passed the potato salad around the table. "Looks like you four are hooked up close."

"I guess," Ty said, "if I understand what you mean. We look out for each other."

"My father used that phrase." Lydia went on. "It comes from the old days when a man hooked up a team of horses close to the wagon so they'd work well together."

"That's us," Ty said. "We'll be hooked even closer now that Rachel is with us."

Bella peered into the face of her brother. When they met again, she'd ask them about returning to Houston with her.

Long after the house quieted that night, Bella whipped off an e-mail to Aunt Debbie. She detailed each sibling, their likes and hobbies and personality.

. . . I could go on and on with the evening. I'm so proud of them and surprised they've done well despite Dad. God is looking out for them. According to Carr, Dad changed shortly after Mair left him. That's good for them, but I don't trust him.

Attached are pictures. Aren't they a handsome bunch?

Aunt Debbie, Dad could be involved in these murders, and I'm afraid of how the kids would handle it. They are so trusting, as though he never did anything wrong. Lots of fears for them are running through my head.

Love,
Bella

She brushed her teeth and washed her face and heard the chirp of an incoming e-mail.

My dear Bella,

Rockefeller and I are up late watching the Lord of the Rings trilogy. Can't get enough of Frodo, Sam, the beautiful Arwen, too-pretty Legolas, and that hunk Aragorn. Makes a woman blush just looking at him—and with me, it's all about hot flashes. Lots of good stuff.

Then I read your e-mail and I'm blubbering. Those precious babies are all grown-up. Looking at Anne is like looking at you. Honey, God is calling you to not only forgive your Dad but give him a chance. I think I hear your stubborn streak coming through cyberspace. But be open, dear one. Who knows what's in the future?

Okay, Rockefeller is at the door, and I need to let him out. He's actually been quite good. I found that one-on-one time with him, along with his special doggy treats, makes him a much better behaved dog.

Love you bunches,
Aunt Debbie

CHAPTER 42

BELLA STUDIED THE ROAD through her car's rearview mirror. She'd left the High Butte at four thirty this morning while the house was dark and quiet. Carr and Lydia would have handcuffed her if they'd had any idea she planned a trip to Junction, about two hours away, where Interstate 10 intersected with Highway 83. An old man by the name of Shep Wither worked at the McDonald's there. He claimed to have information about the Spider Rock treasure possibly being located in Runnels County. Brandt might have milked him for all he was worth, yet she needed the same information.

Wither's shift ended at ten this morning, and he knew to expect her. She'd brought her laptop to work on the investigation until the man was free to talk.

Another glance in the rearview mirror indicated no one was following. She would not have been surprised to see Carr's fancy red F-250 on her bumper or another vehicle that could have been the killer's. Oh, but Carr was proud of that truck.

At the McDonald's, she ordered a large coffee, two packets of honey, and a sausage McMuffin. She didn't need to ask for Shep Wither. He stood a head taller than any of the kids frying hash browns, serving breakfast, or pouring drinks, and he had ancient leather for skin. Lydia and Jasper had described him perfectly. Wither reached over the counter and grasped her hand like it was porcelain and grinned a full mouthful of his own pearly white teeth. *Bet he was a lady-killer in his day.*

"I'll be over there." She pointed to a booth. "I brought plenty of work to do."

"A pretty lady like you should be relaxin'." He drew out each syllable as though they were the only two people in the restaurant.

She smiled and took her sack of food. "I'll remember that." She scooted into the booth and opened the lid of her coffee to cool. After adding both packets of honey, she turned on her laptop.

Hours later, Wither joined her. "Sure would be nice if I could get off work every day to visit with a beautiful woman."

"I'm sure you have no problem attracting women."

He chuckled, and she imagined he had been charming ladies since he was in diapers. "What happened to your arm?"

"Someone tried to use me for target practice."

"What does he look like?"

He wants to defend my honor. "Never saw him."

"Hmm. Interesting. You're curious about why the Spider Rock treasure is buried in Runnels County."

"I am. First of all, I need to tell you I'm an FBI agent investigating four murders in Runnels County." She pulled out her creds. Wither reached into his shirt pocket and fished out a pair of glasses. From the time he took, he surely read every word.

"Am I being recorded?" he said, seemingly convinced of her status.

"No, sir."

"The FBI doesn't get called in on every murder."

"One of the suspects is already wanted by us."

"But you must be close, or you wouldn't have a bullet hole in your shoulder. I read about the killings. One of the men wrote *Spider Rock* in the dirt before he died. Then the sheriff was poisoned."

"Right. I understand others have asked you about the gold."

"Yes, ma'am."

"Do you have any names of those who asked about your theory?"

"No theory at all. It's fact. One of the dead men asked me about the Spider Rock treasure located there—Walt Higgins from Waco."

Until now, Higgins's name hadn't been mentioned as much as the other two men. "Was he the only one who asked you about it?"

"Yep. Most folks in these parts think I'm crazy."

Maybe you are, but I'm enjoying your eccentricity. "So you gave the map to Higgins."

"Not at first. I had to find out if he was Christian. When he told me what church he belonged to, I contacted his pastor. Then I gave him a copy of the map."

"I'd like to see it."

"Can't."

Getting information out of Wither was tasking her brain. "Why not?"

"Got stolen."

She leaned across the table. "I bet you have it memorized."

He leaned closer. "You know I do."

"Can you draw it for me?"

His eyes twinkled. "Not here. Don't trust any of these grease-lickin' folks."

She swallowed her laughter. "Where, then?"

"Follow me to my place, and I'll draw the map for you."

"Am I safe?"

"Depends if my woman is there."

Bella grinned. "I'll take my chances."

She slipped into her car and followed Shep about six miles out of Junction to a mobile home down a dirt road. Shep's woman happened to be about twenty-five and model material. She glared at Bella, probably for any signs of potentially stealing her man.

"Now, sweetheart, this here's a real FBI agent. She's trying to solve those murders in Runnels County. She's not after me." Wither winked at Bella. "And I need for you to promise me you won't tell a soul about this."

"If you do, you could be in danger," Bella said. "There've been four murders linked to this, and I wouldn't want you and Mr. Wither to be added to the list of victims."

The young woman's eyes widened, revealing mascara-coated eyelashes long enough to swat flies. "I promise. Are you sure you weren't followed?"

"I left the area at four thirty to throw off anyone attempting to follow." Bella pointed to her left arm. "As you can see from my shoulder, the murderer plays for keeps. But the road was clear this morning."

Bella spent the next hour waiting on Wither to draw the map. He indicated the treasure was buried where Carr and Jasper had found the three victims on the High Butte Ranch.

"Why do you think the treasure is buried there instead of the other places indicated by previous findings? All the clues point to the triangle of Aspermont, Rotan, and Clyde."

"Because they all read the Spider Rock map wrong." He excused himself and returned with a copy of the treasure map rolled up like a scroll. "This one didn't get stolen. See how the spiderweb circles and connects with itself. That indicates the treasure is outside of the web. My great-grandfather was friends with an old Mexican fellow who insisted the real treasure was buried at the foot of this butte. He insisted anything found within the triangle of Aspermont, Clyde, and Rotan would bring destruction. I reckon you've heard about the curse. Looks like you got a taste of it yourself."

Bella recalled Lydia referring to stories about the treasure passed down from generation to generation. For certain, the three victims believed the gold was buried on the High Butte. And so did whoever had killed them.

"Do you know what to look for? I've been there on more than one occasion, and there are no etchings or rock formations indicating the treasure site."

"But it's there." He reached for a blank piece of paper and drew a sketch of the butte. "According to my great-granddaddy, my granddaddy, and my daddy, it's buried right here, and there's no physical signs of the location."

"Why didn't any of them search for it?"

"They were all Baptist preachers. Believed it was a sin." Wither laughed. "But they didn't think it was a sin to pass on the map."

"And what about you?"

He wrapped his arm around the young woman, who leaned into him. "Different folks call different things their treasure. I've always known what mine was."

Bella smiled and hoped she could contain her amusement until she was in her car. The agents back in Houston would not believe this character. She thanked both Shep and his woman and began the drive back to the High Butte.

If the killer could not get access to the High Butte to dig for the treasure, what else could he do? She grabbed her cell phone and punched in Carr's number.

"Where are you?" His voice indicated his displeasure.

Ouch. "On the road. And for the record, you're not my daddy."

"Point well taken. You're calling, so you must be alive."

"Yes, sir, Mr. Sullivan. I'm driving your way."

"Where have you *been*?"

"Spending time with an old man in Junction."

"I would have driven you." Carr's voice took a level between exasperated and downright angry.

"I needed to do this alone. And I found exactly what I was looking for."

"Which is?"

"Can you keep a secret?"

"For an FBI agent, sure."

"I have the map that shows the Spider Rock treasure is buried on the High Butte."

"Are you kidding?"

"And that brings me to this call."

"You want to borrow a shovel or call in the county sheriff's department?"

"Neither. I'm not the least bit interested in following up on the treasure, but I do want to study the map in hopes of finding more evidence to find the killer. What I want to know is if you own the mineral rights to your ranch."

Silence settled between them.

"Carr?"

"I gave them to New Hope. The church has a building project going for a new education facility, and I thought it might help. I had no use for the rights."

Her heart sank at the thought of who could be behind the killings or working with Brandt. "Did Pastor Kent handle it?"

"No, Aros Kemptor."

She'd heard his name before. "What can you tell me about him?"

"An attorney from Abilene. Outstanding Christian."

"How long have you known him?"

"He lives in Abilene. Joined New Hope about a year ago."

Bella's suspicions raced into overdrive. "Hear me out on this. The victims were killed near the base of the butte while digging for the treasure. Based on the map, their bodies were found near where the treasure is supposedly buried. That tells me they found out where and were killed so the murderer would not have to share the findings."

Carr blew out a sigh. "Makes sense. You and I have talked about that possibility."

"But the real killer cannot dig because he'd be trespassing, and he couldn't risk being discovered."

"But if he had the mineral rights, he could mask what he was doing while digging for the treasure."

"Exactly."

"Aros also has something else of mine," Carr said.

Excitement bubbled inside her, not for Carr but for headway on the case. Aros and Brandt could be working together. "What else?"

"I deeded the High Butte over to the church in the event of my death."

Apprehension changed her excitement into fear for Carr. "Then you're on the hit list. Don't go anywhere today until I receive a full report on Aros Kemptor. Is Wesley there?"

"Of course. This could be the end of the investigation."

"Let's hope so. Do you have Kemptor's phone number handy?"

"Yes."

Once Carr gave her the number, she sensed her confidence easing in. "I'll talk to you after I receive the report from the FIG." She ended the call and got Pete in Houston on the line. "Feed it back to my BlackBerry. This may be our ace." She glanced at the clock in her car. Two thirty. Mr. Kemptor was probably not in his office on a Saturday, but she had his personal cell number.

The phone rang three times and went directly to voice mail. "Mr. Kemptor, this is FBI Special Agent Bella Jordan. I'm working on the murders on the High Butte Ranch and would like to talk to you as soon as possible." She gave him her cell phone number and ended the call.

Exhausted, she couldn't wait to crawl into her guest room bed at the High Butte and take a nap before Zack's baseball game.

CHAPTER 43

BRANDT SIPPED A BEER and contemplated what disguise to use next on Rachel. He'd used a Mexican yardman, a deaf-mute, a maid at the hotel, a mourner at the sheriff's memorial service, and he'd shared an elevator with her—but he'd allowed her to figure that one out.

He swallowed his laughter. If Rachel had any idea how many times he'd walked past her and talked to her since she arrived in Abilene, she'd catch the earliest flight back to Houston.

Oh, but his finest would be his last. All he needed was patience. She'd come around. He'd waited too long for all of this to happen—the gold and her.

Brandt wished Sullivan and Warick hadn't gotten together. This was one of the scenarios that he wanted postponed until closer to *the* day. But since the two met at New Hope Church, their little friendship had progressed to a dangerous level.

Brandt could handle it. His pocket was full of tricks to keep him from being bored. Hmm. It could play right into his hand. His cell phone rang, and the caller ID read *Mair*.

"Why are you calling me?"

"We need to talk."

"I'm busy."

"Oh, really. Where are you?"

"Waco."

"Liar. You're in Austin. Are you with Yvonne?"

How did she find out about her? "Look, I have no idea where you come up with these weird ideas. I'm in Waco, and I'm not seeing Yvonne. I'll see you later on tonight."

"Not so fast. Your girlfriend just phoned me. She said Rachel came to see her."

"We knew that."

"Rachel convinced her to go to the FBI with information about you."

He should have known better than to waste his time with a money-hungry female. "How much does she want?"

"You are having an affair with her."

"I never said anything of the sort. My guess is Kegley told her a little too much about what was going on, and she wants hush money. Which isn't going to happen."

"Then you know what you have to do. And hope it's not too late. I don't care if you sleep around. I do care when your lover threatens me with prison and being an accessory to murder."

Brandt's game had taken a detour. He ended the call with Mair and phoned Aros. "I have a job for you in Austin."

"I'm halfway through my game."

"Do you think you can play golf in prison? Better take a walk away from your golfing partner. I need you in Austin tonight." Brandt waited a few seconds as he heard Aros pant through a fast walk. "Can you talk now?"

"Do your own dirty work. I have troubles enough of my own. Bella Jordan called me this afternoon. We had what she termed an 'interview' via the phone."

"How's that working for you?"

"Very funny. You're not Dr. Phil. She questioned my power of attorney within New Hope Church. She'd seen the paperwork from Kent Matthews that authorized my control of the mineral rights on the High Butte. She also questioned the wording of Sullivan's will that deeds the ranch to New Hope. She demanded copies of both forms."

"So instead of contacting me, you're playing golf?"

"Yeah, with Kent Matthews."

"If you want my help out of this, you'd better finish that game and get to Austin."

Aros cursed. "Once I dispose of her, what about the FBI?"

"The FBI's going to help us with this one." *And help me eliminate you.*

CHAPTER 44

AT LEAST FIFTEEN YEARS had passed since Bella had watched a baseball game from wooden bleachers. In the grueling, near-one-hundred-degree heat, with perspiration trickling down her temples and her back soaked, a strange elation possessed her at watching the third inning of Zack's baseball game. Anne sat on her right with her arm linked in Bella's. The added heat didn't matter; this was her baby sister. Alex sat on her left, and Ty sat behind them with Carr. She felt like a stranger to those who shared the same blood.

To the right of them on the top row sat Stanton Warick. The kids had called out to him, and Anne had left Bella's side to hug him. She was obviously a daddy's girl. Bella couldn't turn around to look at him. Neither could she fault her siblings for their attachment to their father. She'd made progress there. In fact, she envied them. They were able to do what she could not. Or rather, she refused to do. Ah, God had His work cut out for Him. Her siblings had forgiven the man who at one time did not care for his children. He hadn't attempted to sell them, but he'd treated them atrociously too. Why was she hanging on to her hatred? Did she still think he was involved in the murders? Carr touched her shoulder as though he sensed her confusion. She patted his hand without turning to greet him. Some thoughts needed to stay private.

In the past, she'd placed her dreams of a relationship on hold. Frank had tried to break through her wall. But he wanted them to be a suburbia couple with 2.5 kids, while she wanted to be Mr. and Mrs. Dink—double income, no kids. Her priorities had changed, not only with her faith but with Carr and her siblings. Her brothers and sister *needed* her, and they *needed* to live in Houston. Where did Carr fit in the equation?

"Zack is up to bat," Anne whispered.

Ty and Alex shouted like crazy men, and to Bella's shock and embarrassment, Carr did the same, then Anne.

Who cares? She stood and yelled right along with them. Zack adjusted his cap. He had determination etched into his face.

The pitcher threw a fastball.

Strike one.

The crowd roared with a mixture of jeers, attaboys, and you-can-do-its. The pitcher threw again.

Strike two.

The crowd responded the same. Bella sweat more than before. The pitcher, a man who looked to be in his late twenties, grinned at his teammates. He wound up and threw a third pitch.

Crack. Zack smacked the ball way out in left field, past the zone that had *Home Run* whistling on the wind. He raced toward first base while the fans cheered him on. Bella found herself screaming and jumping. And it felt good, so very good.

"I need something to drink. Your brother wore me out," she said to Anne a few minutes later. "Come with me?"

"Sure."

Bella took drink orders from the boys and Carr, and she and Anne hurried to the concession stand. While the volunteers from a local church group fished cans of soda from a huge ice chest, Bella swung her attention to the onlookers.

Brandt could be here. She scanned faces, male and then female, looking for someone who resembled the man who had murdered in his greed, or for her stepmother. No one but good people enjoying a baseball game. No raspy voices or deep-throated laughs. After paying for the drinks, she and Anne wound their way through the crowd toward the bleachers.

An older man stepped in front of them, but his limp halted his progress. "Excuse me," he said. "My grandson's playing ball." He stopped and gestured for her to pass. "Don't let me slow you down. You have your hands full, and those cans are ice-cold."

"Are you sure?"

He nodded. "I don't have far to go."

"Thanks." Bella motioned for Anne to go ahead of her, and she followed. The instant Bella handed out drinks to those waiting, her mind whirled with something that was familiar about the old man—the way he walked . . . the fictitious agent at the Courtesy Inn . . . the day she attempted to speak to the deaf man who limped. Brandt! Her suspicion about his having surgery to repair his vocal cords must have been on target. She could no longer count on his raspy voice betraying him.

Her attention flew to where the elderly man had been standing. He was gone. She rushed back down the bleachers. He'd disappeared. She made her way to the concession stand.

"Did you see an elderly man with a limp?"

One woman said no. The second pointed to the parking lot. "He was moving at a fast clip for an old man."

Bella bent and pulled her Glock from her ankle holster, concealing it so as not to alarm those around her. She sprinted toward the area of the parking lot where the woman had pointed. A few teens leaned against cars.

"Did you see an elderly man with a limp?"

"Yes, ma'am," said a boy wearing a baseball cap and jeans that threatened to fall to the ground. "He was in a hurry. Do you need some help?" She knew he'd seen her weapon by the shock registering on his face.

"Stay right here," she said. "I'm FBI. I'll show you my creds later." The last thing Bella needed was for Brandt to shoot a couple of teens who simply wanted to be of assistance. "Which way did he go?"

"To the right."

Bella left them with a mental note to thank them when she returned. She raced to the right, fully aware if the man was Brandt, he could be waiting for her. Her shoulder ached, but she refused to slow down.

"Bella." She whipped around to see Wesley racing on her heels.

She stopped long enough for him to catch up. "I think Richardson's here."

"Good thing I got another deputy to keep watch on Lydia and Jasper." He shook his head. "Had a feeling Richardson might try something in a public place."

"He's out here in the parking lot, according to those teens."

They separated, but neither was able to locate him. A late-model car and a newer truck left the area. Both kicked up dust, dirt, and gravel. Wesley got the license plates of one, and she jotted down the other.

"You need your rear kicked for taking out after him," Wesley said, taking on the persona of a man in charge.

"It happens to be my job. Had to be Brandt Richardson using one of his disguises." She continued to scan the parking lot. "He could have crawled into one of these vehicles and changed his looks."

Wesley peered out over the area. "Every time I think of Uncle Darren—and the others who've been killed—I want to be the one who catches him."

"I understand. Now I'm telling you to be careful."

"Makes sense that he'd try here since Frank is in Abilene. Carr's probably fit to be tied. He started after you, and I had to order him back. Told him the kids could be in danger."

"Thanks, Wesley. I owe you one."

He smiled his boyish grin, which she hoped wasn't filled with too much naiveté. "All I want is to be with you when Richardson is arrested. Sure hope he doesn't take off until this is over."

"I don't think so. His logic is ruled by his obsession with the Spider Rock treasure."

"Do you believe in those stories?" Wesley studied her as though her response had anything to do with how she worked the investigation.

"Nah. If there ever was a lost cache of gold, I think it was found years ago. And the finder had sense enough to keep his mouth shut."

"Sure seems like a lot of men have died for it. Tell you what: I'm going to walk back and search the far side of the parking lot. Brandt could have ducked between cars."

"Good idea," she said. "I want to talk to those teens. They saw my gun, and I want to explain things." When she glanced toward the small group, she realized she didn't need to waste any time showing her creds. Their imaginations had probably gone berserk.

Carr refused to consider himself a babysitter. But there he was, attempting to calm an overemotional fourteen-year-old and two teenage boys while Bella chased after a possible fugitive with her left shoulder bandaged. At least Wesley was with her. Darren would be proud of his nephew. Roano, on the other hand—or rather, acting Sheriff Roano—would have sent Carr after Bella in hopes Richardson might empty his gun on him. Ever since Roano had blacked Carr's eye, he suspected the man had the potential to put others in danger with his lack of control. *Roano's lack of control?* Carr had come a long way in his climb toward recognizing the height and depth of a man's emotions.

Carr sensed someone behind him. Stanton had climbed down from his perch on the top row. "I saw Rachel hurry out of here and the deputy stop you. Which one of us is going to make sure my daughter is okay?"

"I am." Carr didn't need to venture into a discussion in front of the kids about Bella's resentment toward her father.

By the time Carr located Bella and caught up to her, she and Wesley had parted company, and she approached a small group of teens.

"He vanished." Bella's resentment dripped like a leaky faucet. "I know it was him." She nodded toward the teens. "I need to explain a few things to those kids. They saw my gun."

He listened while she talked to them about her role in the FBI, allowing each of the five to examine her creds. She pulled out business cards from her jean pocket with her uninjured hand. "If you see this man again, please contact me immediately. He's highly dangerous and is wanted for several murders."

The teens were quiet, and Carr supposed they were picturing themselves in some unfolding detective TV drama.

"Ready?" she said to Carr. "We're missing the game."

Once they took a step up the bleachers, Stanton stood and made his way back to the top. Bella didn't say a word. Neither did she turn and toss her father a glance. All Carr could do was pray she soon understood the power of forgiveness.

CHAPTER 45

THE HOUR OF MIDNIGHT fascinated Brandt, the time between night and morning, darkness and light. His mama used to say that nothing good ever happened after midnight. And he'd done all he could to reinforce his mother's theory.

He limped through the sliding glass doors of his hotel room to the private balcony. Mair's snoring and the pain in his knee kept him awake. Sleeping with Yvonne had been more . . . pleasurable. He'd thought long and hard about replacing Mair with her until he had Rachel, but impatience had killed Yvonne. She'd been paid well, but her greed had been the cause of her demise.

No matter. Brandt would have Rachel once he had the gold and got Mair out of the way. She knew too much, and he had no intention of allowing her to hold his past against him. In the beginning, he enjoyed her affections. Then she began reminding him of her sacrifices. Over the years, the nagging and the lines in her face had pushed him to his limit.

Brandt rubbed the throb in his left knee. The late afternoon sprint across the parking lot had cost him plenty. Soon he'd have the knee surgery, but not yet.

Leaning on the metal balcony, he waited for a call from Aros. At 12:41, the room phone rang beside him. He'd dragged it from the nightstand when he couldn't sleep.

"Yes," he said.

"Done," Aros said.

Prudence coursed through his veins in case anyone was able to record their conversation. "Where's the package?"

"Stamped and delivered."

"Good." Brandt ended the call. Time to move on.

CHAPTER 46

BELLA SLOWLY OPENED her eyes. Was that her phone alerting her to a text message? Her gaze flew to the clock radio on the nightstand: 4:00. Yesterday morning had been 4:15 when she climbed out of bed for the drive to Junction. Some days she hated being a light sleeper. Snatching up her phone, she saw Frank wanted her to call him. This could not be good. She quickly pressed in his number on the landline.

"Hi, Frank, what's going on?"

"Yvonne Taylor's body was found outside a bar in Austin. Bullet in her head."

"Oh no." Bella remembered the conversation with Yvonne, hoping the woman would help in the investigation. "Unfortunately, it looks like I was right about her involvement."

"Dead right."

She brushed her hand across her face to sharpen her senses. "How many more will have to die before we catch him?" The memory of the attractive woman who had swallowed Brandt's charms filled her with regret—and anger.

"If she'd come to us, we could have placed her in protective custody."

"Either Brandt followed me that day or she contacted him after my visit. From her expression when I showed her the photos, she recognized one of his disguises. Which confirms that he was the fourth person on the team."

"Bella, do you have any idea who's working with him? Whoever it is has a bird's-eye view of everything we do."

Frank only asked her questions like this when he was fresh out of ideas. "I've suspected Carr, Darren—and he might have been involved, but that means there's someone else. Vic was on my list for a while and Stanton Warick," she said. "Warick has my vote, but he's giving the impression of being an upright citizen."

"I hear the sarcasm."

"Perhaps that's all it is. I'm working from a biased point of view." She let the personalities of those around her settle. "Frank, I appreciate your calling me about Yvonne's death, and I also appreciate your asking me what I think. Yesterday afternoon I asked for a full report on Aros Kemptor, the attorney handling New Hope's legal dealings. A couple of his transactions look suspicious."

"Hadn't heard of him."

"Kemptor may not be his real name. I'll let you know as soon as I learn something."

"What have you found? You know I hate not knowing every detail of an investigation."

"Not sure. It has to do with raising funds for a building project. Carr handed over his mineral rights to the church and willed his ranch to them too. Kemptor is either looking out for numero uno or sincerely interested in growing his church."

"I want that report as soon as you get it."

"I've already asked them to copy you."

Frank sighed, another of his habits when he was changing his topic of conversation. "How are you feeling?"

"Getting stronger every day."

"Ready to move from the High Butte to a hotel?"

No, but how do I explain my reasons? "This location keeps me close to the assignment."

"I can get a two-bedroom suite. No problem."

Not so long ago, she wouldn't have thought twice about such an arrangement. But given her recent decision to draw closer to

Christ, and knowing the standard of purity to which He wanted her to aspire, she didn't feel right about it now.

"I can't stay with you in a hotel room, Frank."

He chuckled. "You don't have any problem staying at the High Butte Ranch with Carr Sullivan."

He had a point. "Jasper and Lydia live here too. Plus Wesley is my bodyguard from seven to seven and another deputy does night duty." She took another breath. "My room is beside Jasper and Lydia's, and Carr's room is upstairs."

"I'm no fool. I see what's going on between you two, and it has nothing to do with the task force or religion."

Four o'clock in the morning was not the right time to discuss personal issues. If there ever was a good time. "Frank, you remember I grew up in church. I never made a decision to follow Christ then, but I have now. No matter how I feel about Carr or you or any other man, I'm not going conduct myself the same way as before."

"Thanks a lot. Good to know our relationship meant nothing to you."

She was starting to feel edgy—real edgy. "That's not fair, and it's definitely not true. What I mean—"

"Never mind. We'll talk about our relationship, or lack of one, when this case is closed. I care enough about you to want the best. Get back with me as soon as you can about Kemptor." He ended the call before she could say another word.

With her mind whirling like an F5 tornado, she climbed out of bed and struggled to slip a robe on over her bandaged arm. Carr had an espresso maker in the kitchen that made single cups of the best coffee in the world. She needed one and could possibly offer a cup to the deputy posted outside the front door. More importantly, she wanted to sort through her notes about Aros Kemptor. The attorney *could* be looking out for the church's best interests. But Bella wanted to find out if he'd taken advantage of other members' financial holdings and mineral rights. As soon as daylight marched across the sky, she'd contact Pastor Kent.

Oops. She'd see him at church this morning. And Aros Kemptor too. For sure, she'd obtain Kemptor's fingerprints. Her first time to church in years and she planned to work on the investigation while worshiping God. Something about that didn't seem reverent.

"Can't sleep?" Lydia's sweet voice brought a smile to Bella's lips. "Or are you planning another escape from the High Butte?"

"No wild morning rides today. Just received a call from Frank."

"Trouble?"

"New information. I need a little caffeine to do some processing."

"Would you like for me to leave you alone?"

Bella remembered Lydia's daughter was the secretary at New Hope's business office. "Actually, you might be able to help me."

"Then I'll put on a whole pot."

A few moments later, the enticing aroma of freshly brewed coffee swirled through the air, and the two sat at the kitchen table in their robes sipping on the most perfect brew known to mankind.

"I have a magnet on my refrigerator that says, 'A morning without coffee is like sleep,'" Bella said.

Lydia rested her chin on her palm. "I agree."

Bella took a breath. "I'd like to talk to your daughter, the one who works at New Hope."

"She's our only daughter." Lydia smiled. "I was wondering when you'd want to talk to her. I assumed since she works for Pastor Kent that you'd want to ask her a few questions."

Smart woman. "Exactly. Does she talk to you about her position at New Hope?"

"Hmm." Lydia handed her a napkin, and Bella placed the spoon on it after she'd stirred more honey into her coffee. "I've heard her say that the devil does his best work in churches."

"Probably so with politics and such. My aunt Debbie says it's impossible for Christians to agree in an argument. Everybody's right because they all prayed about it."

"We must drive God crazy with the way we treat each other. But back to my daughter's position at New Hope. She keeps her views to herself, so I'm not much help. Except I don't want her to know about the threat."

Bella nodded. "Has she ever mentioned Aros Kemptor?"

Lydia shook her head. "I could ask."

"No need. I'll talk to her Monday morning. Wouldn't want to bother her at church."

"Is this a private party?" Carr stood in the doorway. Dressed in jeans and a T-shirt with tousled hair and sleep-laden eyes, he looked . . . well, too appealing. She needed to guard her emotions.

"Sorry to wake you." Bella meant it. She'd put him through a rough time at last night's ball game, and she'd heard him pace the floor above her long after midnight.

"I followed my nose, and the coffee was more enticing than sleep."

"Horsefeathers," Lydia said. "You're nosy."

He proceeded to pour himself a cup of coffee. "I'm a man, and I wanted to make sure that two beautiful women weren't talking about me."

"Men." The lines around Lydia's eyes deepened. "Must it always be about you?"

"Of course." He scooted back a chair and eased into it. He glanced at Bella. "I've been thinking about Aros."

"And?"

"Impossible. No man would spend a year giving away money and volunteering his time and resources unless God was a priority."

Bella took a sip from her mug. "Oh, really? What if he'd planned it that way?"

"Do you suspect every person you come in contact with?" Carr said.

Bella lifted a brow, slightly amused. But she quickly saw his question bordered on irritation. "I suspected you, didn't I?"

He gave her a tight-lipped smile. "You did."

My suspicions really bother him. "Tell me more about Kemptor. Convince me I'm on a rabbit trail. And think about the information he could have given to Brandt about you."

"Nothing points to it. The man has offered me legal advice. And he did not coerce me into giving the church mineral rights or naming New Hope in my will. That was all me. Aros . . ." He stopped. "Maybe not all me."

Good. Carr was thinking through past conversations with the lawyer. "He could have used your generosity to his benefit."

He frowned. "I think you're wrong on this one."

"I'm checking the paperwork tomorrow." She felt the tension. Lydia quietly slipped from the chair and the kitchen and returned to her and Jasper's room. "If he worked for Brandt, then having access to your mineral rights would put them in an advantageous position. They could find the gold and haul it out without anyone knowing. If you caught on to what was happening, then you could be killed, and the ranch would belong to them."

"Then why murder four men—"

"Five, but the fifth is a woman. Daniel Kegley's fiancée."

Carr grimaced. "When did this happen?"

"Frank woke me at four."

He rubbed his palms together, his face grim. "I sure need church this morning."

"So do I." The thought struck her again that worshiping God while gathering fingerprints for a murder investigation might not be exactly what He had in mind. Especially since this would be her first trip to church since becoming a Christian.

"You know Aros will be there," Carr said. "In fact, it's his Sunday to distribute bulletins."

Thank You. "Is he the only one?"

"No. One of the youth will be passing them out too."

"Would you do me a favor?"

When he hesitated, she leaned closer. "This may go a long way in proving Aros innocent or guilty."

"Okay." He breathed out a sigh.

"You take one of his bulletins, and I'll take one from the youth."

"Sneaky, aren't you?" A faint grin met her gaze, and she knew his apprehension had been appeased.

"It's called training."

He took her left hand and kissed it. Not since her days in the hospital had he displayed what she saw in his eyes. "I'll be so glad when this is over. Last night at the ball game scared the daylights out of me. You nearly died on us before, and I didn't want to go through that again. Sounds selfish, I know. But I'm tired of funerals."

"It's my job, Carr. What I do." She placed her other hand over top of his and remembered the flying trip in the ambulance when the calluses on his hands and his audible prayer comforted her. "I know this is difficult for you to understand. The very idea of someone you call a friend being a part of all these murders has to keep you in a panic mode." She remembered Darren, who might have been involved too.

"It's more than that."

She understood what he didn't say. "I think the time has come for me to find somewhere else to stay until arrests are made."

"No way. Here I have some sort of control over your safety. Don't you know how I feel about you by now?"

Bella wished Lydia hadn't left them alone. "Those feelings could put you in danger."

"I don't care."

She desperately needed the right words to convince him of the need to separate. "Aren't you concerned about your reputation—with a single woman as a guest at your home?"

He laughed. "I've been accused of murder. Lydia is here. A deputy is within earshot at all times. Jasper is close by. Frank pops in and out as well. My reputation? You'd better come up with a better excuse than that one, Special Agent Jordan."

"Still, it's a reality." She glanced at the clock. "Can't believe it's six o'clock."

"The youth are having a pancake and sausage breakfast this morning at seven thirty. Proceeds go to church camp."

"I can be ready."

"What about spending the afternoon with me?"

"Doing what?"

"There's an old man who works at the McDonald's in Junction," Carr said. "He likes pretty ladies, and I want to make sure he's not after mine."

Bella caught the twinkle in his eyes. "You've got to be kidding."

"Nope. You said you had more questions for him."

"And if we're followed?"

"I have a one-armed FBI agent to protect me."

If Bella pressured him, she'd probably discover this was a ploy to spend time with her alone. Then again, she did want to ask Shep Wither a few more questions.

CHAPTER 47

BELLA SETTLED BACK in the comfort extraordinaire of Carr's plush truck. She adjusted the seat and the lumbar position, and if she didn't watch it, she'd drift off to sleep. But catching up on rest was postponed until she no longer found it necessary to keep watch through the truck's side mirror.

"I'm sorry Shep wasn't working today or at home," she said.

"Maybe they went to Vegas."

"Doubt it. He and God are pretty tight."

"Uh, but he has a live-in girlfriend."

She tossed him a why-didn't-I-think-of-that look.

Carr laughed. "I've been reading up on my distance-learning FBI training. And I was anxious to evaluate how you handled him—and his girlfriend."

"You would have enjoyed him. Even if you are jealous."

"Ah. Now I know I'll be back. The area reminds me of wanting to drive to the livestock auction in Junction."

What if the only excitement in her life were baseball games, pancake breakfasts, and an occasional livestock auction? Her mind drifted while she continued to focus on the side mirror.

From Junction, the white, rocky hills looked like balding men scattered among mesquite trees. She rolled down her window and smelled the dry air, hinting of another era when air-conditioning was unheard of. She'd spent many an hour as a girl thinking about historical Texas and what it might have been like to live back then.

Bella's mind slipped back in time. She could hear the cattle drivers snapping their whips and calling out to the livestock. *"Rollin', rollin', rollin'. Keep them dogies rollin'."* She inwardly laughed, realizing she was having a good time all by herself. What would Carr say if he could read her musings?

How could she despise a terrain and embrace it at the same time? Memories of the girl who desperately wanted to be loved wrapped around her heart. Would it have been different then if she'd known Christ? Possibly so. Unfortunately, she might have been more easily convinced to obey Dad and marry Brandt.

Her attention focused on the ever-turning windmills pumping water to livestock. Clear blue skies with an occasional puff of a cloud, rising like the smoke from an old man's pipe. She'd forgotten all of this.

They passed huge ranches, many bordered by stone fences that often had fancy gates for the more affluent ranchers. The abundance of stone added to the beauty of homes as the glistening rock exuded natural beauty. The stones had their disadvantages too. Rattlers loved to hide under their coolness, and they also plagued any man wanting to till the ground or a woman who desired a vegetable or flower garden. The realistic person realized the land was good only for cattle, horses, sheep, and goats.

The only thing that bloomed with regularity were wildflowers and the cacti and prickly pear in spring. A few fields held hay and grain, but not many. Those who fancied prickly pear jellies, peppers, and whatever else a creative cook could muster had plenty of produce for the trade. Some ranchers claimed to grow oil— those were the ones who had the money to put back into their land. And any small town worth much to the community had a Dairy Queen, a Sonic, and a camouflage flag waving *Open* for the hunters.

If given a choice, she'd have been a Comanche in this area and pitched her tepee along the Colorado River. Lived out her days keeping her warrior happy and tending to their children. She'd tan deer hide or whatever animal her warrior brought in and never complain about cleaning fish. Sure would beat running down a serial murderer.

"Where are you?" Carr said. "Besides noting every vehicle behind us."

"Daydreaming."

"About us?"

"Don't you wish?" He hadn't been that far off. "Do you like pecan pie? I'm hungry."

He laughed. "I've been tossed aside for a pie. But yes. I own a large pecan orchard in Oklahoma. Want to go there?" He slowed as they entered a small town.

He never ceased to surprise her. "Not today. But it sounds like fun." A large banner stretched across the street and welcomed them with Season's Greetings. "Oh, my goodness. Are those Christmas lights? I didn't notice these the other day."

"Figures," he said. "This is probably where you were talking to me about Aros."

Reality registered. "Thanks for the church bulletin. It's safe in my shoulder bag."

"Your one-hundred-pound purse probably contains land mines."

"Keep thinking that, and we'll do just fine." She noted a Jeep had followed them for the past ten miles or so. "Did you tell anyone where we were going?"

"Only Lydia. The Jeep has your attention too? What if I turn onto the next road?"

"Go for it." She snatched up her cell and phoned the operations center in Houston. "I suspect I'm being followed. Can't read the license plate; I'm—" Her cell no longer had connectivity. "We're on our own."

"Looks like those days of dodging cops while under the influence might have paid off."

She took another look at the Jeep. "That's comforting. Did you outrun them?"

"All but once." Carr turned onto a country road on the left. "I apologize for early this morning. Didn't mean to be so harsh about Aros."

"No problem."

"Kent trusts him, and I do too. But I thought of something during the sermon that I wanted to toss by you. Kent spoke about how King David mourned for those in his army who had betrayed him. Caused me to think about Aros. Kent is a dynamic preacher and counselor. He's a man of vision but not necessarily a man of business. That's why he has surrounded himself with deacons who have the expertise he lacks. However, he has been known to make an inappropriate decision—like all of us."

"What are you trying to say, Carr?"

"Not enough time has elapsed for Aros to present my mineral rights papers to the deacons. On the other hand, would Kent ask him to present anyone's donation? He may want to protect the giver's privacy."

"Fine line of anonymity there. Tomorrow we'll have a better picture of who Aros is and what he represents."

"Impatience is my middle name. How far down this road do we go until we backtrack?"

"Fifteen minutes." Bella's cell phone rang, and she saw the caller was Pete from FIG. "Hey, what's up?"

"Just received an update on Richardson."

Her pulse quickened. "Okay. Bring it on."

"While in Mexico City, he had surgery to repair his vocal cords. From what we've learned, his voice is now normal."

"Thanks. I appreciate this. I'd already figured out that he'd had surgery, and this verifies it. I'll get the info out to the task force." She ended the call and hit speed dial for Frank. While she waited for him to answer, she glanced at Carr. "I'll explain as soon as I talk to Frank."

What if Brandt had said he was Higgins when he met with the old man in Junction? Wither needed round-the-clock protection. Preferably a trip out of Junction. Two items to talk over with Frank.

CHAPTER 48

BRANDT WAITED at a turnoff for Sullivan and Rachel to drive by. He could easily play their game. When they were onto him following them again, he'd quit. His interest had been in why they'd driven to Junction, and it soured him to see they wanted to talk to Shep Wither. By the old man's not working today and not being at home, Brandt had bought time. Higgins had done all of the work and secured the map, but Wither knew the exact location, and he'd tell Rachel and Sullivan. No point speculating how they found out about Wither. The information could have come from a list of locals. However, the time had come for the old man to meet his Maker.

Instead of following Sullivan, he'd drive back to Junction and explore the sights.

Flipping on the radio, he tuned to an old country-western station, then turned the Jeep around. Twenty minutes down the road, his cell phone rang. Recognizing the caller, he made a quick decision not to respond and let the call go to voice mail. Once the message was recorded, Brandt listened.

"Thought you needed to know. New update. FBI is onto your throat surgery in Mexico City. They've also placed Shep Wither under their protection."

Brandt cursed. *Not if I get to him first.*

CHAPTER 49

BELLA WATCHED THE COUNTRYSIDE as Carr drove up 83 toward Ballinger. The flatter the land, the less vegetation, and the stubby trees became more like brush while the grasses faded to brown. Good old Texas. The terrain could change in the blinking of an eye. She could see over the flat plains for miles with narrow rock and dirt county roads breaking the landscape. All the while, her mind twisted with where she'd made errors in the murder investigation.

Brandt had acquired a limp. Was it a disguise or an injury? And Professor Miller's journal indicated the man who called himself Morton also limped. She e-mailed Pete from her BlackBerry and asked him to search out the possibility of an injury. Great, they were out of range; but the message would be sent soon. Oh, the frustrations of West Texas.

"If Brandt really has a limp, there lies the answer to why he didn't walk from the road to the murder victims," Bella said.

Carr blinked. Their last thread of communication had been about the Jeep, which had disappeared. Then Kent's announcement about Darren's burial on Thursday afternoon, now that his body had been released.

Bella realized her less-than-stellar mode of changing conversation topics.

"True. He may not have wanted to drive so he could enter the area undetected."

"All theories," she said, more than a little frustrated. "A jigsaw puzzle is never easy when you don't have the corner pieces."

"You have to try each piece to make sure it fits."

She hesitated, but urgency had taken hold. "Do you know where Lydia and Jasper's daughter lives?"

"Sure. You want to swing by there?"

"I do. This is starting to gel, and I need more information. Naturally it's not protocol."

He raised a brow, and she laughed.

"Agents are not to conduct interviews alone. However, I have a tendency to bend the rules. But since you're with me, I'll call the operations center as soon as I have cell coverage and report in."

"And what will you tell them?"

"Are you worried?"

"Nope. Just curious."

She hesitated, waiting to see if he pursued his curiosity.

"I'm waiting."

She laughed. "I just need to give them stats—the who, what, where, when, and how long stuff. Then when we leave, I'll phone in again. The rule is 'a good agent doesn't put herself in jeopardy.'"

Two hours later, Bella and Carr sat in the living room of Lydia and Jasper's daughter, Wanda, drinking pink lemonade and waiting for her high-school-age twin daughters to leave for a barbecue. When the twins' car pulled away onto the road, Bella didn't waste any time.

"This is not a social call," Bella said.

"I figured as much," Wanda said, a mirror likeness of her mother. "You're FBI and working on the series of murders."

"Right. I have a couple of questions about one of the members of New Hope."

Wanda frowned. "Do I have a choice?"

"That tells me you already know who I'm going to ask about."

Wanda shrugged. "Maybe. Simply makes me nervous—the girls and all."

Bella well understood her apprehension, and Wanda didn't know about Yvonne Taylor. "I hope you choose to cooperate. Runnels County is due for some well-deserved peace. I'm looking for information about Aros Kemptor."

Wanda stiffened, her tanned face tense. "He's the church's attorney."

"Wanda," Carr began in his typical gentle manner, "there's more here at stake than your obvious skepticism about Aros."

"I know." Her voice cracked.

Bella understood the woman's trepidation. Wanda's pale face left no doubt as to her fright. "Anything you say is confidential. But the murderer has to be stopped."

Wanda stood from the beige sofa, took a deep breath, and then seated herself again. "I don't trust him."

"Why?" Bella moved to the sofa and took the woman's hand. She had more of a desire to comfort Wanda than to secure the information. A new revelation about herself.

"Too secretive. And Pastor Kent is much too trusting." She moistened her lips. "When I heard from Pastor Kent about Carr giving up his mineral rights for the building project, I suggested to him that the deacons see Aros's paperwork. Kent agreed and stated he hadn't seen it either. Later I heard Aros claimed the paperwork had already been filed with the county and was unavailable. I'm not a fancy lawyer, but that didn't sound right to me unless Aros had something to hide."

"If it's been filed, we have access to it." Bella patted her hand.

"I know, which also made me question Aros's objection," Wanda said. "I'd planned to check it out at the courthouse this week on my lunch hour. I know Pastor Kent thinks Aros is wonderful—and maybe so—but I don't."

"Thank you," Bella said. "You've been really helpful. Tomorrow we'll have answers."

"Can you call me?" Wanda said. "If Aros has done something

illegal with Carr's paperwork, then he may be misleading Pastor Kent about other things."

"Certainly." Bella glanced at Carr. "One of us will keep you informed. And I don't think it's necessary to let anyone know about our discussion."

"Trust me, I won't. Except my husband. He already knows I don't care for the man." Wanda lifted her chin like Bella had seen Lydia do.

"We'll leave you to your Sunday evening." Bella saw Wanda's face was still pale. "Do we need to talk to your husband?"

"Not at all. He went to see a friend who hasn't been at church recently. Should be home anytime."

★ ★ ★

"My plans for you to have a relaxing afternoon sure went by the wayside," Carr said as he turned out of Ballinger toward the High Butte.

"I *am* tired," she said.

"How about exhausted? A few days ago you were battling for your life, and now you're chasing criminals."

She laughed. "I'm running on pure adrenaline. But we're getting closer to finding the murderer."

"Could be tomorrow." Oh, how he wished so.

"We always say that: tomorrow." She breathed out a sigh. "Remind me to call Frank again before I give in to sleep."

"Better do it now. You're fading like a three-day-old rose."

Bella adjusted the truck seat to an upright position. "You make sense, and my shoulder is killing me—pardon the description."

"Good. Because I have a few things to say to you." When the moment came when he could kiss her, she'd better be ready.

"Frank's already noticed our relationship."

He sobered. Frank had not hidden his caring for Bella, but Carr had ignored it. "Am I in trouble?"

"I don't think so. We dated for a while. I ended it, and he's still pursuing a relationship. Remember? You and I aren't having this discussion until the investigation is over."

"Right. We're only thinking about it."

"I refuse to comment."

"Yes, ma'am." He'd waited all his life for a woman like Bella, and he'd wait a whole lot longer.

Reality always had a way of restraining his emotions. Lately the fear racing through the community seemed to have no end. But today had been a turn for the best. Maybe they were closing in on the root of the evil. At least Carr hoped so.

CHAPTER 50

THAT NIGHT Bella crawled into bed, bone tired and aching all over. The clock read 8:03, but she didn't care. The blinds were closed, and the bed was calling her name. She'd skipped dinner, promising Lydia and Carr she'd devour a full breakfast in the morning.

The day had zapped the last ounce of her energy—well, perhaps the past several days had contributed to the depletion. Closing her eyes, she prayed for God to protect those she loved and for the murderer to be found soon, along with his accomplices. Her mind started to drift when her BlackBerry buzzed a text. She groaned and opted to read it in the morning. This was what had started her day at 4 a.m. But old habits were hard to break, and she decided to take a quick look. *Are you free to talk? Anne.* With a shake of her head, Bella picked up the landline.

"Hi, Anne. You wanted me to call?"

"Are you in bed?"

"Yes, but it's okay. Even FBI agents need their beauty rest."

"I can talk to you tomorrow."

"Nope. You have your big sis's attention, and I'd rather talk to you than sleep."

"I just wanted to say thanks for letting us visit you and get to know you."

Guilt assaulted Bella. "I should have made an effort a long time ago."

"Daddy said for us not to bother you until you were ready 'cause he wasn't a good father."

"He told you that?"

"Oh yeah. He never lets us forget he wasn't following Jesus back then. Sometimes he goes overboard with it."

Bella chose to keep her sentiments to herself. "I really want to be a part of your and your brothers' lives."

"Cool. Does that mean you're going to move back?"

"Not exactly. I thought maybe you and your brothers would want to move to Houston with me."

"Why? Our home is here. And Daddy only knows ranching."

Bella had no intentions of providing a home for her father. "He could stay here. Houston has lots to offer growing teens."

"But this is our home. Wouldn't it be easier for you to live here? I don't want to leave Daddy until I go to college."

Bella sensed her spirit crushing around her. Anne would rather live in this dirt and grit with their father? "Would you think about it?"

"Oh, Rachel. There's nothing to think about. This is home, and I love it here."

"Okay." Bella didn't want to upset Anne. "Are you babysitting tomorrow?"

"Uh-huh. Gotta be there at six thirty. But the little boys don't wake up until eight thirty."

"What do you do for those two hours?"

"Fix them breakfast. Get crafts ready. Pick out books. Things like that."

Bella loved the sound of Anne's voice, the hope and expectations of a young girl who was excited about her future. But Bella could give her and her brothers so much more—education, entertainment, diversity in friends. How could she make them see that they were better off without their father? One of these days, he'd turn on them, and then all four would be hurt. Perhaps irrevocably. She had to persuade them to leave with her, and time was running out.

CHAPTER 51

On Monday morning, Bella wiggled into her jeans and a loose-fitting shirt to take the church bulletin to the sheriff's department for fingerprinting. The fingerprinting examiners would have to take elimination prints from Carr to rule out his involvement and focus on Kemptor. The bandage around her shoulder made showering and dressing difficult, plus the wound still hurt. Forget the pain meds. She needed all of her mental faculties. With the baby Glock at her ankle and the larger Glock tucked in her waistband, she made her way to the kitchen and the wafting smell of coffee.

Once she received the results of Aros Kemptor's fingerprints and Pete's report about him from the FIG, she'd plan the rest of the day. Even if Aros wasn't working with Brandt, he could be cheating the church out of their building fund.

"Whoa." Carr startled when she entered the kitchen. "You're on a mission this morning. It's all over your face, and my guess is your peacemaker is tucked into the back of your jeans."

Smarty. "Might be in your best interest to remember I'm heavily armed and dangerous."

"I'll be your driver so you can fight crime." He had her coffee ready, and one sip told her he'd added a teaspoon of honey. "And I have the keys."

Bella wrapped her fingers around the much-needed brew and directed her words to Lydia. "Is he always this bossy?"

"I'm worse. And he needs to be behind the wheel. Friday scared us all. Wesley wanted to send someone after you, but none of us knew where you'd gone or who to call."

Bella laughed. "I think the High Butte Ranch and Resort has turned into a detention center."

"And don't you forget it." Carr tossed a grin. "I'm thinking about investing in ankle shackles. So what else is on today's agenda?"

She stared into her cup of coffee, black and strong like the hold the killer had on the community. "Depends on what we learn. While we're waiting for the fingerprint check, I'd like to talk to Pastor Kent. Oh, and I'd like to get a list of New Hope's church members."

"I have a list," Carr said. "I'll print it out now while you're having breakfast. By the way, the cinnamon rolls are great this morning. And you didn't eat last night."

She'd smelled the cinnamon and butter combo earlier, but her mind was elsewhere. Working to solve the murders was at the top of her priorities, not breakfast. Those she loved and cared about had been affected, and when she remembered how Darren had been poisoned and how Yvonne had been shot in the head, she wanted the killer found today.

Her brothers and sister were more involved than she wanted to admit. Mair had left them for Brandt, which meant she didn't care what happened to them. No safety net there. He could use any of them to persuade Bella to resign from the case, and Swartzer had indicated that possibility. *I've got to find Brandt and end this rash of killings.*

Too many innocent people had fallen under Brandt's treachery. Some she knew only by name or how they'd died. But she'd give more of her own blood before another victim fell prey to Brandt's insatiable appetite for lost treasure.

Wesley knocked at the back door, breaking her thoughts. Lydia invited him inside with her typical "Breakfast is ready" greeting.

"Mornin', Lydia," he said. "Is Bella where I can talk to her?"

"Right here drinking up your coffee," Bella said. "So you'd better hurry and get some before I finish the pot." She wished she could sound more welcoming, but too much weighed on her mind.

Wesley stopped in the doorway, his gaze capturing her attention. "I heard there's been a fifth murder."

"You heard right." She slid into a chair at the table. "Brandt Richardson is making his rounds. The victim was Yvonne Taylor, Daniel Kegley's fiancée."

"This has gotten crazy," Wesley said. "Do you know why?"

Bella took a sideways glance at Lydia. The dear woman had already heard so much about the investigation. Plus she'd been threatened. But she was strong.

"I interviewed Yvonne almost two weeks ago about the case. She mentioned a fourth man who met with the three murdered victims, but she said he didn't resemble any of the photos we have of Brandt. At the time, I suspected she knew more than what she was telling. From the looks of things, she must have recognized him."

Wesley leaned against the wall. "Makes me wonder who else is behind these killings."

In Wesley's eagerness, would he be the next victim? "Brandt has help. He's quite the manipulator."

"What kind of a lowlife would fall for his bull?" His young face reflected his hatred. "He'd better hope I don't get to him first. I don't know who wants to see him dead the most, me or Roano."

"Keep your head, Wesley." Bella didn't want to lose another friend. "The task force works together." She needed to remind herself of the same thing.

"Uncle Darren taught me well. In case you've forgotten, he was poisoned."

"None of us have forgotten. And every day that goes by increases the likelihood of the killer deciding it's too hot to stay around here."

"He won't without the treasure, and he can't dig at night. We'd see the lights."

"Who knows? If we could figure out how his mind works, then we'd have him." She forced a smile. "Am I shoving my bad mood your way?"

"Nope. It's already there." Wesley took a chair across the table from her. "I also heard Professor Miller's wife turned in his journal. Did the contents help?"

"Nothing there. But I'm running a lead this morning." She held up her hand to stop any more questions. "Can't discuss it right now, but I'll let you know as soon as I have verification on a set of fingerprints."

The moment Carr entered the sheriff's office with Bella, he felt the chill, like stepping into a freezer. Folks new to rural areas always had a hard time fitting in. Some never made the grade. But at this rate, Carr was going to have to hire his own bodyguard to protect himself from the local sheriff's department.

Sheriff Roano leaned back in his chair. "Mornin', Sullivan. Are you here to turn yourself in?"

The next election could not come soon enough. "Old joke, Roano," Carr said.

"Sheriff Roano to you."

I'm behaving as immaturely as he is. "All of us want the murderer found. I'm out to do what I can to help the task force, just like you." How many times did he need to repeat those words?

Roano moistened his lips and took a deep breath. "But you're still my number one suspect. And don't forget it."

Carr chose not to respond verbally or physically. Instead, he'd wait until Roano discovered the real killer.

Roano nodded at Bella. "Glad to get your call this morning. Let's see what you've got and how we can help."

"Fingerprint check and then we'll go from there. I also need to talk to Pastor Kent Matthews."

"He was here earlier. Left his cell phone on my desk, so I doubt if you can reach him." Roano picked up the slim cell phone. "He'll stop back later when he realizes it's missing."

Carr studied Roano. Many times he'd wondered about his loyalty. Since Darren's death, the newly appointed sheriff had made sure half the town knew he suspected Carr Sullivan. Even when Roano blacked his eye, Carr questioned if his grief and revenge were a ploy to throw off any evidence that he was involved in the murders. He still remembered Roano's words. *"You might think you got away with murdering Darren, but I'm smarter than you. You're now a part of the curse."*

★ ★ ★

Within the hour at the sheriff's office, Bella had her answer about Aros Kemptor's fingerprints. She snatched up her phone and speed-dialed Swartzer in Houston.

"I thought you were recovering," he said.

"Soon. I've too much at stake in this."

"Out-of-control emotions can get you killed."

But she had her training and her faith. "I'm being careful, and Frank is hovering over me like a mama. I've got a new development."

"Let's hear it."

"On Saturday, I talked to an attorney by the name of Aros Kemptor out of Abilene, who I suspect is involved in these murders. I lifted his fingerprints and found they matched Professor

Howard MacGregor, who taught law at the University of Texas until about eighteen months ago, when he disappeared. He was associated with Brandt and the Spider Rock treasure. He didn't leave a forwarding address in Austin. Frank and I are putting together a team to pick him up for suspicion of murder."

"Call me once he's arrested. Do I need to have you arrested in order to get you well?"

Bella hoped he wasn't serious, and she wasn't about to quit when they were so close to apprehending Brandt. "Give me a little longer. Kemptor doesn't seem like the type who'll go down without leading us to Brandt."

"I agree, and we need him in custody. Got a lead on Mair in Waco. I'll get back with you on that. Probably notify the Dallas office to pick her up."

For the first time in her career, Bella thanked God for the leads in solving the murders. She asked Him to protect her team and to lead them to those involved in the crimes. The more she trusted God, the more peace filled her. What a great equation.

Bella made her way to Roano's vehicle. With her bandaged arm, she needed the sheriff to drive her to Abilene to join Frank and Abilene's police department in arresting MacGregor. Roano would then return to Ballinger. Carr opened the passenger door. She understood his trepidation. If the situation were turned around, she'd want to accompany him too. "I'll call later."

"I know. Be careful." His eyes betrayed his feelings for her.

"This is my job." Did he hear what she could not say?

"A part of your life that scares most of us."

"Oh, but it sure gets the adrenaline going." She plunged forward. "Would you check on the kids? make sure they're okay?"

He touched her arm. "Whatever it takes."

"Gotta get going. Frank's waiting with Abilene PD." Maybe someday they could talk about what they really meant.

CHAPTER 52

BRANDT SKIMMED A STONE across the creek and watched the ripples spread farther and farther. Effortlessly. Like this last hurdle of obtaining the treasure and joining Rachel so the two could spend the rest of their lives together. Brandt needed to grease up Aros's pace so the digging could begin. The weasel thought he had the edge with the mineral rights and Sullivan's will. But Brandt knew the exact location at the butte, and he had Shep Wither's map. Stupid old man, as if Brandt ever had any intentions of handing over a cent of the gold to anyone.

However, keeping one step ahead of the FBI had begun to wear on him. His left knee burned when he walked, and the surgery couldn't be postponed much longer. If he could trust Aros, he'd slip down to Mexico City for a while and have it taken care of. But that was impossible.

The estate in Brazil had cost over two million dollars, but it was ready for Bella. She'd be so pleased. Ten thousand square feet of luxury—everything she'd ever want. They'd be happy there.

Brandt's cell phone rang. The caller was unknown.

"We've got problems."

Brandt recognized the voice. "Give it to me."

"Aros's fingerprints have been traced to MacGregor. Bella and Frank are on their way to arrest him. Abilene police are assisting."

"Have you called him?"

"Yes. He's left the office and is on his way to the hotel."

"He'll name all of us. You'd better get to him first."

"I've been on the road since I saw the fingerprint check. I'm on it."

Brandt refused to let this go south, not when he'd staked the last two decades of his life on it. "Call me when you're done. We need insurance."

"Which one of them?"

"Anne. Just keep an eye on her."

"What about Mair?"

"I'll handle her."

CHAPTER 53

BY THE TIME Bella and Frank arrived at Aros's office on the south side of Abilene, police and SWAT had staked out a perimeter around the building. The law enforcement officers waited for a signal from her and Frank to enter the premises. MacGregor had not been involved with anything illegal prior to his association with Brandt, which meant no one knew how he'd react to an arrest.

"You're still the lead in this investigation," Frank said.

"Don't think so. Go for it."

"Sorry. You worked him. You charge him."

Being near the end did have a lot of satisfaction. "We need him alive," she said as the two stepped from opposite sides of the car.

They made their way with several members of the police force inside the black-glass building and up to the third floor housing Aros Kemptor's law firm. She expected a locked door, but Frank had his own method of opening inaccessible areas. A barren office greeted them. Nothing but furniture. Even an empty trash can.

"Let's check with the security guard in the parking garage." Disappointment diminished her expectations to conclude the investigation. "And I want a sweep of this office. Someone notified Aros within minutes of the fingerprint confirmation for Howard MacGregor.

"Only a handful of people knew about this," she said to Frank.

"That should narrow it down—Roano, the four or so deputies inside the sheriff's office, Carr, you, and me."

She studied Frank. In the heat, his sunglasses had slipped down his nose. "You forgot Kent Matthews. No man is ever beyond being seduced by money."

"I'll call for a report on him."

"Make it fast." The thought of Kent's possible involvement would upset a lot of people in the community.

Patience was not one of Carr's finest traits. He'd paced his library, the kitchen, the back porch, and now the stables. How long did it take to arrest a man? Over four hours had passed since Bella had left Ballinger. His head rang with all the possibilities of what could be happening, interrupted by flashes of *Why aren't you trusting God?* Bella had taken the lead on this investigation for two reasons: her abilities as an FBI agent and her familiarity with the case. She had Frank with her and Abilene's police force. This was candy. Then why was he twisted in apprehension?

Bella hadn't called, and the news sites carrying the latest happenings in Abilene were void of any FBI arrests. Twice he'd fished his cell phone from his pants pocket to call or text her, but he could be putting her in danger.

"You doing all right?" Wesley leaned against the side of the stable door, his lanky frame blocking the sun streaming through.

"Hardly. Wish someone would call."

"Roano is as antsy as you are." He made his way toward Carr, his boots tapping on the concrete. "I'm as shocked as everyone else. Aros Kemptor spilled a lot of money into this community."

"Looks like he had reasons." Now Carr understood why Aros had attempted to deter him from probing into the Spider Rock treasure and manipulate him into giving up mineral rights. And then there was the matter of his will. "My hope is he spills his guts about Richardson."

"If he doesn't, he could be charged with four counts of murder—and that's just for starters. He nearly killed Bella and shot you. So many times today I wanted to be out looking for him, but I understand my responsibilities."

Carr briefly recalled all that had happened since the Monday afternoon he and Jasper found the dead bodies. "I appreciate you, Wesley. Darren was proud of all your accomplishments."

The young deputy smiled. "All our lives have been on hold while we wait for this to end."

"Yeah. Soon. Maybe right now."

"Oh, I nearly forgot what I came out here for. Lydia got back with groceries and wonders what you want for dinner tonight."

His appetite had left him early this morning. "I'll help her put things away. Gives me something to do."

"All right. I have a phone call to make, and then I'll be right there."

Carr made his way across the yard to the back porch and inside the house. Wesley must have already carried the groceries inside. At least Carr could help her while they all waited to hear from Bella.

Lydia had already separated pantry items from the food that would be stored in the refrigerator and freezer. If he could only be as organized. "Point me in the right direction," he said as lightly as possible.

She glanced up, pale. Sometimes he forgot she'd been threatened and how that must be constantly on her mind. "Pantry items. The shelves are labeled. Have you heard from Bella?"

"Not yet."

"Hopefully soon. Do you have any requests for dinner?"

"I don't think either of us is hungry." He gathered up a handful of items and carried them into the walk-in pantry that was more like the size of a small bedroom. He sorted through her dry goods and noted a large box of specialty chocolates. "Who's the candy for?"

"Wesley loves Godiva," Lydia said. "I make sure I have a stash for him. Poor guy. Having to stand over an old woman all day has to be boring. The least I can do is supply his favorite chocolate."

Chill bumps raced up Carr's arms. *The candy wrapper found at the beginning of the investigation that had Darren's fingerprints on it.* The same brand. Surely not. Paranoia had attacked his logic. This was a coincidence and nothing more. Darren could have seen Wesley's interest in the chocolate and had one himself. He'd ask Wesley about it later.

"Where was Wesley earlier? I saw one of the other deputies when I came back from Ballinger." Carr stepped out of the pantry, his thoughts racing.

Lydia opened the refrigerator and placed carrots and parsnips inside the vegetable crisper. "Said he needed to purchase an engagement ring for his girlfriend. Guess he works during the store's normal working hours."

"I'll have to congratulate him."

"Oh, he asked me to keep the information to myself until her family has an opportunity to make the announcement."

Less than a month ago, Darren said Wesley complained about the lack of girls around Ballinger. Carr swallowed his fears. What a joke. Darren's nephew involved with something illegal? No way. Wesley was rock solid. Had been for a long time.

"Sure glad that nephew of mine changed his outlook on life," Darren had said.

Carr recalled Darren telling him about Wesley's habits prior to Carr's move to the High Butte. *"Underage and always in trouble. Once that boy hit the age of fourteen, he didn't have a lick of sense."* According to Darren, the local police couldn't prove Wesley had been involved in a convenience store robbery, but they strongly suspected him. Drinking became a problem as well as fighting.

That's when Darren stepped in and helped Wesley make some changes.

Taking a deep breath, Carr remembered his own failings. God had picked him up, dusted him off, and sent him on his way with a new purpose. Much like Darren had done for Wesley. But as much as Carr tried to shove away the nagging thoughts about Wesley, the thoughts persisted.

Darren trusted Wesley. Loved him like his own son.

Wesley had access to all of the task force's communications.

Where was Wesley when Bella's tires were shot out?

Where was Wesley when Bella and he were shot?

Where was Wesley when the rattler was placed in the hotel room?

Where was Wesley when Darren was poisoned?

Who could have stolen Carr's rifle and then later returned it?

Wesley had been present at Zack's baseball game. Had even called his replacement for Lydia because he had a hunch about Richardson attending the game.

And where was Wesley earlier today?

The morning of his death, Darren was concerned about something regarding the case, and he hoped he was wrong. Later he told Carr that "it" was worse than he expected.

Or was Carr nuts? He didn't have anyone to call about his qualms except Roano. And knowing him, he'd toss Carr's concerns. He finished putting the pantry items away and waited. If Aros or MacGregor—whatever his name was—had been picked up and Wesley was implicated, it would be only a matter of time before Bella and Frank made their way to the High Butte for another arrest.

In the meantime, Carr would write down his every thought and lock it in his safe.

CHAPTER 54

BELLA AND FRANK drank double espressos while they tossed back and forth where Howard MacGregor could have gone. He hadn't booked a flight out of Abilene, Austin, or Houston. For certain an informant had warned him about the FBI, which meant he'd left by car. Except the authorities hadn't been able to locate it.

Most likely Brandt had arranged for his death. The race sped on as to who would get to MacGregor first.

"I need to call Carr," she said.

Frank lifted a brow.

"You already phoned Roano. This is a courtesy call."

"Right." Frank's surly attitude was about to rub off on her.

"Swartzer is doing all he can, and the Abilene police are chasing down a few clues."

"Right. So call Carr."

She didn't want to discuss their personal relationship right now. But Carr did have a right to an update. He answered on the first ring.

"You have MacGregor in custody?" Carr said.

"Nope. He's gone. We're following up on a few things now." Not exactly. They were sitting in a Starbucks—regrouping.

"Are you headed this way?"

"I know you're anxious, but we can't leave without some answers."

"This is different. I have a few . . . suspicions or conclusions to discuss with you and Frank."

Her pulse sped into air travel. "What's happened?"

"Maybe nothing. Maybe a lot."

"Are you in danger?"

"I don't think so."

"Wesley's there."

"Uh-huh."

She relaxed. "If you think this is serious, we'll wrap this up and drive your way."

He blew out a long breath. "If what I'm thinking is a false alarm, I'm going to feel stupid. MacGregor is the real thing. This is . . . speculation."

Bella noted Frank was following the conversation the best he could. Then his phone rang. "It's Abilene PD," he said. "They've located MacGregor's car outside a hotel."

"Carr, I gotta run. Talk to you later." She ended the call and snatched up her shoulder bag.

Fifteen minutes later, Bella and Frank approached a hotel door where Howard MacGregor was supposed to be. This time the hotel manager had given them a key. "Howard MacGregor, this is the FBI. You are under arrest. Open the door," Bella said.

When he didn't respond, she handed Frank the key. Weapons ready, he opened the door and swung it wide.

The room reeked of vomit. MacGregor lay facedown on the bed, his face in a puddle of his own excretion. The memory of how Darren had died crept across her mind.

Frank felt the man's neck for a pulse. "He's dead."

"A wild guess here says it's thanatoxin." She studied the room and the bathroom. A half glass of water was by the sink. "It may be in that," she pointed.

Another body.

Number six.

★ ★ ★

Carr took a chance. What did he have to lose? Bella and Frank were driving back from Abilene and would be at the High Butte by early evening. The man he'd known as Aros Kemptor was dead. Wesley sat on the back porch reading yesterday's paper from Abilene—at least that was his normal habit. Time to mosey on down from the library and be friendly-like, as the locals said. He put the landline on Do Not Disturb since Lydia had opted for a nap—her usual way of handling stress—and Jasper was riding fence, which was where Carr should be.

Turning his cell phone ringer off, he snatched up a pitcher of lemonade and two glasses on his way through the kitchen and stepped onto the back porch.

"Are you as bored as I am?" Carr set the pitcher and glasses on the table.

Wesley let the newspaper rest on his lap and rubbed his eyes. "By this time of the afternoon, I'm ready to call it quits. And day-old news doesn't cut it."

Carr poured them a glass of lemonade. "This is the strongest I can offer."

"No problem. I'll have a cold beer when my shift's over." He wrapped his fingers around the glass. "Sure is a shame about Aros."

"I liked the guy. Never had a clue he was working with Brandt Richardson."

"You don't think he was working alone?"

Carr kept his gaze focused on Wesley and sat down across from him. "Not at all. Neither does the FBI. Heard Aros made some accusations before he died."

"What did he say?"

"According to Bella, he named who else was working with him."

Wesley took a long drink. "I wonder who."

"Beats me, but they're finishing up in Abilene and then on their way here." Carr *hoped* they were on their way to the High Butte.

"Too bad my shift is over early today. I'd like to hear about it."

"Won't Roano give you the information? But I can call if you like."

"That would be good. Sometimes Roano is slow."

Carr settled back into the chair and crossed his legs. He peered at Wesley's feet. "Boy, you got some big feet going there."

"Got those from my daddy. Size thirteen."

Bella stated the boot print found near the candy wrapper was a size thirteen. "Are your folks living? Never heard you mention them."

"Mom is. Dad died of a heart attack when I was eleven."

"Is that when Darren took over?"

"Not until later."

"Darren told me once you were spiraling down a twisted path for a while."

"Oh yeah. Once my dad was out of the picture, I didn't care what I did or who I hurt. Uncle Darren got me on the right road."

"I'm glad. He has you and his sons as a part of his legacy."

Wesley flinched, and Carr saw it. "At one time when Mom remarried, I was supposed to live with Darren and Tiffany, but she didn't want me around her kids."

"I'm sure she had good reasons. But look how well you've done."

"Tell her that."

"Sorry to hear there were problems."

"Uncle Darren took her word for everything. Happened a long time ago, but it still fries my rear. She was afraid I'd get my hands on her family's money."

"Well, seems to me you proved her wrong." Carr smiled and finished his lemonade. Once the two talked a few more minutes, he excused himself to place a call to Tiffany Adams.

CHAPTER 55

BELLA HAD STEPPED over the threshold of cranky into the realm of wanting to tear something—anything—apart with her bare hands. Brandt had left another body for them to uncover, and Howard MacGregor had been working for him under the name of Aros Kemptor.

She massaged the back of her neck as though it would give her clarity of thought. Staring at Frank as he drove toward Ballinger, she wondered how he could look so calm. "This just gets worse and worse."

"We have to be getting close or MacGregor wouldn't be dead. Brandt didn't trust him to keep his mouth shut."

"Carr has a suspect."

Frank's attention swung to her. "Since when?"

"When he called earlier. Remember?"

"Who?"

"Said he'd tell us when we got there."

Frank pressed his lips together, then nodded at her. "Let's hope he's still alive."

Bella's stomach flipped. "I think he was simply speculating. You know Carr. He's always trying to help. Wesley's there, Mr. Andy of Mayberry himself." She pulled out her phone and pressed in Carr's number. The phone rang four times and went to voice mail. "Carr, call me. Frank and I want to know what you're thinking."

"Does this happen often?" Frank said.

"He normally answers on the first or second ring." She shivered, and it had nothing to do with the air-conditioning in Frank's car. "It's a first."

"Try again."

When Carr didn't respond to her second call, she phoned the landline. "Oh, I'm getting a text."

★ ★ ★

"Did Tiffany give you an earful?" Wesley leaned against the library's doorway, his 9mm aimed at Carr's chest.

Carr's presumption had been right. But this wasn't how he wanted to find out who murdered Darren. *Lydia, stay asleep.* "All this time, we thought you and Darren were closer than father and son."

"Hated that man. Hated his wife more."

"But he tried to help."

"Oh yeah, by doubling my community service over and above what the judge dished out. Lecturing me for hours about right and wrong. Making me go to church. Giving me curfews when I was eighteen years old." Wesley shrugged. "I got even, though."

"You've been busy."

"I have."

"Was it worth it?"

Wesley smirked. "What do you think?"

Keep him talking. "Got to hand it to you. How did you trick him?"

Wesley stepped into the room and closed the door. "Doesn't matter now since I'm about to shoot you in self-defense."

Carr didn't move a muscle. Wesley didn't need an excuse to pump a bullet into him. And he was right. No one would doubt his integrity for shooting a suspect in self-defense.

"I followed dear Uncle Darren that morning," Wesley said.

"We'd had words the night before, and I knew he'd suspected me of working with Aros. Especially when he caught me meeting with him after my shift on the west side of the High Butte. Anyway, I pulled off to the side of the road and parked where I knew he'd see me. It was a gamble, but it paid off. I had other plans if that didn't work. When he drove by, I waved. Good old Uncle Darfen turned back around and parked beside me. I apologized for taking the case into my own hands and consulting Aros about the possibility of your guilt. Then I offered to buy him a cup of coffee. Told him I appreciated him and all he'd done for me. He agreed to the coffee, and I whipped my car back into town, bought a cup at the convenience store, and dropped the poison into it." He laughed. "I even offered him another candy bar, which had been my first thought of where to place the poison. But he played right into my hands that morning."

Someone had to have seen Wesley at the convenience store. "So you and Aros were working together?"

"Were." Wesley snickered. "We had our areas of expertise."

Carr shook his head. Time. He needed more time. "Who else?"

He laughed. "I have no idea."

"Who killed the three men at the butte?"

"You can figure that one out yourself."

"Richardson or Stanton Warick?"

"Warick? Are you kidding? He's a Bible-thumper. Worthless. Wouldn't waste my time on him."

"Did you shoot out Bella's tires?"

"Shut up. You've heard enough."

"You're one smart man, Wesley."

"And I'm about to be a rich one too."

From the way Wesley narrowed his eyes, Carr realized the man's patience was dangerously thin. "Are you sure Richardson is going to let you live to spend any of the money?"

"I'm following his instructions and doing exactly what I'm told."

"Even this one?"

Wesley nodded slowly. "Open your bottom desk drawer on the left, nice and easy. Inside is a revolver."

Carr slowly pulled on the drawer. There it was. Another one of his guns from his supposedly locked case, a Colt .45. The weapon gleamed wickedly at him.

"I had lots of time to figure out where things are kept. Thought about planting the poison, but Richardson didn't like the idea. Lydia told me where you kept the key to your gun cabinet. Stupid woman."

Now it had all come together. "How much are you getting paid for this?"

"Plenty. And I'm going to be the local hero. Pick up the gun. It's not loaded. I'll take care of that part later."

"You have a problem. Modern technology will show a discrepancy. You shoot me; then you load my gun. What happens if Lydia or Jasper hear you?"

"Jasper is gone and Lydia is about to get herself killed by her trusted boss. If I had thoughts of staying around this dust bowl, I could end up as sheriff."

"Or you could end up on death row."

"I need less than two minutes to pull this off."

Carr leaned onto his arms on his desk. Time was running out, but he had nothing left to stall Wesley. "I do have something to say."

"Make it fast."

"Since you walked in the door, I've had my phone on speaker. Bella and Frank have heard every word of your confession."

Wesley's face reddened. "Liar."

Carr pointed to the phone, where a small red light indicated the activated speaker phone option. "If I were you, I'd be getting out of here. Doesn't take but a few minutes for Roano to close the distance between Ballinger and the High Butte."

Wesley swore and aimed his weapon.

Dogs barked, momentarily snatching Wesley's attention. His eyes narrowed.

"Look out the window behind me," Carr said, much more calmly than he felt. "I advise you to take the back door."

"They might take me, but you'll go in a body bag."

CHAPTER 56

MOMENTS AFTER ROANO and two other deputies quietly entered the front door of Carr's home and another deputy hurried around to the back, Bella exited Frank's car with him right beside her.

"Let's take the rear." Bella raced to the back of the massive home with her Glock drawn, wishing she had both arms free to help apprehend Wesley.

Carr and Lydia had to be all right. They had to be. What if Brandt was there too? What if . . . ? She shook off her fears and concentrated on her job.

The deputy gently tugged on one of the two doors that led inside the rear of the house lined with glass. Locked. She wrapped her fingers around the doorknob that led from the deck into the kitchen. Locked. Perspiration dripped down her temples.

Gunfire burst from inside the house.

"Break down the door, the glass, something," she said. "We've got to get in there now."

Through the window she saw Lydia stumble through the kitchen. The three pounded on the doors and glass. She startled and hurried to open the closest door, where the deputy stood.

"Stand aside, ma'am," he said.

Lydia, clearly shaken, did as she was told. "What's going on? Where's Carr? Wesley?"

"Roano," Bella called, hoping they weren't too late to help him or any of the deputies.

"We got him." Roano's voice rang from the upper stairway. "Wesley fired his weapon, but no one's hurt."

Thank You. Bella glanced up at the winding staircase to see Wesley in handcuffs. His cocky attitude had been his downfall.

Lydia gasped. "Not Wesley."

Bella made her way to the woman's side and wrapped her arms around her trembling shoulders. Lydia had the strength of ten women, but being betrayed by a young man who'd professed to be her friend and bodyguard was a heavy dose of shock. "It's over, Lydia. Roano has Wesley in custody. He's one of the killers."

Bella assisted Lydia into a chair. "But how? He was devoted to Darren. Where is Carr? Is he okay?"

"He's fine." Bella knelt beside her. "I'm sorry. I know you're fond of Wesley."

Lydia covered her face with her hands. She glanced up at Bella. "He lied to me so many times, saying how much he wanted to catch the killer. And how much he loved his uncle Darren. How could he fool us like that?"

"For some, it's easy," Bella whispered. "None of us ever want to be taken advantage of."

Carr entered the kitchen, and Bella fought the urge to go to him. Instead she moved aside so he could comfort Lydia. He embraced the tearful woman. No doubt he was shaken up too.

"Mi hijo." This was the first time Bella had heard Lydia speak Spanish, and the words were the endearing *my son.*

Brandt hadn't been apprehended, but two key persons had been identified: Howard MacGregor and Wesley Adams. Now to keep Wesley alive and persuade him to point the FBI to Brandt.

Roano escorted Wesley down the stairs in handcuffs. Roano handed him off to two of his deputies. "I'll be there in a minute," he said to them. "First I need to talk to the FBI and Carr." Roano nodded toward the open door of the kitchen that led to the deck. "Can we talk outside?"

"Sure." Bella patted Lydia's shoulder. Frank and Carr followed her into the torrid heat.

"I owe you an apology." Roano's reddened face mirrored his humiliation. "All of you." He hesitated, then blew out a sigh. "In my gung ho effort to seal this case and charge Carr with the murders, I kept my suspicions to myself." He nodded at Bella. "Pastor Kent came to me the other morning and said Darren was having problems with Wesley, and he wondered at times which side of the law he was on. Kent said he didn't want to tell Carr or the FBI because he didn't really have a basis to accuse Wesley."

Bella remembered the flippant remark she'd made about Carr possibly being a delusional psychotic. She'd slammed the door on Kent's displaying any confidence in her. This could have been brought to an end sooner if she'd guarded her mouth. Her own fault. As soon as she had an opportunity, she'd make amends with the pastor who found it impossible to trust her.

The jigsaw puzzle had now fallen into place. Wesley, the earnest and conscientious young deputy who claimed to idolize his uncle Darren, had been the infiltrator for Brandt. He'd been privy to the discussions about the investigation. Been Lydia's bodyguard. Offered information that threw them off.

Roano reached out to shake Carr's hand. "I've been a jerk. You took a bullet like Bella. That should have cleared your name, but I was after revenge for Darren without any sense."

"No problem." Carr gripped his hand. "It's done and over."

"I don't deserve to take Darren's place, not with the mistakes I've made."

"I think that's how we become better law enforcers," Frank said. "You've done an excellent job on the task force."

"I'm grateful you came as fast as you did today," Carr said. "I was sweatin' buckets before you arrived. I talked to Wesley until there wasn't anything left to say. I'd have been dead if you hadn't rounded those stairs when you did."

"Was close. After getting the call from Bella, we headed out this way. The shot fired at us could have been aimed at you."

"Or you. Don't care to be that close to a killing again," Carr said. "Thanks."

Roano disappeared inside the house, leaving Bella, Frank, and Carr to catch their breath.

"We've got a lot of threads yet to untangle, but we've made progress." Bella took a deep breath to steady her emotions. Wesley claimed her father wasn't involved, but she didn't believe it. Not really. Peering at Carr, she didn't want to think about nearly losing him. "Sure glad you're okay."

"I was afraid we'd lose our phone connections, but it worked out."

She wanted to kiss him but not in front of Frank. Carr put his arm around her waist, and she didn't try to stop him. She needed him in some tangible way that she'd fought all along. He complemented what she possessed and added to what she lacked. And it felt good. Very good.

CHAPTER 57

BEFORE NIGHTFALL, Wesley revealed all he knew about Howard MacGregor—alias Aros Kemptor—and Brandt Richardson. A lot of gray areas remained due to Brandt's doling out information in small bites to his protégés, but Bella relaxed in the knowledge that an arrest would be made in Mexico City.

She had a report to wrap up before leaving West Texas. Right now she was awaiting instructions whether to fly to Mexico City in an official capacity to bring in Brandt or drive back to Houston.

Her emotions jumbled between relief and satisfaction that the investigation neared the end. But she had a valley full of regret for having to leave Carr and her siblings. She planned to see the boys and Anne later on this evening to make plans and consider the future. She hadn't been able to convince Anne of the need for them to move to Houston, but the boys might be more easily persuaded.

Bella's relationship with Carr was another matter. She'd shoved the discussion about them aside until the murders were solved, but now what?

Bella stared at the sun glistening off Carr's swimming pool. She sensed him beside her, but she chose to keep her thoughts private. "How do you feel about some treasure hunting?"

Carr laughed. "Since when are you into lost gold?"

"Since I wondered where Shep Wither's map led." She hadn't shown it to him or anyone, but this morning she wanted to see what might lie buried at the butte. Six people were dead, and it all led back to the Spider Rock treasure. "Let's throw a shovel into the back of your truck and see if we can figure out this mess. Oh, and a camera, too."

"And a ladder in case this is a really deep hole."

She laughed. "Maybe I should pack a picnic."

At the butte, Bella sat inside the air-conditioned truck and unfolded the map with Wither's instructions.

"I've never seen anything unusual here," Carr said. "Can't figure out what's been missed."

"That's because there's nothing to see." She stared out into the shimmering sunlight, then lifted her sunglasses to her head to study the butte. Peering in every direction, she took a moment to wonder if she'd lost her mind. "What time is it?"

"Twenty minutes to one." He looked over her shoulder. "Why?"

"I want to tell you what Shep told me the day I met with him in Junction. His story is fascinating, and who knows? It may be the truth. We're about to find out." She pulled out another folded piece of paper, a copy of the Spider Rock map used by the treasure seekers. "To the best of anyone's knowledge, no one has ever deciphered this map. Lots of men have come close, and artifacts have been found, but no one claims to have discovered a cache worth $64 million." Bella handed him the map.

"With all of modern technology, it seems strange that hieroglyphic experts couldn't figure it out," he said. "And my thoughts about contacting those who understand the area and history of the Incas have already been done. So what did Shep have to say?"

"He said that his great-grandfather got his information from an old Mexican priest. The priest claimed the three rocks in Aspermont, Clyde, and Rotan represent the Trinity, and in the middle was another map that indicated the *true* treasure was here." She pointed to the butte.

"Did he actually use the word *true*?"

Bella nodded. "Not *real* or *gold* or *artifacts* but *true*."

"Strange."

"I agree. According to Shep, the one who buried the treasure was not the Spanish soldier but the priest who traveled with them."

"Maybe he saw how greed was destroying the souls of the soldiers."

"Since history doesn't tell us how they died, you might be right."

She considered all those who had given their lives for a glimpse of treasure. "Enough people have died over it."

He picked up her left hand, then trailed his fingers up her arm, the one that would always carry a scar.

"It's over," she whispered. "Mair's been picked up, and I bet she'll sing to plea bargain. Took a little persuasion to convince Wesley to help us, but now we know Brandt is on his way to Mexico City to have knee surgery. Sure glad Frank and the authorities are waiting there to pick him up."

A hint of sadness spread over his chiseled features. "Brings us back to the *true* treasure. All of the senseless killings and lost souls for gold."

"I think Shep has the best perspective about it."

"How do you figure?"

"Grab your shovel." She opened the door and walked toward the right corner of the rock fortress. "Let me know when it's straight up one o'clock. Actually, it used to be noon, but daylight saving time altered Shep's directions."

Carr studied his watch. "Now. What now?"

Bella pointed to the left of where the rock shimmered like diamonds. "See how the sun lightens that section?"

He nodded. "Dig there?"

"Not yet. We're supposed to take seventeen steps to the left." Which they did.

She bent and examined the spot and the rock. "This is supposed to be it. The same spot where Professor Miller's body was found. Where he wrote *Spider Rock* in the dirt."

Carr shook his head. "Good thing I care about you because I wouldn't dig out here in this heat in rock-hard ground for just anybody."

"And I doubt if you'll find a thing. I'm only following Shep Wither's map and instructions. Have no clue where the number seventeen came from, except the original map had a seventeen on it. Do you want to mark the spot and come back early evening when it's cooler?"

"Not on your life. Curiosity will drive me nuts." He clamped his foot onto the shovel and drove it into the dry earth.

Bella sat on the ground opposite him. "I'd help if it wasn't for this bandage. I'll be the water girl."

He chuckled. "I always knew I was good for something. What are we going to do with the $64 million in gold?"

"Open a home for at-risk teen boys."

"Are you going to stay out here and help me run it?"

His voice held a ring of hopefulness, and for the first time in her life, she was ready to say yes to a man. But not until Frank phoned her about Brandt's arrest. Earlier she wanted to talk about her and Carr's relationship. Now she was doing two steps backward. No wonder women were labeled as fickle. "I might. We'll see."

"So you're an old-fashioned girl who'll say yes to a marriage proposal before agreeing to a kiss?"

She wagged a finger at him. "Maybe."

He leaned on the shovel and wiped sweat from his face on his shirtsleeve. "For that, I'd dig for a long time."

She felt delightfully smug, and it was an incredible feeling. She drew up her knees to her chest and watched him dig where Shep Wither believed the Spider Rock treasure lay buried. In the

West Texas heat, Carr deepened the hole to three feet, stopping for frequent water breaks at her insistence.

"Let's come back later," she said. "Maybe bring Jasper or someone else to help. I'm afraid you're going to have a heatstroke. And digging with a bandaged arm has to be excruciating."

"Nope. I'm into this now."

"Keep digging." Another male voice sent shivers up her spine.

Bella's attention whipped to the man standing behind her and the young girl in his clutches. "Anne." She sucked in a breath.

The girl's eyes were glassed over in terror.

"Let her go, Brandt. She has nothing to do with this."

"She has everything to do with it." He grinned at Anne. "If your big sister doesn't cooperate, you and I have our own destiny."

Not my Anne. "Okay," Bella said. "Whatever you want."

"Take your left hand and ease out that Glock in your ankle holster. Then toss it over to me. Anything else, and I'll have to shoot little sister."

Bella complied, her injured arm burning while her mind spun with how to free Anne and Carr.

Brandt limped toward them. "I warned you to stay out of this. I had you covered."

"You what?" Her pulse raced with the deranged man before her, the man who would not think twice about killing Anne, Carr, or her. She had to outthink him, stall for time. But no one knew their location.

"I've worked hard to protect you, to give you everything a woman could want."

"But you tried to kill me."

"That was Aros, and he paid for his stupidity. You should have stayed away from the investigation until I had everything ready. I called you. I did everything but lock you up."

Ready for what? "I don't understand, Brandt. Explain this to me." She poured compassion into her voice. If he was obsessed with her, then she'd use it against him. Maybe she could get him to release Anne.

"For fourteen years, I've searched for the gold and planned for us to be together. Everything I've ever done since meeting you has been for you."

"For me? Why?"

He limped a few steps closer, the pain evident in the tightened muscles of his face. Yet he didn't relinquish his hold on Anne. He couldn't have walked from the road. With no vehicle in sight, he must have ridden from the road on horseback with Anne—just as he'd done when he murdered the three men. But where was the horse?

"How did you hurt your knee?"

"Slipped and fell while climbing mountains in Peru."

"I'm sorry. Was Mair with you?"

"Are you jealous?"

The thought sickened her. "I might be."

He stared in her face rather pathetically. "No need, sweet lady. You've always been number one."

"I wish you hadn't killed those three men who were digging here."

"Them and others who got in my way. They outlived their usefulness. It was all part of my plan so you and I could live the rest of our lives together with no financial worries." He motioned to Carr. "Keep digging. We've waited a long time for this, haven't we, Rachel?"

"Of course he needs to dig." Bella continued to lace her words with tenderness. "The gold is here for both of us. Anyone else involved has to be eliminated."

Anne's eyes widened. Bella feared she might faint. But better that than become hysterical and have Brandt hurt her. She avoided looking at Carr for fear Brandt would see the emotion between them.

For the next two hours, Carr continued to dig. He widened the hole and pointed out that it would have to be widened even more so he could step inside and dig deeper. Possibly might need to add the ladder. Every swish of the shovel cutting through the hard ground brought all of them closer to whatever Brandt had planned for them.

"I like what you've done to your voice," Bella said.

"Do you?" His face softened, a face she knew could distort to whatever disguise he so chose.

"It's pleasant—deep, manly."

"I wondered if you knew it was me." The moonstruck look on his face displayed his deranged mind.

She forced a smile. "Of course. A few times I questioned if you were following me, like the landscaping man at the hotel."

He laughed, and she remembered fourteen years ago, when his laughter preceded terror. "What else?"

She searched her mind for those times she tingled . . . and wondered. "The man in the elevator. The older man at Zack's baseball game."

"And of course, the phone call from 'Vic.' You didn't even question the number I texted you to use."

She stared into his face, undaunted. "What's next for us, Brandt?"

"I have plane tickets to Mexico. We'll be married there, and I'll have this bum knee taken care of. Then I have a wonderful surprise for you."

Stall him. "What kind of a surprise?"

"A mountain estate for us in Brazil. It's beautiful and filled with the fine things you deserve. The gold here will be our comfort cushion."

She nodded and captured his gaze. "I'm excited. Thank you, Brandt."

"I knew you'd be pleased. Now we wait until Sullivan here pulls up the gold."

"It's terribly hot. Are you okay in this heat?"

"Yes, my sweet lady."

She wanted to throw up, and poor Anne must be thinking her sister was a criminal. "Did you ride?"

"I have a horse waiting for us on the other side of the butte."

Just as she'd thought. "May I stand?"

"I don't think so." He stared at her with a faint look of admiration. "I'm so proud of you. Your experience with the FBI will help us stay out from under their radar once we're in Brazil."

Her experience was going to help her, Anne, and Carr get out of this mess. "Thank you. I'm glad. What about Anne? Will you let her go?"

"Not sure. Depends on how well Sullivan cooperates. I heard what you said to him. Clever. I mean the part about marrying him."

And I meant it. Every word. "I've learned how to get what I want."

"I've changed my mind. Why don't you come over here a little closer? Sullivan might grab you."

Disgust bubbled up her throat. She had the martial arts skills to apprehend him. Maybe she could get to her weapon in the dirt and free Anne. "Okay."

"You have to earn my trust, Rachel. That's the way it works."

"I understand."

"So when the time comes, you'll be the one to put a bullet in Sullivan's head."

She masked the horror, the repulsion of what Brandt was asking. *Dear Jesus, help me.* "I've never murdered anyone before. I don't think I can do it."

"Oh, but you will."

Without her weapon, she was defenseless. And that meant she'd need to use defensive tactics. Was this what trust in God was all about? All she could do was wait while Carr continued to dig. Time dragged on, and the sun traversed farther across the sky. She feared he'd pass out from the heat and work.

A dull thud alerted her attention to Carr's digging.

"Was that a rock?" Brandt said, eagerness tipping his words.

Carr stepped into the hole and wiped away the dirt. He'd dug to about five feet. He cleared the dirt around it, widening to a huge piece of pottery. "If I'm not mistaken, it's some kind of earthen jar."

"About time." Brandt sucked in a breath. "I've spent the last eighteen years looking for this."

"The question is what?" Carr's response held no sign of fear. Could he have a plan as well? "Can't be a cache of gold here unless the pottery opens to a room or tunnel."

"The legend speaks of a huge room filled with Inca gold," Brandt said.

"Come see for yourself." Carr hoisted himself out of the hole.

Bella saw her opportunity. Brandt limped closer, insane greed glazing his eyes. She caught Carr's attention. *Anne, watch me.*

Fifteen feet.

Twelve feet.

Ten feet.

Eight feet.

Come on. Just a little closer. Carr could use the shovel as a weapon. Anne could wiggle from Brandt's grasp.

Six feet.

She could almost reach out and touch him.

"We could finish this by ourselves," Brandt said to Bella. "We could open the jar and take the tunnel to the gold." He turned his gun on Carr. "Since Rachel hasn't ever killed a man before, guess I'll have to do it myself. She can prove her trust in other ways."

"No." Bella started to reach for Brandt, but he swung the weapon toward her.

His eyes flared. "What's the problem? Have you lied to me?" He jerked Anne between them. "Why not let me take care of little sister first?"

Bella drew in a sharp breath. "There's no point in killing either of them. He could help us get the gold out of there. I mean with your knee and all."

"Drop it, Richardson."

Bella startled at the sound of her father's voice.

"I told you years ago that you'd better never mess with my family again. And that means leaving my daughters alone."

Brandt laughed, but he didn't lower his gun. "You gave Rachel to me. Remember? You sold her to me."

"That was before I got smart."

"You mean became a religious cripple?"

"Yes. But since I have a gun aimed at your back, I don't think I'm a cripple."

"How's that? I have my gun on Anne's pretty face. Or I can kill Rachel. Which one is it going to be?"

"Turn around and face me like a man instead of the snake you are. Leave women and children alone."

"Big talk for a little man. Let's be reasonable."

"Not when it comes to my daughters. Drop it now."

Brandt hesitated long enough for Carr to whip the shovel from the hole and into his midsection. Brandt lost balance and fell over the hole, his body sprawled out like a pagan tribute to an idol. Anne screamed and scrambled away. Bella grabbed Brandt's gun, but he grabbed her foot, causing her to fall.

"You'll always be mine," he said. "Don't you forget it."

"I don't think so." She jerked free of his hold, the gun trained on him. Her gaze flew first to Carr and then to Anne and her father. She'd been wrong, oh so wrong. She stared into her father's leathery face, not knowing what to say or even where to begin. He had his arms around Anne, but his focus was on Bella.

"Are you all right?" her dad whispered. "He didn't hurt you, did he?"

"I'm fine."

Carr anchored his boot on Brandt's back. He glared at Brandt, who stared at him pitifully. Bella could only imagine what Carr was thinking—the murders, Darren, the threat on Lydia's life. He turned from Brandt and reached to help Bella to her feet. She trembled, her knees shaking.

"Thank you," she said to her father. "I'm so sorry. I've been wrong. I should have been able to tell from the way the kids turned out that you were sincere."

His eyes moistened. "You had every right not to believe me. Just glad I got here in time. When I went to check on Anne at her babysitting job and learned she'd been nabbed, I realized what had happened."

"How did you know we were out here?" Carr said.

"I stopped at the ranch house to get Rachel to help me. Told the woman there who I was and why I needed to find Rachel. She had no idea where you two had gone. I had a feeling that I shouldn't call your cell phones or have Lydia raise you on the radio. So I took a chance and followed the truck tracks."

Bella's eyes filled with tears, and she didn't know which emotion had caused them. But she knew she needed to reach out to this man who had carried a burden of guilt for too many years. She reached for her father. He released Anne and clasped her waist while tears flooded his eyes and poured down his cheeks.

"My dear Rachel Bella." His voice broke. "I'm sorry for all I did to you. I was so very wrong."

And that's when she realized she'd truly forgiven him, and she'd finally come home.

CHAPTER 58

ONCE SHERIFF ROANO had Brandt in custody and her dad and Anne had left, Carr and Bella lingered at the butte. The relief caused by Brandt's arrest and the reconciliation with her dad had left her weak. And yet she wanted to stay beside Carr.

"Sure was good of Roano and his deputy to lift the jar from the hole," she finally said.

"Shall we find out what's in it?" Carr bent to study the large globe-shaped pottery. Nothing lay beneath, no tunnel or hidden room filled with gold. "I wouldn't want to break the handle."

He's as uncertain about what Brandt's arrest means to our relationship as I am. "We're both too curious to leave it alone."

"Yeah. Driving me nuts to see the contents. Especially since you haven't told me what Shep said."

"I was afraid of sounding like a treasure hunter." Bella knelt beside him.

Vestiges remained of what looked like a blanket that had been used to protect the pottery. Carr continued to wipe the dirt from the top of the jar, revealing a diamond pattern painted in red and yellow. "Look at the etchings," he said. "My guess, it's Inca."

Bella lightly traced her fingers over the pattern encased in black. "I have no idea, but that makes sense. The lid looks like a huge ring or a stirrup. This is incredible."

"What did old Shep say was in the jar?"

"A treasure worth more than silver or gold."

Carr leaned in closer to the lid's seal. "My guess is candle wax was used to seal the lid to the pottery jar on the inside and then sealed again on the outside." He sucked in a breath. "I don't believe this, but I see fingerprints embedded in the wax."

"You're kidding." Her heart pounded. "I bet they belong to the priest who buried it." She studied the indentations. "I'll be anxious to see what the radiocarbon testing shows. The prints are smaller than what I'd expect."

He picked up his camera and took several pictures. "I don't want to break the seal in the area of the fingerprints." He studied the jar a little longer. "It's soft in the heat." He hesitated and gingerly touched the wax. "I think I can remove this section without damaging the fingerprints."

For the next several minutes, he worked with the wax until the sections containing fingerprints lay on the ground. Together he and Bella lifted the lid.

She peered inside the pottery. What had they found? "It's a book. Maybe two of them. Remember history records the priest carrying a Bible. I wonder if these are written in Spanish or Latin."

"One way to find out," Carr said.

Bella rubbed her hands on her jeans. "I wouldn't want it to disintegrate in my hands."

"Candle wax would have preserved the contents in the jar."

"I can't wait. And I can be careful."

Carr laughed. "You remind me of a kid at Christmas."

"This is better." She reached into the jar and pulled out one fragile, leather-bound book. It looked to be approximately ten by eleven inches, nearly square. Age had taken its toll, but the wax had preserved it very well. Another book lay beneath it. Trembling she opened the cracked cover of the first one to the vellum pages. "Latin," she said. "If only it were in Spanish; then I could read it."

"I might be able to help there." When she startled, he

continued. "I've been taking a few Latin classes in order to read translations of the Bible and other antiquities."

She handed the book to him. "Be my guest."

"Oh, my goodness. It's *The Imitation of Christ* by Thomas à Kempis."

"What?"

"Some view this as second to the Bible," Carr said. "For Catholics and Protestants, this has been the heart of meditation and inspiration for over five hundred years. Come to think of it, this manuscript is probably that old."

"What is the book about?"

"Reflections of Christ's life and His teachings. It's been translated into several different languages."

"Now I'll need to read it." The moment felt reverent, beautiful.

While Carr leafed through it, she thought about Brandt's insatiable desire for treasure. "You know, I don't hate Brandt anymore. Haven't gotten to the forgiveness part yet, but I'm making progress."

Carr glanced up. "It'll come."

With her heart still in meditation mode, she reached for the second book and handed it to him. She thought it was a Bible, perhaps nine inches by thirteen.

"The Vulgate." Carr breathed the words as though they were a prayer. "A Latin Bible. Finding these two books is a miracle."

Beneath the heat of a hot Texas late afternoon, Carr read a few passages he was able to translate.

"A treasure worth more than silver or gold," she repeated Shep Wither's words. "Those searching for gold are going to be very disappointed."

"I imagine they'll keep looking for the cache." He sat back and studied her. "To me, what we've found is worth more than money could ever buy."

"And to think God knew we'd find it."

"These are a priceless addition to any museum, and the pottery too. And look what else we've found," he said.

Her attention snapped to his eyes. "What do you mean?"

"I was referring to what else God has shown us."

"Do you mean that the case is solved?"

He shook his head. "Try again."

She searched her thoughts. Perhaps she was too tired and hot to follow him. "You can proceed to build the home for at-risk teens?"

"That's a good one. But not what I'm thinking." He reached out and she willingly settled in his arms. "Do you know how long I've wanted to do this?"

"Couldn't possibly be any longer than I have. However, our left arms are in the way."

"Those will heal." He kissed the tip of her nose. "So will you stay here on the High Butte and help me run this place? even continue with the plans to build the home for boys?"

"In what capacity?"

His lips met with hers gently, then deepening until she shivered in the heat and broke away.

"There's an FBI office in Abilene," he said.

"You've looked into it?"

"I have. And in answer to your question, the *capacity* I'm speaking of is as my wife."

She wanted to laugh and cry at the same time. Words formed in her heart, but she couldn't utter a single sound.

Not only had she really come home.

She'd found God.

She'd found her family.

She'd found Carr right here in West Texas beneath a butte marking Spanish treasure. And she wasn't about to let him go.

A NOTE FROM THE AUTHOR

Dear reader,

As a child, I spent lots of warm summer days looking for buried treasure. While digging in a pasture, I would envision who'd buried the treasure and the amount of gold and jewels beneath my feet. Some childhood dreams never change.

A few years ago, while visiting a friend in West Texas, I was told about the legend of the Spider Rock treasure. My friend even knew people who continued to look for the lost Spanish gold. Immediately I became interested, not to embark upon a digging expedition but to write a contemporary story about this legend. I snatched up every article and book I could find about Spider Rock, and I began interviewing treasure hunters and dreaming about a romantic suspense novel that used this information.

I made a second trip to West Texas for the sole purpose of setting the stage for my story and visiting sites mentioned in the Spider Rock research. What fun! I lived Bella's life vicariously while my mind spun with possibilities.

Pursuit of Justice weaves a generous thread of history with a greedy treasure hunter—and the woman who helped to stop him. I hope you enjoyed Bella and Carr's story. They found a real treasure, the kind that time and man cannot destroy.

Now what did I do with my pick and shovel? I think they're beside my trusty hoe—the one I use to kill rattlesnakes. LOL!

Expect an Adventure
DiAnn Mills
www.diannmills.com

ABOUT THE AUTHOR

AWARD-WINNING AUTHOR DiAnn Mills is a fiction writer who combines an adventuresome spirit with unforgettable characters to create action-packed novels. DiAnn's first book was published in 1998. She currently has more than fifty books in print, which have sold more than a million and a half copies.

Six of her books have appeared on the CBA best-seller list. Six of her books have either won or placed in the American Christian Fiction Writers Book of the Year contest, and she is the recipient of the Inspirational Reader's Choice award for 2005 and 2007. She was a Christy Award finalist for *Lightning and Lace* in 2008 and for *Breach of Trust* in 2010.

DiAnn is a founding board member for American Christian Fiction Writers and a member of Inspirational Writers Alive; Romance Writers of America's Faith, Hope and Love chapter; and the Advanced Writers and Speakers Association. She speaks to various groups and teaches writing workshops around the country. DiAnn is also the Craftsman mentor for the Jerry B. Jenkins Christian Writers Guild.

Her latest releases are *A Woman Called Sage* and *Sworn to Protect*.

DISCUSSION QUESTIONS

1. Have you ever hunted for treasure? What are some of the moral implications of treasure hunting?

2. Carr discovered that following Christ didn't make him immune to tragedy or crisis. Do you think that's fair? Why or why not?

3. Why did Bella throw all of her energies into her work and ignore personal relationships? How valid were her reasons for doing that?

4. Have you ever been interested in investigative work? How might the accepted means of obtaining information conflict with a Christian's commitment to truth and honesty? In what ways could investigative work fulfill a Christian's mission?

5. How well do you read body language? Do you find it helpful or threatening that others may be able to discern your thoughts and motives by observing your nonverbal communication? Why?

6. Bella treasured her aunt Debbie. What did she offer that Bella desperately needed? Is there someone in your life who meets a similar need for you? Have you ever filled this role in someone else's life?

7. Bella battled with wanting to be a part of her siblings' lives, but she feared confrontation with her father. If you were her best friend, what would you have suggested?

8. Brandt was a hardened man, motivated by greed. Why is it that some become better people when they face adversity, while others sink into evil?

9. Bella and Carr realized they were attracted to each other, but so many problems stood in their way. What did Carr and Bella have to give up in order to be together? Would any of the obstacles they faced have stopped you from following your heart?

10. Where is your treasure? Is that where you want your heart to be? If not, what changes will you try to make in the coming year?